THE
CRIMSON
SPARK

WILLIAM HASTINGS

Cover art by alhexz/jervy bonifacio

Map by Cédric Hamon
https://thefantasymapsforge.pb.design

Edited by Kat Rocha
https://KnightEditor.com

Proofreading by Heather Fitt
https://overviewmedia.co.uk

Interior design by Kevin G. Summers
https://kevingsummers.com/

Fonts used in this work:
Body: Adobe Garamond Pro
Headline: Metamorphous

For Christopher, this book is part of your legacy, sewn upon the hearts of your kin, that you may walk the green road forever.

CENTRAL FORTUNA

1

Tooth and Nail

THE SHIP ROCKED back and forth in the churning sea, carried up one wave and hurled down on another, creating a sickening rhythm even in the bowels of the great wooden beast. A beam of rich evening sunlight shone down through the solitary porthole, barely illuminating the ship's hold and the crumpled forms within.

There were at least three hundred of them inside. Children, shackled and packed together in neat rows like livestock. The ship took on more and more at every port, gorging itself on this horrible cargo. They had been at sea for over two weeks, headed north to the Kengean Archipelago and their new life in chains.

Leo had been flitting between the strange moments where one is neither awake nor asleep. Though his entire body hurt, he dared not close his eyes. He didn't trust himself to wake up. His stomach gave a small groan, but he ignored it along with the chill that filled the hold.

Huge shadows clung around Leo's dark eyes and his olive skin had turned a sickly pale. His bandaged right arm hung from the tatters of his shirt in a sling he'd made himself. With every jolt of the ship a fresh wave of pain shot through it. Crippled as he was, the slavers had only shackled his ankles. The metal had chafed his flesh, leaving his feet caked in dried blood. He shivered like a frightened animal and when he stood, his shoulders were forever hunched in submission. Leo was broken. They all were.

Throughout the hold the children lay, discarded playthings, defeated. Their stories were all the same. The slaving companies, the grassers – they would find you. Any lost child wandering the Southern Isles was easy prey for them, so long as you were small enough and poor enough that nobody would miss you. And though at first you might

1

resist them, no matter how brave you were, how strong you were, the grassers would drain your spirit until you were an obedient little husk. Did he think it would be different for him?

In the months since he'd run away, Leo felt his personality being broken down piece by piece. The only thing keeping him sane were his memories of Nico. Dreams of the endless exploring they used to do together through the abbey. Chasing each other through the church and library, whispering after lights out, getting scolded by the nuns. That had been their whole word.

The sound of raised voices caught his ear. A boy was hurled down the stairs and into the hold. A few of the children opened their eyes to see what was going on, watching him crash to the floor. He scrambled to his feet, trying to run. But there was nowhere to go. A pair of grassers descended behind him, seized him by the arms, and dragged him down the line of slaves. The boy kicked, screamed, bit, and swore. Fighting to get away but he had no chance. They slammed him down across from Leo, shackling his legs tight and giving him few kicks in the gut for good measure.

"Amount of bloody trouble you caused us!" growled one man. "I ought to break your fingers."

He spat at the man's feet, still thrashing. They laughed, the other grasser rattling the chains with his billy club. Leo flinched and crawled away as far as he could.

"Next time we have to chase you down, we might not be so nice!" he said as the two disappeared up the stairs.

The jeers stayed even after they had gone, hanging in the air like a foul odor. Muttering a few more choice threats, the boy brushed himself off and glared at their retreating backs. Leo didn't recognize him, he must've been one of the more recent arrivals still working above deck.

He was taller than Leo, and in the dim light seemed a couple of years older. Fourteen or fifteen at most. His filthy tunic hung loose on his thin shoulders and the boy's brown hair was short and jagged, as if he'd cut it himself with a rusty knife. Lines of experience crossed his young face. Still, his bright brown eyes burned with defiance. Those eyes — there was something familiar about them.

He flashed a look at Leo.

"What you staring at?"

His voice was raspy, and he spoke with a strange accent. Leo looked away, recoiling as if someone had struck him.

"Whoa, it's all right," said the boy, his words losing their harsh edge. "Didn't mean to scare you. Grassers got my blood boiling you know?" he smiled.

It was small, but it warmed Leo down to his core, as if reminding him his heart was still beating.

The lad drew a water skin from a pocket of his ragged pants eyeing it like a prize. He took a swig of its contents and Leo became acutely aware of just how dry his mouth was.

"Thirsty?" he asked, as if reading his mind.

Leo said nothing; nobody had spoken to him like this in ages.

The boy tossed him the skin. "It's okay, take it."

Leo reached out his good hand, grasping the skin. He drained it, the cold water falling on his throat like rain on a desert. It was so perfect, the beginnings of tears started forming as gratitude threatened to overwhelm him.

He wanted to say something; all he could manage was, "How?"

"I stole it off one of those grassers when they brought me in," the boy whispered rather proud. "Christ knows, you look like you needed it more than me." He looked Leo up and down, squinting through the dark. "You Infernian?"

"Half," Leo hadn't known his parents, but the nuns had told him that since his skin was darker, his mother or father must have come from the eastern most nation of the Kengean Archipelago. The endless desert of Inferno.

The boy's eyes homed in on his mane of crimson hair. "I figured. That's not red is it?"

"Yes, it's red." Leo shrugged; it had always earned him a share of strange looks.

"Bet they don't have that in Inferno," said the boy. "What's your name?"

"Leo." The word sounded alien. He hadn't heard it in months.

"I'm Nea."

Leo didn't know what else to say, it had been so long since he'd talked to anyone, finally he decided on, "Did you … did you try to escape?"

The boy nodded, grinning. "Yeah, again. Grassers had me working top side, and I made to scarper, you know how it is."

"Sorry they caught you."

"Don't be, happens all the time. Haven't you ever tried?"

Leo shook his head.

"Not even once?" Nea pressed him.

Leo glanced at his sling, Nea followed his gaze, eyes fixing on the long scars that ran up his arm. "Did they do that to you?" he asked, some of his fire returning.

"No it's been like this for a while, it was bad when they caught me, got worse along the way."

"Sick bastards like to throw us around don't they?" Nea scowled. "When did they get you?"

"Two months, maybe three." Leo glanced out the porthole. "I can't really keep track of time anymore."

"Yeah, I had that problem at first," Nea shrugged. "Got you headed to the mine in Fortuna?"

The words sent a chill down Leo's spine. Fortuna, the second nation in the Archipelago. The final destination for all the vagrant children snatched by the grassers. It was there that the great opal mines were found. A hoard of wealth and prosperity locked away so tight in the earth that only the smallest could reach. It was because of this that child slaves were the among most sought-after products in the country.

"I don't know. They said I might not be able to. What happens then?"

Nea's face darkened, and he changed the subject. "Where are you from, anyway?"

"Meridus,"

"Not surprised, I hear that place crawls with them bastards?" Nea shot a sidelong glance at Leo. "Any family?"

"No ... no, I ..."

Nea's smile slipped and he reached forward, Leo winced and made to draw back but the boy just ruffled his hair, like Nico used to. The contact was familiar and gentle; he hadn't felt that in so long. Leo let himself smile, he'd no idea the last time he'd managed one.

"I lived in a ..." He paused, looking for the right words.

"Home for strays?" Nea offered.

"Something like that."

They sat for a moment, in a kind of happy silence. Then Nea leaned in and whispered. "How'd you like to get the hell outta here?"

Leo stared at him. "What? We can't—"

"Yes we can." Nea reached into his pocket and pulled out a ring of keys, his smile widening with wicked glee. "I stole them from the grassers while they were tossing me around."

He looked down at the chains that bound his bloody feet. Was it possible? "Then what?"

"I heard those drunken idiots talking, they say we'll reach Fortuna in less than a week. If we pick the right moment, we can creep up on deck, snatch a lifeboat. Most of the grassers'll be asleep. We paddle to shore and nobody's the wiser."

"You sound as though you've been planning this for a long time."

Nea's eyes darkened. "Very long. What do you say?"

"T… together? Where would we go?"

Nea beamed at him. "Conoscenzia."

Conoscenzia the third nation in the Archipelago. Stories of its technology and civilization had reached even the abbey on Meridus. It was said that there was no slavery in Conoscenzia. Could they be free there? Free, what a strange idea. He had so many questions and it seemed impossible. But when he saw the confidence in Nea's eyes, Leo thought he would believe anything the boy told him.

"Nothing will go wrong," Nea insisted. "You don't have to be afraid, Leo. That's what they want."

And despite months without hope, without contact, without joy, Leo nodded.

Nea beamed at him. "All right then, here's what we're gonna do."

*

When night had fallen and the sounds of drunken reverie at last died out, Nea unlocked their bonds. Helping Leo to his feet just as the ship gave a lurch. Leo stumbled forward but Nea caught him before he fell, accidentally grabbing him by his wounded arm. It seized with pain but he refused to let himself cry out.

"Oh damn, sorry," Nea whispered, eyeing the useless limb. "That's in a bad way. Are you sure—?"

"Yes!" Leo said, not wanting to second guess himself. "Let's go."

Nea had a decent idea of the ship's layout, the grassers had chased him around it all morning. Any useful supplies would be one level above on the orlop deck. Leo kept close behind him, following silently up the steep stairs. They passed through the crew's quarters and into the galley. Nea stopped and poked his head around the door. Leo copied him. Only a few of the grassers were still awake, drinking and playing cards at a solitary table.

"I'll go," Nea hissed. "Keep an eye on them."

Before Leo could say anything the older boy slipped off down the corridor, leaving Leo to cling to the wall and listen.

"You're out of your damn mind if you think I'm going ashore in bloody Fortuna," said a younger man, his voice full of barely disguised fear.

"Oh what's the matter?" teased his companion. "You believe all that guff do you?"

"Don't chu?"

"No, I bloody don't. I've been to Fortuna more times than I can count and I never saw anything strange."

"What about all those stories a while back, bout the raiding party? Turned up with all their throats cut, still in the saddle, I heard."

The grasser shrugged, taking a long draft from his mug. "Probably just bandits. Fortuna's a rough place, opium, delvers, all kinds of ways to get killed."

"Very reassuring."

They continued their game as Nea reemerged clutching a bit of rope, some dried rations and gloves. They wouldn't get far without those. One look at their left ring fingers would identify them as slaves, runaway or otherwise. Slaves were given a circular brand around that finger, binding them to the trading companies forever in a twisted marriage. It was from this that it earned its name, The Nuptial.

*

The other children barely looked up at them when they returned.

"What about the rest of them?" Leo asked. "Do you think they'd come with us?"

"We'll leave them the key," said Nea grimly, "but they've been here a long time and I'm not sticking my neck out for people who don't want to be rescued. You get locked up for long enough, eventually you forget how to escape. Grassers don't even need chains to keep them around."

"Broken," said Leo, remembering how close he'd been to that himself. "Like a horse."

"That's right. I've seen it before." Nea's face shifted, as if he was remembering something terrible. "You gotta look out for yourself," he said, chaining their legs back up like nothing had happened.

They spent the next few days memorizing patrol routes, guard shifts, and docking procedure. All reports were that the ship would arrive in the dead of night. That meant they would have to drop anchor outside the harbor until it reopened at dawn. This would be their moment, Nea said.

While Leo's heart raced with fear and anticipation, somehow he managed to keep it under control and push forward. Perhaps the older boy's confidence was rubbing off on him. When they weren't creeping about the ship, he and Nea would talk. Leo hadn't talked so much to another person since Nico's death, it was strange but wonderful at the same time.

"So," said Nea after they'd locked themselves back up for the night. "You like old stories?"

"Old stories?"

"Yeah old stories, vagabonds, delvers, monsters, and heroes you know?" he grinned. "You seem like that type."

Leo thought back to the abbey. "Yes, I used to read those all the time."

"Stayed in the library until the sun came up?"

"How did you know?"

Nea laughed. "Cause that's what *I* used to do. What's your favorite?"

"Sujec and Perora." he said instantly. Leo knew that story so well he could almost recite it by heart. He and Nico read it together dozens of times, doing different voices for all the characters.

"Didn't figure you for a romantic," said Nea approvingly. "Want to go see the boulder they cut in half, when we get out of here?"

"That's just legend isn't it?" Leo said frowning.

"All those stories from the Archipelago become myths and legends by the time they reach the south. My Dad was a fisherman, and you wouldn't believe the things he saw, things that he thought were just stories."

"Y … your dad?" Leo asked, before he could help himself. "Are your parents …?"

"Alive?" Nea shrugged. "Honestly I've no bloody idea."

"Sorry."

"Don't be, I asked you the same thing." Nea looked up at the ceiling, listening to the sounds of water slapping against the hull.

"Nea?" Leo asked, before his courage left him. "Why me?"

"Sorry?" he blinked.

"Why are you doing all this? Wouldn't it be easier to get away by yourself? You said—"

"I know what I said," Nea grumbled, not looking at him, "but I'm not going to leave you behind."

"Why not?" Said Leo, the question sounding almost like an accusation.

Nea shot him a curious glance. "You used to people leaving you behind?"

Leo looked away. "I…"

"Yeah, me too," said Nea, leaning back and closing his eyes.

Morning came, their final day at sea dawning bright and clear. They spent the afternoon swabbing the deck with some of the others, keeping an eye out for land on the horizon. The huge white sails caught the wind, pulling the ship closer and closer. But it wasn't until night had fallen and they were nestled back in the hold that land appeared.

Standing on the tips of their toes to peer through the porthole, at first all the two of them could see was pitch dark. But through the murky spray of the sea, Leo began to make out tiny specks of light fighting to pierce through the night. They had entered an inlet. Stretches of land spread out on either side of the bay like the pincers of a giant crab. And soon, the massive harbor came into sight. Ships large and small, rocking in the rough waters, floated along countless docks that rested at the feet of an enormous city. The port town nearly stretched across the entire inlet and back, well into the lands beyond. It seemed to cascade down the hilly landscape until it was almost level with the sea.

"Limani," Nea whispered. The largest port in southern Fortuna, all Leo could do was stare.

They waited until the anchor dropped and the noise above slowed to a dull rumble. Now was the time. At first Leo wasn't sure his legs would obey, but Nea was having none of that, he pulled Leo to his feet and took him by the hand. Leo's knees shook and he stumbled often but Nea held him firm. Before taking the stairs, Nea looked back and tossed the keys to the nearest boy. Leo's heart twisted when he didn't even glance at them.

They crept up through the belly of the ship, their research paying off. Not one grasser crossed their path until they reached the deck.

Lights from the distant harbor cast the shifting forms in shadow. Those few awake and sober grassers were finishing the final preparations for the next day's docking. The cool spray of the sea felt wonderful on Leo's skin as he breathed in the thick salty air. Nea pulled Leo up and, moving between cover, they crept towards the side. The ship bobbed up and down, the old wood creaking in protest as Leo and Nea fought to keep their balance.

But when they reached the spot where the lifeboat should've been, they found nothing but ropes and an empty winch. "What the hell?" Nea's hissed, eyes wide. "It was right here! Just a few hours ago you—"

A hand closed around Leo's bad arm. The grasser yanked him back, squeezing on the ruined muscle until Leo cried out in agony. Nea sprang back at the sound, just dodging being grabbed himself.

"Well well," the grasser snarled at him. The man's breath smelled like whiskey and rotting meat. "Ya' wouldn't be thinkin' o' leavin' us would ya'?"

Leo struggled and flailed, fighting to get away, the pain in his arm only growing worse. Through his streaming eyes he saw Nea staring at him, one foot hovering on the rail. Then something in his face shifted. Nea shot forward, ducking another swipe, he slipped between the man's legs. Nea leapt up onto the grasser's back, wrapping his arms around the man's throat, biting and scratching every part of him he could reach. The grasser reeled in shock, sending Leo sprawling to the deck. Nea clawed at his eyes as he thrashed back and forth desperate to throw him off. More grassers were running towards the commotion. There would be no other opportunity. Nea screamed a single word.

"Go!"

Leo couldn't, he wouldn't leave Nea behind. Not after everything that they'd been through. He had to—

"Get out of here stupid! I'll be behind you, honest!"

Nea and Leo locked eyes. Leo wanted to believe him, he needed to believe him. Slowly, unwillingly, Leo stumbled towards the edge of the ship, ignoring the agony in his arm, the painful thumping of his heart and his shaking legs. He kept going despite the protests of his mind and body. Then he was over the side and falling.

2

A Face in the Crowd

OF ALL THE pig-headed, idiotic, self-righteous things to do! You had to try and be noble didn't you! Never mind all the damnable work you've put in getting this far, no let's risk it all for some stupid kid you're probably never even going to see again.

Nea continued this internal berating, as the grassers drove them forward to join the rest of the children on the stage in the middle of the square. Half-starved ragged ghosts with staring eyes and trembling knees, clapped in irons, snatched from all over.

The ship had made port at dawn, right on schedule. And aside from some new bruises, Nea had nothing to show for all that work. They had marched the children through town like thieves to the gallows, all three hundred of them. Locked in filthy cells under the merchant district and left to stew for hours. Nea sat in silence, face aching, staring in contempt at the others.

Stupid little things. One of them probably sold you out, got an extra ration or something.

They were to be auctioned off in groups of fifty throughout the day. Nea was among the first batch selected. No doubt the grassers were tired of all the escape attempts and wanted him out of their hair as soon as possible.

Good.

The auctioneer stepped up onto the stage. Upon which stood the prospective sales, guarded on all sides by armed grassers.

Limani was a strange town for sure. Mismatched buildings of every color and size imaginable lined the square at the center of the merchant district. Here vendors hawked their wares, loud as could be, and the masses milled about buying whatever caught their fancy. Nea saw no signs of the poor here, just people selling and shopping. The city guard were everywhere, patrolling the streets in formation, breaking up pricing disputes and hauling off those who got too heated. Limani seemed blissfully unaware of the children on sale before her eyes. It was a beautiful place, and somehow that made everything feel worse.

Twisted country full of twisted people.

Twisted or complacent. Nea wasn't sure which was more reprehensible.

The town square was packed with people, all eagerly watching as the well-dressed auctioneer began to speak.

"Greetings ladies and gentlemen," he said, his voice like a tiny little bell, shrill and fluttering. "Thank you all very much for taking time out of your, no doubt hectic, day to come and participate in our trade show once again."

Oh, is that what they call it?

"As you can see, the fine men of the Grassen Trading Company have outdone themselves. The crop this year seems finer than ever, do you not agree?"

The audience broke out in a smattering of applause, none too impressed with the ragged lot before them. Nea felt sick. Sick with anger. Anger at the crowd, anger at the grassers, and anger at Leo. If it hadn't been for him…

You wouldn't be here. You could've escaped just fine and been on your damn way.

Nea's thoughts trailed off. That boy, what had it been about him? Nea had always done things alone, never needed anyone else. What changed? It must've been his eyes. Those big sad eyes, someone who had seen too much too quickly and didn't quite know what to do with it. They were so familiar, but Nea couldn't say why.

Hope he's all right.

Nea blinked, shaking away these thoughts.

Pull yourself together, you've still got to get out of here. This isn't the time to go soft!

Nea's plan was still there, a fixed point on the horizon, and damned if this would change anything. Conoscenzia was waiting, it was so close. The more enlightened nation to the west, with all its wondrous new ways of living. Technology, innovation, art and culture, so unlike the world back home. Nea had lost count of the number of times the reading candle had burned itself out after a night pouring over the books, those remarkable tales of the west. Maybe it was a stupid dream, but it was the only thing keeping Nea going.

The auctioneer began his little speech. "The Grassen Trading Company stands forever as the economic backbone of this mighty nation. Through their efforts does wealth flow out of and into good Fortuna. They strive to make lives better for the people, keep the nation prosperous and indeed provide people with an honest living."

Nea snorted at that part, prompting a kick in the ribs from a nearby grasser.

The stupid little man prattled on, but Nea wasn't listening. A quick scan of the crowd revealed a few contemptuous packs of gossiping women, several merchants attempting to set up a cart amidst the cluster of humanity, and city constables leaning against buildings half asleep. None of them objected to the cruelty they were observing. In the front, unmistakable, stood the potential buyers. These men represented the mining companies.

You can smell the blood money from here, can't you?

Fortuna sat atop veins of some of the most precious and valuable stones in the world. It was how the country had gotten its name. These mining companies had established quite a network of profit with grassers' product as their workforce. With them, the tycoons produced nearly a third of the Archipelago's wealth. At least that's what Nea's old books had said. It was a sickening economic backbone that Fortuna didn't confront nor expunge, a nation made fat on the blood of the slave.

Even better, you're not sticking around.

Once the grassers caught the children, they would be branded and then evaluated based on their size and condition. If a child was small enough and able-bodied, he or she would be snatched up by the mining companies. They would then spend their childhood lost in the dark of the earth, scratching for the faintest trace of opals in the stone. When they grew too tall or broad to fit in the mines anymore, they were returned the grassers. The girls, grown now, and able to bear children of their own, could be sold off. Those who'd kept their maidenhood intact as brides, and the rest as whores. Some boys were auctioned off as cheap labor, working in cities and farms, attempting to earn enough to buy their freedom. But the grassers would keep the strongest among them, those tempered by the mine and keen of wit. These boys would be trained to become the legendary Grassen Hunters. It was their job to deal with the enemies of the company, and keep the monopoly in functioning order.

As Nea looked up and down the stage, it became clear that many of these children wouldn't be fit to work in the mine. Some were too frail, others had grown too much during their captivity, or were wounded in one way or another.

It was for them that Nea's heart ached. Some of them, the lucky ones, usually those who'd hit growth spurts early, would be snapped up by a farmer without a son, or a shopkeeper looking for an apprentice; they were often freed young. The crippled or frail, they would become the playthings of aristocrat perverts. Subject to the sick abuses of the decadent and depraved; most of these took their own lives.

Leo

Nea hadn't told him on the ship, but with his arm he'd be no use to the slavers, nor any good for labor, but he was a pretty thing. With his long red hair and olive skin, there was no doubt he would end up in one of these houses of debauchery.

Not anymore. At least you saved him that.

Nea's eyes swept once again across the expanse of people, but this time someone met the gaze. A man in the crowd stared at Nea, un-blinking. He was tall with dark, amber-colored skin and jet-black hair pressed to his skull. A full-blooded Infernian man, his eyes, dark as his hair, passed over Nea, his mouth curling in the smallest hint of a smile. He wore a tunic the color of ochre, with a thin translucent red sash as a belt. On his forehead was a piece of black stone, embedded in his flesh. Jewelry, or a religious mark maybe, Nea had never seen anything like it. Black-cloaked bodyguards surrounded him. Their hoods hung low, concealing their faces, and they wore brooches set with opals the size of a robin's egg.

Who're you supposed to be then?

As if hearing these thoughts, the stranger winked at Nea, inclining his head. Slowly, his men began to move through the crowd, striding towards the stage. The Infernian man followed them, a pleasant smile still playing on his face, as if he were on just another mid-morning stroll.

A spatter of frightened muttering broke out as the black-clad men drew nearer. The crowd parted, giving them a wide berth. The grassers on the stage shifted nervously and the city guardsmen began trying to maneuver their own way through the throng. The auctioneer's voice trailed off as he watched the men spread out to surround the stage. There were far fewer of the men than there were grassers, but they gave off an aura, there was something unsettling about them.

"Yes, as I was saying," the auctioneer continued, gesturing for some of the grassers to cut them off. "These strong young souls come to you from throughout the Southern Isles, selected specially for—"

It happened so quickly. The black-clad men dashed forward and leapt onto the stage, like a colony of giant bats. In that moment every grasser's face contorted in terror. More screams sounded from the crowd as the men in black fell upon the grassers, cutting them down.

Yes!

The gathered throngs scattered as the city guards attempted to rush the stage. Before they could even make it half way up the steps, the Infernian with the unusual stone set in his forehead, hopped up onto the platform. He spun on his heel to meet the approaching soldiers, his face as tranquil as could be.

A light flashed from the gem in the man's forehead. Illuminating the oncoming guards for the briefest instant. As the light fell upon them, they stopped dead for a moment. Before scrambling away from the stage and screaming. Their eyes were out of focus, staring at something that wasn't there.

They ran, knocking over civilians and merchants' carts, fighting and pushing each other aside as they desperately tried to outrun... nothing?

What in the hell?

Back on the stage, the Infernian whispered something to one of the men in black, a pale young man with white hair. He barked an order at the others, who began to undo the slaves' chains, plucking keys from the dead grassers all around. As each child's shackles fell to the ground, the Infernian checked their faces and ran his long fingers through their hair, as if he were looking for something.

The children stood dumbfounded as the men freed them one by one. They would stare at their hands, at their feet unsure of what to do. All save for Nea. The second the iron released its death grip, Nea knew it was time.

Move!

Nea leapt from the stage, not daring to turn around to see if anyone was following. Nea met the cobblestone with a roll and took off through the masses and into the city. Refusing to revel in the triumph of escape, Nea kept moving. Trying to out-run the impossible things that had just happened.

3
Mercy

LEO WALKED THROUGH the sand, his bare feet burning with every step. He crested a hill and looked out across an endless desert. Stars glinted in the night sky, a curtain of deep blue inlaid with countless precious stones. Nico held his hand, and they continued. The world was large, glorious and theirs to know together. Leo gripped his brother's hand tighter as they went, convinced Nico would let go.

For a time, the two of them pressed on. Leo savoring the closeness, the love. Fires danced over the dark desert hills, and he could hear chanting and wild music. Leo smiled and turned to his brother, but Nico was no longer there. In his place, stood a child's skeleton. No expression came from its hollow eye sockets, or crossed its lipless mouth. The skeleton just stood there holding Leo's hand tighter and tighter in its long white fingers until he cried out in pain and the stars burned out.

Bells echoed over the city, jolting Leo from his restless sleep. He was drenched in a cold sweat and gasping for breath, his arm throbbing. The dream had come again, striking at his weakest moments, when he was the most frightened, the most alone. Waking left him with the same horrible ache in his heart. A pang of pure loneliness and grief that time refused to heal.

The previous night was a blur, the icy water, the cries of slavers and the howls of dogs. He had crouched cold and wet under the docks and in old warehouses until he was certain it was safe. Even then he'd only gotten an hour or so of sleep inside a coil of rope. Leo had lost his sling and now his bad arm hung limp at his side, throbbing with pain made worse by the frigid morning. How he'd managed to swim to shore with the injury was a miracle, whether it was the adrenaline or Nea's final empty promise, Leo couldn't be sure.

Countless times during the night's chase, his mind had gone racing back to Nea. Though he tried not to, every time he thought of the boy's face his stomach turned with guilt. Perhaps that's why he'd had the old dream again. It wasn't fair. Nea was the one who had been kind. It had been his plan, his courage. He deserved to escape, and Leo left behind. He was free for the first time in months but Leo found he could take no joy in it, knowing Nea was suffering even now.

It was almost enough to make him stay hidden away, but he knew that was the last thing his friend would want him doing. Nea would've slapped him and told him to stop being such a child. Besides, he couldn't risk getting sick. There must be somewhere in this city that was warm and secluded. Leo wiped his freezing nose and hoisted himself out of his hiding place. The cloudy morning carried a chilly wind that bit and stung his face. The summer was growing cold much quicker this year.

He'd seen very little of Limani during the night, just flashes of the harbor. He didn't know a lot about cities, but knew he was likely to draw the least amount of attention if he stayed in the more run-down and shabby parts of the city. So he made his way from the harbor and into the slum district that covered the claws of land he'd seen from the bay. Here the ramshackle buildings sat so low in the ground he was amazed the sea hadn't washed them away.

It was in Limani that they were to be auctioned off to the mining companies that owned the opal veins to the southwest and supplied most of the nation's wealth. The grassers acted as liaisons to them, gathering the children, selling them and transporting them, as well as rounding up deserters. Even once you were sold, if you managed to escape, the grassers would find you – the Nuptial made sure of that.

When the grassers branded him with it, they said that if anyone saw a child bearing the mark without an escort, they were bound by law to report it to the city guard. They then had to turn runaways over to the grassers. Leo would've been skeptical if he hadn't seen it for himself growing up in the abbey. The nuns often tried to shelter these escaped slaves, but with no kind of long-term sanctuary nearby it was only a matter of time before the guards came pounding at the door. He remembered watching them being dragged away in the dead of night, screaming for help while the sisters were forced to stand by and watch. Once or twice Nico tried to push past Leo and help. Nico had always been the brave one.

He adjusted the gloves Nea gave him, making sure they concealed the mark.

In the cramped alleys of the slums Leo blended in fairly well, but he needed to get off the streets as soon as possible. The city guard would have heard of his escape by now and would be looking for him. It wasn't just grassers hunting him anymore.

Leo passed, what looked like, a tavern. A faded sign swung above a staircase that led, below the street, to a door made of rotting wood. It didn't look inviting, but Leo was too cold to be picky.

He ducked down the stairs and stumbled into the pub. A bell jingled as he entered, ruining any hope of being quiet. It was gloomy, with glimpses of pale morning light seeping in through windows level with the street outside. Around the small room several tables had been set up, but they were covered with dust and looked not to be used much. A line of stools stood along an oak counter, behind which, was a large man cleaning out glasses.

Leo was having second thoughts, but when the high black boots of a city guard passed the window, he mounted one of the stools and sat at the bar, still shivering. The bartender glanced at him, as if only now realizing he was there.

"On your way," he growled, looking Leo up and down. "Unless you've got money, you've no business here."

Leo's shoulders slumped, unable to look the man in the eye. He tried to say something but couldn't find the words.

"Nice glove," said the bartender. "Shall we take it off and have a word with the guards?"

The barkeep's focus broke only when the bell jingled, signaling a new customer.

"Lo' what can I get for you?"

Leo followed the bartender's gaze. A man entered the tavern. He was tall and slim, dressed in dirty travelling clothes; he wore a long, dark-green cloak that fell to his knees, with the hood up, concealing his face. Over one shoulder he carried a heavy leather pack that bulged in strange places. What drew Leo's eyes most though, were the two swords hanging from the man's belt, one long, one short.

"Milk, if you have it," replied this stranger, taking the stool beside Leo. His voice was melodic and no louder than it needed to be.

"Milk?" The bartender was taken aback. "Been a few days since the last shipment. I'll go check. And as for you—"

"Let him stay," said the man, not looking up. "I'll pay for what he drinks."

"You sure?"

The stranger nodded.

"What'll you have then lad?"

Leo did his best to avoid making eye contact, lowering his head on instinct as if this man would strike him.

"Milk as well, I think," said the stranger.

With that, the bartender stepped into a back room, leaving Leo alone with this man. He sat, lacing his fingers together on the wooden counter. His palms were covered in scars.

"I'm called Seiyariu," said the man.

"You hear about this bit of noise downtown?" said the bartender as he returned with the milk.

"What noise might that be?" asked Seiyariu.

Leo prayed that the bartender wasn't talking about his escape.

"Slave auction got attacked, guards and grassers were killed and a whole bunch of the little ones up and vanished."

Nea? Was it possible? Had he gotten away?

"Never a dull moment in this town," replied Seiyariu.

The bartender shook his head. "Didn't expect to be entertaining a vagabond in my pub this morning to be sure."

Vagabond? Leo should've realized it the moment he saw the man's cloak. Vagabonds were criminals, thieves, and murderers. He'd seen them in the old city, the nuns careful to keep them away from the children. These men, they all wore the same green cloak, patched and frayed. Without so much as a backwards glance at Seiyariu, Leo hopped from his stool and stepped out of the bar.

Leo hurried down the streets in a panic, darting down a deserted alleyway. He wandered for a few minutes trying to put more distance between himself and the harbor. Before long he'd entered the artist quarter of Limani.

There was so much color. It was nothing like the old stone city that surrounded the abbey back home. The artist quarter crackled with life. Music filled every corner of the winding cobbled streets, joining into a single chaotic tune. It beat Leo over the head with its constant energy. Wonderful smells came wafting down every alley, causing his mouth to water. The streets were crowded with large clusters of people gossiping, working, living away their lives. He even saw a few slaves, branded as he was, but too old for the mines, escorting their masters through the throngs.

Leo forced his way through the mass of humanity stumbling out of the crowd and into a group of men chatting to one another. Leo's mind went blank. Standing in front of him, looking down in amazement, were three large men. They were dressed in tunics emblazoned with the mark of the Grassen Trading Company. He'd walked straight into the arms of three grassers. Leo was frozen solid, he wanted to run but his legs weren't responding. Suddenly he was back here, at their mercy. He was bombarded with a host of terrible memories. He felt his shoulders slump in submission. The effects of his time with the grassers had left scars that a few hours of freedom couldn't heal. Had Nea set him free for nothing?

"Where did you come from then?" said one grasser, the leader.

"Did he get away from the auction you think?" asked his companion, moving to block off Leo's avenue of escape.

The man squinted at Leo for a moment.

"Forsyth?" the third grasser said. "What is it?"

"That ship that just got in. Said they had an escape, before the auction," said the man they called Forsyth. "Red hair, bad arm."

His eyes swept over Leo, sizing him up like meat on a stall. He felt naked, alone, helpless just like he always was.

The crowd jostled Leo, knocking his arm and causing him to cry out. The pain was like a bucket of cold water on his face. He couldn't stay here, what was he doing? What would Nea say if he saw him now?

Leo scrambled backwards and took off down a narrow alleyway, fast as his legs would carry him. He turned and burst onto a side street that ran up a small hill. Behind him, he could hear the shouts of the men. He doubled back on himself and veered right only to crash head-long into another person.

Leo tumbled to the ground with a grunt of pain, his arm throbbing. He looked up at the man he had hit, certain the grassers had caught him. To his astonishment, it wasn't the slavers that stood looking down at him. It was the vagabond, Seiyariu. He didn't seem surprised to find Leo crashing into him at all. In fact, he gave him a pleasant smile and removed his hood.

The face underneath had soft features that contrasted with the hatching of thin scars that ran along his bare arms. His eyes were brown, somber and calm. He wore a black headband, binding his thick, shoulder-length mess of tangled dark hair.

"Are you all right?"

As soon as he was up, Leo tried to run again but Seiyariu held him fast.

"Let me go!" Leo begged.

The slavers cries were growing closer, and how had this peculiar man made his way from the bar so quickly? Had Seiyariu followed him?

The strange man glanced over Leo's shoulder and as he did, his face changed. Gone was his look of simple curiosity, in its place lay a kind of stern resolve.

"Stay close."

Seiyariu took Leo by his good arm and, taking quick strides, led him down another alley, and out into a cemetery.

It had undoubtedly once been part of the surrounding country-side, but as the city expanded it had been swept up and had buildings constructed around it. No tombstones were inlaid into the soft earth. Instead, great stone crypts rose like teeth. Each crypt was marked with a family name and crest, they obviously did not contain paupers. Leo wondered why they had been buried above ground. Perhaps because of flooding. The grass had been allowed to grow thick and wild, weeds and flowers sprouting at the base of many of these tombs. Seiyariu strode forward, leading Leo deeper into the graveyard. The morning fog seemed somehow thicker here, collecting about the tombs and giving the place an unnatural glow.

Seiyariu pulled him down a walkway of chipped stones, set into the grass and half-concealed by the overgrown foliage. Leo looked back and saw the approaching shapes of men. When they were only a few yards away Seiyariu stopped and turned around, placing himself between them and Leo. He put an arm out, guiding Leo behind him. Leo didn't need convincing, he gripped Seiyariu's cloak. Whoever this strange man was, Leo couldn't go back with the grassers – he wouldn't, but why was this man protecting him?

There were three of them. Two carried swords, one an axe. All of them were broader than Leo's strange protector. The slavers stood facing Seiyariu, waiting.

"Gentlemen," Seiyariu gave a little bow, a hint of authority behind the words. "May I help you?"

The men shot confused and annoyed looks at one another. This hadn't been part of their plan. The man called Forsyth took a step forward, a dented sword in his hand. "Stand aside vagabond. That's private property you've got there."

"Property?"

"Aye property, you not hear? Let us go about our business and there'll be no trouble."

"And what business is that?" Seiyariu asked, steel in his voice.

"No business of yours."

The men began to advance. Seiyariu tossed his pack to the ground and threw back his cloak to reveal his swords.

The slaver spat. "Have you any idea who you're dealing with?"

"The Grassen Trading Company if I'm not mistaken," Seiyariu said. "I'll give you one chance. Run back and tell your masters that this boy is no longer your property."

"Damn fool," muttered one. "Step aside, or we'll make you."

Seiyariu rested a hand on the hilt of the larger of his two swords. "I would very much like to see that."

Leo stared in horror, the grassers had the high ground and numbers; they'd cut him to shreds!

Forsyth ran at them, steel flashing and before Leo even realized what was happening, Seiyariu darted forward. He moved with superhuman speed, kicking off the ground and launching himself at the grasser. Before Forsyth could so much as raise his weapon, Seiyariu brought down a massive two-handed strike, cleaving the grasser's chest open. Forsyth fell to his knees, eyes white, blood seeping from the wound in his torso. Seiyariu flicked his sword clean as the slaver's corpse collapsed.

"That will be all, I think."

They ran. Whatever they'd been expecting, Leo could tell it wasn't death. He watched them go, dumbstruck. Seiyariu's face had returned to the serene expression Leo had seen earlier. He surveyed the body lying on the steps, a pang of regret in his eyes.

"I'm sorry you had to see that." Turning to Leo he asked, "What's your name?"

"You... you saved me."

Seiyariu looked him up and down. "Should I not have?"

"Why?" The tears were coming now. "Why you too?"

It was too much, thoughts of Nea imprisoned, maybe even dead, because of him. But, just like Nea, this man had saved him. He had killed another person to save a frightened child with nothing. Between choking sobs, Leo felt Seiyariu's hand on his shoulder.

"Listen to me very closely. I don't know, or care, what you've heard about my kind, none of that matters. You're an escaped slave and now an employee of the Grassen Trading Company lies dead hunting you. No matter where you go, no matter what you do, these men will come after you until they get what they want."

Leo stared at the corpse lying in the tall grass just a few feet away. Then turned his tear-streaked face to Seiyariu. "What can I do?"

"You have two choices. You can try to escape on your own. Or you can come with me, and I will get you to safety. Choose now."

Leo met the vagabond's gaze. The man in front of him was a murderer. He'd split a grasser almost in two with a single blow, true to his reputation as a vagabond. But he had done this to help Leo. Why was that? And even now he was offering more help. He dressed like a vagrant but he carried himself like a warrior. There was a quiet nobility in his actions, and a sincerity to his words that Leo was unaccustomed to. Leo realized he'd already made his choice.

"Where will we go?"

4
Reflection

The shop was deserted. The owners perhaps off traveling. It lay on the edge of the garment district, removed enough for Nea's purposes. The door was locked, and the blinds drawn, but the side door provided little resistance. The old wood hadn't been reinforced in some time and Nea broke the handle off with a few kicks. It was just a matter of knowing where.

Nea was still in shock. Barely more than an hour had passed since the chaos at the auction. Since that …

What was he? A delver? An illusionist? Like in the stories?

Since that Infernian and his men had attacked the grassers. During the flight, Nea wondered if perhaps it was a mistake to run from them. What did they have planned for the other slaves? Had Nea left them to die?

Doubt it. Anyone who kills a grasser can't be all bad. Besides, it's you, you gotta worry about.

The store was for a lower-class clientele. Few custom jobs here, just wall-to-wall clothes. A counter and money-box stood guard over a door to, what Nea presumed, was a storeroom. This door was unlocked, inside were lines of shelves with countless different garments draped over them in an order that probably made perfect sense to whoever had left them there, but it took Nea ages to find the necessities.

The rags had to go. They would attract too many odd stares, every slave wore the same grubby thing, and they were easy to spot in a crowd. Nea selected a plain shirt and tunic, as well as a long pair of pants with high black boots, something durable for the road. Then all that was needed were gloves to hide the Nuptial. A brown waist-length cloak was lying on a shelf nearby; Nea took it too for good measure.

Nea bundled everything up and dumped it on a table in the back of the room. Resting on the table, Nea noticed several spools of fine white linen. Perfect.

Nea had no idea if the grassers had seen through the disguise. What did it matter to them? So long as you were scrawny enough to fit in the ground the grassers didn't care what was between your legs. But it mattered to her.

Trying hard not to look in the mirror, Nea disrobed and removed the old binding, it was filthy and worn down, loose in its age, but it had been invaluable. Nea was only fifteen and her breast, weren't that large yet. A baggy shirt might've done the trick, but Nea needed to run, move quickly, and that meant tighter clothes. So she bound what she had, wrapping the cloth around her chest. When she'd first started binding, it had taken ages to adjust to the pressure on her lungs, but now the restrictive ache brought her a strange comfort. It was her armor.

As for the rest of her body, Nea was a spindly girl with little in the way of curves. A person would have to be looking very closely to notice that her hips were a bit larger than a boy's, her legs a bit longer. But Nea never spent enough time around people for that to become a problem. Leo might've noticed something was off if he'd stayed with her for long.

Then again maybe not, naïve little thing.

She rolled the spool of cotton up and stuffed it down her trousers, completing her disguise. She managed a quick look in the mirror to make sure everything was in order.

There you go, a boy for all the world can see.

A small squeak sounded behind her. It was a girl, standing in the doorway. She was a year or so younger than Nea, with blond curls, and her soft face wearing a mixture of confusion and fear.

"What are you doing?" she asked.

A violent, hot rage began bubbling through Nea.

She saw you.

Nea wanted to rush at the girl, hurt her, hit her hard enough to make her forget. But Nea fought back these urges. She took a deep breath and looked down at herself. She did look like a boy, remarkably like a boy.

But not to her.

26

Nea made to walk past the girl, trying to contain the anger just beneath the surface. The girl, heedless of this, reached out and grabbed her by the cloak.

"Hey," the girl said, indignant at being ignored.

Nea stopped and slowly turned around.

"You can't just take that."

Nea looked at the girl's rosy cheeks, her big, stupid eyes.

She looks just like them, like all of them.

One look at the girl and Nea was back at that place, at the mercy of those bastards. Trapped and frightened, ruined and alone. Surrounded by girls too weak and foolish to do a damn thing about it. Their faces swam over the girl's, a dozen familiar stares. Nea felt nothing but hatred for the girl.

She saw you. She saw you.

"Well?" The girl put her hands on her hips. "Aren't you going to—"

Nea exploded, seizing the girl by the hair and slammed her head into the wall as hard as she could. There was a horrible crunching sound, and the girl went limp. Her head lolled to one side, blood dripping from her nose.

"Oh God."

Nea's anger was fading fast now, what had she done? Nea put a hand to the girl's neck.

"Don't be dead, damn it please don't be dead."

The girl was not dead, but Nea had crushed her nose, it was bleeding so much...

"I didn't mean to... to hurt you, I just... oh God."

But you did. Don't lie.

Nea *had* meant to hurt the girl. The memory of her feverish rage was still fresh in her mind. The girl hadn't meant to stumble upon Nea; she was probably just checking on the shop while the owners were away. She'd no idea Nea was even there.

"I tried to leave, I did. Why didn't you let me, stupid thing?"

You could've shoved her off and been on your way. Now look what you've done, you monster.

Nea knew she should run but what if she was leaving this girl to die? She'd never treated a broken nose before, but she had a basic idea of what to do. She propped the girl's head up and grabbed some more cotton from the storage closet, using it to clear the blood as best she could. All the while cursing to herself.

"I'm sorry," she muttered, when it was all finished.

Nea hurried from the shop and tumbled out onto the streets. What in the hell was wrong with her? If she was willing to do that to a person, just for seeing her …

Don't act like that's all it was.

But it wasn't just for that was it? The girl had looked so much like the women Nea had known in that other life. It had roused something in her, something awful.

You liked that didn't you? Knocking her around, like they used to do to you. You feel strong now, don't you?

Nea bit her lip and kept walking.

A monster, that's what she was. Her years at Glatman Finishing School had made her that. It had sounded like such a grand adventure when her Ma had first told her. The chance to get a proper education, earn a place in society. Nea had come from nothing, a tiny fishing village in the middle of nowhere, so the prospect of her child moving beyond this simple life had thrilled her mother. When Nea arrived she soon realized that it wasn't a school at all. It was hell.

She hadn't gotten far when a pair of freezing hands seized her and yanked her into a side alley before she could cry out. A young man stood before her. Couldn't have been older than twenty, yet his hair sparkled a brilliant white. His skin was unhealthily pale. If it wasn't for his sharp blue eyes, he might've been an albino. Instead he looked like a statue carved from ice. Nea tried to run, but he put up a hand to block her path, shifting his black cloak to reveal a pair of daggers in his belt.

"Listen very closely," he whispered.

His voice was as cold as the rest of him and his breath sent shivers down Nea's spine. She held perfectly still, terrified but refusing to show it. She remembered this man, he'd been with the Infernian at the auction. Who in the hell *were* these lunatics?

"What's your name?"

"Nea." She tried to sound defiant.

"We are looking for someone; a boy."

"A… a boy?"

"Yes a boy, younger than you. He'd be about thirteen or fourteen years old. Small, red hair."

"Ginger hair?" asked Nea.

The icy man shook his head. "Dark red hair, almost like crimson. Very odd."

Leo!

"Why are you looking for him?"

"I'm asking the questions here, Nea, not you. I want to know where this boy is and why he wasn't with the rest of you? Just a warning; if you lie to me, I *will* know."

"What makes you think I know a damn thing?"

"The little ones at the auction," he said simply. "They said he spent the most time with you."

"How did you find me?" asked Nea in amazement.

"You're not as sneaky as you think you are."

The chill in the air seemed to deepen.

"Are you going to hurt him?" Nea asked.

The icy man scowled even further but he let her go. "The Black Briars? Hurt a slave? Don't insult me."

"Am I supposed to know what that means?" Nea scoffed, panic rapidly becoming irritation. This icy fellow wasn't that much older than she was, yet he talked to her like a child. "That's you? The Black Briars?"

"Have you not heard of us?"

"Can't say I have."

"You will."

Nea looked at the man, evaluating every line on his face, his cold blue eyes utterly serious. "What's your name?"

"Quinnel," he answered without pause. "Quinnel Votrow, left hand of Djeng Beljhar."

"Fancy names. Why should I trust you?"

Quinnel seemed to have been waiting for this. He pulled off his glove to reveal the Nuptial, branded across his finger.

"Because I'm just like the two of you. I want to help. Please, for his sake."

Nea thought about this. She had no idea who these people were. This man however, had freed slaves, had killed the grassers. He was strong. That was all right by her; and if he was a former slave himself…

Maybe he can help.

"He escaped from the ship before we docked. I was with him, gonna escape myself, but I did something stupid and helped him get away instead."

Quinnel swore. "So you've no idea where he is now?"

"None, but I'll bet you he's in the city someplace. He was small, his arm was hurt. He couldn't have gotten too far." She paused, "Look, if you find him, please…"

Quinnel gave her a curt nod. "We will keep him safe, I promise."

"Thank you," Nea mumbled staring at her feet.

"You're quick," he said slowly. "Took me longer to find you than I expected. You've got spirit too, you were the first to run. You're strong, too strong to be a slave. If ever you feel an urge to set the world afire, go to the town of Foresbury. You'll find our trail beneath the holy stone. Confess our liturgy and the trail will become clear."

Nea blinked. "What?"

"If you ever see a body, strung up in your view. Take care and leave it strung, else the Briars string up you."

The words hung in the air, the poem as chilling as the man who spoke it. Then he was gone, leaving Nea to wonder whether what he'd said was a threat or a clue.

5

The Vagabond

GLEAMING LANTERNS HUNG like sparkling necklaces over the market, though night-time was still a ways off. Throngs of people were a constant no matter where Leo looked. Seiyariu had led him north, almost to the city wall. He wasn't sure where they were heading. But they were passing through more residential areas now, fewer guards and grassers. How long would it take for word of Seiyariu's victim to spread?

All through their trek Leo had to fight the urge to run, to dive into the exotic chaos that surrounded him; to try and escape this mysterious man in green. Seiyariu's hand was a constant presence on Leo's shoulder, tight and firm, guiding him through the crowd. As much as the vagabond scared him, Leo knew that he wouldn't get far, not with his arm. He'd seen the speed that Seiyariu moved at. Besides, he had chosen this.

They were passing through a market, most of the vendors' stands here sold some kind of food; Seiyariu selected one operated by a large, beefy man, ladling soup into wooden bowls.

"Sit."

"But won't people be looking for us?"

"We'll be long gone by then."

He sat Leo down at the counter and passed him a bowl of steaming broth. "You need to eat something."

There was something about the way Seiyariu spoke – they were more commands than suggestions.

As the warm scents wafted past his nose, Leo suddenly became aware of just how hungry he was. He hadn't eaten a thing since a few scraps on the ship the day before; all the panic must've pushed it to the back of his mind. He dove into the soup, slurping away noisily.

"I imagine you have a lot of questions. But allow me the first. Who are you?"

Leo looked away. "Nobody."

"Oh come now, you still don't trust me?" Leo didn't answer. Seiyariu shrugged, "Well that's probably smart, you only just met me. Trust must be earned after all and what have I done, besides save your life, I mean?"

Leo glared at him, confused. Every instinct he had told him to clam up and get away, but there was just something about Seiyariu. Leo did trust him, no matter how much he didn't want to.

"I don't understand," he muttered.

"I don't expect you to just yet," Seiyariu replied with a twinkle in his eye.

"Fine, I'm a runaway slave."

"I pieced together that much." Seiyariu laughed. "Where do you come from?"

"I grew up in…" he remembered Nea's words and smiled. "…a home for strays."

"Oh?"

Leo nodded. "I was born in The Southern Isles, on Meridus. In an old city I don't know the name of. I grew up in an orphanage, in an abbey run by the local church. But…" he searched for the right words. "…I had to leave."

"I see," said Seiyariu, his face expressionless.

"But I didn't get far, my arm is no good and Meridus is full of grassers. They caught me barely two nights after I left. I was with them for a while, I started to… slip."

Seiyariu was still looking thoughtfully up at the sky. "You've got an incredibly brave heart to have made it through all that. Many a person in your place would have simply given up."

"I had given up, a lot of us had," Leo said sadly, remembering the pale lifeless children in the hold of the ship.

"What changed for you?"

Leo thought of Nea's swagger, his confidence, his sacrifice. "I met someone."

"Oh?"

Leo nodded. "His name was Nea. I… I think we were friends. He wanted to escape and decided to let me come along." Leo's voice was shaking now. "I got away, but only because he didn't."

"I see," Seiyariu nodded solemnly.

Leo was grateful not to be pressed further.

"Alright, now your turn. Ask away."

Leo didn't think much of this little game, but he had a question nevertheless. He looked into Seiyariu's kind face. There was something strange about all this. "Why are you helping me?"

Seiyariu raised an eyebrow, "I need a reason?"

"People don't do things like this without one," Leo said frankly. "You killed that man."

"As you keep reminding me," Seiyariu laughed. "I'm afraid when I see a child being chased by large men with swords, my first instinct is to help."

"That's kind of you," Leo murmured.

"That's the vagabond way."

"I thought vagabonds were criminals," said Leo. "The sisters always told us to stay away from them."

"Smart ladies," said Seiyariu, a playful smile on his lips. "Vagabonds are criminals in the legal sense certainly, but I like to think we answer a higher calling than that."

"A calling?"

"We are watchers in the shadows, wandering guardians tasked to keep this land and its people safe. That is why I helped you, it is the duty of a vagabond." Seiyariu paused for a moment, lost in thought. "You will come with me and I will help you disappear. There is a sanctuary for runaway slaves a fair ways to the north. My turn now; why did you run away from your home for strays?"

Leo stared into his bowl of soup. He couldn't tell Seiyairu. The shame was too much. "It…"

"It just wasn't home anymore?" Seiyariu offered.

Leo stared at Seiyariu for several moments. It was as though the man had pulled out his heart and showed it to him. Seiyariu knew what Leo was feeling before even he did and was able to use whatever he needed to prove his point. The vagabond was right, and Leo would trust him.

6

Binding

THERE WAS NO chance in hell Nea was getting on another ship, let alone one headed for Conoscenzia. After what had happened that morning all ships would be subject to a thorough check from the grassers before departing. Besides, Nea had had her fill of boats, so it was the north road for her. For that she would need supplies. Fortuna's landscape was not unfamiliar to her, she'd read about it and its neighbors constantly in the long hours she had to herself back at Glatman. Nea had a pretty good idea of what she would need.

Nea had a quick hand and was able to pinch most of what she needed from unsuspecting merchants. A traveling pack, tinderbox, a bedroll. Everything she wished she'd had when she first escaped from Glatman. She would need a weapon as well. Eventually she decided on a bow; she'd probably need to catch food and she had the most experience with a bow. When she'd left Glatman, Nea had nothing but the clothes on her back. She would've starved to death if she hadn't learned to shoot.

When Nea's quest for supplies was done, the sun had begun to sink over the horizon. The road to the gate eventually led her through Limani's pleasure district. A luminous playground of intoxication, lit with red lamps and filled with the ladies of the evening, already plying their trade. Their bodies, their cooing in Nea's direction, the smell of their perfume; Nea almost lost it. She hated them, every single one. They were just like all the other women: weak, stupid, and at the mercy of those stronger than them. But they seemed to revel in it, making their coin, being subjected and abused.

Nea thought back to the children on the ship. How many of them had been damaged beyond repair by the same things these tramps were actively plying themselves for? Nea remembered the expressions that the other women and girls at Glatman had worn; stupid, complacent, uncomprehending, just like the girl in the shop. She clenched her fists tight.

Stupid, stupid and weak.

That girl had seen through Nea's disguise like it was nothing. Disguise. The word made her laugh. Dresses, skirts and braids had always felt like the disguise, one she'd vowed never to wear again. To the world she was a boy. She'd fooled everyone, probably even the grassers. Not a soul in this world had to know that she was one of them, as pathetic as any of the whores she'd passed. But Nea had been sloppy. Now there *was* someone who knew her secret, and there wasn't a damn thing she could do about it.

Stop thinking about it, get on the road. You're not far now. Almost free.

Free… Nea thought of Leo, was he alright? He was such a fragile, frightened looking, little thing. Could he really survive out there alone? There was no way. Nea realized she'd stopped walking.

What in damnation do you think you're going to do eh? Hunt through a city full of grassers, guards and who knows what the hell those Black Briars are? Find another escaped slave in all that madness and be on your way? Stupid.

Nea shook her head. She prayed Leo was ok, and that Quinnel would find him, but whatever came his way he would have to face it himself. She had plans of her own.

Nea followed the river north towards the main gate. Here in the wealthier, residential part of the city, people seemed almost happy. The northern quarters seemed blissfully unaware of the day's events, everyone going about their business as usual. Nea would've liked to have stayed and gotten a better look at everything, but there was no time. The main gate would likely be shut the second it got dark and she was going to have enough trouble getting through as it was.

When Nea reached the stone gate of Limani, her worst fears were confirmed. The place was crawling with guards, out in numbers enough to match the huge queue of civilians. Most were farmers and merchants, headed home for the night after a day of selling their wares. For a moment Nea thought she might be able to slip through in the crowd, but as she drew closer it became clear that the city guard were funneling the people into lines, checking faces, and most importantly, the left ring finger of everyone that went through. Carts and wagons were being pulled aside and searched. Nea swore under her breath.

This is gonna take some doing.

She wondered how Quinnel and his men had gotten out. Had they even left the city? For all she knew they could be haunting some bar, waiting for everyone to calm down. Not a bad idea.

No. Not an option. You're leaving tonight, you're getting out of this bloody country remember?

"No, you're making a mistake!" The cry came from towards the front of the crowd. Nea craned her neck and caught a glimpse of a boy her age being pulled aside. His left hand was coated with a thick bandage. The guards paid no mind and tore it off. There was nothing under the bandages, but Nea saw a small dark circle around his left ring finger. An obvious trick.

Stupid.

She watched the guards drag him off. That would be her in a few moments if she didn't think of something. Perhaps she could hurt her hand, maybe damage it to the point the Nuptial couldn't be seen. She scrapped this idea immediately; she needed her hands. Maybe if she put on a convincing enough show the guards wouldn't check under her gloves.

I won't lose, I can't lose, not after this.

"Name?" asked a guard, barely looking up.

He was a bored looking man wearing the same red tunic and plate that the rest of the city watch wore.

"Niall," she said, not making eye contact. Her da's name would have to do.

"Just off the boat are you?"

"Yeah," she said. "Visiting my da."

"Good, he'll likely need your help. I've heard the winter months are going to be hard this year. Where are you arriving from?"

"Meridus."

It was a gamble. The place was so full of grassers that an actual slave would be a damn fool to say that's where they were coming from.

"I see."

The man looked down at his book and did a bit of scribbling.

"What's all this then?" she asked, pouncing on the idea. The more questions she asked, the less like a slave she would look.

"We had an incident in the city center this morning," replied the guard. "Tell me, have you seen any of these men?"

He handed her a stack of papers. Each one bore a detailed illustration of a man's face – wanted posters. Nea immediately recognized one. The first face on the stack was the same she'd seen in the crowd. The Infernian man with the gem in his forehead.

Djeng Beljhar
Commander of The Black Briars.
Terrorism and Conspiracy.
Dead or Alive.

There was the name Quinnel had told her, Djeng Beljhar.

"Who are the Black Briars?" she asked, unable to help herself.

"Blimey you really *aren't* from round here are you?" said the guard. "They're terrorists who target the trading companies. Attacked an auction in town today."

Terrorists who target the grassers; sound like your kind of people after all.

She flipped to the next poster. There he was, the icy young man who'd jumped her on the street.

Quinnel Votrow.
Second In-Command of The Black Briars.
Terrorism and Murder.
Dead or Alive.

"Have you seen any of these men?"

"No," Nea lied.

"Go on through then," Nea's heart leapt and she made to step from the throngs but...

"Oh, wait just one moment if you please."

This was the moment. The moment when she didn't know if success or failure waiting, only that one of them was crashing down upon her and there was nothing she could do about it.

Don't panic, he'll see it on your face.

It felt as though Nea had been drenched in ice-cold water. He was going to ask to see her hand he was—

"Your surname," said the guard. "I forgot to ask you."

"Oh," Nea prayed that her relief didn't show too much on her face. Her real name would do, not like the grassers kept track of that stuff. "Dúlaman,"

"Dúlaman," said the guard scribbling on his pad. "Alright off with you now."

Nea turned to go when a voice broke over the dull murmur of the crowd, loud and commanding.

"Stop!"

No. Not now.

Nea couldn't help herself, she turned back and felt the bottom drop out of her stomach. Stepping from the crowd were three guards and they were pointing directly at her.

"You there, boy," they called. "You're under arrest."

Weak, said the cruel little voice in her ear. *Stupid and weak.*

7

Lionheart

THE FIRST THING Seiyariu did was take Leo to get some new clothes. His slave rags were discarded for a black doublet and brown traveling pants that were baggy enough for him to grow into, or so Seiyariu had said. The vagabond let him keep his gloves, to conceal The Nuptial from any wandering eyes. The ensemble was completed with a pair of tall boots, and a long brown cloak with a hood that Seiyariu had insisted he wear up.

"They'll know you by your hair; it's a beacon," he said.

The vagabond paid for these clothes without a fuss and like that, the two of them were off again.

"You'll need a pack for the road. It's nearly two weeks on foot."

Seiyaru found him a pack, not unlike his own, and filled it with what he claimed were all the necessities of the road. These necessities turned out to be a single bedroll, a pocket knife and a spyglass. Leo was instantly suspicious of where a homeless wanderer like Seiyariu managed to get the money to pay for all of this, but he didn't want to press the issue.

As night began to fall, Seiyariu didn't take them through the main gate. Instead he led Leo to an area of the wall some ways from the crowds and activity of the city. There was a sizable missing stone in the wall here, surrounded by strange symbols Leo didn't recognize. He watched in amazement as Seiyariu reached through the hole and pulled open a door concealed in the stones just large enough for the two of them to squeeze through.

"One in every city," Seiyariu muttered. "Try to remember where."

Leo crawled out of the makeshift exit and out into the world, then he felt his jaw drop. The rolling green landscape gave him a wild sense of freedom, an endless expanse of hills, trees, and looming mountains. So this was Fortuna. Seiyariu strode out into the dark world, his face like that of a singer about to perform.

They traveled down the road for an hour before Seiyariu turned and led Leo up a winding path through a dense canopy of trees that eventually burst out into a wide meadow.

"We'll camp here tonight," Seiyariu said, throwing his pack down.

"Out in the open?" asked Leo. He didn't know very much about survival but if they were being hunted surely it made sense to find somewhere less exposed.

"I'm not an easy man to sneak up on," Seiyariu replied. "Besides, from the look of things they're more concerned with what's going on inside the city than out. I heard more talk about that auction. If we're lucky, the incident in the graveyard will be shunted down the list of priorities. Though come tomorrow we will have to be on our toes."

Leo sank to the ground and stared at the forest, bathed in shadow. As the night wind blew in, he was thankful for the clothes Seiyariu had given him. The grass was soft and Leo was exhausted, but he knew sleep was a ways off. His mind was spinning.

"How are you holding up?" asked Seiyariu, sitting down beside him.

"I'm fine."

"What about your arm?"

Leo winced. He'd hoped Seiyariu wouldn't notice, but he'd seen Leo struggle to get the doublet on over the injury; seen the pain on his face. Would the vagabond leave him if he knew he could barely use it? Would Leo be alone again?

"It's fine, just acts up once and awhile."

"Give it here."

Leo hesitated, but Seiyariu's face invited no suspicion. He proffered his arm to the vagabond, silently wishing he'd not lost his sling. It had hidden the worst of the damage from view. Without it, it was plain to see that Leo's arm was covered in thick deep scars up to his elbow. Seiyariu looked the wounds over calmly, running his fingers along one of the marks.

"Who did this to you?" he asked, simply.

"It was an accident," Leo lied.

"I see." Seiyariu's expression was unreadable.

"It's not as bad as it looks," Leo lied. "I won't slow you down. I promise."

The vagabond gave him a curious look but said nothing else of it. "Good, help me gather some wood, and I'll show you how to make a fire."

Seiyariu gathered stones and placed them around the wood to prevent the fire from kindling the surrounding vegetation. He then lit the pile with a tinderbox from his pack. He whistled, at peace with the world. Leo, however, had begun to shiver. The cold of the night was creeping in. A heavy warmth surrounded him as Seiyariu wrapped his green cloak around Leo's small shoulders.

"Stay close to the fire," Seiyariu muttered. "You'll get used to it soon enough."

Leo did as he was told, the warm patch was the only part of his body he could feel. In a vain effort to distract himself, he gazed up at the stars.

Seiyariu noticed his gaze. "Leo, can you tell me what that constellation is?" He pointed to several stars shining beautifully in the cold dusk. Leo shook his head. He couldn't connect the stars, no matter how he looked at them.

"I don't see anything," he said frowning.

"Leo."

"Yes?"

Seiyariu smiled, "No, you misunderstand me, that constellation is called Leo."

Surprised, Leo looked up at the stars once more. Seiyariu drew across the stars with his finger and this time Leo noticed them taking a shape. It was an animal, a lion with its head held high, roaring defiantly to all creation.

Seiyariu stared at Leo through the glint of the fire. "Is that your full name?"

Leo shook his head. "Leonardo."

"Just Leonardo?"

"Fortunato. Leonardo Fortunato."

"The fortunate boy in the fortunate land," Seiyariu chuckled.

"I suppose," Leo mumbled, letting himself smile a little.

"That's not a name common to the Southern Isles. Tell me about your parents Leo, are they still alive?"

The question came as something of a surprise. Why did he want to know that? "No," Leo replied simply. "I told you I grew up in a home."

But when Seiyariu wouldn't stop looking at him he elaborated. "My mother died before I was born."

"Before you were born?"

Leo nodded. "A few minutes before I was born. That's what the sisters told me anyway. They said she was sick."

"How did you survive?" Seiyariu raised his eyebrows.

"Why do you care?" Leo replied more savagely than he meant to. He didn't talk about this with people.

"Isn't it enough that I *do* care?"

Leo shrugged and turned away. "She had been staying with someone in the mountains. My father maybe. He managed to save me." Leo thought that was just enough. He didn't want to talk about Nico unless he absolutely had to.

"I'm sorry," Seiyariu said sincerely.

"It's not your fault." Leo blinked, as the crackling flames danced before his eyes. "Seiyariu?"

"Yes?"

"Where were you going exactly? Before I ran into you, I mean."

Seiyariu laughed, "I wasn't *going* anywhere!"

Leo looked at him, somewhat confused. "What do you mean?"

"Leo, that is the life of a vagabond. I'm never truly going anywhere. I go where the world draws me," he said, staring thoughtfully up at the rising smoke.

"I don't understand."

"Ever since I was your age, I've never been happy with a sedentary life. I need to travel, see new places and sights. It's part of who I am but... you're looking at me like I'm crazy."

"Doesn't that get lonely? Don't you... don't you ever wish you had a home?"

"The first thing you need to learn Leo, is that home is a not a place, it is a feeling. It's a feeling you get from being with those you care about and doing what you love."

Leo stared down the road, his eyes misty. He hadn't mentioned Nico, yet it was like Seiyariu could read his mind. Nico had been home. Without him, Leo had no idea where to go or what to do. An image of Nea and his kind smile flashed in front of his mind's eye. He shook it away; this was not the time to worry about things he couldn't help.

Seiyariu drew his sword, and began to run a whetstone over the blade. Now that he could get a good look at it, Leo saw that this sword and its miniature counterpart were like nothing one would find in the Southern Isles.It was a long two-handed weapon. Its pommel the same width as its grip. The cross-guard was a simple steel disc and the blade curved out slightly. Most curious of all though, was that only one side of the blade had an edge, the other was essentially blunt.

"I've never seen a sword like that before," said Leo.

"I would be shocked if you had," said Seiyariu with a smile. "They're very rare in these parts. Crafted for speed and power by some of the finest smiths on earth. These two were given to me in my travels across the sea, far from the Kengean Archipelago.

"You've left the Archipelago?" Leo sat upright and stared at Seiyariu, his calm demeanor suddenly out of place.

Seiyariu blinked. "Yes, several times in fact. I went about as far east as you can go."

"Was that where you learned to fight?"

Seiyariu laughed again. "Leo, you're never finished learning to fight. But I learned to use it there, yes. If you'd like, I'll teach you to use it."

"Really?"

"Certainly, it is a useful skill for a vagabond to have."

"Am I a vagabond now too?" Leo asked with a little smile.

"We shall see, perhaps a fine one in the making." He pulled a bed-roll from his pack and rolled it out by the fire. He stretched out on it with a sigh. "Get some sleep," he said. "Tomorrow, we're off."

8

Down Vagabond Road

THE SUN WAS up and no matter how Leo shifted it wouldn't go away. With a yawn, he sat up. The bedroll Seiyariu had given him had at one point been used to feed an entire colony of moths but it kept out the worst of the autumn chill. Leo stretched, rubbing his eyes, unable to remember the last time he'd fallen asleep with a full stomach.

He looked around for Seiyariu but the vagabond was nowhere to be found, nor were any of his things. Leo jumped up in panic, but as he did, a note tumbled off of his bedroll. Curiously, he picked it up.

Gone to get breakfast, keep fire going.

Leo breathed a sigh of relief. The vagabond was a mystery to be sure, but to be lost alone in Fortuna all by himself? The thought made him shiver. Leo glanced at the smoldering ashes where the fire had been. Beside them Seiyariu had left him a knife. Leo weighed it in his hands; it was heavier than it looked.

Leo wasn't really sure what he was doing, but he began hacking off a few branches from the surrounding trees; the knife didn't go through them instantly like he thought it would; he had to really hack at it. When he'd collected enough, Leo dumped the branches in the fire pit. Remembering an old trick he'd seen the paupers in the old city use, Leo picked up a small branch and, placing it on a larger one, he began to turn it. Slowly at first, and then faster and faster. Soon enough, smoke began to rise from the wood.

"Very good," Seiyariu said, strolling up, a pair of dead rabbits swinging from one hand. "But you've forgotten something."

He crouched down and picked up several dry leaves and twigs. He aligned the branches into a point and placed the leaves underneath. Then he took the tinderbox from his pack and struck a match. Seiyariu tossed it into the kindling, which ignited instantly, eating away at the branches. He then straightened up, eyeing his handiwork.

"Why couldn't you leave *that* here?" Leo demanded.

Seiyariu raised an eyebrow. "Because you won't always have one with you."

He then showed Leo how to prepare the rabbits. Together, they constructed a spit and sat back to watch the meat cook. Despite himself, Leo smiled. Seiyariu was quite proud of his efforts. The meat was dry, but to Leo it tasted wonderful.

*

Seiyariu and Leo spent most of the day on the road. The sights and sounds of the world swept over Leo like a cool breeze; there was so much to see. They passed thick forests, some that had already begun to change color. Rivers ran through the countryside, reflecting the sunlight off their mirrored surface. Small towns were scattered here and there on the road and they would often pass other travelers. Leo saw young families in horse drawn wagons, rich men on horseback followed by an entourage of servants, silent men carrying swords, and loud, happy merchants striking up a merry conversation with anyone who'd listen. Among these travelers, Leo noticed several men in long green cloaks adorned with patches, other vagabonds no doubt.

At about midday they stopped and ate some dried fruit Seiyariu produced from yet another compartment in his pack. Perched on a rock, they ate heartily and watched the faces passing by.

"We'll follow this road for a bit, head northeast through the swamps and then cross the inlet I think," Seiyariu said. "It gets a little bit muggy but nobody takes that road. Besides, there's an old friend I need to look in on."

"Who?"

Seiyariu merely smiled and pretended he hadn't heard. Leo frowned. He was still adjusting. Despite his hesitations, he felt resigned to go with Seiyariu. One thing still played on his mind however, a question that needed asking.

"What happens when we get there?"

"Leo take my advice, fretting about the future, or the past for that matter, leaves you distinctly unsatisfied with the present. We'll take everything in our stride, I think."

This answer was unhelpful, but honest. Leo actually liked the idea. He'd always worried, more than Nico certainly. The sisters at the orphanage used to say that he fretted like an old man. They were right. He'd constantly been on edge about what was to come and how he'd deal with it. It had been Nico who greeted the new day with curious excitement rather than anxiety. It seemed all Leo's decisions had been made either by Nico or the butterflies in his stomach. Seiyariu's suggestion was intimidating, but there was a liberation in it. Leo watched him stare at the clouds as though there was simply nothing else in the world and found himself envious.

As the main road grew more and more crowded, Leo felt Seiyariu's hand on his shoulder. "What does that tell you?"

Leo looked across at the traveling crowds. There were more of them certainly, but why weren't they moving? The merchants had dismounted their horses and were rummaging in their wagons. Men searched their saddlebags for papers and families stuck close together as the crowd began to slowly inch forward. Leo thought back to the city, how everything had been locked down. "A checkpoint?"

Seiyariu nodded, "The military will be checking everyone for papers and Nuptials, no doubt. Come Leo, something tells me we should take a detour."

Seiyariu's detour, as it happened, involved cutting through the nearby forest. "This is the eastern path; we'll reach the swamps soon. See this here?" he remarked, pointing at a symbol carved into one of the trees on the edge of the wood.

Leo peered closer. It was a tiny picture; to him it looked a bit like a dog turned on its side. "What is it?" he asked turning his head.

"Peregrine Runes." Seiyariu knelt down. "That's what we call them."

"We?"

"Vagabonds."

Leo blinked. "You've got a secret code?"

"I suppose you could say that," Seiyariu chuckled. "We who walk The Green Road have symbols that inform each other of the perils and pleasures that the road ahead might contain. This is one of those marks. One of our Peregrine Runes."

"What's The Green Road?"

"The Green Road is what vagabonds walk, the aimless trail of justice. Our solitary and nomadic lives."

"Oh," said Leo, not sure he understood. "And this symbol?"

"It means game is to be found deeper in this wood," he grinned. "Perhaps it will make for another good lesson."

Leo, clumsy enough when everything was flat, tumbled over the winding tree roots that covered every inch of ground. If indeed there was a forest path, Leo certainly couldn't see it. Roots clung to the side of giant ditches and the trees were unusually far apart.

Seiyariu put a finger to his lips. Beckoning Leo to follow, Seiyariu disappeared in between the tree trunks. Leo scrambled after him. Leo's noisy tumbling probably scared off every living thing for miles. Seiyariu however had no trouble moving silently. No twigs, no leaves, crunched under his boots and his pack didn't so much as rattle. Seiyariu blended into the forest, just as he had in the city. Leo was still an intruder. They'd been walking for only a few minutes when a small rabbit came hopping onto a root some thirty feet away.

The vagabond silently pulled a short-bow from his pack, strung it and let an arrow fly through a gap in the branches, catching the rabbit in the belly. The animal fell dead to the ground, impaled by the arrow. Leo felt a bit of remorse for the little thing.

"Don't elevate yourself."

"Sorry?"

"Over the creatures of the wood. Don't assume that just because we walk on two legs and not four, you and I are immune to the laws of nature."

"I don't understand."

"We have to hunt and kill, the same as any creature on this earth. Life is about survival, for every living thing on this planet. Try to remember that."

"Okay," said Leo, thinking about these words. "Can I try it then?"

Seiyariu eyed his injured arm. "Are you certain?"

Leo nodded, eager to impress the vagabond. Surely it couldn't be that hard. Seiyariu tossed the bow to Leo, who promptly dropped it.

"Sorry," Leo muttered, picking the weapon up. It felt good, the smooth wood of the handle. Still, how was he to draw it?

"See if you can hit the center of that tree," said Seiyariu pointing.

Leo took aim and pulled back on the string with clenched teeth. The pain was instant and white-hot, his bad arm shuddered, causing the shot to miss by several feet.

It didn't take long for Seiyariu to write off shooting as a lost cause.

"Let's try a different approach," Seiyariu suggested after Leo's fourteenth shot ricocheted off a nearby branch. "See this?" He pointed to a mark in the ground.

Leo peered at it, "It doesn't really look like anything."

"A deer passed by here not long ago, female and slow, possibly sick."

Leo laughed. "You can't tell all that from this, can you?"

He nodded. "I spent two years living in the wilds of the continent. I learned that nature gives you enough clues if you only look hard enough. You have to learn to not just look at something but hear it, smell it, feel it, taste it."

Leo frowned, it felt like an impossible task. Seiyariu sensed this. He placed his hand on Leo's shoulder.

"I don't expect you to learn this all at once, I certainly didn't. You just need to be patient. Don't worry Leo, we've got all the time in the world."

*

After a few hours of learning the finer points of identifying animals based on their tracks and droppings, they came to the edge of the forest, beyond which lay what looked like an open field. Eagerly Leo strode forward.

"Leo wait!"

Seiyariu's warning came too late. Leo's feet met nothing but air and he stumbled and fell. He rolled for a few terrifying moments before coming to a stop at base of the slope. He sat up, clutching his throbbing arm. Then he realized where he was sitting. It was overrun with grass and flowers but its shape was bizarre, like a great hole cut into the ground.

"Seiyariu," Leo started, looking around in astonishment. "What is this?"

"A crater," said Seiyariu, sliding down to join him. "They probably didn't teach you this at your little home for strays."

Leo frowned, "Teach me about what?"

"This is a scar Leo. Fortuna is covered with thousands of them. All left behind by The Clash of Comets."

"The what?" said Leo. "I've never heard of it."

"I'm not surprised," said Seiyariu. "It's not a tale that travels far from the Archipelago, and if it does, it's very easily transformed into myth."

Leo thought about what Nea had said about tales from outside the isles. "Will you tell me?"

"Of course." Seiyariu sat down on the incline of the crater and leaned back to look at the setting sun. "A thousand years ago, or so I'm told. The Kengean Archipelago was a single solitary land mass. One united nation, hard to imagine now I'm sure. For the purposes of our story let us say it was a grand time indeed. An age of peace and unity. Until a man appeared from the deserts of what is today called Inferno. This man had the power to control, commune with the stars. Vagabonds call him the Astrologue."

"Astrologue," Leo tasted the strange word. "What do you mean control?"

"I'm still not entirely sure myself." Seiyariu grinned. "Some people believe he was a Delver."

"Delvers are real?"

"Please Leo, let me finish. Others believe that he created grand machines the likes of which even the great minds of Conoscenzia cannot comprehend. Some even venture to say he was a god made flesh. Whatever he was, it was he who ignited the Clash of Comets."

"Comets." said Leo. "You mean like falling stars?"

"They rained down upon this land, breaking it apart. Massive earthquakes and tidal waves annihilated entire cities, countless people were killed."

"Why?" asked Leo.

"Pardon?"

"Why did the Astrologue do it? Kill all those people?"

"I'm not sure what could compel anyone to cause such suffering. The Astrologue had every intention of letting this planet be consumed by his power."

"But it wasn't."

Seiyariu's eyes twinkled. "No, the Astrologue was stopped."

"How? By who?" Leo found himself enthralled by the story, not least because he was sitting in the middle of evidence of the tale. This was no myth, this was history.

"A soldier," said Seiyariu, "by the name of Romulus Caloway. He killed the Astrologue before his plans could be completed. The land had been ripped apart. Transformed into the three nations as we know them today. The word Kengean means 'broken land' it's a word from the continent."

"The broken land," said Leo, looking around in amazement.

"Craters like this, are the only evidence that remains. In the aftermath of this great battle, chaos erupted. The once unified people descended into in-fighting and civil war. Caloway decided that there should be guardians to watch over these new lands. Romulus Caloway you see, became the first of the vagabonds. He recruited others to his cause and they too chose to walk The Green Road. Romulus believed in decentralized power. He declared that the vagabonds should never have a leader or official form of control, that they must exist as an ideology and a lifestyle in order to survive. And survive it has. We operate under the structures he laid down. The green cloaks, the Peregrine Runes, the legacy patches and so on. Vagabonds are intrinsically linked to the history of The Archipelago."

Seiyariu was done with his story and was striding to the other end of the crater, squinting into the distance. "Come here."

Leo did as he was told. Seiyariu pointed off back towards the wood. Leo heard them before he saw them, the thunder of horses. And there they were, Leo plucked his spyglass out of his pack for a better look.

The riders were making their way through the forest. They wore beaded leather armor emblazoned with the crest of the Grassen Trading Company and carried crossbows and swords. Leo hid a bit lower in the crater even though the men were much too far away to see them in the dying light. A raiding party, almost identical to the one that had captured him back in the Southern Isles.

"Are they looking for me?"

"They're looking for slaves. More must've escaped during that riot than we heard." Seiyariu pursed his lips, "They'll be out hunting all night, and for days to come."

"Seiyariu I can't go back there—"

"You will not be going back there Leo, I guarantee it. These men are adept at tracking runaway children, let's see them try to follow a vagabond."

9
Conscripted

NEA HAD BEEN dragged back to the fortress in the center of town. She'd fought; Nea always fought. But these were men; she wasn't going anywhere. Her mind was awash with panic and confusion, and it wasn't to be abated any time soon. She was tossed in a cell and left to rot for three bloody days. Sitting in the dark thinking of all the horrible things that were waiting for her, it was enough to make her go mad.

At noon on the third day she'd been taken to the interrogation chambers. Small square rooms with nothing but a door, a table and some chairs. At the table sat a wiry-haired man wearing spectacles and sorting through papers. Nea was forced into the seat across from him, hands bound and flanked by two city guardsmen. They were standard fare, working men, wearing basic plate and mail. Nea had snuck past their like many times before.

So how come you couldn't do it this time?

The wiry-haired man shuffled the papers about, casting his eyes over Nea. He was getting on in years, but he still wore the red uniform of the city guard. Though he wore no armor and carried no weapons. This man worked inside the fortress, that was plain.

"Lieutenant Auditore of the Limani City Watch," said the man. "What is your name?"

"Piss off," she said, glaring at him. "I've got nothing to say to you."

"Nothing to say in your defense then?" he asked, cocking an eyebrow.

"I don't even know what I was bloody arrested for," she scowled.

During her time in the cell a thought had occurred to her. What if someone had found the girl in the shop and put out a warrant on Nea for the assault. Despite herself, Nea felt cold sweat on the back of her neck. If that was the case then her secret was as good as out.

"You haven't any idea why we've brought you here?" asked Auditore, unconvinced. "You're an escaped slave, attempting to flee the city."

It was not a question.

"Damn right I am," she spat. "You bring us all in for questioning now?"

"Not usually no. But we're attempting to piece together what happened at the auction three days ago."

"What makes you think I know?"

"Because you were there, don't play games with me," replied the lieutenant, sounding bored. "I would like your name, and your account of what happened."

"Why do you need it?" said Nea. "Thought there were plenty of people there, probably your own men."

"Ah, well there you see we've run into something of a problem. My men have been giving conflicting reports of what they saw there, as have many of the people that were in the crowd. Whatever that Infernian did, it made piecing this whole thing together extremely difficult."

"The Infernian?"

"Yes, Djeng Beljhar. No doubt you've at least seen his poster. He is the leader of the Black Briars. The men who attacked the auction."

Nea remembered that calm face; it was burned into her mind's eye along with Quinnel's. "If I tell you my story, what's in it for me?"

"You're one of the only slaves from the auction we've managed to recover. Your testimony is vital."

"Why?"

"And," he continued, "because it is vital for the investigation, the grassers cannot claim you until it's over. So it's in your best interest to show us that you're valuable."

Got a point there. Might as well play along.

"Alright then. My name's Nea," said Nea.

She launched into her account of what she'd seen at the auction. Beljhar in the crowd, his men jumping the stage. The way he'd sent the guards running with nothing but a look.

Auditore stopped her there. "A look you said?"

Nea nodded. "He turned around, stared at them, and the thing in his forehead flashed. Then they all just ran."

He sighed. "Would you like to hear what those guards claim that they saw?"

Nea didn't say anything but the lieutenant took her silence as affirmation.

"The men claim that a pack of wolves the size of horses appeared as if from nowhere and chased them off."

Nea blinked. "What?"

"Yes, my reaction as well," said Auditore. "The only versions of this story I have heard without the wolves, come from what few slaves we were able to recover. Those who were out of Beljhar's line of sight, not struck by this light you described."

Of all the damndest...

"What did he do exactly?" asked Nea.

"It's no concern of yours. But thank you for cooperating."

Something was bothering Nea. "At the gate, how did you know I was at the auction, or that I was a slave without seeing my Nuptial?"

"Because you were seen conversing with this man." He slid Quinnel's wanted poster across the table to her. "Quinnel Votrow."

Nea froze. "It's not—"

"You'd best be very careful boy," said Auditore. "You're associating with some very dangerous men. And—"

One of the guards came up and whispered something into his ear.

Lieutenant Auditore blanched. "Very well. I'm afraid our discussion will have to wait. We've a member of the Royal Guard here, sent down by the King himself."

What?

Fortuna's military, as Nea understood it, was separated into three tiers. At the lowest, there were these city watchmen. Above them was the nations army and its commanders. And at the very top was the Royal Guard, the elite soldiers of Fortuna who answered only to the King. What the hell was one of them doing here?

"And?"

"Watch your cheek boy, they have been listening to our conversation, and wish to speak with you." He gestured to one of the guards.

"And for God's sake try and be polite. This will likely find its way back to Captain Cain."

Nea had heard of Captain Cain. Whenever she had read or listened to someone talk about Fortuna the Captain always came up. It was said that Cain was a Conoscenzian that the King had ensnared to his services during the war fifteen years ago. The Captain had forged the Royal Guard into a national peace keeping unit, far more efficient and focused than Fortuna's infamously shoddy military. Cain was said to be an eccentric genius, beloved by the guard and the King as well.

Nea braced herself, wondering what a member of this storied guard might look like. But her expectations were shattered when the door swung open and in strode a woman.

No! That's not possible. She can't be one of them.

The lieutenant stood. "I'll give you a moment then M'lady."

He bowed and stepped outside, the guards following him. The woman took his place at the table. Sure enough, she wore the blue feather, the symbol of the Royal Guard.

The woman had far-away blue eyes and her shoulder-length golden hair was shiny and clean. She had soft, delicate looking features and was only about a head taller than Nea. She wore the stiff blue uniform of the Royal Guard. Her hands were covered in a pair of heavy looking steel gauntlets. An intricate series of designs covered these. The metal work was precise, and they clicked heavily whenever the lady adjusted her fingers, as if there were moving parts inside of them. Nea had never seen their like.

"You're—"

"Maria," she said sharply. "You are Nea, yes?"

It wasn't a question. The woman looked at her expectantly.

"I am," Nea replied, glowering at her.

Stupid cow. Who the hell does she think she is?

"I have several questions for you and very little time, so let's keep the answers short shall we?"

"Beg pardon?"

"Are you, or have you ever been, a member of The Black Briars?"

Nea blinked. "Sorry?"

"Why was the auction chosen selected as a target?" said Maria. "Is it to be the first, or have the Black Briars moved on?"

"Slow down; what are you?"

"Don't play dumb with me boy. I've no time for games. How is it the Briars managed to get out of the city?"

"Look lady I'd never even heard of the Black Briars before three days ago," said Nea, folding her arms.

"Then why were you seen speaking with Quinnel Votrow?"

"Piss off love, I've got nothing to say to you."

Maria narrowed her eyes. "Shall I throw you back to the grassers then?"

"Let's not keep them waiting," she muttered. "I'll escape again, I always do."

Maria looked at her seriously. "I think I may actually believe you. But then what? Have you any idea what they do to escaped slaves in this country, Nea? There's not a place you can go where they won't find you."

"You think I don't already know that?"

Good thing you don't plan on staying.

"In that case perhaps we can help each other."

What's she on about?

Nea glared at Maria. "These men are enemies of the grassers yeah? You want me to rat out the people who attacked those bastards and set me free. Why should I tell you a damn thing?"

Maria shot a glance at the door, then leaned in closer. "Because if you do, I'll get you out of this place."

"What?"

Maria nodded. "You're the property of the Grassen Trading Company, but I'm in the service of the King. I've the power to confiscate you from them. The slaving companies won't dare cross the Royal Guard."

Nea stared back at Maria's eyes. Loath as she was to accept help from anyone, let alone a woman, Nea's survival instincts were kicking in. There was no way in hell she'd get a chance like this again.

"These Black Briars, the man at the gate said they were terrorists?" Nea asked.

"For lack of a better word. I doubt they see themselves that way. They're a private army that has been operating out of somewhere in Fortuna for the better part of a decade. Nobody is quite sure how many there are or what it is they want. Though their targets give us some clue. The Black Briars' hatred for the slaving companies is apparent."

"Then we have something in common."

"Oh certainly," replied Maria. "Though they've never been this open in their attacks?"

"What do you mean?"

"When they strike it's mostly silent, quiet. Very rarely do we have an attack like this one; one with their leaders actively participating, in broad daylight, with dozens of witnesses. Hell, you even had a conversation with the second in command. It's odd, disturbingly odd and His Majesty has sent me to find out just what game Djeng Beljhar and his men are playing."

"You?" Nea asked incredulously. She'd thought that the irritating woman was at least of low rank in the guard, was she really working with the King? "But you're..." Nea trailed off awkwardly.

"I'd watch my tongue if I were you, boy."

Nea snorted but didn't press the issue.

How does a stupid girl like her get up to a position like that? Probably bedded every single commander in the guard to get this post. Maybe the Captain or even the King.

"Well?"

Nea stared into Maria's eyes, sizing her up. "Get me out of here and I'll tell you what I know."

"Very well."

"After that I want you to put me on a boat."

"Wherever you please."

"Then I'll do it," said Nea.

"I know you will. Where is this boat going?"

Nea scowled. She wasn't eager to share the company of this infuriating woman but if it meant getting out of this city and putting some distance between her and the grassers, maybe even getting her west, then she had to take it.

"Conoscenzia," said Nea flatly.

"Well that makes things a great deal easier for both of us then," said Maria smiling and getting to her feet.

"What do you mean?"

"I grew up in Conoscenzia," she said. "Getting you there will be no trouble at all."

Nea looked at Maria, a wild thought suddenly occurring to her.

No, no she can't...

It wasn't possible. "You're not..."

"I am," she offered Nea her hand. "Captain Cain, Captain *Maria* Cain."

10

Growing Pains

"Seiyariu are you sure we're not leaking?"

"No more than we were the last time you asked."

Their tiny boat drifted smoothly over the murky green water. Seiyariu brushed aside reeds and low hanging branches as he rowed through the swamp. The water writhed and twisted with plants and animals. Strange looking fish swam past Leo's reflection and then vanished before he could get a good look at them. He was constantly swatting away insects seeking refuge in his mane of hair. Overhead, the tops of the dark trees knitted together in a dense canopy blocking out the twilight glow. Their only constant guide was the lantern that hung from the boat. The air was hot, muggy, and stank of mold and dead things.

"Sorry, it's just..." Leo craned his neck, convinced there was something moving out there. The hot, heavy air combined with the droning of the insects was making him feel tired.

"Relax Leo," Seiyariu said, not looking back. "If any of your grassers were following us, I'm certain they'll have given up by now."

Leo nodded, as out of the corner of his eye a scaly... something crested the surface for the briefest moment then dipped back under. He edged closer to Seiyariu, eyes wide.

It had been two days since they stood in the crater together. In that time, they'd left the grasslands for the thick swamps that made up the western coast. The sanctuary that Seiyariu had spoken of was still a few days away. Their progress had slowed to a crawl in the mire. As ever, the path Seiyariu took was erratic, wild and confusing. Undoubtedly it made sense to him, but Leo could not get his head around it. At least, Leo thought, no grassers would follow them through all this.

The sound of raucous laughter carried over the swamp. Leo raised his sleepy head and looked across the water. On the edge of the shore stood a dilapidated building, supported precariously over the water by large wooden beams. It was several stories tall, with light streaming from its many windows and the holes in the badly thatched roof. A long dock extended out towards them. Several boats were moored there already but there was just enough room for one more. Trumpets could be heard, loud singing, and even a piano. The music was rocking the already shaky foundation and joining with the merry laughter to echo across through the night, unfamiliar and inviting.

Leo sat up, very much awake now. "What is that?"

"Where we'll be staying tonight, I hope." Seiyariu grinned. "It does tend to be full this time of year."

The boat drifted over to the dock and Seiyariu hopped out to tie it off. Leo scrambled after him. On their way in Leo noticed several small Peregrine Runes, as Seiyariu had called them, scratched next to the door.

"What do those mean?" he asked.

"That," Seiyariu pointed at the first one, which looked like a crackling fire, "Means that you stand outside a sympathetic home, sympathetic to vagabonds, that is. And this one," he pointed to the symbol below it.

This one was more complicated, Leo thought, perhaps it was a hand raising a single finger to ask for silence.

"This means that you stand outside a good place for sharing secrets. When these two symbols are together you are in the safest places for our kind in Fortuna, so do not pass them by; they are few."

It was packed and raucous, the bar and all the surrounding tables were crowded and then some. Men were shouting, laughing and fighting in at least three languages. In the corner, a band was playing on the instruments Leo had heard outside. The music was so loud and the voices so numerous, that it all blurred together into a mass of noise and confusion that made Leo feel dizzy. Nevertheless there was a wonderful energy about the place and almost everyone was smiling. He noticed a fair number of men and women in green cloaks, just like Seiyariu's.

"Seth!" Seiyariu called, sidling up to the bar.

"Well I'll be damned," cried the innkeeper, a wall-eyed old man with a patchy beard. "Seiyariu! Where the hell have you been?"

He had a very thick accent that sounded much like the poorly tuned instruments roaring in the background.

"Away on business," Seiyariu replied with one of his strange smiles. "I only just returned."

Leo was hanging back, staying slightly behind Seiyariu, when he noticed a statue resting on the bar. It was an alligator, carved to perfection. Leo drew closer to it, curious as to what it was made of. He was about to touch it when the alligator snapped at him. Leo jumped backwards so quickly he almost fell over a chair. The innkeeper burst out laughing.

"Sorry about that lad," he wheezed. "It's his favorite game."

The alligator had already gone back to pretending not to be real.

"Room six is free," he said, wiping a tear from his eye. "Top floor."

"Thank you," Said Seiyariu. "I'll come down and join the fun a little later. I've some new stories."

The innkeeper nodded happily and Seiyariu led Leo up the stairs. They were as run down as the rest of the inn and wobbled with every step, growing slimmer and slimmer as they climbed past two floors to the attic.

"He fooled me with that damn alligator the first time too," Seiyariu told Leo as he approached a door with a crooked brass six on it.

The room inside was cramped but cozy. Two small beds lay below a sloped ceiling so low that Seiyariu brained himself on the way in. Mumbling some choice curses, he sat down on one of the beds and tossed his pack to the ground. Leo dropped onto his bed. The mattress was lumpy and the pillow smelled like cats, but to Leo it felt like heaven. The days of travel on the road had left him stiff and dirty. But as he lay back, letting his muscles relax, Leo thought that perhaps wandering had its luxuries.

"Don't get too comfortable," said Seiyariu as he rummaged in his pack. "There's still time for one more lesson."

"Right now?" Leo sat up, his muscles complaining.

"I was always of the opinion that one can learn better by the light of the moon." His now resident mysterious smile was in place again. "I'll let you choose the subject, if you wish."

This piqued Leo's interest. "Will you teach me to fight like you? With a sword?"

Seiyariu shot him one of those sweeping looks. "No."

"What, but you said—"

"You can barely hold a pen in that arm of yours, let alone a sword."

Leo felt his cheeks flush with shame. Seiyariu was right, but Leo's awe at what Seiyariu had done back in Limani overshadowed his apprehension. The idea of being able to move like the vagabond, to defend himself. It was too tempting to resist.

"I'm left handed," he said, hopefully. "If I don't put too much strain on it, it won't get in the way."

"Very well, who am I to keep you from trying." Seiyariu unbelted the smaller of his two swords. "Here."

He handed it to Leo.

Leo unsheathed the weapon, letting out a frightened little squeak as he did. The feel of the blade in his hand was otherworldly. It gave him a sense of potential, confidence, and power. He practiced unsheathing it a couple times before Seiyariu led him outside, away from the inn and to a patch of the most solid ground they could find.

By all rights Leo felt he should've been shaking. Yet something kept him calm, likely it was Seiyariu's smiling face. The sword felt awkward in his hand and he was unsure of how to hold it properly. It weighed more than he'd expected.

"What do I do now?" he asked, feeling rather stupid.

Seiyariu stepped behind him and helped adjust his grip so that he had the blade pointed out in front of him. "Turn your shoulders; there you are." He eyed a rotting old tree. "Ordinarily I'd have us try sparring but in your condition I don't think that's a good idea. At least not yet. Try and strike at the bark here," he pointed. "Fast as you can."

He did, bringing the blade across as he'd seen Seiyariu do. He stumbled, the weight of the sword shifting his balance, and he missed the tree by a few inches.

Feeling even more stupid, Leo straightened up to try again. This was much harder than Seiyariu had made it look. But the vagabond had years of training; had been in countless fights. Leo swung again, making contact with the wood this time. But the sudden impact jostled his right arm, causing him to drop the sword. Before Leo knew what was happening, the pain returned and he collapsed to the ground, clutching at his arm as if trying to keep it from coming apart.

Seiyariu stared down at him, a curious look in his eyes. "You lied to me."

"I'm sorry," Leo hissed through gritted teeth.

Seiyariu crouched down beside him. "The wound is old, but it's deeper than you let on. And it hasn't healed. Tell me the truth Leo, how did you hurt your arm?"

Leo tried not to look Seiyariu in the eye. "Glass," he said, relenting. "I put it through some glass."

"Why is that?"

"I was angry," Leo replied. It was technically the truth, if not all of it. He was afraid the full story might make the vagabond think he was mad.

"Why didn't you just tell me?"

"I was scared." Leo turned away. "I thought you'd leave me, if you knew I was broken, I mean."

Seiyariu's eyes looked far away and misty. "Battered Leo, not broken. Never broken."

He took his short sword back and belted it on. Reaching inside the folds of his tunic, Seiyariu produced a third blade. This one was much smaller, curved like the other two but without a cross-guard. It's sheath and hilt merging almost seamlessly together.

"I'm supposed to carry this with me; I don't imagine I'll need it as much as you."

He handed Leo the dagger, scabbard and all and showed Leo how to belt it on.

"This will suit you better I think. It's not as heavy. If you're in a fight, you'll need to do all you can to protect your injury. The enemy will see it as nothing more than a target. I suspect you have some nerve damage in that arm, so defense will be paramount."

Leo unsheathed the dagger. Just like Seiyariu's other weapons, it only had an edge on one side. He tried swinging. Sure enough it was lighter, easier to control. He managed to slice the bark from the tree this time, leaving a long thin scratch in the wood.

"Much better," said Seiyariu, folding his arms. "Though I think you'd better practice a bit more before we try to spar."

Leo weighed the dagger in his hands curiously. "Why carry three weapons?" he asked, confused. Surely a hidden dagger was redundant for Seiyariu when the vagabond was carrying a sword at his fingertips.

"This little one isn't meant for battle," said Seiyariu.

"What then?"

Seiyariu's brow furrowed. "To wear swords such as these means to follow a code."

"Like The Green Road?"

"I suppose in a way," he said. "But these rules are far more ironclad than any vagabond custom. When I agreed to wield them I pledged myself to a certain standard. This dagger is for the moment I fail to measure up to that standard."

Leo stared at the blade in his hands, horror gripping him. "You mean it's…"

"For suicide. Yes."

Suicide. The word hung in the air as Leo stared at the blade in his hands. In that moment, Leo felt certain that Seiyariu could see right through him.

11

Steel Grip

CAIN AND NEA rode out of Limani in a merchant convoy heading north. The two of them blended in quite well with the travelers and even when a posse of grassers insisted on checking the wagons and supplies for escaping slaves, they took little notice of her. Though if they had, Nea was grateful that Cain had let her keep the bow and arrows she'd stolen back in town.

Cain had been true to her word; she gotten Nea out of the fortress, out of the city. Nea even had her own horse now, a calm, but rather dim palomino. Cain's own horse was dark brown and fierce; it snapped at any hands that weren't its master's.

They met up with the caravan and blended right in. Cain had changed from her uniform into a set of simple traveling clothes. Nea wasn't sure why, but she didn't feel like asking. She kept silent most of the day, letting her rage smolder.

This was Cain? This small woman was the legendary captain that so many people spoke about? It was impossible.

All those stories and in the end she's just a noblewoman out playing soldier.

Women weren't even permitted to captain in the army let alone the Royal Guard.

It's an insult.

As the sun began to set, Cain split off from the caravan and headed down an eastern road into the woods. That night they made camp on a little hill overlooking the road, sheltered by trees. Nea watched as Cain fiddled with her over-packed saddlebags. These were square, and seemed to weigh quite a lot, based on the protests of her horse.

"Why did you bring so much?" Nea asked.

"Ah," she said, noticing where Nea was staring. "My inventions." she explained. "I'm something of an engineer."

"Of course you are," muttered Nea, this whole thing was becoming ridiculous. "Those things on your arms too?"

Cain adjusted the gauntlets fondly. "Possibly."

Nea avoided the knight's gaze and began to gather wood for a fire. All the while fuming to herself.

Stuck up, self-important cow.

Cain was so small, so weak, yet she carried herself like a true aristocrat.

Pathetic.

When she'd found enough kindling she returned to the clearing and let Cain ignite them with a tinderbox she'd plucked from the saddlebags.

Cain yawned as the fire started to rise. "I'd love to get to sleep and I'm sure you would as well. But we've got to talk properly if only for a little while."

Nea just scowled. The pompous ditz was lucky Nea hadn't scarpered the minute they'd gotten out of town. Still, Cain had gotten her out, just like she said she would. Nea could at least fulfill her part of the bargain. "Where do you want me to start?"

"We have reason to suspect that the Black Briars were looking for something, or someone, during this little operation."

Leo.

"Ah so I'm right then," Cain grinned, catching the panic on Nea's face before she could hide it.

Damn!

"I think that you know exactly who that someone is," said Cain. "Are you going to tell me?"

"Why should I?"

"Because I got you out of there," Cain's voice dripping with a cockiness that made Nea's toes curl. "And because I'm the only chance you have of getting away from the grassers. You've got a choice here Nea, you can be stubborn and go back to being a slave. Or you can tell me what you know and be on your way to Conoscenzia."

You think you're so damn smart. How'd you like it if I just clubbed you on the head, took your damn bags and rode off?

It was a lovely thought, but Nea wasn't stupid enough to ignore the truth in Cain's words.

"What did Quinnel say to you?" Cain asked, feigning patience.

"Not much." Nea shrugged. "He told me they were looking for someone, like you said. A boy."

"And?"

"And what?"

"Come on Nea don't play dumb with me; we're past that point I think."

I hate you.

"Fine," Nea glowered at Cain. "He said he was looking for a boy with red hair and a bad arm."

"And what did you tell him?"

"I don't…" Nea sighed. It was becoming apparent that this woman wasn't going to be weaseled around with tricky words. "I told him the truth."

"Oh?"

Nea bit her lip, unsure of how to explain this. "I met a boy named Leo, on the ship coming here. He was young, small, kinda sick looking. He had the red hair and his arm was all limp-like, covered in scars. He wore it in a sling."

Cain nodded, not interrupting.

"Anyway, I screwed up. I was supposed to get away, but I did something stupid and helped him."

"How noble of you."

"Shut up," she snapped. "If it wasn't for him I'd be halfway to Conoscenzia by now. I wouldn't be stuck here talking to…"

"To what?" Cain asked.

To a woman.

"To you." Nea looked away.

"Leo," said Cain softly. "And do you have any idea what they want with him?"

Nea shook her head. "But he did tell me something else, something odd. He said…" Nea tried to remember Quinnel's exact words. "…that if I ever wanted to set the world on fire, go to a place called Foresbury, and confess his liturgy beneath the holy stone."

Cain sat back mulling these words over. "It sounds to me like he was trying to recruit you."

"What? Like to be one of them? Why?"

"You're a resourceful boy and the Briars are known to recruit escaped slaves. Did he say anything else?"

Nea shook her head. "No, but he didn't seem keen to hurt Leo or anything. And he didn't hurt me either."

"The Black Briars never hurt slaves," said Cain.

"So far that's better than anyone else I've met in this damn country. I'm not seeing much reason to be hunting them."

"Kidnapping and murder of public officials, theft of the property of the crown. The attack in Limani was the final straw. His majesty decided something had to be done. The Briars must be found and eliminated, and I intend to do just that. And you're going to help me."

"Hold on, I thought we had a deal."

"We did," said Cain. "And I have no intention of going back on it. But if Quinnel Votrow seeks to recruit you, then you may be my only lead in finding the Black Briars."

Liar! She tricked you!

"Oh no," Nea was on her feet now. "I'm not getting caught up in your stupid investigation. I've got to get out of here."

"Foresbury," said Cain thoughtfully. "That's north, it's a quiet town, not much goes on there. As for the rest," Cain frowned. "A church, confessional probably."

Nea was already striding away.

Stupid soldier girl thinks she can walk all over you. Well—

Something cold and metallic locked around Nea's wrist. She turned to find Cain's armored hand holding her fast.

"Let me go," Nea hissed.

"I'm afraid I can't do that," she said. "I need you and you need me if you want to get to Conoscenzia. You won't last ten minutes out there by yourself. You saw them on the road. They'll find you. I don't care how smart you think you are. Surely you don't want to go back to that."

"Anything is better than listening to you," Nea snarled.

"You're not going anywhere."

"You're gonna stop me then," said Nea.

"Yes," Cain replied, her face set.

68

How could she be so sure of herself?

"You're stupid, you know that? You think just because you've got a fancy title that makes you a warrior. You're a lady, and even the weakest man can overpower a lady. And you're no different!"

Cain gave her a curious look then. Nea had expected rage, indignation, but what Cain wore was something else entirely. Pity.

Nea felt the rage ignite in her gut once again and she swung at Cain, trying to wipe that stupid look off her face, just as she had the girl in the shop. But Cain ducked, stepping around Nea and sweeping her legs out from under her. Nea tumbled to the ground and Cain locked her arm in a steel grip, pressing her face down into the grass.

"Not fast enough," she said with a bit of a laugh.

"Let me go!"

"What's that?" Cain said. "Can't overpower a lady? Seems your theory is found wanting my little man."

Nea screamed and thrashed, trying to get away but Cain held her fast. Her words were a garbled mess of cursing and threats. Cain gave no indication that she heard.

Stupid whore! You can't let her do this to you, you have to...

But Nea knew there wasn't anything she could do. Despite everything, this damn woman was stronger than she. Cursing her own weakness, Nea relaxed her body. If her fists weren't going to get her out of this, she would need to be more diplomatic, no matter how humiliating it was.

Cain loosened her grip and let Nea sit up. Nea scrambled a few feet away, massaging her scraped wrist.

If she's so weak, what does that make you?

"I'll not do that again," said Cain, holding up her hands. "So long as you promise not to run."

"How long?"

"You take me to Foresbury and we follow the trail to the Briars. All I need from you is to confirm the location of their headquarters. That will satisfy His Majesty. Sound like a plan?"

"And after that?"

"You'll be on the next boat to Conoscenzia."

You won't last that long. The second she turns her back, you'll run again.

But Nea could see in Cain's eyes that moment of weakness was not coming. She could run, but Cain would catch her as surely as the grassers. Somehow, she knew that.

"Fine, I'll do it."

"Good choice," said Cain with a smile.

"Do I have any other choices?"

"Many, but you know that this is the smartest."

Nea glared at Cain. She wasn't quite sure what annoyed her more, Cain's constant assumptions that she knew what Nea was thinking, or the fact that she was right.

12

Kokaleth

THE DREARY LITTLE fishing town loomed out of the fog. At first, Leo took it to be a burned-out ruin, but as they drew closer he saw a single muddy street lined with small grey buildings on either side. At the end of this little road the sea stretched out before them, a great steel sheet, vanishing into the fog. A smell of rotting fish filled the thick air and what few people did wander the streets, glanced suspiciously at the two of them. A post sticking out of the muddy ground told him the town was called *Udra*.

"Your friend lives here?" said Leo. The town was remote, even by Seiyariu's standards.

"Of course not," Seiyariu gave a mischievous wink. "That part comes later."

Leo shot a few nervous looks at the townsfolk. Did they perhaps recognize him? Seiyariu sensed his worries.

"Relax," he said. "We won't be here for long."

It had been over a week since the pair of them had left the tavern in the swamp. Beyond the marshlands was the coast; they would need to follow this north to reach the sanctuary. All along the coast were tiny little fishing villages just like this one.

Despite Seiyariu's patient teaching, Leo was still struggling to learn the vagabond way. He could cook, and reading the Peregrine Runes came fairly quickly for him. But, when it came to hunting, tracking and fighting, Leo was a dreadfully slow learner. It infuriated him. He wanted to impress Seiyariu, to see his face light up with pride. This drove him to keep trying even in the face of his failures.

Seiyariu led Leo straight past the town and onto the dock. He sat on the edge and unwrapped a loaf of rather stale bread. Leo stood for a few moments, looking out at the great black expanse before him. The ocean in its pure immensity never ceased to overwhelm him. Memories of his time at sea still burned hot in his mind but he refused to let that spoil the unrivaled beauty before him. He took a deep breath, filling his lungs with the refreshing sea air, and sat down beside Seiyariu.

The vagabond handed Leo a chunk of bread and the two began to eat quietly. It was nice, sitting there with Seiyariu as though they were the only two people on earth. Now and then he noticed the vagabond looking up at the increasingly ominous looking sky.

"This friend of yours," Leo began. "Will you tell me a bit about him please? You're being very mysterious, more than usual I mean."

Seiyariu laughed. "Well, he's a vagabond."

"Then why does he live here?" asked Leo. "I thought vagabonds didn't live anywhere."

"He doesn't live *here*," Seiyariu said.

"What does that mean?"

"You'll see," Seiyariu replied, clearly enjoying himself.

"Why are we stopping to see him? Will he help us get to the sanctuary?"

"The sanctuary is well within our sights Leo, we won't need his help for that."

"Why then?"

"Before I found you Leo, I'd been traveling abroad. I'm woefully ignorant of what's been going on in Fortuna during my absence, and not a soul pays more attention to the comings and goings of this land than him. He specializes in investigation, and hoards the information and secrets he uncovers. I'm hoping he can fill me in on what I have missed these last few months before we continue north."

"Oh," said Leo, rather disappointed. "That's all?"

"Vagabonds must always be aware of the land they protect Leo, it is my responsibility. Besides, I think you'll find him... interesting."

Seiyariu rummaged around in his pack. He took out a tiny crystal bottle, uncorked it, and tipped it over, a few shining grains of what looked like salt slipped out into the sea. Where they had landed, a bubbling green froth erupted and steamed.

"You may want to stand back," said the vagabond helping Leo to his feet.

They did, Leo looking at the water and back to Seiyariu, with no idea what was happening. Bubbles began to rise from the depths, breaking in rapid succession, as though the sea itself was boiling. It grew and grew until it reached such a pitch that a tumultuous explosion of water erupted, dowsing the pair of them. Leo wiped water from his eyes and turned back to see something perched before them on the edge of the dock.

It was shaped like a man, only a good foot taller than any man should be. The creature's skin was the same color as the sea, a dark forbidding gray-blue, covered in tiny scales. Long webbed fingers stretched out from its hands, flexing and grasping at nothing. It wore a cloak – at least Leo thought it was a cloak – tattered and shredded, hanging over only one shoulder, and made of tightly wound seaweed. Around its waist the creature wore more seaweed in a loincloth and a black belt covered in pouches.

Atop its head, it wore something resembling a crown made of red coral. Gills pulsed on its throat, and instead of ears, sharp pointed fins shot out from its skull. Its eyes burned with a deep glowing green. Despite all that, its face was closer to a man's than a fish or a frog. The creature's lipless mouth opened and a throaty, garbled voice emanated.

"Where in the hell have you been?" it said.

Leo sat down, unable to comprehend the thing that stood before him.

"Kokaleth!" Seiyariu beamed at the strange creature. His arms raised in greeting. "How are you my friend?"

"Don't change the subject!" The thing called Kokaleth replied, face contorting in fury. "You picked a fine time to go gallivanting about the Southern Isles, let me tell you."

"What are you talking about?" Seiyariu's face has fallen, he looked worried and confused. "What's happened?"

"Seiyariu, Knail has been stolen!" Kokaleth roared, his eyes bulging.

Seiyariu's face changed, all its color washing away. A look of fear that Leo had never seen him wear before.

"What's been stolen?" Leo asked.

"Are you certain?"

"Without a doubt," Kokaleth replied. "I've been looking into it as best I can."

"What've you found?"

"No clues, no trail to follow, and no witnesses. And I can't get in contact with the man who was supposed to be guarding it."

"So what can we do? It's just gone without a trace?"

"Well that's where my investigative skills come in Seiyariu. For the past couple of years I've been keeping tabs on a string of artifacts, stolen under similar circumstances."

"Well that's not unusual," Seiyariu said, folding his arms.

"I think you'll find that it is quite unusual," snapped Kokaleth. "All these artifacts come from the same time period. Before The Clash of Comets."

"Weapons?" Seiyariu asked.

Kokaleth nodded, a shadow passing across his face. "They are being stockpiled somewhere in Adis."

Adis, the words left Kokaleth's mouth with a mix of fear and disgust.

Seiyariu's face was unreadable. "And you think Knail is among them?"

"I'm all but certain. The pattern is unmistakable."

He shook his head. "I am going after it, with your consent and a full partnership of course." Seiyariu offered his hand and Kokaleth shook it. "Do you have more salt?"

Kokaleth produced a bottle from one of the pouches on his belt and tossed it to Seiyariu. "I know you wouldn't be out this far if you didn't need it." Kokaleth frowned as his gaze fell on Leo. "Who is this whelp?"

"Oh, I'm sorry where are my manners?" Seiyariu said, gesturing at Leo. "This is Leo. I rescued him from some unsavory types back in Limani. I'm taking him north to the sanctuary."

Leo was baffled by the conversation that had just taken place, but he was feeling more relaxed now that he saw Seiyariu and this creature were friendly. Leo raised his hand in greeting. Kokaleth looked him up and down unimpressed. Though there was something behind his gaze, an understanding that Leo couldn't quite place.

Seiyariu continued with the introduction. "Leo this is Kokaleth, he's an old friend of mine."

Leo wanted to say something polite or at least nothing at all, what came out of his mouth was, "What… what are you?"

Kokaleth snorted at this. "Listen well, boy, for I am master of the tides, lord of the sea." Seiyariu rolled his eyes, but Kokaleth continued. "I am the rider of the arctic whales, the…" He noticed Leo's bewildered expression, "I am a Mariner," he said more calmly. "More importantly I am a vagabond."

"You?" Leo asked incredulously.

"Is that so terribly hard to believe?"

"Well," Leo looked Kokaleth up and down, sure enough his cloak did seem rather similar to Seiyariu's. "You do kind of stand out."

"Charming little thing, Seiyariu, congratulations," said Kokaleth as Seiyariu suppressed a laugh. "I would recommend against taking him with if you are going after Knail."

"You don't have to tell me."

"Yes I do," Kokaleth smirked and with that, he flung himself back over the edge of the dock and disappeared beneath the waves.

For a long time, Leo just stood there. "What was that… that thing?"

"I thought he told you in rather explicit detail," replied the vagabond, a twinkle in his eye.

"I've never seen anything like him before," Leo persisted. "I didn't know anything like him even existed."

"You may find, that there are great many things that the rest of the world is quite content with ignoring."

The sky opened up and a light fall of rain came pattering down on their hoods. Together, they made their way back through the town. Leo bubbling with excited questions the whole way.

"Are there more of him?"

"Oh I assure there is only one of *him*."

"I mean Mariners."

"I am inclined to believe so, though I've never met them."

"What's Knail? And what's Adis?"

"Adis is a city, built within an old system of catacombs deep below the forest of Styx to the northeast. Leo, those catacombs have become home to the most foul examples of humanity, a home to the darkest, most ancient arts."

"And we're going there?"

"*We* are not going there."

"But you said…"

"*I* am going there. You are going to the sanctuary."

"What?" Seiyariu wasn't serious, he couldn't be.

"That was the deal was it not? You wanted to disappear; we have. I told you I'd take you as far as sanctuary overlooking the edge of Mavrodasos. I will."

"But…"

"Leo you don't want to venture into a place like that," he stated flatly.

"No I don't I just… I thought were going to be together longer. I thought I was becoming, I don't know, your apprentice."

"You are!" Seiyariu said, his eyes genuine. "I'll come back and resume your teachings once this whole matter is settled. I don't want to put you in any more danger."

Leo thought about this. What Seiyariu said sent chills down his spine and Leo had no desire to hike to the darkest corners of Fortuna to recover something he knew nothing about. But his time with the vagabond had been… happy. The first time in ages that he'd felt any kind of joy. He didn't want it to just end. He didn't want to be alone again.

"What is Knail?" Leo asked again, stalling for time. If Seiyariu was kept talking perhaps he'd stay with him a while longer.

"A terrible weapon. A weapon vagabonds are sworn to protect." Seiyariu knelt and took Leo by the shoulders, a strange look in his eyes. "I've made many mistakes in my life. Consider this journey my way of atoning for them. I can't say more, and I won't ask you to go with me."

"What do you mean you can't say?" Leo was trying very hard not to cry now. "You can't just take me away, promise to teach me all about being a vagabond and then just leave. You can't!"

"Leo I…"

"I'm going with you," Leo said flatly.

"Look at this from my perspective. If anything happened to you…"

"You said I'd be safe with you."

"Leo in a place like Adis even I cannot be sure of that."

76

"Is it… is it because of my arm? Because I can't use a sword?"

"Leo…"

"I'll learn!" he said desperately. "I don't care how much it hurts. I'll learn to fight if you'll take me." Leo hadn't known he'd felt this strongly until the moment he needed to say it.

"The sanctuary is a good place Leo. They'll look after you better than I ever could. Weren't you the one who said you wanted to find a place to stay, a home?"

"Weren't you the one who said that home is a feeling?" Leo had tears in his eyes now. The strange happiness he'd felt on the road with Seiyariu, was that what home felt like now? Whether it was or not Leo would be damned if he'd let that feeling go now.

Seiyariu glared at him for a few seconds, then his expression melted into that familiar calm serenity and he took Leo in an embrace. "Fine. Damn you, Leo. You can come with me. But you must swear that you will do exactly as I say."

13

Captain Cain

WHEN NEA WOKE the next morning she couldn't quite remember where she was.

Still in the jails of Limani?

She rolled over, and realized she was too comfortable for that. Nea sat up and fought her eyelids open. A beam of soft sunlight slipped through the trees and she could feel an autumn chill in the air. She yawned and stretched. She hadn't slept that well in some time.

She'd slept in her clothes, as usual. Swinging her bow over her shoulder and stifling another yawn, Nea got to her feet, looking around. The stupid woman was already awake and dressed, clearing the campsite and putting away her bedroll.

"His Majesty didn't pack the lady a fancy tent?" Nea sneered.

"You're awake," Cain said, ignoring the jab and infuriating Nea even further. "Good, I want to go over the plan."

"The plan?" Nea frowned, Cain was speaking like their conversation the night before had never ended.

"Yes the plan," she continued. "On the King's business secrecy is vital."

"That why you're not wearing your uniform?"

"Indeed, and I'd prefer not to attract any more unwanted attention on the road."

"I attract unwanted attention, do I?"

"Not so long as you keep that hand hidden. Tell me, what would you say if we passed a checkpoint, like the one that nabbed you in Limani, and you were asked what our relationship was?"

"I…"

"Precisely, and that's likely to lead to more questions. Hence why I think we should decide on your role."

"You could say I'm your son," Nea offered, loading up her horse.

"My son?" Cain laughed. "You're a bit too old to be my son."

"Oh," Nea hadn't thought about this. "Your squire then?"

"Squire?"

"Don't knights have squires?"

"I'm not a knight, I'm a Royal Guardsman. Besides do you have any idea what a squire does?"

"Of course I do. Help her divine majesty put her armor on, brush her hair and make sure her feet don't get cold." Nea gave a mocking little bow.

"Charming," said Cain. "But that's work for a lady-in-waiting don't you think?" Nea nearly dropped the saddlebag. "Besides, I don't like to parade my name and station around."

"You didn't have a problem with that yesterday."

"Oh the pin is fine in the company of men of service, but I'd prefer to keep it off on the road, especially if the Briars' spy network is as robust as they say."

"And those?" asked Nea gesturing at Cain's hands. She was still wearing those strange metal gauntlets.

"I like to keep those on," she said simply. Then, looking Nea up and down, Cain said, "I think you shall be my delinquent brother, escorted from his violent boys school by his kind elder sister for the holiday."

"Whatever," Nea muttered, hoisting herself into the saddle.

"Oh come on now," Cain imitated her. "We're going to be sharing each other's company for some time; we should at least make the most of it." She gave the animal a kick and they cantered down towards the road. "I'm sorry you feel so betrayed, hitched to a lady like me, but remember at the end of the day we're doing the other a service."

Nea met this with a fair amount of grumbling and the day continued without much fanfare. All Nea managed to do was get herself more worked up over Cain's calm demeanor. Several times she thought to just run her horse off the road and leave the daft lady to her stupid errands. But she didn't.

Coward.

Few travelers were walking these paths. Despite her present company, the crisp, cold air made her feel alive. Was this what freedom tasted like?

No.

She shot a scathing look at Cain's back. She'd just traded grassers for this damnable knight. As soon as the thought materialized Nea found herself regretting it. Cain was a stupid girl, but she wasn't cruel. Without her Nea knew she couldn't reach the coast. Not with the slaving companies after her, the previous day's events had proven that much.

At least the lady doesn't ask questions.

The only traveler who spoke to them that morning was a wizened old man in a dark green cloak covered with patches. He inclined his head as they passed, and murmured something to the effect of "M'lady."

Nea frowned at his retreating form. "Do you know him?" she asked Cain, who didn't look the slightest bit amused.

"No, but they know me."

"They?"

"Vagabonds, you can spot them by the cloaks usually."

Nea spun back to get another look at the old man. Vagabonds, the homeless drifters who kept watch over the Archipelago; they were infamous. Nea had never met one before. She watched the man make his way down the road. Cain still had that sour look on her face.

"What's wrong with you?"

"Nothing is wrong with me," Cain snapped. "I've just got very little patience for that lot."

"I thought they kept Fortuna safe."

"No," she replied flatly. "*I* keep Fortuna safe, His Majesty keeps Fortuna safe. What those vagrants do is interfere where they're not wanted and make more trouble for everybody. Take my advice on this Nea. Do not trust vagabonds. They're no better than The Black Briars at the end of the day, though they'd like to claim the moral high ground I'm sure. They operate in lies and deception, dispensing vigilante justice on a populace that never asked for their help."

"Oh," was all Nea could figure to say. Though she liked how frustrated it made Cain.

If they bother pompous fools like her, then they can't be as bad as all that.

"Sorry they bother you, M'lady."

*

Around midday they came to a checkpoint on the road. The flag of the Fortuan army, the horse in the storm, billowed overhead as the soldiers checked papers. There were around twenty of them there, armed and ready. These were no dozy city guardsmen to be sure. They sized up each traveler with a sweeping gaze inquiring about local brigands and escaped slaves.

"Is it always like this then?" asked Nea.

"Yes, we've a far lower tolerance for outlaws than The Southern Isles."

But not grassers.

The soldiers looked them up and down. "What's your business in these parts?"

"Heading home," replied Cain her voice high and flirty.

The soldier glanced at Nea. "And you?"

You're her delinquent little brother, escorted from your violent boys' home by your kindly elder sister for the holiday.

Nea just blinked, and muttered, "My sister."

The soldier frowned, "All right then. Off you go, have a nice day miss."

"Oh, and you as well," Cain said waving.

When they were out of earshot Nea grumbled, "What the hell was that anyway?"

"That?"

"That voice," she scowled. "Batting your eyes and preening like a—"

"Notice how few questions he asked? A little kindness can work wonders."

"Not exactly becoming for a knight."

Of course the girl would try to rely on charms.

"I'm just being friendly, Nea," laughed Cain. "No need to be jealous."

Nea's face went scarlet. "I'm not jealous, I just…"

"I'm teasing, come on let's go."

They continued down the road.

"Army seems tense, those weren't your men I take it," said Nea, once the checkpoint was out of sight.

"No, my men are all over Fortuna."

"Spread thin are you?"

"We go where the King needs us."

"I've been wanting to ask about that," said Nea with a frown. "Why did His Majesty send you on your own?"

"It couldn't be that I'm simply the best at my job?" Cain said, shooting her a sly look.

Nea rolled her eyes. "Fine don't answer."

"Alright don't get fussy," said Cain. "If you must know, The Black Briars dabble in my area of expertise."

Unbearable smug self-entitled nonsense?

"And what's that?"

"Weapons," Cain replied. "His Majesty believes that The Black Briars are behind a series of thefts lately. Thefts of powerful weapons and artifacts. Something I'm very knowledgeable about."

Sure you are.

"One more reason he sent me."

"Not because you're his favorite?"

"Ah," Cain laughed. "Here we go. Go on, I know you're dying to ask."

Nea didn't waste the opportunity. The question had been nagging at her ever since they'd left Limani. "Is it true that he stole you away from Conoscenzia during the war?"

Cain blinked. "Oh, oh no, of course not." She began to laugh.

"What?" Nea scowled.

"That's not the question most people ask me," she replied. "Generally, there's some gossip involving His Majesty's lack of a wife and my lack of a husband."

"Oh," Nea hadn't even thought about that. "I didn't know you were so close, all the stuff I read about…"

"Ah well, there's your first problem, stories of our meeting have been greatly exaggerated."

"How did you meet?" Nea asked, despite herself. "During the war, right?"

Cain nodded. "Because of the war, in many ways. Lord Chiron assumed the throne when he was quite young and inexperienced. His father had been killed and all the blame pointed to an outside attack from my home, Conoscenzia. Acting on this, he launched a massive invasion. It cost both sides countless lives and, in the end, the country that he had ravaged had been innocent. The murderer had been one of His Majesty's own advisers."

What in the hell?

"And you serve this man?"

Cain laughed. "I said it's quite a long story."

"But…" Nea couldn't get the words out.

He invaded your home, killed your people.

Nea had known that there had to be something off about the strange knight but this? This was too much. How could anyone be so stupid?

"Nea relax, you look like you're going to explode."

"What were you thinking?" Nea exclaimed.

"Maybe I think that my presence here will do far more good than it would elsewhere." Cain gave Nea a serious look. "Don't mistake my fealty for blind acceptance. You don't understand the…"

"Don't understand what?"

"Look," said Cain pointing.

Nea squinted. "Is that another checkpoint?"

More people had stopped moving further down the road. As they drew nearer Nea could see that the path ahead was blocked by a deluge of fallen trees. Many of the riders were dispersing now, doubling back the way they'd come. She and Cain would have to cut through the woods again. Why did Cain look so concerned?

"What's happening here?" she demanded. Her cheery demeanor was gone in an instant as she cantered her horse to the front of the remaining travelers, two men on horseback, and a shrouded figure sitting atop a horse drawn wagon filled with hay.

"Road's blocked miss," said one of the men.

"Fastest way north now is the Borgia Pass," his companion chimed in.

He pointed. Nea hadn't seen it at first but through the trees on the side of the road there was another jagged path strewn with rocks that led into the forested hills beyond.

Cain gave him a serious look. "So it is. And do you intend to take that road?"

"Of course." He grunted.

"Just the three of you?"

"What are you getting at lady?" snapped the guard.

"Have you not heard the stories?"

"Miss, our abbey tells stories of the Spook Legion to frighten altar boys. I thought a grown woman might be a bit less gullible."

The Spook Legion?

"I assure you they are no mere stories," said Cain. "Or did you not take a good look at those trees?"

Cain led them over to the fallen trees and Nea followed. Nea had assumed a storm or something had passed through. But Cain dismounted, passing the reigns to Nea. She strode towards the wreckage, brushing leaves aside to reveal marks in the wood. These trees hadn't fallen, they'd been cut.

"It seems someone means to lure hasty travelers like yourself through the pass."

Nea could see the fear and apprehension in the men's eyes now. She stared farther up Borgia pass. What was it that waited in those hills?

"Plenty of people cross through every year," said one. "They never see anything."

"I imagine not. But tell me, do they travel with a force as small as yours?"

"Enough," said the traveler barking an order to the figure driving the wagon. "Celia, turn it."

The woman named Celia hesitated slightly then flicked the reigns and the wagon began to move. Cain however strode out in front of them.

"Hold on. You should at least have a proper escort."

"We don't have time," muttered one of the men reaching for his sword.

"Please miss," Celia lowered her hood and Nea could see that she was a nun. "Please you must let us through."

Nea watched all of this, confused. If it were truly as dangerous as Cain said, then there was no reason not to just turn around and go back. Nea froze,

Unless…

"You're hiding slaves."

Cain, Celia and her two companions all turned to stare at Nea.

"Nea what—"

"Escaped slaves, churches give sanctuary to runaway slaves, but the runaways need help getting there, especially with checkpoints."

Nea knew this all too well. When she'd first caught wind of the grassers, she'd tried desperately to reach one of these sanctuaries but to no avail.

The man's eyes narrowed. "We don't know what you—"

"Yes!" said Celia, an air of desperation in her voice. "Come out children, it's alright."

Slowly, from inside the mass of hay, a few small heads emerged to look frightfully at Nea and Cain. Nea couldn't bear to see the looks of terror on their faces and removed her glove, showing the Nuptial. This soothed them a little. Nea avoided their gaze all the same. The little ones brought up unwelcome feelings.

"They escaped, found sanctuary in our church. But we've been raided twice already and threatened with worse."

One of her escorts cursed and spat.

"We have to get them to the sanctuary in—"

"You'll never make it through the pass by yourselves." said Cain shaking her head.

"We must try," said Celia.

Nea only now realized just how young she was, barely older than her.

Brave thing. Stupid, but brave.

"There is no other way, they are searching for us even as we speak."

Cain sighed. She looked at the path, then at the sky, then finally at Nea. "Very well. We'll help you."

"You will?" Celia gasped.

We will?

Nea stared at Cain, what was this mad woman playing at now?

Cain smiled and dismounted offering Celia a metal hand, revealing the blue feather of the Royal Guard. Celia's eyes grew wide and her companion quickly sheathed his weapon.

"M'lady," she whispered, shocked.

"Maria is fine," said Cain gently. "I'm Maria and this is Nea; he's… my squire."

14

Gathering Dark

SEIYARIU HAD SENT Leo on ahead, told him to wait by the hilltop just outside Udra. The vagabond had wanted to double back to ensure they weren't being followed. The rain picked up fiercely as Leo walked. The storm recast the country surrounding Udra in a far more sinister light. Winding hills covered in yellow grass stretched for miles. Rainwater pooled at the base of these hills into deep puddles. A bolt of lightning lit the sky followed by a crash of thunder. The lightning threw the hilltop into relief, Leo was grateful, he wasn't sure he'd have been able to find it in the dark of the storm.

There wasn't any protection from the rain atop the hill, just an old well. It looked like it hadn't been used in years, the stone around it was crumbling and it wasn't covered. The vantage point gave Leo a nice view of the little town from here, or it would've if it hadn't been growing too dark to see.

He leaned back against the stone with a sigh, allowing the rain to fall against his skin. Seiyariu was going to take him along. The thought filled him with so much joy. Any fears he might have had about their quest had been washed away. He wasn't going to be alone again.

There was something cleansing about the flecks of cold water tumbling into his eyes and into his hair. That is until the sound of the thunder crashed once more and the rain picked up. Leo pulled up his hood and wrapped his cloak tight.

"What brings you out in this mess?"

Leo leapt back. There was a man standing beside him. Where had he come from? Had Leo simply not noticed him? Surely not; he was far too peculiar looking for that. Young though he was, his hair was pure white. His eyes were a chilling blue, and he wore a black tunic and shirt wrapped in a dark black cloak bound with a brooch, inside of which rested a large gem, smooth and polished. His skin was alabaster white and seemed to shine in the dark.

"Sorry kid, didn't mean to startle you."

His voice too was cold, throaty and chilling, but awkward as if he wasn't comfortable using it. The strange, icy man sat on the edge of the well and laced his fingers together.

"I... I should go," Leo said. "I need to find my teacher and—"

"I wouldn't recommend it. You could miss each other in a storm like this."

The strange man had a point, it would be safer to wait for the vagabond than to go looking for him in the downpour. How much longer would Seiyariu be? Cautiously Leo took a seat on the well beside him.

"Quinnel," the man said, offering his hand.

Leo didn't take it. The man scared him. They sat in silence for a few moments, under the torrent of rain.

"Aren't you cold?" he asked Quinnel. The man had his hood down and his arms were bare under his cloak.

"Always."

He drew out a steel flask from his coat. Quinnel unscrewed the cap, releasing a torrent of steam. He took a long draft and wiped his mouth. "You a traveler?"

Leo shrugged and said nothing. This man disturbed him, he thought it best to keep his head down.

"Go on," said Quinnel. "Bit of talk to weather the storm."

Leo bundled his cloak even tighter. "I'm heading south with my teacher."

"What kind of teacher?" asked Quinnel, taking another sip from his flask. He offered it to Leo, who shook his head as politely as he could, not sure how much would be left of him after drinking something that hot.

"Bit of everything really."

"He teach you to use that knife?" Quinnel's breath rose in a pale cloud as he let out a sigh.

Leo jumped, realizing that his dagger had been showing. "Y... yes," Leo lied.

"Where do you come from?" Quinnel asked.

"You ask a lot of questions," Leo replied firmly. "I don't even know who you are."

Quinnel shrugged. "Besides my name, I'm from the north. Ran away from home when I was twelve."

He removed his glove and held up a pale hand, the Nuptial burned into his flesh. "I'm sure you know how that story usually goes."

Leo felt himself relax slightly. "I do." He took off his own glove to show Quinnel his Nuptial as well. "I'm sorry."

"Well what are the odds of that?" said Quinnel, he didn't smile but his voice had a bit more levity behind it. "You teacher help you escape?"

Leo nodded, "He saved my life."

"That's kind of him. What's his story?"

"Sorry?"

"Tell me about this teacher of yours, what do you know about him."

Leo paused, thinking. "I don't really know anything."

"Anything?" asked Quinnel.

"N-no."

"Why do you suppose that is?"

"I…" Leo trailed off. Suddenly acutely aware of just how little he knew about the vagabond. "I guess he doesn't like talking about himself."

"Suppose."

"How did you escape? From the grassers I mean?" asked Leo, eager to change the subject.

"In a manner of speaking. I was freed."

His eyes misted over as if staring at something that wasn't there. "Freed by a man called Beljhar."

"Why did he free you?" asked Leo, trepidation forgotten in the face of this story. "Was he a vagabond?"

"Pegged you for a vagabond's apprentice," said Quinnel. "You don't have the cloak yet, but I'm sure that's not far off. No, he wasn't a vagabond. He was the leader of a group of young men. All escaped slaves like you and me. Took me in, gave me reason to go on."

"I see."

Quinnel took another draft from his flask. Then, staring across the dark landscape he said, "He wants to do the same for you."

Leo froze. "What did you just say? Who are you?"

"Just a messenger, at the moment," Quinnel replied, his icy blue eyes fixed anywhere but Leo's. "We've been having a hell of a time trying to find you. Ever since you gave us the slip in Limani."

Leo was on his feet now, backing away with his hand on the knife. "Get away from me."

"Hold on now kid, I don't mean you any harm. That day in Limani, we were trying to free you."

"What?" said Leo, stopping.

"You've become of interest to Djeng Beljhar. He can save you Leo. He wants only to give you a home, a purpose."

Leo felt his hand leave the hilt of his knife despite himself.

Quinnel didn't waste the opportunity. He got to his feet and took a few steps towards Leo.

"Without him, I would have never crawled out of the hole that this world put me in. He gave me hope and he can do so for you as well."

"I… I don't understand," said Leo truthfully.

"You will," said Quinnel. "If you come with me and join us. Nobody will ever be able to hurt you again."

"Leo!" Leo looked back to see Seiyariu racing towards them, moving faster than Leo had ever seen him. In seconds he was at Leo's side, eyeing Quinnel up and down.

"Who in God's name are you?"

"What do you say?" Quinnel asked, ignoring Seiyariu.

There was an enormous boom as lightning ripped across the sky once more, the rain falling in curtains on the trio. Leo looked at Quinnel, torn. A home, a place for him to belong, safety. For a moment Leo wondered what that would feel like, then he looked into Seiyariu's worried eyes and the vagabond's words came drifting back to him. Leo realized that he had his answer.

"I'm sorry." Leo said to Quinnel. "I'm happy here."

Quinnel pursed his lips and gave a curt nod. He fiddled with his belt for a few seconds before saying, "If you refused, I was told to improvise."

Seiyariu, reached for his sword. "I don't know who you are, but he's given you his answer. Leave us."

The cold that radiated from Quinnel seemed to pick up, biting at them. There was a glint of metal at his belt and, in a flash, twin daggers were sparkling in his hands. The sky darkened as the two faced each other. Seiyariu pushed Leo back and Leo obeyed.

"My task is the boy vagabond." said Quinnel as the two men began to move along the stone well, back and forth, neither of them daring to strike the first blow. "I've no desire to kill you."

Why was Sciyariu hesitating? He'd killed that slaver in Limani so effortlessly.

"He is my charge. My student. My responsibility. If you want to take him, it will be over my corpse."

"So be it."

Quinnel darted forward, his daggers moving faster than Leo thought possible. Seiyariu parried the blows and swept his sword across the man's chest. Quinnel dodged, leaping back and drove his blades forward, forcing Seiyariu to sidestep towards the slope, sacrificing the high ground. Quinnel didn't let up, cleaving the rain out of the air as he slashed at Seiyariu's defenses. With every blow Quinnel forced the vagabond down the hill, Seiyariu's boots here already beginning to sink in the mud. Why was Seiyariu letting Quinnel gain so much ground? Something was wrong, there was no way Seiyariu could be losing, could he? His face was set, teeth bared as he weathered Quinnel's endless assault.

Leo's hand tightened around his knife, knees shaking. What should he do? Leo had never fought an actual opponent before. Quinnel could kill him. Seiyariu knocked one of Quinnel's attacks aside and swept in vain at his legs. Worse, if he did nothing, Quinnel could kill Seiyariu. Leo drew the blade.

Seiyariu struck a massive, two-handed blow, forcing Quinnel to step back. Before the icy man could regain his footing, Leo stabbed at his shoulder. Quinnel saw the blow coming and kicked Leo hard right in his bad arm.

Leo's vision went dark, the world exploding into a cloud of pain and he felt himself go limp. Quinnel took Leo by the collar and tossed him away. Half conscious, Leo felt himself crash into the mud and rainwater as he rolled down the hill. Seiyariu let out a roar and the sound of metal on metal picked up again, louder and more intense than ever.

His vision blurry and confused, Leo became aware that he was half submerged in one of the giant puddles at the base of the hill. Thunder roared and a fresh curtain of rain fell harder and faster, the sky, now pitch dark. Leo crawled his way from the pool, gasping for air. His arm was on fire, the pain screaming with the slightest movement. Seiyariu and Quinnel were still on the hill, feet set, digging into the muck, trading blows with the same ferocity as the lightning that crackled overhead. Leo's fist tightened, mud squelching as he forced himself to his feet.

He scrambled up towards the duel, fighting against the current of rain every step of the way. Seiyariu, his footing regained, was sending Quinnel stumbling with every alternate blow. He stepped into one of these strikes and brought his sword up across Quinnel's chest spraying blood and water. Quinnel dropped one of his daggers, clutching at the wound. Seiyariu shot forward, sword plunging in for the kill, but Quinnel kicked, knocking Seiyariu's legs out from under him. The vagabond fell, slamming his head into the stone well.

Leo let out a cry and Quinnel turned. He drew another dagger from his belt and spun it through his fingers. Leo wanted to move but he couldn't, again feeling that terror in the pit of his stomach. Quinnel stared down at him, a look of pity on his face.

"Your weakness betrays you," Quinnel said coldly. "We'll teach you to master it." He raised a hand, but it was caught. He spun round to stare into the bloody face of Seiyariu.

The vagabond seized Quinnel, a look of undiluted venom in his eyes. Quinnel's eyes met Seiyariu's, there was no fear in those icy blue stones. Whether he sensed the vagabond's intentions or not, Quinnel had no time to react. Seiyariu spun, hurling the younger man over his shoulder and down into the well. Quinnel let out a strangled cry that echoed as he fell through the abyss, until he was cut off with a sudden, terrible splash.

15

The Spook Legion

Nea's horse skittered nervously as she brought up the rear of their strange little caravan. The path was too tight for them to ride abreast with the wagon, the men rode first, swords out. Their names were Roderick and Sebastion, and neither of them looked like they'd be much help in a fight, swords or not. Cain and Nea rode behind. Nea would've thought the lady knight would want to go out in front after all that big talking she'd done but it soon became apparent that Cain wanted the wagon in her sight at all times. Nea could see the children inside, peering out in terror at every cracking twig, every loose rock. She didn't blame them. Nea clutched her bow tight as she could, her knuckles white. Beside her, Cain rode slowly and deliberately. Gripping the reigns of her horse with an iron focus. Why didn't she have a weapon?

No weapon, no armor except for those gloves. What the hell kind of knight is she?

Nea scowled at herself, now wasn't the time.

The moon was out but it was only a sliver, forcing them to carry lanterns. The road had been cut into the side of a steep hill. It was frightfully narrow, one false step would send them crashing down into the woods below. Nea's eyes hardly ever left the rocky hillside or the dark road ahead. Cain's warnings still fresh in her mind.

"What the hell is so dangerous about this pass exactly?" Nea had asked before they had set out.

"You saw those trees," Cain replied, not looking at Nea. "This is a road that someone wanted people to take. Borgia Pass is infamous for blind corners, hidden ridges and caves just out of sight." She cursed quietly. "It's home to a group called The Spook Legion, at least that's the name given to them by the locals. Fitting I suppose."

"What are they? Bandits?"

"Perhaps," Cain replied.

"What's that supposed to mean?" asked Nea,

"Nobody is quite sure who or what they are. Superstitions keep the hill largely unexplored."

"Hasn't the army ever…"

"Once," said Cain darkly. "A sizable force from what I've heard. They went up and down the pass, even ventured through some of the caves, didn't find a damn thing."

"Well then, how the hell do you know that these spooks are even real?" said Nea.

"I don't. For all I know the stories are the work of some very clever bandits. Nevertheless, we must be on our guard."

Cain's words had shaken her. Even through Nea's cynical shell she felt the fear behind the lady knight's words.

You didn't sign on for this.

If those church fools were determined to get themselves killed, let them, it made no difference to her. Why had Cain offered to help? Nea caught one of the little slaves looking at her and she was reminded of Leo. Instantly, she had the answer to her question,

Amazing what big sad eyes do to your common sense.

Keeping her lantern close, Nea strained her eyes against the darkness. Aware of every rock, every branch, and every clump of fallen leaves. She wasn't sure what she was looking for, but it would come. The waiting was the worst part of it.

Waiting for the axe to descend on your neck.

Something loomed out of the darkness and Nea felt her heart skip a beat. Celia let out a shriek but clapped a hand over her mouth.

Nea notched an arrow. The thing wasn't moving. As they drew in closer, Nea heard Roderick curse violently. It was a scarecrow, old burlap stuffed with straw. A tiny little thing mounted on a roadside pole. Naked, save for a tattered red cloak and hood. It stared blankly down the road at them. Nea shivered, the scarecrow's face was painted bright white. It had two spots of dark for eyes and a long, strangely bulbous nose. Worst of all was the lurid grin had been drawn or, more accurately, carved in the thing's face.

"What in the hell…"

"Hush!" Cain held up a hand. "Don't—"

An ear-splitting howl erupted behind them. Nea felt her whole body turn itself inside out as the noise split the night. Roderick and Sebastion's horses shrieked and bolted forward in a terrified gallop. Nea and Cain's mounts would've run too if the wagon hadn't been there. Nea pulled back on the reigns, trying desperately to calm the panicked animal. The howl came again, and this time Celia's horses went into a craze, racing forward as fast as they could and dragging the wagon behind them.

"After her!" Cain barked.

Nea didn't need to be told, she turned her panicking horse and took off down the road. Their animals were in such a state, they didn't need encouraging to sprint.

Celia had lost her grip of the reigns and was clinging to the wagon for dear life. The children screamed, their tiny voices muffled by the hay. Roderick and Sebastion were farther down the path, riding at break-neck speed.

What happened next was over so quickly that Nea barely had time to register what it was. One moment the two men were ahead of them, riding like death itself was on their heels, then something flashed level with their throats, and the next moment, their heads gone.

Cain loosed her foot from the stirrups and flung herself bodily over her confused horse and onto the wagon. She grabbed Celia and pulled her back into the hay just as the glint of steel was upon them.

Cain ducked and Nea imitated her as the wire shot overhead, just grazing the end of her hair. There was even more glinting ahead and in desperation Cain yanked the reigns, turning the horses and the wagon off the road, sending it careening down into the woods. The screams of the children echoed through the trees.

Just ahead of them, a whole host of wires were spread taught across the road. And there were Roderick and Sebastion's horses, strung up in the middle of the road like flies in the web of a giant spider. Nea dove from the saddle just as her own horse crashed into the wires.

She staggered to her feet, checking to make sure nothing was broken. She still had her arrows, her bow. The sight before her made her gag. Unlike with Sebastian and Roderick, the wires hadn't cut cleanly through the poor beasts. Nea could see one of them still twitching. She made to put an arrow in it. Only then did she realize that it wasn't the horse that was moving, it was the wires. She felt her blood run like ice as a dozen small forms scampered across the wires to observe.

They were about the size of a child. She couldn't see much of their bodies, they all wore the same little red cloak. But the way they moved, it was as though their legs were too short, their arms too long. Nea had never seen a human being in her life move like that. It wasn't a walk, or a run, it was more like the mad lope of a rodent. Worse still were their faces, all of them wore the same luminescent white mask. With the same blank stare, long nose, and carved grin she'd seen on that little scarecrow.

Terror gripping her, she raced off down the hill, following the screams. She ran as fast as she'd ever run in her life, vaulting over gnarled old tree roots and ducking under low hanging branches. Celia and the children couldn't be far, where was Cain? Cain, Nea cursed.

The hell are these things? Not bandits, what the hell kind of bandits do that?

As she moved, Nea became aware of something like a great wind through the trees overhead, but no wind could ever make a noise like that. She didn't have to run far. The remains of the wagon were wrapped around a tree, hay tossed everywhere. The children huddled in its shadow with Celia, who was holding her hands up pleading, though with the Spook Legion or Christ, Nea couldn't tell.

What the hell are you doing? Just leave them! You're going to get yourself killed.

But even as these dark whispers crept into her mind, Nea remembered another terrified face. This one had been on a ship, in the claws of a grasser. She'd had a chance to run then too, but she didn't. Why not?

"Where's Cain?" she asked, skidding to a halt at the foot of the tree.

Celia just shook her head. Nea set her teeth as a rustling sounded from all around them. Little red forms darted about, surrounding them. Despite every impulse in her body screaming at her to run,

Nea planted herself between the Legion and the slaves. She met the haunting white gazes looming out of the darkness towards her. If they swarmed her, she could get a few shots off, maybe even enough for some of the others to make a run for it, perhaps Cain could—

There came a scream from behind her. Nea spun around and saw more grinning white faces descending from the trees above towards the helpless children.

No!

She shot an arrow, everything in her being behind it. The thin bolt buried itself in the chest of one of the spooks. The creature let out a little shriek, tumbling to the ground in a heap.

The creatures hesitated, but Nea didn't. Whatever these things were, they could be killed. She let another arrow fly, striking one right through its mask. One of the spooks leapt at her.

Her arrow missed the beast by a hair's breadth and it crashed onto her. It was heavy, and strong too, driving the air out of Nea's lungs as they went down. It scratched and clawed madly, before something smashed into it with such force that the creature went flying off of her, collapsing in a little red pile.

What in the hell did that?

Nea stumbled back to her feet and spun to face the rest of the hoard, but they weren't there. The legion were busy throwing themselves at someone a few yards away, and they were losing.

It was Cain. The legionnaires were falling upon her again and again, but she was repelling them with nothing but her hands, driving her armored gauntlets into the bandits, and sending them flying back through clouds of blood. Nea watched in amazement as Cain struck a legionnaire in the head; there was a crunch and its mask shattered as the thing went limp.

How hard is she hitting them? That's impossible.

Each blow she landed rang like a bell through the gloom. Nea added her arrows to the chaos, keeping any and all of the beasties away from the wreck. The Spook Legion began retreating into the hills with that dreadful scurrying gait, howling in despair. The last thing Nea saw was the glowing white of their masks, disappearing into the darkness of the wood. Then they were gone, and a hush fell upon the hills. Cain watched them go, her armored hands dripping blood onto the dirt.

Nea stared, agog. There had been so many and Cain, with her hands… She'd never seen anything like it, never even imagined something like it, and from Cain.

She's just a woman. How on earth could she do those things?

The adrenaline faded, and soon Nea felt something else running through her body, a new and unwelcome feeling. Admiration.

16
Licking Wounds

LEO SANK HIS mud-caked clothes into the river. The grime slowly began to fade, staining the rushing water a dirty reddish brown. The sky overhead was gray, a remnant of last night's storm. Resting his wet clothes on a rock to dry, Leo knelt and stared at his reflection in the passing flow.

The person looking back was unfamiliar to him. He'd eaten better on the road than he had in months. His new reflection was healthier. He couldn't see his ribs anymore and his skin no longer had that sickly tinge to it; its dark olive color had begun to return. The scars on his arm looked worse somehow. Maybe it was because of how they'd held him back the night before. He yawned and sat on the sandy riverbank, letting the cold water run over his feet.

The previous night had been a wild half-remembered flight through the torrents of rain and unceasing wind. It took hours for the storm to blow itself out. Unsure of whether or not Quinnel had been traveling alone, they'd gone for miles upon miles, cutting across the countryside all roads forgotten. Until at last, they'd stopped for the night. Seiyariu's head had a nasty gash on it, but he'd refused to do a thing about it until he'd tended to Leo, who was fine, save for a few cuts and bruises.

The vagabond stood against the rail of a stone bridge overlooking the river. He was locked in a fevered conversation with Kokaleth. The Mariner was standing waist deep in the rushing water. Seiyariu had called him the second he'd gotten the chance, using the same salt as before. Leo couldn't hear what they were saying, though he was dying to try and listen in.

The night's battle had shaken him deeply. Quinnel's scream, that terrible look in Seiyariu's eyes. It didn't make sense. Everything Quinnel told him, Leo just couldn't fathom. What could this Beljhar person want with him? Leo was barely thirteen, with no family to speak of, no debts, no connections except to the slaving companies. And that man had been no grasser. Leo dressed and made his way towards the bridge where Seiyariu stood arguing with Kokaleth.

"You don't know how many of these men there are," Kokaleth interjected. His gurgling voice was stranger away from the sounds of the sea. "How can you can't just—"

"We're still going on to Adis, Kokaleth, that's final," Seiyariu said calmly. "We have to. It's far too important."

Kokaleth crossed his arms. "I'm still not sold on you taking the boy."

"Why not?" Leo cut in.

Kokaleth ignored him. "You can't honestly tell me that the two of you are fit to be poking around that subterranean hellhole after last night. From the sound of what that loon said, the boy is marked. Seiyariu, I don't know what your little friend did to get on these people's bad side but—"

"I don't think that's it," said Leo.

"Oh?" The Mariner gave Leo a look. "And what *do* you think?"

Leo shifted uncomfortable under the mariner's gaze. He glanced over at Seiyariu but he too was waiting for an answer. "Quinnel said that he wanted to take me with him, he said that his master, he said his name was Beljhar, he would—"

"He said his name was what?" Kokaleth barked.

"Beljhar."

"Djeng Beljhar?"

"I think so. You know him?"

"Know him?" Kokaleth roared. "You would be hard pressed to find someone who didn't know the name Djeng Beljhar. You've left the boy poorly educated on the affairs of Fortuna, Seiyariu."

Seiyariu nodded. "Djeng Beljhar is the leader of a group called The Black Briars."

"The Black Briars?"

Seiyariu nodded. "Whenever a slave ship goes missing, or a rich merchant turns up with a knife in his back, chances are they're the ones to blame."

"They exist as a kind of private army, and not one that you can hire either," Kokaleth added darkly. "The Briars seem to have their own, convoluted agenda."

"Quinnel said he was part of a group of escaped slaves."

"Sounds like them," said Kokaleth. "At least that's what the rumors say."

Leo's head was spinning again. "What do they want with me?"

He felt tears in his eyes but he blinked them away, it was too much to handle but he wasn't about to let Kokaleth see him cry.

To his surprise however, Kokaleth's expression was one of understanding, not contempt.

"I know it's hard," said the mariner slowly. "Look lad, just concentrate on this foolish errand that Seiyariu is dragging you on. Against my better judgement, I might add. But from what he tells me, you've a strong desire to learn. Whatever the trouble your body may give you, that desire is the truest requirement for a vagabond."

"Kokaleth…" Seiyariu prodded.

"I take it you won't be persuaded against going to Adis then, even with all of this?"

Seiyariu shook his head. "We're going, aren't we Leo?"

Leo smiled and nodded.

"Very well, have it your way. But if you're committed to bringing him with you, it'd be best not to put off performing the rite any longer."

"I understand."

"Good, and I'll see what I can dig up on what the Briars are up to. In the meantime, you two get Knail someplace safe. And for God's sake stay out of trouble."

"Thank you, Kokaleth," Seiyariu beamed at him.

"Oh, one more thing." The mariner gave a great leap and landed on the bridge beside Leo. He reached into one of his pouches and pulled out a vial. Drawing a finger up to the thing that Leo had thought to be a crown made of coral, Kokaleth reached into one of the holes. A look of concentration on his face. Leo was unsure whether he should be fascinated or nauseous. The mariner removed his finger, which was now covered with a bright, sparkling substance. He placed it in the bottle and sealed it. It was just like the vial Seiyariu had used.

"This is summoning salt," Kokaleth said sternly. "Seiyariu has some already, but I get the impression you'll need this sooner than you think. It is through this that we mariners commune with the sea. Pour it into a body of water and as long as that water is connected to the ocean somehow, I will be able to find you. The farther away you get from the sea, the more you need to pour, understand?"

Leo nodded. "Thanks."

He took the vial gingerly and slipped into his pocket. He wasn't sure why he'd need this if Seiyariu had some. Surely the mariner didn't expect them to get separated. Still, they had been separated yesterday. The idea hit Leo hard and hung there like an echo.

"Take care friend," said Seiyariu fondly, clapping the fish man on the back.

"It was, erm, nice to see you again." Leo added.

Kokaleth let out a throaty, gurgling laugh and flung himself into the air. He did a magnificent flip backwards and plunged into the rushing water without so much as a goodbye. Seiyariu seemed quite used to this however.

"Are you ready to go?" he asked.

Leo nodded and the two of them set off over the bridge and down the eastern road.

"What did Quinnel say to you, before I showed up?" Seiyariu asked.

"He told me he was a slave once. Like me, he showed me the Nuptial and everything. He said this Beljhar person freed him, gave him purpose among these…"

"Black Briars," Seiyairu finished for him.

"Right. And he said that Beljhar wanted to do the same for me."

"Why?"

Leo frowned. "I've no idea. What use would I be to a force like that? I'm…" He felt the tears again.

"Leo…"

Leo became very interested in his boots. "I'm useless. You saw, my arm gave out again."

"I'll not have you blame yourself for this Leo, I won't. Your arm is a part of you Leo, you must learn to play to your strengths, and strengthen your weaknesses. Especially on this quest we've set ourselves. If anything, I should be the one apologizing."

"For what?"

He raised his eyebrows. "I shouldn't have sent you off alone. I was careless. And you were hurt because of it."

They continued on in silence. The wooded and rocky landscape of Fortuna returning in full as they moved farther from the coast.

Leo's mind was fighting to take it all in. By the time the sun began to dip, all he'd gotten was a headache. When they finally made camp that evening Leo decided to ask, "What rite was Kokaleth talking about?"

Seiyariu looked through the fire at him. "The Vagabond's Rite, your initiation, as it were. It's necessary if you're going to come with me and be my student, my little vagabond in training. But I need to know, is this what you want, truly? You don't want me to take you to the sanctuary? You want to follow me and learn this life?"

Leo had no qualms in his mind about this. "More than anything."

He beamed. "Then you shall be my student through and through, and must be recognized as one."

From his pack, Seiyariu produced a forest green cloak, like his, only smaller and with only two small patches on the inside.

"Is that… is that for me?"

"If you'll have it."

Leo's eyes lit up and Seiyariu took that as a yes. "Give me your hand."

"My…"

"Your good hand don't worry. Your knife as well."

Leo did as he was told. Gently, Seiyariu slid the blade across his palm, drawing blood. Leo winced from the pain but didn't shy away. The vagabond then did the same to his own palm, before untying his headband and using it to bind their bleeding palms together.

"Repeat after me. I, Leonardo Fortunato."

"I, Leonardo Fortunato."

"Give myself to The Green Road."

"Give myself to The Green Road."

"I accept the Rite of the Vagabond. Until the clash comes again, I will walk The Green Road, a wanderer and guardian. A son of Romulus. Not alone, but as the legacy of those who came before."

"I accept the Rite of the Vagabond," Leo repeated, fascinated by the words. "Until the clash comes again, I will walk The Green Road, a wanderer and guardian. A son of Romulus. Not alone, but as the legacy of those who came before."

"I will not shy away from pain, inside and out."

"I will not shy away from pain, inside and out." Leo thought of his arm, his fears, his memories of Nico.

"For Pain begets Power."

Leo felt emotion swelling up inside, but he kept himself together. They had accepted him, despite all his failures. Were Kokaleth's words true? Could he be a vagabond with only a desire to learn? And those words he had spoken in the Rite. Would his pain give him strength? Was that even possible?

"For Pain begets Power."

Seiyariu straightened up and stared at Leo proudly. "Students aren't unusual, many vagabonds have them. But I... I just... I never thought I would be one of them."

He draped the green cloak around Leo's shoulders and fastened it about his neck.

"Welcome to The Green Road, vagabond."

17
Flowers of the West

THE SLAVE SANCTUARY had once been a monastery, but the old dormitories had been repurposed. Now the church and the dorms formed a single connected structure, not unlike a school. A stone wall had been erected around the grounds, complete with a portcullis. It was like a tiny little island in the chaos of Fortuna. A place for children to grow up, to live normally. Nea couldn't get the grateful little faces of the children out of her mind.

Would've been nice, if that had been you a couple years ago.

After the local priest had finished ringing their hands, Nea and Cain retired to a rather cramped guest room in the eastern wing of the dorm. It was small, but warm, a fire crackling in the grate, with a pair of clean smelling beds and a little table. Cain didn't stick around, eager for a hot bath and a change of clothes. Nea honestly didn't care at this point, the stench of the road had become such a constant, it was hard for her to notice anymore. She stretched out on her bead with a groan. She felt like she'd run a hundred leagues.

By the time they had reached the sanctuary, it was the darkest hours of the morning. When the walls of the church at last came into view, Nea felt as if she'd woken from a nightmare.

More than once, during their flight to the sanctuary, Nea caught herself looking at the back of one of the older slaves, imagining for a moment that she saw a mess of dark red hair. What was Leo doing now? She wondered sleepily. Had he made it to a place like this?

Hope so.

"Bath's yours," said Cain, striding through the door in a dressing gown, running a towel through her hair.

"I'm fine," Nea murmured into her pillow. "Did you bring food?"

Cain raised her eyebrows, "You are not fine. I'll not have you smelling like a goat anymore Nea, now go."

Nea grumbled something.

"Trying to get a look at me changing are you?" shrugged Cain, unlacing her dressing gown.

"No!" Nea said, sitting up in alarm.

Cain laughed at her, that unbearable smug grin on her face once again. "Then off with you. And take these." She tossed Nea a small brown package. "New clothes, courtesy of these kind people. And you'd best be clean when you come back, or I'll scrub you down myself."

Nea was already out the door, scowling viciously to herself. The damn woman and her teasing, did she treat everyone like this?

No wonder she travels alone.

Nea spent most of her time smelling bad. At Glatman they had kept her so clean, smelling so nice. She'd come to hate it, but even she had to admit she needed a bath.

Cain, there was something different about her now. Nea had thought her stodgy, pompous and privileged, carrying a pretty title with little to back it up. But after the events in the pass, Nea's perception of the woman had been shattered. Cain was a soldier through and through, and a damn good one.

Doesn't mean you have to like her though.

*

When Nea returned to the room she found Cain sitting at the table in her nightclothes. A variety of baskets and plates had been brought up, full of what food the church could spare.

"That dinner or breakfast?" asked Nea, yawning.

"Sun's not up yet," said Cain buttering a steaming roll. "Come on, you must be hungry."

Nea was hungry. They ate in silence. Cain looked even more tired than Nea felt. Still, for all the madness in the plan, Cain had done it. They had done it. Nea felt a flame in her chest, whether it was pride or relief, she wasn't sure.

Cain drew a small flask from inside her doublet and took a long swig of whatever was inside.

"Can I have some of that?" asked Nea, breaking the silence. She knew that filthy smell; it could only mean good things.

"You're a touch young," said Cain, raising an eyebrow.

"Old enough to keep up with you," Nea smirked.

Cain laughed. "Believe me you don't want this; have some wine."

"I can't stand wine," said Nea. It was true, the fruity smell reminded her far too much of Glatman. But real drink, Nea had a weakness for that.

Cain shrugged and passed Nea the flask. It was bitter, and terrible, and Nea loved every drop. She had to keep her eyes from rolling over in a combination of joy and revulsion.

"Go easy on it at least," said Cain. "It's pretty strong."

Reluctantly Nea stopped herself from draining the flask and tossed it back. Then she leaned back in her chair, happy and full.

"So, Nea," said Cain, tucking the flask away. "When was the first time you killed a man?"

Nea about fell out of her chair. "What?"

"Come off it Nea, I was far older than you when I killed my first man and I couldn't sleep properly for weeks. Yet I saw you kill at least two of those things without batting an eye."

"Are they men then?" asked Nea. "The Spooks I mean."

Cain shrugged. "I wish I knew. But don't change the subject, you killed them, men or not. With an efficiency I'd expect from my soldiers, not from mouthy slave boys with a curious fondness for terrible homemade rum."

Nea didn't know how to answer that. Though she hated to admit it, there was a part of her that wanted to tell Cain. She hadn't spoken about it to anyone since she escaped from Glatman. It was as though the whole thing had been some terrible dream. "Fine, I'll tell you. Not everything, I'm not just gonna bear my life story to some lady in pants because she barks an order."

Cain smiled. "Tell me what you are comfortable telling me."

"It was when I left Glatman." Nea blinked, not sure if she'd ever said those words out loud.

"Glatman?"

Damn it all, what are you thinking?

"It's the place I was being held before I got picked up by the grass-ers and sent here. I killed some people when I escaped."

"How many?"

"Three."

"By yourself?"

Nea nodded. She was dancing dangerously close to the edge here; she needed to protect her secret. But Cain was done questioning her. Perhaps it had been the expression on Nea's face as she soaked in bad memories.

"I saw the way you stood between those slave children and the le-gion. That was very brave of you," said Cain.

Nea sniffed, "Just doing a job."

There was a long pause. "You know Nea?" Cain said finally. "I don't think you're as selfish as you want people to think."

Nea blushed. "Shut up. Besides I didn't do much good. We would've died if it hadn't been for you."

"I suppose you didn't believe I could fight?"

Nea looked at her feet. "I did. I just…"

"Of course, it's only natural to assume, I suppose, that the Captain of the Royal Guard is utterly defenseless and must rely on men to do the fighting for her, hmm?"

Nea went a little red. "No, it's not that. I… I needed to think you were weak."

"Because I'm a woman." It wasn't a question.

"Are you though?" asked Nea. "Never seen a lady hit that hard."

Women aren't supposed to be strong.

Cain snorted. "Very funny, take a look at this." She held out one of her gauntlets. Nea took it cautiously. "Touch the knuckle."

As soon as Nea's finger made contact with the metal, a small steel cylinder blasted from just above the knuckle, only for a moment, and then it retreated. Nea tried it again, and again with each of the knuck-les, each one did the same thing save for the thumb.

"What on earth…" she muttered.

"The hammers activate on the first punch, then act as a sec-ond blow, breaking bones, crushing armor and the like," said Cain. "Conoscenzian technology, of my own invention."

"Conoscenzian," muttered Nea. "Brilliant."

"I'm glad you think so. There's not much of our work floating around Fortuna. Here such machines are lovingly called Flowers of the West."

"Nice name."

"From the way the metal flows. Like petals you see."

Nea ran her hand along the gauntlet, admiring the finish and detail that had been put into every inch of it. "And you made this?"

"Must you always act so surprised? I may be an empty-headed lass out playing soldier, but—"

"I don't… I didn't mean any of that."

"Yes, you did."

"Well I don't now," Nea said, avoiding her gaze.

"Oh?"

"Yeah," she grumbled, her ego screaming in protest. "I don't like women. But you're not like the others. I …" She bit her lip. "You're different. I dunno." She trailed off miserably.

No point in going back now.

"Would you, maybe teach me?"

"I may. But before I do, you asked me about Chiron and how I could possibly serve under the man who attacked my homeland."

"Are you going to tell me?"

"I wouldn't be babbling like this if I wasn't." Cain's eyes flashed as Nea watched her dive into the memory. "During the war I was young, only a little bit older than you. I was only just getting started with my inventions. Chiron, young as he was, made a fool's error and was left on a deserted battlefield to rot among the corpses, mortally wounded and resigned to death. I found him, and I saved his life."

"You what?"

Cain held up a steel hand and allowed it to catch the firelight. "With the help of my machines, I helped him live and fight again. He in turn helped me end the war and save my home. When he returned home, I came with him."

"Because he made you?"

"Come now Nea, you know me better than that."

"Sorry," muttered Nea, embarrassed.

"He asked me. It meant leaving my friends and family, and the country I had fought so hard to save. But I said yes."

"Why?"

"Because I felt I was needed here."

"Do you miss it? Conoscenzia?"

"It was my home, certainly I miss it sometimes."

Nea frowned at her, confused. "What do you mean *was* your home?"

"Home can sometimes be more than just a place," said Cain thoughtfully. "Sometimes it's just being with the people you care about the most."

Nea glanced at the knight, seeing her differently for the first time.

Don't get too close.

It had always been hovering in her head, whenever she met someone new or came to a new place.

Never ever get too close.

Ever since she began her stay at Glatman, Nea had stopped feeling happy around people. She'd forgotten what it felt like to desire company, but as she looked at Cain now, a part of her remembered.

18

Sounds of the Forest

AFTER THEIR HARROWING encounter with Quinnel, Seiyariu was on edge for several days, jumping at shadows and never letting Leo out of his sight. But as the days passed with no sign of any of these "Black Briars" the vagabond relaxed. Still Leo did not let his guard down. Quinnel had been so strong.

And they're looking for me.

The thought gave him chills. Still, the cloak now fastened around his neck, made him feel stronger somehow. As the days went by and the events at the well were left behind them they'd begun to enjoy themselves again.

Day and night Seiyariu instructed Leo in everything imaginable, leaving Leo desperately trying to remember everything from trapping squirrels to removing leeches. He was getting slightly better; each failure pushed him to try harder, to Seiyariu's delight. Though he still couldn't swing a sword to save his life. He had his knife; that would do for now. They'd crossed several of the rivers that ran like veins through every part of the land, passing over marshes, and through a daunting series of moors. But wherever they went, one thing was always the same – the craters.

They peppered the land every couple miles. Some were so deep they couldn't see the bottom. A few, filled with water, had towns built alongside them; some of the dry ones actually had towns built inside them. Between the craters, the rivers and gulfs, Fortuna was like a ceramic that had been dropped, leaving the pieces strewn about with no particular rhyme or reason.

When at last they left the moors behind them, the pair was greeted by something even less encouraging. Leo felt his stomach twist as they neared the edge of a forest, one made of massive trees as tall as the mast of a ship. "What is that?"

"Mavrodasos," said Seiyariu, not breaking stride. "The Pinwheel Forest, it acts as something of a shortcut into eastern Fortuna."

"How long will we be in here?" Leo asked, uncertainly staring up at woods edge.

"If we cut through we shouldn't be more than a few days."

"Couldn't we just go around?" Leo asked, sounding more timid than he'd meant to.

"If we had an extra week or two to spare," Seiyariu replied. "But the trail through is faster and I want to get to Adis as soon as we can."

Leo stopped walking. "I don't like it," he murmured. "There's something wrong about it… it's too…"

"Ancient?"

Leo shrugged. "What did you call it before, The Pinwheel Forest?"

Seiyariu nodded. "A nickname, probably comes from the stories."

"What stories?" Leo couldn't help but ask, not wanting to know the answer.

"They say it has a nasty habit of playing tricks on hapless travelers."

"You talk like it's alive."

"All forests are alive," Seiyariu grinned. "But this one, there's something special here. With a vicious sense of humor."

"You're making it sound worse and worse." Despite his trepidation, Leo couldn't help but laugh.

"Just stay close," said Seiyariu. "I've been through this place before and if we stay together nothing will go wrong, I promise."

As they followed the road into the forest, the whole world closed in around Leo. The mass of trees formed a thick canopy overhead, through which the fading sunlight could only drip like water from cupped hands. The trees' branches wound together as did their thick roots. This made the going slow. The Pinwheel's leaves had not yet begun to change, even though the end of October was fast approaching. The trees weren't packed closely together, but they could still see only a short distance in front of them due to a combination of thick bushes and vines.

Leo shivered. The hairs on the back of his neck were upright. Every snapped branch, every birdcall made him jump. A chorus of unknown sounds followed them farther and farther into the dense wood. The noises set his senses on high alert, his little heart hammering fast with anticipation.

"Slow down," said Seiyariu. "Relax your breathing."

Leo gulped, he hadn't realized how ragged his breath had become. "Sorry."

"Don't apologize." He stopped and put a hand on Leo's shoulder. "It's safe, just stay close."

The touch reassured him. Seiyariu pushed on and Leo followed, sometimes holding the hem of his teacher's cloak just to be sure he wouldn't lose him. When at last of the light slipped away, they made camp in-between the roots of an ancient oak tree.

"Do we light a fire?" Leo asked awkwardly.

Seiyariu nodded. "Gather some branches, but stay where I can see you."

Leo did as he was told, fumbling about the roots of the trees. It was amazing to him that the forest was even louder with the sun down. A cacophony of insects and other nameless rumblings could be heard coming from all around them. As he bent down to pick up a good bit of kindling, Leo caught a glimpse of something moving between the distant trees. It was little more than a shadow, until a pair of red eyes bloomed in the dark.

Leo screamed and tore back to Seiyariu. As he ran, his foot caught on an unseen root and he crashed to the ground at the wanderer's feet. Pain lanced up his arm and he swore, rolling onto his back.

"Leo, what happened?" Seiyariu helped him up.

"There was something out there!" Leo gasped. "In the trees."

Seiyariu's face darkened. "I know." He sat Leo on one of the roots and got the fire going himself. In moments the orange light was dancing against the surrounding trunks.

"What is it?" Leo asked, trying to hide the panic in his voice.

"A takabran," Seiyariu replied, stoking the fire. Leo frowned, the word was gibberish to him, but Seiyariu wasn't finished. "They're widely thought to be a product of farmers with overactive imaginations, but I've several scars that would suggest otherwise."

"What do we do?" Leo hugged his knees close to his chest, trying to make himself smaller.

"It won't come near the fire." Seiyariu leaned back against the large root. "And it won't press its luck so long as we outnumber it."

"But—"

"All will be well Leo. Get some rest, I'll keep watch."

Leo did not go to sleep. He pretended to, wrapping himself in his cloak and turning his back on Seiyariu. The vagabond sat, facing out into the darkness, one hand on his sword. Leo tossed and turned but though he was as tired as he'd ever been, his eyes refused to shut. The forest was alive all around him, and he dared not look away.

19

Beneath Holy Stone

"WHAT DO YOU mean you've never been to confession?" Cain asked, tinkering away.

"What do you think I mean?" Nea scowled. "Never had time for stuff like that, sorry if m'lady's offended."

"You know an actual squire would show some respect to his lady knight."

Nea rolled her eyes. Despite repeatedly saying it was incorrect, Cain enjoyed calling Nea her squire. No matter how hard Nea tried to sound insulting, every time she called Cain "M'lady," it only made her laugh. Nea found herself enjoying the teasing all the same. Though she prided herself on not needing anyone, Nea had to admit that this would be a difficult road to travel by herself. What animosity she'd had for Cain for besting her outside Limani had faded away when she'd seen Cain in battle. Never had she thought someone like the knight could exist. Strong, brave, confident, yet unmistakably feminine. It made her feel very strange.

They had arrived in Foresbury that morning with little trouble. The town was a picturesque little place overlooking a lake, not an ordinary lake either. This was one of the craters ripped into Fortuna during the Clash of Comets. Centuries of collecting water from rain and nearby streams had filled it up. The town on its edge was little more than a single curved street. But there was an inn all the same with a cozy parlor and a set of soft armchairs. Cain and Nea had made themselves at home before venturing out again.

Cain had one of her gauntlets open, fiddling inside it with a tool Nea didn't recognize. With every twist, Nea saw the weapon convulse, all its inner machinery being adjusted. She still couldn't believe that Cain had made those bloody things.

"Can't be that hard, kneel and tell him what a bastard I am yeah?" Nea asked. She'd never had any patience for Christ or the church, not after Glatman.

"Yes, but I'd advise against doing it in that tone," said Cain, raising an eyebrow. "The good father might just throw you out on your ass. You mentioned that Quinnel said something to you, something like a song or a poem?"

Nea had turned the words over in her head a thousand times or more. "That's what he means by confess the liturgy?"

She nodded. "It will likely be the password for whatever awaits you in there. You're certain you remember it?"

"You sound like a fussy mother."

Cain blushed, "I just want to make sure you're taking this seriously."

"I am," said Nea. "Can't be as hard as that business with the legion right?"

"A rough way to get the journey started to be sure."

"How is that working exactly?" Nea asked, peering at the gauntlets.

Cain smiled. "The hammers are wound so tightly that I've got to maintain the springs and clockwork, else the whole thing just comes apart."

"Brilliant," hissed Nea.

"You know if you keep humoring me I'm going to want to keep you on as my squire."

That made Nea smile, at least a little bit. "Your guardsmen not keen on hearing you prattle on about your machines all day?"

"They all act like it's some kind of magic." Cain laughed.

"It might as well be," said Nea. "How does someone so obsessed with tinkering become a knight then?"

"I'm not a—"

"I know, but if your toys are that important to you, why are you a guard?" Nea gestured around aimlessly. "Why do all this?"

"Aside from my oath to His Majesty? Would you believe me if I said I just don't trust anyone else to use my tools?"

Nea laughed. "I'd believe that, yeah."

"You're quite a decent hand with a bow, you know that?" said Cain.

"Glad M'lady noticed," said Nea, "but what's that got to do with anything?"

"Well since you've been eyeing my tools like a hungry puppy," Cain's eyes glinted. "I thought I might give you a little something."

"Me?" said Nea sarcastically. "M'lady is too kind."

"If you're going to get big headed about it then perhaps I'll just keep it to myself."

"Keep what to yourself?"

"Oh no, no, if the little squire can't even humor his lady then I suppose we're done talking."

"Fine, fine, fine," said Nea rolling her eyes. "Tell you what, if M'lady will do me the honor of telling me just what the chuffing hell she's on about, I'd be inclined to listen to you prattle about your toys until it puts me to sleep."

"Very well then," said Cain, putting her work aside and rummaging around in her bag. "There aren't too many but…"

Cain produced a bundle of leather and unrolled it. Twenty arrows tumbled out, but they weren't like any Nea had ever seen. For a start they were made of metal. She leaned over and picked one up gingerly. It was light, just like the gauntlets had been. Perhaps the shaft was hollow, and the arrowheads were strangely angled. The steel points were a slightly different color the rest of the head and the shafts were covered in lines where the metal had been worked into shape.

"What are these?" asked Nea, fascinated.

"An invention of mine," proclaimed Cain proudly. "I call them burrowers. When the arrows make contact with a target, the head will break off and drill into your opponent's body, shredding whatever gets in their way."

Nea cradled it her hands, studying every inch of it. "And these are for me?"

"Well I keep a few on me in case I need to hunt, but after seeing your skill with a bow, I think this may be a match made in heaven, don't you?"

She didn't know what to say, nobody had even given Nea anything quite so special.

Nobody truly gives anything away.

But despite the mutterings in the back of her mind, Nea was happy. She had a little piece of Conoscenzia with her now, her own flowers of the west, to remind her of where she was going and why.

"Do be careful with them though," said Cain. "Once the arrowhead breaks off there's no way to retrieve it."

Nea nodded eagerly and slipped them into her quiver. "Thank you."

"You're very welcome," Cain beamed. "Don't think I've seen you this giddy before."

Nea blushed and quickly began studying her feet. "I like them."

"I'm glad. Now as I recall there was some kind of agreement involving me prattling on about my inventions to my heart's content."

Nea nodded. "Please do, I might even stay awake."

*

The old church was tucked away out of sight on the edge of town. It lay in a glade of trees with a view of the lake. Moss and lichen clung to the stone building, coloring it various shades of green, which clashed rather beautifully with the faded stained-glass windows. It stood watch over a little cemetery, the inscriptions on the graves long faded, alongside a ramshackle bird coop. She recalled reading that some of the churches used birds to communicate over long distances.

Nea let herself in gingerly, careful not to make too much noise. The inside of the church glowed in the light of oil lamps on either end of the one room. It had a high ceiling, but there were so many pews it felt cramped all the same. In the light, Nea could better see the pictures in the windows.

She'd expected stories from the gospels, but didn't recognize whatever the windows were supposed to be representing. At first glance they might've been scenes from scripture, or perhaps church history. Portraits of a war or crusade, full of images of carnage and suffering, out of place in such a peaceful place.

Behind the altar there was no cross, just names, thousands of names carved into the stone. This place was obviously some kind of memorial.

Nea's eyes fixed on the confessional just off to the side of the pulpit. Not for the first time, she wondered if Quinnel hadn't been taking her for a ride, but she slipped inside all the same.

Here goes nothing.

She knelt, as Cain had told her to do. In the opposite stall, sure enough she could hear a man's breathing.

"Forgive me father, for I have sinned."

There was silence for a moment. Then an older man's voice came from the other side of the screen. "When was your last confession my child?"

"Er, never."

"I see," Nea couldn't see the face behind the words but she could visualize the expression of disapproval perfectly. "Go on then, tell me your sins."

Nea took a deep breath, and then she recited the liturgy. "If you ever see a body, strung up in your view. Take care and leave it strung, else the Briars string up you."

There was a long silence. Nea began to worry that the priest wouldn't say anything at all, but sure enough the voice came again. "I didn't expect to hear that from one as young as you."

"I'm not that young," Nea grumbled, half to herself.

Not anymore.

"What's your name?" asked the priest. "And why do you seek the Briars?"

Honest to a point, thought Nea. Quinnel had said he could tell if she was lying, there was no reason for her to doubt his companions could do the same. "Nea Dúlaman. I was told to follow this trail if I wanted to set the world on fire."

"And do you?"

"More than anything," Nea said.

No lie there.

"Why?"

"I was a slave. The Briars freed me."

"Show me."

A small panel slid out of place, revealing a hole just large enough for Nea to reach through. Warily, she took off her glove and presented her hand. The Nuptial was still there as dark as the day they branded her with it.

"Very well," said the father as Nea withdrew her hand. "What were you expecting to find here?"

"I… I've no idea. Didn't think Quinnel looked like he was part of the church."

"Quinnel? I see you come highly recommended. The Black Briars are not part of the church."

"Then what is this place?"

"Another grave. Tell me Nea, what draws you to our cause?"

"Your cause?" asked Nea.

The priest sighed. "I see Quinnel was as cryptic as ever. Let me ask you something Nea. Do you believe in evil?"

"Yes," said Nea instantly.

"And why is that?"

"I've seen it." At Glatman, among the grassers, Nea had no doubts in her mind what evil looked like.

"Do you believe that evil is something men are, or something men do?'

This one gave Nea pause but only for a moment.

You know the answer.

"Something men are."

"I see," said the priest. "Very well, then I think you'll appreciate this story."

"A story?"

"Yes, one that will help you better understand our organization and why we fight, that will pull the cobwebs from your eyes and let you *truly* see the cruelty of this land."

"I've already seen plenty of cruelty, thanks. Just tell me where to go next."

"You cannot join our order without hearing this."

Nea's curiosity was piqued. "Alright."

"When you came in, did you look at the windows?"

"I did," said Nea.

"What did you think of them?"

"I don't know," said Nea, confused. "I didn't recognize them."

"You wouldn't have," said the priest. "It's not a tale that is told in polite company in this land. You are familiar, I take it, with the great war between Fortuna and Conoscenzia fifteen years ago?"

"Yes, but what does that—"

"Quiet, and I'll tell you."

Nea scowled but shut her mouth.

"It was prompted by the assassination of the King of Fortuna, not a good man but not a wicked one either. His son, Chiron, in his youthful arrogance, took the throne and immediately threw his country into a bloody war against the nation he believed responsible for his father's death. Sending thousands of men to fight for the sake of his revenge."

Nea listened silently, comparing it to the tale Cain had told her.

King sounds more and more like a bastard every damn day.

"Lord Chiron knew that they would not be able to fight the Conoscenzian army technologically; he chose instead to drown them in his force's sheer numbers. However, numbers only provide an advantage so long as one has the resources to maintain them, the new king did not. That is, until he was approached by the Grassen Trading Company. A decision was made and an order given. Of the slaves captured, a new force was to be formed, made of children."

"What?"

"They were made up of children from all across the Archipelago. Just like the slave crops of today, the young homeless, the runaways, the destitute. The disposable. They were not expected to fight, merely to distract and hold off the Conoscenzian forces out of fear, but such things rarely go according to plan. What followed was called the Dashing of the Innocents. Having formed this child army, it was moved into position off the coast of southern Conoscenzia. Before landfall could be made, word reached the Conoscenzian forces. They did not know the details of the approaching force, how could they? Their machines showed no mercy."

Nea didn't believe her ears.

No!

There was no way that something like that could happen.

Is it that hard to believe? You've seen what this place does to children.

Yet not once, in all the books she had read about Conoscenzia, had she ever stumbled upon even a footnote mentioning this.

Cain, Cain was there!

Cain hadn't said anything about it. A horrible chill ran down Nea's spine.

Did she know? She was close with the King after all, was it possible?

No, it couldn't be. Cain had helped those children, helped her, she was different.

Is she?

"After the end of the war The Dashing of the Innocents was buried by both nations involved. They were rightly afraid of what the population would do if word got out that such an atrocity had been committed." The priest said finally. "This place is one of the only clues that it even happened. The Black Briars built it to serve as a memorial, and a warning."

"A warning?" Nea thought about all those names on the wall, and the stained-glass pictures of child soldiers being marched to their deaths. It was too horrible.

"I tell you this so that you might know why it is that the Briars fight. You understand now that the government of this land is an unjust one and must be overturned by any means necessary. That is what The Black Briars fight for."

"Revenge?"

"Justice. Be warned, should you continue down this road you will see more examples of the wanton cruelty of this land. Are you prepared to face that?"

"I... yes I am."

"Very well, go west, to the town of Ventain. Seek the council of Mortimer Brumani. He holds court in a den of sin, wrapped in fumes."

Another strange clue, what could that mean? A den of sin; Nea had known lots of places that could be called that, but fumes...

"I hope my words have resonated with you Nea. This nation cannot exist under the thumb of such a king, nor can the companies that aided him be allowed to persist. Will you take up arms to prevent such horrors from being inflicted upon the world?"

"Yes," said Nea softly.

"Swear it."

"I swear."

*

"There you are!" said Cain eagerly. It was late and Nea was just getting back. She'd walked around the lake for hours, thinking about all that the priest had told her.

Cain was in the sitting room, nestled into one of the armchairs by the fire. The warm room was less inviting than it had been hours before.

"How did it go?" She saw the look on Nea's face. "What's happened, what's wrong?"

Nea looked up at her, unsure of what to say.

What can you say?

Nea's face was ashen, her eyes exhausted. She looked like she hadn't slept in days. Desperate as she was to have an answer, when she looked into Cain's big eyes, she couldn't bring herself to ask the question.

20

Devil in the Dark

"I THINK SOMETHING'S made a nest in my hair," grumbled Leo swatting at the mosquitoes looking for a midnight snack. A dull fog hung so tightly between the thick trees Leo could taste it. "Shouldn't we make camp soon?" They'd been walking since first light that day after all.

"It's not as cold as it's been," said Seiyariu. "And the moon is out, I thought we could get a few more hours in before we sleep."

"This is worse than the swamps," Leo muttered.

"Oh without a doubt," Seiyariu smiled.

Leo didn't return the cheer. "Nothing bothers you does it?"

"I wouldn't say that." Seiyariu replied still smiling. He stepped under a low hanging branch. "Nature can throw what it will at us. If a bit of murk and a few bugs are all we've got to worry about, I'm perfectly happy."

"And the takabran?" Leo hadn't caught sight of the strange creature again, but the memory of those red eyes still haunted him. Even when he'd finally drifted off to sleep the night before, they were all his dreams would show him.

"I can't say, but remember, we'll be fine so long as we stick together."

"I guess," Leo looked at his feet. He didn't share Seiyariu's optimism.

"Is there something wrong?" Seiyariu asked. "You look worried again."

Leo *was* worried, everything about the forest made him worry. He felt trapped, strangled by the closeness. "How do you stay so cheerful?"

"I've had to get used to savoring what little peace I can find."

They walked in silence for several more minutes. Seiyariu didn't miss a stride and despite the vastness of the wood, he never seemed to be lost. It was as though he were reading signs that Leo couldn't see. He wished the vagabond would share these with him; show him the road they were following, if only to ease his nerves. There was a lot he wished Seiyariu would share with him.

"Seiyariu?" Leo asked finally, if only to get his mind off the darkness all around them. "What exactly is Knail?"

Seiyariu blinked at him. "I thought I told you."

"You told me it was a weapon that the vagabonds keep safe." Leo bit his lip pensively. Seiyariu seemed as though he was trying to avoid this question at every turn. "You didn't tell me what it was or what it did."

"Perhaps it's better that way."

"Why though?" Leo pushed. "Why can't you *say* what you mean, rather than dance around it?" He hadn't meant to sound so angry, perhaps the forest, and his own anxiety, was affecting him more than he'd thought. The vagabond's incessant vagueness was beginning to truly annoy him.

Seiyariu's face fell. "Have I upset you?"

Leo didn't look at him. "You expect me to trust you. Why keep secrets from me?" Quinnel's words were ringing in his ears now, the subtle questions about the vagabond's identity that Leo had been utterly unable to answer. Though he was grateful he hadn't given Quinnel any useful information, the fact that he barely knew Seiyariu had been biting at him.

"You've only just started to walk the Green Road, Leo. There are certain things I'm not sure you're ready to…"

"Is that because you don't trust me?" The words left Leo's mouth before he could stop them.

Seiyariu stared at him for a moment, looking hurt. "I thought we had an understanding, if I took you with me to Adis, you would follow my instructions. If there are things I keep to myself, it's because I wish to keep them to myself." Seiyariu's voice was so stern, Leo had to look at him. His face was reserved, cold even. "You'll forgive me if I choose to omit things I don't expect you to understand."

The words hit Leo hard. He turned away from Seiyariu, trying to hide his hurt face. Seiyariu walked on. Leo stood there a few moments, and then made to follow. He wanted to say something back, something sharp. Something that would hurt Seiyariu, but he couldn't think of anything.

Leo moved to catch up but as he did Seiyariu's form seemed to retreat. Leo sped up, yet he wasn't getting closer. He couldn't have been that far away a few moments ago, could he? Were Leo's eyes playing tricks on him? Was Seiyariu pulling ahead on purpose?

"Seiyariu!" He called out. The dark was closing in and the fog was growing thicker. The last he saw of his teacher was a fleeting backwards glance, which quickly turned into a look of horror. Seiyariu spun on his heel and ran back towards Leo, as he did there was a rumbling and the whole forest gave a great lurch. Leo was thrown to the ground, as everything around him became a blur. The forest was spinning, the trees racing around and around in a mess of color and sound. They spun faster and faster, until he thought he might just be thrown off into nothing. Desperately trying to block it all out he wrapped his arm around a tree root and shut his eyes, praying that it would stop, whatever it was. Was he sick? No, this was real, he could feel it. From a long way off he heard Seiyariu's voice cry out. Then it was gone and he was thrown off the root, flying into the spinning mess of branches and leaves as the forest finally came to a stop.

His arm gave a spasm of pain and he groaned, clutching at it in vain until it subsided. Dizzy and bruised, Leo tried to get to his feet, only to fall back to the ground, his head still spinning. Blearily, he looked around. The forest began to take shape again. Trees, brambles, and roots but not at all like how they had been when he'd fallen.

Panic rose in his chest. This wasn't the same part of the forest. He'd moved, or the forest had moved. But that was impossible. Yet his teacher was simply gone. Leo's heart began to speed up and his breath came in gasps.

I'm alone.

His mind began screaming at him.

Alone again, all alone. Just like before.

His panic was such that he felt as though he might vomit. A mad fight or flight response pulling him in all directions until all he could do was curl up, shaking. How would he get out of this damn wood now? He had no idea which way was north or south, which way he'd come from, which way they'd been going.

"They say it has a nasty habit of playing tricks on hapless travelers." Seiyariu's words rang in Leo's mind. Was that what was happening? Had the Pinwheel Forest spun them around for a laugh? Or, had it perhaps heard them fighting? The thought made Leo's stomach turn. They'd been harsh with each other; what if that were the last thing he'd ever get to say to Seiyariu?

That in itself was enough to get Leo to his feet. He stumbled drunkenly forward through the underbrush for a little while, aimless. Still battered, he leaned against a rock to catch his breath. The moon was looking down through the canopy here, bathing him in a soft white light. What was he to do?

Leo bit his lip. There were few things that scared him more than being truly alone. Growing up, he and Nico had been inseparable; Leo could hardly even remember a time where they had been without one another. After Nico's death, he'd been split down the middle, left a half of a person wandering aimlessly through a world he didn't understand, couldn't understand, without being whole.

He gazed up in despair. Only to find himself face to face with the constellation of the lion Seiyariu had shown him on their first night together. The sight of the creature made Leo feel a little less alone. Lost in thought, Leo ran his fingers along the rock, through the lichen and across the smooth… he paused, his fingers tracing something unnatural, something carved. He crouched and scraped the lichen away and his heart leapt to see a series of Peregrine Runes etched in the side of rock. Seiyariu was gone, but he was not alone after all. He pulled the green cloak tight about his shoulders as he attempted to read the marks, feeling for the first time that he was part of something larger than himself.

He knew these marks. Leo replayed the lessons he'd had with Seiyariu over in his head. What was the vagabond who carved these trying to tell him? The first symbol was a twisting line, the road, followed by a perfect circle, the mark for safety. Beside it was a broken chain, freedom.

The Road to Safety and Freedom

Then beneath that he saw a pair of human shapes inside one another, follow, and the image of a bird larger than the other rune. Ordinarily a bird was the Peregrine Rune for flight, but that was drawn differently, this was a bird proper. What was it saying?

Follow the birds?

Leo got to his feet and looked around, sure enough, there they were, birds etched in the side of the trees, barely visible but for the light of the moon. They sometimes included arrows, pointing in the direction of the next tree, sometimes a small rune or two with phrases like, *forward* and *west*.

It was slow going, he didn't want to accidentally take directions from a knot in the wood or a scratch from some animal. Leo followed the invisible path for what felt like hours, making sure not to double back on himself. His fear was still there, buzzing like a wasp's nest. but as long as he was doing something, he felt he could keep it at bay. He silently thanked the vagabond, whoever he was, for leaving their marks for fellow vagabonds to follow. But what was waiting at the end of this trail? As he went further into the wood, new messages emerged beneath the markers. There was one phrase that was repeated over and over again. Leo thought it looked like the mark for rest or sleep with a cross through it.

Stop for nothing.

Taking this phrase to heart, Leo didn't break stride. Though the forest around him was growing darker and colder all the while, the light of the moon and stars helped him feel safe. His mind was determined not to stray into unhelpful worrying, but he couldn't help but feel there was something wrong, something he was forgetting.

The sound of the animals had faded away. Leaving him with only the pattering of his feet. The fog was thinning but the trees overhead were growing thicker. Just as he was beginning to get tired and out of breath, Leo came across the last thing he'd expected to find in this endless wood. A building, or something that used to be one; he'd stumbled upon the ruins of an old stone hut.

The roof had long since collapsed, as had two of the walls. The others were broken and jagged but still standing. Leo took a few careful steps forward, avoiding the bits of wall that now lay strewn about in the bed of needles and leaves.

Against the wall, a small human form was draped. It was not moving. As he drew closer, Leo's heart nearly stopped when he saw that it wasn't a person at all, just a skeleton. Leo tried not to look at the pale white bone. Thoughts of the dream, of Nico's corpse holding his hand, filled his head. He shut this out, it wasn't the time. He commanded himself to resist the urge to run away.

"How long have you been here?" he asked the corpse softly. The moon drifted out from behind a cloud and cast the ruins of the house into light. Leo gasped, the skeleton wore a green cloak, patched and frayed just like Seiyariu's. He was a vagabond! Or at least, he had been one in life. Was this the same vagabond who carved the path that brought him here, or merely an unlucky soul like him, that didn't reach the end?

Then he heard it, a low, guttural snarl. He felt his heart catch in his chest and leapt to his feet, eyes darting around madly. The takabran! Had it been hunting him this whole time?

Stop for nothing!

Leo cursed. He stared into the woods beyond, straining his eyes to see even the faintest hint of those eyes.

The terrible noise came again, louder and closer. Leo pressed his back to the wall and drew his knife, eyes darting about the ruins looking for any signs of motion. None came, the noises stopped. Leo choked on his own breath; the silence far worse. Then he felt the terrible sensation of eyes on the back of his head. Slowly, Leo turned to see something perched atop the jagged remains of the wall. Something that looked as though it had stepped out of a nightmare.

Burning red eyes shone within a long thin skull. The creature's snout was lined with gleaming teeth. Its skin clung to it loosely, and even the dark hair that covered its body was unable to hide its skeletal frame. An array of spines protruded along the takabran's back down to its small tail. Its thin legs were bent, ready to spring. Its unnaturally long arms hung down to its feet, claws at the ready as it leered down at him with those terrible eyes.

Leo stumbled back, half mad with terror. Then the takabran sprang at him. It was all Leo could do to throw himself out of the way. It landed on the ground, shifting its weight to attack again. It didn't run like any animal he'd seen before. It hopped unnaturally towards him, its large legs propelling it forward.

Leo drew his knife as the creature lashed out at him with one of its claws. Leo made to dodge again but didn't account for the length of the arms. It tore through the threads of his jerkin, brushing deathly close to his throat. Leo stabbed with his knife, but the takabran was faster than he was. He felt the claws again, this time the beast's aim was true, its claws ripped through his shirt and into his flesh.

Pain burst through his chest like fire. Leo staggered back, clutching at the wounds, feeling the warmth of his own blood. The takabran was emboldened by this. It hopped around him, sizing up its prey.

Leo cursed inwardly, why was he so weak? Was this it then? Was he going to be another skeleton in a green cloak, lost and forgotten? Would he never see Seiyariu again?

No!

Leo tightened his grip on the knife and braced himself against the wall. He would not die here.

The creature lunged at him again, and Leo caught it with his knife. They tumbled to the ground in a whirl of hair and blood. He felt its claws dig into his shoulders as it snapped at his face. But he brought the blade up, blocking the gnashing teeth from closing on his throat. Then with all the strength he could muster, he twisted the blade. The beast let out a howl of pain and paused in its attack. Leo struck again, slashing the monster's face and driving it back. The takabran thrashed, mad with pain and Leo stabbed with everything he had left. For a moment, Leo thought he had done it, and then a dreadfully familiar agony exploded in his right arm.

The takabran had latched onto his wounded limb with its jaws. Leo could feel its teeth moving, ripping into the damaged nerves and tendons like a thousand tiny knives. He slashed blindly, clipping the beast's eye and forcing it to let go. The pain in his arm was unimaginable. Had the takabran ripped it clean off? Leo collapsed on the ground clutching at the wretched, useless thing. White-hot pain blurred his vision as he felt the blood pouring. The takabran was bleeding, but still on its feet. Despair filled his heart as Leo realized that this was the end.

Leo watched as the beast leapt at him. At least now he'd see Nico again, but that thought brought no comfort. He'd been so damn close.

Then, from the trees, a dark shroud came diving down onto the takabran, driving a gleaming sword through its heart.

The creature screamed its dying breath. Leo stared in astonishment. Was he hallucinating? No, surely not. The corpse of the takabran lay on the forest floor, impaled by a bloody sword. Standing over it, was a figure. As Leo began to lose consciousness, it turned to face him and he could see that it was a woman, a woman in a green cloak.

21
Den of Sin

"ARE WE NOT staying in town?" asked Nea as Cain dismounted.

"No," she replied, fussing with the saddlebags. "I think it'd be better if we made camp here. You'll understand once we're inside."

Nea wasn't sure what Cain meant by that, but she shrugged and looked around. The campsite was as good a place as any, large stones jutted from the earth, concealing them, but if Nea climbed to the top of one, she'd have a perfect view of the road and the town beyond.

Slowly she and Cain got to unpacking, the midday sun bright overhead. They didn't say much. In fact, they hadn't said much since leaving Foresbury. The story she'd been told, part of her had wanted Cain to tell her it was all a lie made up by the Briars, but that church, that'd been all too real. She had told Cain nothing but the Briars' clue.

How do you even ask about something like that? Still, you've gotta find out sooner or later.

"Ventain's a port, not a large one but an important one," said Cain as they unpacked.

"I didn't realize we were back on the coast," said Nea staring off into the distance, but the morning was cloudy and she couldn't make out much.

Cain nodded, "It's a place of terrible poverty, possibly the worst in Fortuna."

"Why's that?"

"A great many reasons," Cain sighed. "The wealth that comes from trade is concentrated in the port, bars, brothels and gambling dens, all under the thumb of the local criminal element. The slums beyond, they were constructed poorly, making sanitation difficult. As such, disease spreads easily, and it's in Ventain that much of the trade with the continent is carried out, which means foreign diseases that the people can do little to prevent."

"And people live there?"

Cain leaned against a tree, looking off into the distance at the dark shape of the town. "It's a home for those with nowhere else to go, the crippled, the sick – you understand. Lepers and the deformed, those who are too broken even for the slaving companies all come here, like so much drainage."

You'll feel right at home then.

Nea followed Cain's gaze, even from this distance the town was run down. "That's horrible, why doesn't your king…?"

"What Nea? What would you suggest he do?" snapped Cain, her tone suddenly defensive.

"I…" For once Nea was at a loss for words.

Cain had a terribly sad look in her eyes. "Ventain has become a haven for continental opium traders. That is what I think your contact meant by a den of sin, wrapped in fumes. He's sending us into an opium den."

Opium? Christ.

Nea knew all about opium, that strange drug from the continent. It had been a constant at Glatman. She remembered how it got its claws into some of the girls there, how they shriveled up and wasted away.

But can you really blame them?

"Let's not waste time then," said Cain.

"You coming along?"

"I am," she replied, leading her horse down the hill. "Ventain is no place for a child."

"I'm not a child," said Nea darkly. "Besides I grew up poor, poor family, poor village. I won't stand out. I should go alone."

"You've proven that you can keep a cool head in a fight, even if a delicate lady such as myself gets in the way."

She's a fool. But is she a liar? Does she know?

*

The first thing Nea noticed was the smell. She'd picked up on it on the walk down and it had only gotten stronger. Ventain was absolutely filthy. With nowhere for it to go, waste had been left to pile up in the streets, filling the air with a noxious odor that made her want to vomit.

The wooden buildings were full of holes; doors hanging off their hinges and walls cobbled together with whatever material could be salvaged. A fair few others walked the streets with them, mercenaries, sailors and the like, no doubt on their way to the port. There were no animals on the streets, not a single one. Nea had a nasty suspicion as to why that was as they passed the lines of poor impoverished people, sick and starving down to their ribs. They lined the filthy streets, scavenging, begging. She looked away as they passed a boy spread out on a bit of cloth. His arms and legs were gone, whether from birth or some terrible accident Nea couldn't tell, but he just sat, watching people go by. Every so often a coin would be thrown onto his blanket, only to be snatched and pocketed by the fragile looking woman beside him.

Even Glatman wasn't like this.

Nea had half expected the beggars to swarm around, but they were either too weak or too sick to do much more than proffer their hands and cry out.

In the distance she could make out the warehouses and masts of the port. "So that's where the drug comes in, yeah? Doesn't seem like the people here could afford it,"

Cain scowled. "The trading companies take more than money as payment, as you well know."

That hairs on the back of Nea's neck stood up as Cain continued. "They got the population to become addicted to something they couldn't afford, snatching up all the land, buildings, and people that they could along the way. The only real structure and rule comes from the slum lords who run the opium dens; those can afford enough of the drug to keep the population indebted to them."

Nea wanted to be sick. It was horrible, to see human beings reduced to this, little more than animals.

What kind of king would allow this to happen?

The briar in Foresbury had been right. At the time Nea hadn't been sure what he'd meant. First his story and the memorial to the lost slaves, then this horrible display of, what had he called it? Wanton cruelty? Nea didn't know what to think. Would Mortimer Brumani send her to yet another haunting showcase? Force her to look at even more evidence of the grassers' death grip on this country? And when she got there, would it merely lead her to another?

Nea shook her head; how could anyone look at all this and not be filled with anger, not want justice for all the wrongs. She did. She wanted to find the men who did this, one by one and hurt them like they'd hurt these people. She wanted them blind and crippled, mewling for mercy from the people they'd tormented.

Like those bastards you killed at Glatman.

Nea stared at Cain's back. Who could stand by and watch as their king did nothing? The Briars were the ones who spoke up, the ones who'd actually taken any real action; time and time again she caught herself replaying their attack on the auction in her head.

What if she's wrong about them?

Cain was a decent woman sure, Nea had seen that first hand when she'd helped those slaves get passed the Spook Legion. But would those slaves have been there were it not for the state of Fortuna? Fortuna, the name was a cruel joke. Nea felt that old familiar anger burning in her chest, and she didn't know what to do with it. She wanted to lash out, to fight, break something, but everything here was already broken.

The few beggars who would, or could, talk to them, had heard the name Mortimer Brumani before. He must've been one of these slumlords Cain had mentioned. All the beggars they talked to pointed them in the direction of an opium den near the waterfront. The dens were the easiest buildings to spot; they were the only ones that weren't completely falling apart.

"You should wait here," said Nea, eyeing the place.

"I don't want you going in there by yourself," Cain replied.

Nea shook her head, "I know that but if we're going to do this right I've got to be on my own. They're expecting me."

Cain frowned. "Yes I suppose, we can't risk the trail going cold. Fine I'll wait. But if I hear anything – anything – I'm coming in after you."

Nea nodded and made for the door. "See you soon, M'lady."

Inside the den, silent forms lay slumped about in every corner, little plums of white smoke illuminating their gaunt faces. Even the rancid smell from the street was blotted out by the cloying, overpowering stench of the drug. Nea had expected to be more afraid, instead all she felt was pity.

Poor bastards here can't hurt anyone anymore.

Indeed, the only movement they seemed to be capable of was pressing the pipe to their lips. She took a few more strides into the den, looking around. No attendant, he too was probably off smoking.

Nea had no clue which of these ghouls might be Mortimer Brumani, but she didn't feel like asking. Instead, she took a deep breath and again recited, "If you ever see a body, strung up in your view, take care and leave it strung, else the Briars string up you."

For a few moments the lyrical words hung in the air with the smoke. Then a door Nea had taken just to be a patch of wall, slid open. Nea approached it warily. The room beyond was tiny, little more than a closet, cloaked in shadow. The walls were mirrored, and Nea had to be careful to avoid catching the eye of her reflection, now wasn't the time.

The man, who could only be Mortimer Brumani, sat in the corner of the dark room, resting on a pile of cushions, a pipe in his hand. He was far gone, a ghoul for the drug like all the others. Little more than a skeleton with yellowing, pockmarked skin, his bones jutted out at odd angles and his hair was completely gone. His eyes were open, and fixed on Nea, unblinking.

"And what can I do for you?" The man's voice came like a death rattle, so faint that Nea barely saw his lips move. His huge staring eyes followed her as she sat down before him.

"You can tell me where to find The Black Briars," said Nea.

"Is that right?" He took a long draft on his pipe and let the smoke free of his mouth slowly, savoring it as much as possible.

Then he spoke again. "You did well, finding this place on your own, Nea Dúlaman." Nea's breath caught in her chest and she stiffened. "Relax," he croaked. "I had a bird from our friend by the lake, he said that you might be coming."

The smell of opium in the room was unbearable. She longed to be anywhere else, even the filth-covered streets, if only she could get away from the cloying sickeningly sweet smell. It brought back the worst kind of memories.

"What do you think of my home?" he asked, drawing back on his pipe once again. "Do be honest."

"I think it's the worst place I've ever seen."

Mortimer cracked a smile, revealing dozens of missing teeth. "Go on."

"I hate it. I want to leave. But… but I also want to…"

"Burn it to the ground?"

Nea blinked, "Yes."

More than anything.

"Don't feel guilty on that account boy. For the truly wretched, death is often a mercy. Wiping this town from the face of the earth would certainly be a mercy. This place is a monument to human suffering. You have the trading companies and his divine majesty the King to thank for that."

Nea was desperately trying to avoid the man's gaze but it followed her, like the eyes of a painting. It was true, all of it. The town made her so angry and sad she didn't know what to do with herself. "Why doesn't anyone stop them?" she asked softly.

Mortimer continued to look her up and down. "If you could stop them. Would you?"

She met his gaze now, her anger and hate almost completely overriding her fear. "Yes."

"What would you do to stop them?"

"I'd fight."

"Would you kill?"

"Of course." said Nea, her nasty smile imitating the ghoul's. "For the truly wretched, death can be a mercy."

Mortimer let out a garbled laugh and puffed again on his pipe. "You're smart. And you speak with a weight of experience I don't often hear from one as young as you. You are exactly the kind of solider we need."

"Kind of you," replied Nea, her face set.

"Let's get right to what you're here for then, shall we? Information. You see Nea, the Black Briars are a sanctuary. We take in those who have nowhere left to go, the frightened, lost souls of this land. And we train them." he said. "Do you know why?"

Something told Nea that Brumani didn't really need an answer.

He continued, "With the scattering of the land comes the scattering of military might. The King knows that and that's why he's trying so desperately to find us now. But it's too late. Soon we will be ready to strip them of the power they so selfishly squander."

"You mean..."

"To take control, yes, in one swift strike, Fortuna's chain of command will collapse. The nation will fall to us, then Inferno."

"Inferno?"

They're mad, that's not possible.

"The Twelve City-States of Inferno have grown weak since the murder of their king. Warring with one another over their religious disputes. They won't be able to form up against the Fortuan army. One by one the twelve will fall to us, and with the combined strength of Fortuna and Inferno we will seize Conoscenzia. The Kengean Archipelago will be united for the first time since before the Clash."

Nea stared at him, the ghoul's face unreadable. "You're mad if you think a small army like that can take over one country, let alone three."

His smile grew. "That's why we need fierce, hungry young soldiers like you counted among us."

"It won't be enough."

"Our leader, Djeng Beljhar, is quite prepared. Both to seize the three nations and defend them. You've seen his power first hand, have you not?"

Nea thought back to the illusions Beljhar had cast at the guards. How powerful was he truly?

"And that's why you've stolen the weapons?"

Brumani's eyes widened. "Indeed, Mister Beljhar is gathering artifacts of the old world, weapons of such great destruction not a soul has dared use them. Until now."

"People will—"

"People will rejoice, when we hang every last slaver in the land high for all of them to see. Wouldn't you? Tell me that's not a future you would fight for."

"I..." Nea trailed off, unable to force the words together.

Damn right you would.

"I'll just ask you one more question; if I like the answer then you'll have your clue and be on your way, sound fair?"

Nea nodded.

"Will you go to war?"

Nea sat in the fumes, thinking about her answer. The ghoul waited patiently, a look of genuine curiosity on his mutilated face. Finally, Nea's eyes fell upon her finger, on The Nuptial, the brand marking her as the property of the slaving companies for the rest of her life.

"I'm already at war."

22

Patches

"Boy? Wake up child, you're safe now."

Leo's eyes slid open. As his vision swam into focus, a face took shape before him, a woman's face. She was Infernian, her dark amber skin and long black hair shining in the sunlight. Her features were sharp, her eyes dark and unreadable. She wore jewelry, hoops of gold in her ears and rings on her fingers, which combined with her red and gold tunic gave her a fiery appearance. This was muted somewhat by the faded and patched vagabond's cloak she wore like a shawl. The woman was so incredibly beautiful that, for a moment, Leo wasn't sure where he was.

She smiled weakly, as though it was something she didn't often do. "I am glad to see you're alive."

Leo looked down at himself, his rescuer had treated his bad arm, and the bleeding had stopped, although it ached with every beat of his heart.

I wish the takabran had just taken the whole thing off.

The sun was blinding after being in the dark of the wood for so long, the endless blue sky greeted him like an old friend. Sitting up in amazement Leo saw he was in a meadow. Pure emerald grass grew tall, and wildflowers of every color imaginable lay scattered about, painting gorgeous pictures with every flutter of the wind.

"Where are we?" he asked, trying to get up.

The woman pressed her hand against his good shoulder, "Stay down, do not exert yourself just yet." She sat beside him, carrying herself with grace and simplicity, as though she were at peace with all the life around her.

"Are we still in Mavrodasos?"

"Yes, but there is no danger to be found in this part of the Pinwheel." Sure enough the large trees of Mavrodasos bordered the meadow, and kept it hidden away like an oasis in a desert. "I am sure you have many questions," she said, removing a pile of green rags from one of her pockets.

It looked familiar, "What's that?"

"The cloak, I took it from that dead soul in the woods. He is a fallen compatriot to you and I. We must give him the honors."

"The honors?"

The woman raised an eyebrow. "Are you not a vagabond? Forgive me if I was quick to judge but you are—

"Oh no, I mean yes, I am, er I think. But I haven't been one for very long." he admitted.

"You are a student? Then where, if I may ask, is your teacher?"

Leo shrugged sadly. "We got separated in the woods. Or maybe *by* the woods, I'm not sure."

She nodded. "Quite ill to strangers no?"

"Y-yes." Then, unsure of what else to say, "I'm Leo."

"Zhenamansa," she said offering him her hand. He shook it; her hands were soft and her grip firm. Bracelets rattled on her wrists and her fingernails had been painted a deep violet color.

"It seems Leo, that we have been made the butt of a joke."

"Have we?" He watched as Zhenamansa began to rip up the old cloak as gingerly as possible.

"Not maliciously so; I believe the Pinwheel simply gets bored. Sitting here for thousands and thousands of years with nothing to do but play tricks on the odd travelers that dare to enter."

"Sounds more lonely than bored," said Leo, glancing at the surrounding trees.

"A generous perspective, considering it made you lose your vagabond."

Leo shrugged. "It led me to you I guess, it can't be all bad."

She gave him a warmer smile. "I suppose not. But you are lucky I came around when I did. Tell me, what is the name of the vagabond you travel with?"

"Seiyariu," said Leo, wondering where he was now; was he still alone in the woods, looking for him?

"Seiyariu." Zhenamansa nodded, as this confirmed something to her, her smile vanishing. Why was that?

"Do you know him?"

She nodded. "I suppose you could say that, yes."

"Everyone seems to know him, and he seems to know everyone." Leo said rather wistfully.

Everyone except me, he wanted to add.

"How did you come to be travelling with such a famous vagabond?"

Famous?

Leo told her; he didn't see any reason not to. The woman was kind and she was a vagabond. She didn't seem to mean any harm.

"And you have been with him ever since?" Zhenamansa asked when he finished. Leo nodded. "I am sorry you lost one another, but please do not worry. There is a town not too far from here." Zhenamansa pointed east, to where the meadow sloped off. "Hunter's Hollow. Those lucky enough to find their way out of the Pinwheel sooner or later wind up near there."

"Hunter's Hollow." The name didn't sound familiar. Seiyariu hadn't mentioned it at least.

Leo had been watching Zhenamansa's hands this whole time. She tore the old cloak into small bits of fabric, then drew from her pockets a needle and thread. "What are you doing?"

"Seiyariu has not taught you this?"

Leo shook his head.

"Give me your cloak."

Leo did, rather reluctantly. Zhenamansa took a piece of the old skeleton's cloak and pressed it against his own.

"Do you know how to sew?"

"Yes," said Leo rather proudly. Nico had been constantly ripping his clothes, so Leo had taught himself.

"That is good, then you can do this one yourself if you like. Hold it like this, there, very good. You see Leo, when one of our number dies, we shred his cloak and sew the pieces into our own. These are called the legacy patches."

"Legacy patches," said Leo softly, watching as Zhenamansa carefully sewed the patch onto hers.

The patch stuck out like dead grass, old and faded against the cloak's natural color.

"Why do you do this?"

"Why do *we* do this, Leo," she corrected. "Because as vagabonds we have nothing to our name but our deeds and our companions. We are the legacy of those who came before, you understand. That is why we carry them with us. A vagabond's legacy never truly dies, it is sewn into the hearts of his kin that he may walk the Green Road forever."

Leo thought about this more, staring at the patch. He found himself wondering about who that skeleton had been, and what he would think knowing that Leo was carrying a bit of him around now.

"That's nice," he said finally. "I like that."

"Be sure to remember it if you come upon any more slain wanderers or if, and I pray this doesn't happen, one of your companions is to fall."

"I will," said Leo.

"Is something wrong?" Zhenamansa asked.

"It's nothing," Leo's thoughts of Nico had lingered longer than he would've liked. "I just, I lost someone, someone important, before all this. I would've liked to have something to remember him by is all." After Nico's death, all he'd taken with him were the nightmares.

"Is that when you tried to kill yourself?" Zhenamansa said gently.

Leo dropped the needle, "What?"

"When I was wrapping your arm, I found your scars. I am sorry if that was supposed to be a secret."

Leo just stared at her, unsure of what to do. He hadn't told anyone. Not a soul.

"The scars are deep. And they overlap on themselves enough to make me think they were self-inflicted." Zhenamansa paused, perplexed by the look of horror on Leo's face. "I am not angry with you child, I just—"

"Please don't tell him," said Leo softly.

"It is not my business to tell Seiyariu anything. But I must ask, why keep it a secret?"

"He'll think I'm mad." Leo's voice was wavering now. "Or that I'm not fit to stay with him."

Zhenamansa stared into Leo's eyes for a few moments. Then she opened her cloak and pointed to a patch sewn into the fabric that covered her heart. "My husband," she said simply. "Sometimes when those we love take that journey, it seems easier just to follow them, no?"

Leo turned away from her, shaking. "I needed him," was all he said but the words had been floodgates, he felt the tears come.

Nico's death had come from nowhere, a few coughs one day, then he was standing over his bed, looking at a brother he didn't even recognize. After Nico died, it was all too much. He had been lost in a world he didn't want to brave alone. As the hole in his heart grew with every passing day, he began to realize just how much of the world his brother had been protecting him from. He had been too naive to realize just how much of a target he had been; now he was alone. He still recalled the night, sobbing alone in the attic of the old church, his eyes had fallen upon a mirror. The sight of his reflection, the face of his twin, of Nico, had been too much. In his anguish, he'd driven his fist through it, the glass tearing at his arm. Then as despair threatened to overwhelm him, he pulled his arm back across the broken glass, cutting even deeper. He hadn't cared anymore. He just wanted to be with Nico. It wasn't to be. Waking in the infirmary, his arm bandaged and useless, Leo had decided to run away. And run he had, right into the arms of the slaving companies. Why hadn't he cut just a little deeper? In the months that followed he'd been unable to work up the courage to try again. Nico had always been the brave one.

Zhenamansa let him cry, continuing her work in silence. When he managed to swallow the last of the tears, she said,

"I will not tell Seiyariu a thing. But I think perhaps you are not giving him enough credit. Vagabonds know loss better than anyone walking this earth Leo, Seiyariu is no exception."

"What do you mean?"

She shook her head. "It is not my place to tell. I will do him the same courtesy I do you. Agreed?"

"Agreed," said Leo sniffing. "Thank you."

"There is no need to—" she began.

"There is," said Leo honestly. "I think I probably needed to tell someone."

"Perhaps," she said kindly, getting to her feet. Leo couldn't help but notice the curved sword that hung from her belt in an ornate scabbard that shone like gold. "You should go, you want to get there before dark."

"You're not coming with me?" said Leo tentatively. "You said it's not far, right?"

"Not particularly no," replied Zhenamansa. "But you see, I have a student of my own and she is expecting me back soon. Besides, Seiyariu and I have not spoken in quite a long time. I would rather not trouble him, you understand."

"Oh," Leo didn't quite understand but he had a feeling Zhenamansa wouldn't give him a real answer even if he pressed her.

"Be safe Leo," she said gently. "I wish you the best, truly." With that, she turned on her heel and disappeared back into the woods.

23

Loyalties Lie

THE EVENING SUN descended over the dark outline of Ventain. The sky was a perfect prism of orange and red, cascading their little campsite in color, before it slipped away for the night. The pair of them were sitting atop the rocks, watching the sunset.

"So they're planning a coup," said Cain, once tinkering with her gauntlets. "I suspected as much. Especially with the disappearing weapons."

"Do you think that's how Beljhar was able to make people see things at the auction? With one of those weapons?"

"I wouldn't be surprised. Artifacts from before The Clash of Comets often carry strange powers."

"Enough power to overthrow a government?" asked Nea.

She'd left the den of sin unscathed and returned to the outskirts of town with Cain. She'd said almost nothing along the way. That old ghoul Brumani, his words haunted her even more than his face. The state of this land, it was something to be ashamed of, something to be fixed.

And what the hell is she doing about it? Not a damn thing. Her royal love sends her traipsing after the only people making a lick of bloody sense.

"Perhaps. Let's hear his directions again."

Nea sighed. "Take the ship, Stella Amora, from the capital to meet The Last Innocent."

"Hmm," said Cain, brow furrowed.

"What's wrong?" asked Nea, suppressing the fire in her gut.

"I didn't think it was possible that the trail would lead us to the capital. Let alone end there," said Cain finally. "I've lived in Equius for years; to think it's been under our noses this whole time. Still, something about this seems wrong."

You, the King, this country, the whole damn thing is wrong!

"What do you mean? We're almost done with this damn crusade of yours," said Nea.

Cain frowned, "Perhaps I'm being paranoid, but this strikes me as far too easy."

"How do you mean?"

Cain got to her feet and started back down the rocks to the campfire. The cold had come rushing in very quickly. "This hunt we've been on doesn't feel like a way to test worthy recruits. The clues are simple, childish, and the contacts haven't put up any resistance. I feel like we're walking into a trap."

"A trap in your own capital?" asked Nea, following after her. "That's bold."

"The Briars are nothing if not bold, don't you think?" she said pensively.

"What if…" Nea bit her lip.

"What if what?"

What if they're right?

"Never mind," said Nea quickly.

"No, go on, I want to hear what you've got to say Nea, you're as much a part of this as I am."

Nea thought back to everything she'd seen so far. "What if it's not a test?" Cain gave her a quizzical look and Nea continued, staring out across the horizon. "The priest in Foresbury said that if I keep going down this road it will show the 'wanton cruelties', I think it was, of Fortuna."

"A showcase of horrors," Cain said thoughtfully. "To pull people into their way of thinking. That makes sense but why stop at just Ventain? There are many such places in Fortuna."

Of bloody course there are.

"You don't think that means the Briars have a point?"

Cain shot her a look. "I've never denied that the Briars have a point, Nea. But that doesn't give them the right to wage a vigilante crusade in which innocent people can and will get hurt."

"I suppose that's the job of His Majesty then," said Nea without thinking. "Crusading through the innocent."

Cain stared at her for a few moments, not understanding, then her eyes grew wide. "Nea, you—"

"It's true, isn't it?" she asked, knowing the answer. The look on Cain's face told her everything. "What they said about the King? About the war?"

"Nea…"

"Is it?" Nea was on her feet, fists clenched. All the anger and distrust that had been building up over the past few days came frothing the surface.

"Yes. It is." The lack of emotion in Cain's eyes was worse than screaming. "They told you the whole terrible story I take it?"

"And you didn't."

"No."

"But you knew."

"Yes."

She knew! She knew and she still serves him, why?

Nea turned away. She couldn't bear to see Cain's face. "I thought so."

"Nea—"

"Shut up!" she yelled. "I should've run away from you the first chance I got!"

"Then why didn't you?"

Nea froze.

That's a damn good question.

Why had she stayed? She'd distrusted Cain from the moment they'd met, resisted and belittled her at every turn. She'd taken barely any convincing to believe she had known about the atrocities committed in the King's name. Yet she'd stayed with her all the same, and it damn sure wasn't for safety.

You know why.

Nea glared at the ground, still refusing to meet Cain's gaze. "You saved those slaves when we fought the Legion. You didn't have to, but you did. After all that, I figure I owe you at least a chance to explain yourself. Plus," she added. "I was hoping you'd tell me it was a lie."

Cain took out a flask and silently nursed it for a few minutes. "When did you first learn of this?"

"The church," said Nea gruffly, "It was a monument, all the kids names were carved into the wall."

"My God," Cain took another sip of her drink to steady her hands. "I had no idea. But that confirms some of my suspicions about the Briars, they—"

"Cain," said Nea seriously. "I swear if you had anything to do with it…"

Cain let out a hysterical little laugh. "How little you must think of me Nea. No, I had nothing to do with this, it happened before I even met Chiron."

"But you knew about it, and you still saved the King's life?"

How could you after that? How could you serve him? How can you even look at him?"

Cain wiped her eyes. "Yes I did. I found him in the aftermath of a terrible battle. Though the Fortuan numbers were great, my nation's technology was too powerful. It was a losing war from the very beginning. I was ready to kill him, and I wasn't the only one either. But when I finally found him, there he was, crumpled under his horse, both legs in pieces, hovering over the door to death. I couldn't bring myself to see anything other than a stupid child thrust into a role he wasn't ready for."

"So that's why you keep his secret? Why you do nothing?"

"The people would turn on Chiron and—"

"He'd deserve it."

"There would be fighting, blood, even more innocents lost. It was not him alone that brought about this tragedy. But it was he that I swore myself to him Nea. I am honor bound to protect his interests. My own opinions are irrelevant."

"How can you say that? You're not his slave," said Nea. "Sounds like you just don't want people to see your love for what he truly is."

Slap. Cain struck Nea full in the face.

"You don't know a damn thing about me boy."

Nea blinked, stunned at first. She wanted to throw herself at Cain to beat her like she had that girl back in shop. Like she had their first night together. But she didn't, for once in her life Nea held her composure.

"If it's not love, then what is it?"

"It's because I have no choice!" Cain shouted. "My loyalty, my pledge to the King was part of our peace treaty with Fortuna. He promised to withdraw everything, pay the reparations, if only I would serve under him."

"And you... you said yes? All that stuff about thinking Fortuna was better off with you around. Was that—"

"That was the truth," said Cain. "But my loyalty to the King goes deeper than that. I am a living treaty between our nations."

Christ, she is his slave.

"Christ, you are his slave."

Cain stared at her for a moment, then got to her feet. "Yes, I suppose I am." And with a turn of her heel she was off, striding down the hillside, leaving Nea alone with these words.

You thought she was different didn't you? You stupid, gullible little thing. When will you learn?

Nea realized there were tears in her eyes.

24
Nesting In The Hollow

Leo made his way to Hunter's Hollow without much trouble. It was truly right up on the lip of the woods, the Pinwheel forest curving around the town protectively, like an animal keeping her young safe. Nestled away, the town was quiet and inviting, little wooden houses lined the dirt roads, with shingled roofs and brightly painted doors.

The streets weren't busy, but the people out and about all knew each other. They were a tough looking sort, lumberjacks, tanners, and hunters by the looks of their wares. They lived off whatever the forest would give them.

The townsfolk shot curious looks in his direction as Leo shuffled nervously down the street. He was a real sight. His clothes dirty and stained with blood, skin broken all over. A few small children actually drew back from him as he passed. Were they scared?

Leo made straight for the inn, following a sign swinging in the breeze. Before he entered, he made sure to check and see if any Peregrine Runes had been carved into the building, trying to form the habit permanently. To his luck there were two small runes cut on the inside of the doorframe. Craning his neck Leo made out the symbol for "woman" as well as a second symbol, one that looked suspiciously like the one for "carnivorous."

A small bell rang when he opened the door. As he entered, he almost immediately collided with a desk, behind which sat a rather scrawny woman with her back to him. On one side of the desk was a staircase leading up, on the other a door was cracked to reveal a small living area complete with armchairs, a lit fire and a bearskin rug.

"Yes, what can I do for you?" the woman drawled, not looking back.

"Um, I need a place to stay."

"Fifteen a night, water's an extra five."

"I…" Leo only now began to realize just how little he'd thought this through. "I'm afraid I don't have any money."

"Then I'm afraid, you ain't got a room."

Leo frowned, carnivorous indeed. What would Seiyariu do? The wanderer was never short of money, but surely he had some secret for when he was in trouble. Leo turned around, and caught a glimpse of his reflection in the window. An idea blossomed in his head, so despicable and brilliant that he could feel Seiyariu beaming at him.

He turned to face the woman again putting on an expression akin to that of a stray puppy, all quivering lips and welling tears. "Please miss."

"I thought I told you." The innkeeper spun around and her expression changed immediately. "Well you're about the smallest vagabond I've ever seen." Then she took in the whole picture, wounds and all, "Christ what happened to you?"

"I'm sorry," Leo sniffled. "I got separated from my teacher in the woods and…"

The woman's face softened, she stepped around her desk and knelt to get a better look at him. "Those are some nasty scratches you've got." She checked his shoulder and gasped. "Are those teeth marks?"

Leo nodded melodramatically.

"These are horrible," she cooed. "I've seen this kinda stuff turn nasty, we best get you cleaned up."

A few hours later, Leo was clean, full, bandaged up and nestled into a tiny room at the top of the inn. Its ceiling was low and sloped, likely to hit a grown man in the head if he wasn't careful. A bed was tucked into one corner, a dresser in another. Two large windows hung on both sides of the room, other than that it was empty. Benya, the innkeeper, told Leo that it had belonged to her son.

"He's grown now, probably off getting into all kinds of trouble," she'd grumbled, not unsmiling. "There's some old clothes of his in the dresser; you're welcome to them. Yours are about worn out I'd say."

That night, as Leo wrapped himself in blankets, alone with his thoughts, his heart settled. He positioned his bandaged arm so as not to put any pressure on it. Lying there, he thought back to his talk with

Zhenamansa, her frankness still sent a chill down his spine. The way she had known – instantly. Still, it felt good to tell someone, especially someone he probably wouldn't see again. Zhenamansa's words on Seiyariu had forced him to reconsider some things. Leo hadn't told Seiyariu the truth about his arm, or Nico, or anything really. Yet he'd had a fit over Seiyariu not wanting to tell him about the artifact in Adis. It would be easy to blame the heat, or Quinnel's prodding, but Leo did neither. He'd acted like a petulant child and resolved to do better.

As he stretched, he felt his body ache from his fight with the tak-abran. There had been a moment during the battle, a small one to be sure but unmistakably there, where he had felt his fear fade. Not completely; it had merely stepped back to allow him to act. Leo had never felt that way before; since Nico's death, everything he did was through the haze of fear and anxiety. Why had that instant been so different? It hadn't. He'd been different, if only for a moment. He glared down at his arm again. What was the point of beating back his fear if he was just going to be defeated by his body? Leo didn't feel in control, of himself, of his situation, of anything. He let these worries go for now as he burrowed deeper under the covers. Next time he needed to fight, Leo swore he would be ready.

25

Dishonor Bound

CAIN AND NEA stopped in one of the larger crater towns, as they were called, in central Fortuna. She hadn't bothered to learn its name. The great recess in the earth left by The Clash of Comets had grown verdant over the centuries, the stream of several rivers flowing into the basin. Here their waters collected in a moat surrounding the town and were swept off in cut channels to irrigate the crops. It was a breathtaking sight, not so much living against the land as bending it to suit the needs of the people.

The town was at an important junction, connecting central Fortuna to the northwest, where the capital and their passage to the Briars waited. As such it was growing impossible for Cain to keep her low profile. So she'd taken to wearing her uniform more often, her pin on full display; it attracted attention but the kind that meant they wouldn't be bothered by curious guards or grassers. Though Nea noticed that the further north they went there was less and less evidence of the grassers' presence.

Out of sight, out of mind, for His Majesty's delicate sensibilities.

She and Cain had barely said a word since leaving Ventain the night before. They'd rode the entire day in silence before stopping at an inn in the heart of the crater town. The two of them never shared a room, for which she was grateful. Nea wasn't certain she would've been able to keep her secret if they had. It was hard enough when they were camping. Besides, she didn't want to talk to Cain, didn't want to even look at her.

The next morning, Cain slept in, so Nea decided to make herself at home at the bar downstairs. The barkeep wouldn't serve her anything strong, but Nea managed to swipe a whisky bottle when he wasn't looking and fill her mug.

The drink brought her no comfort, however. She just sat and scowled into it. Cain was complicit in everything; she kept the secret of a murderer.

But you stayed with her.

She was a part of the system that had brought so much suffering upon the people of this land. Still Nea had stayed. She'd truly wanted to believe Cain was different.

Don't lie. You stayed because you're a slave and a criminal. Figured it'd be safer to stick with her so long as it benefits you.

Nea shook her head, trying to make the voices stop. It would be over soon. She'd be on her way west and would never have to see or think about Cain again.

"Oi, you there!"

Nea blinked, a gaggle of boys at a nearby table were beckoning her over. The hell did they want with her? There were five of them. A boy with ginger hair and a pimply face, two large boys Nea took to be brothers, a smaller boy who looked quite out of place, and a tall, dark haired youth with broad shoulders. Nea didn't need to ask to know who the leader was. The dark-haired boy exuded authority, the biggest dog in the pack.

"Watch yourself," mumbled the barkeep. "Those boys' fathers own a good bit of land around here, makes them think they can go where they want and do what they please."

But curiosity got the better of her and she maneuvered her way over to the table. "What do you want?"

"Sit with us," the dark-haired boy kicked out a chair for her. When Nea took it, he held out his hand, "Jason."

"Nea."

"And I'm Rupert," said the ginger-haired boy. "This is Ian, and they're Claudio and Matteo." He gestured at the brothers.

"Pleasure," Nea said coolly.

"We saw you come in last night with that woman. Was that the Captain of the Guard? Lady Cain?"

Nea nodded, "That famous eh?"

"This close to the capital everyone knows the colors of the Royal Guard," said Ian meekly.

"And there's only one woman that is allowed to wear those colors," finished Jason.

"I suppose there is."

"Are you her servant then?" asked Rupert.

"Her slave actually."

The boys laughed at this, unaware of its truth.

"Yeah?" asked one of the brothers. "She a hard-ass?"

"You've got no idea," Nea found herself laughing as well; it was nice to be able to be honest for once.

This could be you. If you get away from this damn land, go to place nobody can find you. This can be you. One of these boys, sitting and laughing, not a care in the damn world.

"I bet she has to be," said Rupert thoughtfully. "What with her being the only woman, y'know? Otherwise people won't take her seriously."

"Well I don't take her particularly seriously," said Nea with a smirk.

"What do you do for her?"

"Listen to her bullshit all day. I suspect I'm the only soul in the kingdom that can stand to be around her," Nea said and the boys laughed again. It felt good to rail against Cain, to vent some of the frustration she'd been feeling.

"I always heard she had a bit of an attitude," said Jason, arms crossed.

"A bit?" Nea snorted. "There's not much *but* attitude there. A lot of showing off."

"Does she ever do any fighting?" asked the other of the two brothers.

"Not if she can avoid it," Nea lied. "That's what she has her guard for, plus her dear Majesty."

Jason scowled. "She's got that post because she's the King's lapdog, everyone knows that."

"And an obedient one," said Nea. "I suspect she'd fetch his slippers in the morning if he asked."

The boys' laughter filled the pub. Nea joined them but it felt as though something was stuck in her throat. Thoughts of the things Cain had said on the road, the experiences they'd shared filled her head. A knot of guilt wound itself around her stomach.

"I heard that she's actually a prisoner," said Rupert, eyes wide. "A hostage, so that we never go to war with the west again."

"You've got it all wrong," laughed Jason. "The King brought her back for one reason. He fancied having a golden-haired western girl as a trophy, that's it."

She said as much herself.

"She ever talk about the King?" asked Rupert.

"Sure did. Mooning over him every chance she got. I half expected to catch her kissing his locket." Nea smirked, wanting to delight in the wickedness of her words. But the rush wasn't coming as strong now, the words just made her feel sick.

"My mum says they're in love," chimed in Ian.

Jason laughed. "Bloody typical, it's a nice story but I think she's just there to keep His Majesty's bed warm."

Nea felt her fists clench under the table.

Oh what's the matter? Now you care? Want to stick up for the lover of a child murdering despot? Or do you just feel guilty you joined in. You thought the same damn things about her, they're just saying it out loud.

"But His Majesty's got no legs," said Ian with a frown.

"That don't mean he can't still have a woman."

"Must be a desperate lass to bed a cripple, king or not," said Matteo.

"Well you know what they say about those western girls."

"They'll take it however they can get it," Jason laughed.

"No," said Nea suddenly.

"What?" asked James.

"I said no. She's not a whore."

She's not a whore. That's just you right? Don't want the lady dragged down to your level?

"Oh?" The boys seemed taken aback by Nea's change in tone.

"Please," Jason snorted. "I'm surprised you didn't catch her ru—"

"Shut up."

Jason blinked. "What did you say to me?"

Without realizing it, Nea was on her feet. "I said shut up."

Jason raised his eyebrows. "What's the matter? This getting under your skin?"

Rupert's smile slipped a little. "Yeah, come on, we're just playing around."

"You don't know a damn thing about her," Said Nea.

What the hell are you doing?

Where was this coming from, this anger? After everything Cain had done, why did their words sting so much? She'd said similar things to Cain herself, why was it upsetting her so much now?

Because they're wrong, just like you were.

"You don't like us insulting your lady? Why's that, Cain pretend you're her king when she gets lonely at night?"

Nea's nails dug into her palms, white-hot anger filling every vein. "Say it again."

Jason stood up. He was a good head taller than her. "Scrawny little thing, aren't you?" Jason muttered. "You should watch how you're talking."

"Jason…"

"You lot stay out of this," he said cracking his knuckles. "I won't need you."

The boy was much larger than her. Each of his broad shoulders was the size of her head. Nea quietly went through all the fights she'd ever been in, recalling what had worked and what hadn't.

"Take it outside boys," warned the Barkeep.

"Shall we?" Nea beckoned condescendingly.

Jason scowled and followed her out the door onto the street, the other boys in tow. They surrounded Nea and Jason, as the two faced each other. "You should've kept your mouth shut, now I'm gonna have to beat you until even that western slut won't–"

Nea hit him in the jaw, sending him reeling back. For a brief second she thought she had him, but he came back swinging. She tried to catch one of his blows with her arm, but his weight was too much. She did a quick hop backwards, running through her options quickly. She needed to use her speed, her legs. Every strike needed to carry the full weight of her body if she wanted to stand a chance.

The rush of adrenaline made her feel alive. This was what she needed, what she wanted. A chance to burn off all the excess hate and rage that had been simmering away.

Jason came rushing at her again, anger flashing in his eyes. He'd not counted on a spindly thing like her putting up a fight. Nea stepped into his assault; she was only going to get one chance at this. Plowing her fist into his stomach, knuckles out. He spluttered and coughed, guard broken. She dug in deep and twisted, then heaved him back. Jason stumbled but stayed on his feet, and to her surprise spun around and caught her in the face. Even as she felt her lip swelling up, the boy's knee landed in her ribs and sent her tumbling to the ground. All the air left her body and she let out a strangled cry.

"Had enough?"

"No!" Nea coughed, hoisting herself up shakily.

"Lady Cain's little man still has some fight, eh?" Jason taunted, a nasty smirk crossing his lips.

Nea wiped the blood from her mouth and faced the boy again, taking hold of the anger bubbling inside her. Teeth grinding against each other, she waited. Sure enough, the boy darted forward. Nea spun around him and pushed, using his own weight to send him stumbling to one side. She punched him, but met only his hand. The boy snatched her arm and began to twist.

Christ he's strong.

"Give up?"

"Nope," Nea spat a mouthful of blood into his face. She drove her leg into his ribs, once, twice, three times. Each time she hit harder. He may have her in raw strength, but she was faster, her legs were longer, and she could do this all damn day if she had to.

And you'd bloody love every second of it. You monster.

She ignored the voice, embraced it even. When her fourth kick connected, she felt something give. But Jason was too strong, and by now he was all adrenaline. He moved in, wrapping his arms around her brutally tight and began to squeeze. Her limbs pinned together she could only wriggle as he pushed the air from her lungs. He squeezed harder, his face wild and mad.

Crack!

There was an audible gasp from the boys as Jason's legs gave out and he fell to the ground, stunned from Nea's headbutt. She stayed on her feet, but barely; the whole world around her swimming.

That was stupid. Least it worked.

Jason was on his feet again, there was anger, madness in his eyes. She knew exactly why. Nea had made him fall, in front of his boys.

Jason raised his fists again and Nea braced herself for another round just as a figure in blue burst out of the inn.

"Nea!"

It was Cain. Of bloody course it was; she couldn't let Nea just beat her frustrations out on this idiot and his friends. The boys were already backing off, but even as they did, Jason looked back. The anger and madness had gone from his eyes, replaced with a kind of confusion.

What's that look mean?

"Nea," Cain reached out for her hand but Nea knocked it back.

"Get away from me," she said, turning on her heel and heading down the street.

"For god's sake Nea, what were you thinking?" asked Cain striding to catch up with her.

"What?" Nea scowled, shaking the fog her head.

"Are you out of your mind? We're not even a week from the capital and you start fights with—"

"I didn't start anything," said Nea, scowling. "He was looking for a fight."

"If you were to get tossed in jail you'd be sent right back to the grassers," she sighed. "I can't always be there to make sure you don't get into trouble, you know."

"I got along just fine without you, y'know. So don't lecture me," she said. "You know about what the King did and you…"

"Know about it? Nea I saw it."

"W…what?"

Cain stopped walking. They'd wandered into a back alley full of kegs and crates. She leant against one of them and looked up at the sky, a mad look in her eyes.

"I was a refugee at the time, most of us in the south were, that's where Fortuna first landed you see. I'd lost everything, home, family, but I was determined to survive all the same. I'm sure you can relate to that."

Nea said nothing.

"I fell in with criminals. Pirates, thieves, killers and the like, we would raid battlefields after the fighting was done, to steal whatever we could. We came upon the beach where it happened. When I saw the bodies…"

Nea could see that there were tears in her eyes now.

"I think I went a little mad that day."

"I…I would have too," said Nea awkwardly.

Don't, don't break now, you have to hate her.

She'd wanted Cain to stand her ground, so that Nea could scream and hate all she wanted, but this was so much harder.

"Then how can you stay with him?"

"Besides my vows?"

Nea nodded, "You could just run away."

"So could you," she said. "There's always something that keeps us staying with the one's we love. And make no mistake I do love him more than life itself."

Nea looked away awkwardly. "Why didn't you tell me earlier?"

Cain's eyes flashed away for a moment, as if she'd left her body. "Aren't there moments in your life that you try not to relive?"

Glatman, every damn day.

"I still have nightmares about that day. Sometimes it's the only thing I can see when I close my eyes. It's because of this that I have to stay with him. I can't let anything like that happen ever again. If that forced me to leave my home, so be it. I'll not stand knee deep in the corpses of children, nor will anyone else for as long as I am on this earth. Do you understand me Nea?"

"Y…yes." Nea stared at Cain, as if seeing her for the first time. She didn't see a posh lady playing soldier, nor a lady knight decent in a scrap. She just saw a girl doing what she thought was best in a terrible world. Then came something Nea was most unprepared for. Empathy.

"That's noble of you," she said simply.

"I'm sure you would do the same."

They made their way up the streets in silence while Nea thought about this. Would she have made the choice that Cain did? Would she give up her freedom to save others?

Of course not you selfish little—

Nea shut the voice out, realizing that for once it was wrong. She had done just that, on the ship with Leo. That memory, that solitary good deed, it seemed to keep the voice at bay.

"What started the fight?" asked Cain, as they walked.

"They were saying things."

Cain raised an eyebrow. "What?"

"Those boys I was fighting, they were saying things about…"

"About what?"

Nea looked away. "About you."

But I started it.

"Nea I don't give a damn what anyone else thinks of me, frankly it's none of my business." She looked over Nea's bumps and bruises.

"But they were saying—"

"What? That I'm a tramp? That I'm the King's whore? Words Nea, just words," Cain sighed. "They may have bothered me when I was younger, but I've learned better."

"They bothered me," Nea mumbled.

"What?"

"They sure as hell bothered me." Nea scowled. "You're not like that."

Cain's face softened a little bit. "I seem to recall you having a few choice words for me yourself."

"Maybe that's why I got so mad. They were wrong, like me."

A wicked smile crossed Cain's face. "What's that now, I couldn't quite hear you."

Nea finally let herself smile. "I said I was wrong, M'lady."

Cain put an arm on her shoulder. Nea allowed the contact. "You're a strong boy Nea. That's a good thing sometimes, but remember to sometimes take your armor off."

Nea didn't say anything, what could she say? Nea looked away, embarrassed. The words pierced Nea right through the heart, and it occurred to her then just how much the two of them had been through together. That wall of ice had been in her head, a way of avoiding things Nea didn't feel comfortable talking about. Cain understood this too. Whatever her feelings about Cain now.

"There's just one more thing. About all this briar stuff," Nea muttered.

"Go on then."

"If you and His Majesty are so concerned with keeping it a secret, how did the Briars find out, do you think? One of the grassers?"

Cain shook her head, "Even within the Grassen Trading Company, very few people talk of it. Opinions might sour on them if people knew they'd marched children to their death."

"Who else knew?"

"One other person," Cain said slowly. "I had an idea that he might still be alive, but I couldn't be sure."

"Who?"

"The Last Innocent," said Cain simply.

"What, like in the clue?"

"Yes," Cain nodded. "The only survivor from that day fifteen years ago. I plucked him from the corpses myself. I believe that boy now calls himself Djeng Beljhar. And I believe that boy is the leader of the Black Briars."

26

Familiar Faces

LEO SPENT A couple days nestled in the warmth of Hunter's Hollow. Benya kept him busy, letting him pay off his stay by working in the inn, running errands for her and tiding up. When he had a free moment, Leo helped with odd jobs about the village, cooking, gutting and cleaning the day's fish, and anything else his arm would allow. He found that he liked being busy – there was something liberating in honest work. It kept his thoughts away from Seiyariu and freed him from the doubts that clawed at his mind. Was this what it felt like to live a normal life?

The nights were more difficult. The warmth and comfort of a bed couldn't stave off the doubts. There was still no sign of Seiyariu. What if the vagabond wasn't coming for him? What if he'd had been so furious with Leo he'd just decided to leave him behind, or worse, what if Seiyariu was hurt? Leo tried not to imagine him in the place of that old vagabond skeleton. What would Leo do if Seiyariu never came?

The villagers were a nice lot, a little suspicious of him at first, but after some prodding from Benya they had taken to him as well. After the day's work had ended, Leo spent the evenings sitting in the tavern, enjoying the dim glow of the oil lamps, as the shadows grew long and the voices soft. He listened to the travelers tell their stories and sing their songs. Every night he watched the door, hoping he would see a green cloak, but he never did.

The seemingly cold innkeeper met every new explosion of song with rolled eyes and a secret smile. She'd pressed him for his origins, to which Leo offered some vagaries about the abbey in The Southern Isles. In response to this, Benya revealed that she herself had once been a Nun.

"Why did you leave?" Leo asked, realizing how childish the question sounded the moment it left his lips.

Benya shot him a cold but calculating look, then smiled. "Why did you leave your orphanage?"

Leo looked away and adjusted his glove, as if making sure it was still there. Benya hadn't seen the Nuptial, and though there were no signs of grassers in this town, he didn't want to put her in danger. He thought perhaps he should make something up; he was a vagabond after all. Any story would do, but all clever excuses dried up under her sweeping gaze.

Benya laughed, "Fine have your secrets. If you must know I left because I fell in love. I wanted to get married and have a child of my own."

"You broke your vows."

"Too right," she winked. "Thought it was about time to feel the Lord's graces for myself I suppose. Now the husband is dead and the son's gone off," she laughed. "But I tell you what little secret keeper, I'd do it all over again. Now why don't you go get some rest."

"All right then," said Leo smiling back. He hopped from the stool and started up the stairs. As he reached the landing the door opened and a trio of men entered. They all wore the same black cloak and brooch, and carried weapons.

"Welcome," he heard Benya say, casually. "What brings you gentlemen through our little town?"

An elderly man with a face like a sheepdog sidled up behind the three black clad strangers. Leo had met this man in the days before, his name was Vincenzo and he was a fairly important man about the town. It was strange to see him acting so haggard.

Benya raised an eyebrow at Vincenzo's expression. "What's got you all worked up then?"

"Show a little respect Ben, for once in your life," he said. "We've got guests."

"We've always got guests."

Vincenzo glared at her. "These men are bloody heroes."

"Oh, well pardon me," she said with a mock curtsy. "We don't get many heroes through here, hope you understand."

"We're not heroes sir," said one of the strangers, lowering his hood. He was a slim man with dark hair, his eyes small green dots in a sea of white. "We're merely doing what we think is right."

"Well you're welcome in this town long as you like sirs. Hunter's Hollow will always be a sanctuary for The Black Briars."

Leo's entire body went stiff. *No.* It couldn't be. They couldn't have found him, not here, not now. The Black Briars. The men Quinnel had been working for? Of course, the brooches were the same; Leo had been stupid not to notice.

"The Black Briars," said Benya approvingly. "Forgive me for being fresh sirs, your lot are always welcome here."

"Thank you ma'am."

"Have you business in the Hollow?"

"You might say that."

Leo leapt up the last few steps, praying that they hadn't seen him. He could feel his heart hammering out of his chest. The Black Briars knew what he looked like. These men sitting downstairs, knew what he looked like. He needed to get away, out the window.

Leo threw open the door to his room, grabbed his knife and his cloak as the sound of raised voices came from down the stairs. He heard a crash, then a scream. Before he could do anything, the door to his room was thrown open. The three men strode in, spreading out around the room. An icy chill ran through his entire body as Leo realized that he knew one of them.

"She said we'd find you up here," said Quinnel pulling his hood down.

Leo went for his knife. "You!" He felt the edge of the bed against his back. There was nowhere he could run. The man with the dark hair was between him and the window. "How? I thought—"

"Thought he killed me? Made a try of it." Quinnel's knives were in his hands, twirling dangerously as he stood in the doorframe.

Benya had told them where he was, just like that? Why? Weren't these evil men? Why had Vincenzo said they were heroes?

"You know what I was thinking crawling out of that well, as my nails scraped away to nothing but blood?" Quinnel's daggers stopped moving, and Leo saw that indeed his hands were wrapped in bandages.

"I was furious. With myself you understand. I failed in my mission. I didn't bring you back. Tell me, where is the vagabond?"

"Gone," said Leo, thinking quickly.

"Good," Quinnel growled. "That will give us the chance to talk properly this time, without being interrupted."

"Why?" Leo asked, stalling for time. "What do you want with me?"

Quinnel sighed and leaned on the doorframe. "I'm not the right person to explain that to you kid. I'm a thug. But don't worry, he'll help you understand everything."

"D…Djeng Beljhar?"

"That's right," said Quinnel. "The light in the darkness for this miserable land. The greatest man I've ever known, and you lads?"

"Yessir," said the man with dark hair. "An inspiration."

"A hero," said the other.

"Heroes…," said Leo. "They called you heroes."

"That's because we fight for them. Them and their children. We're an army for the people. You'll find most of them are just as keen to be rid of the grassers as you."

Was it possible Quinnel was telling the truth? The only person he'd learned anything about The Briars from was Seiyariu. Was the vagabond keeping more secrets from him?

Quinnel saw the hesitation in his eyes. "Enough talk. Take him."

The man with the dark hair darted forward. But Leo had been waiting for that exact moment; he slipped under the man's legs and threw himself through the open window. The pain in his arm flared up as he twisted, hitting the slanted roof, the next he knew he was tumbling down fast. He planted his feet and skidded to a halt seconds before plunging to the street below.

Leo sprang across to the neighboring house, a good ten feet below. From there, he let himself fall back, skidding against the wall into the alley between the houses. His legs throbbed violently as he landed, but he shook it off and began to run. He didn't look back, he knew what was there. He broke from the alley and ran skidding into the street, only to be cut off by three more Briars, emerging from the shadows.

"That's far enough boy," Quinnel leapt down from the rooftops, his cloak flying back like a set of wings. He landed softly, unflinching and rose to face Leo.

"Give up," he hissed. There was no mirth in his eyes now, no joy. "You've done enough running."

Leo was trapped, blocked on all sides. "Please." He fought to keep his voice from cracking, even as tears formed in his eyes. "Please, just let me be."

Quinnel sighed. "*He's* trying to help you." There was an affirmative murmur amongst the Briars. "End it Leo and come with me."

Leo stared into Quinnel's cold eyes. This man, he truly believed what he was saying. His conviction, it was unflinching, like a man of the church. What wouldn't Quinnel do to bring Leo to his master?

A distant sound of galloping met Leo's ears, he lowered his knife as Quinnel drew closer.

"I knew that you'd see reason, you—"

Suddenly the sound began to grow louder. The Briars turned, shouting, even Quinnel glanced down the street. Leo saw his moment and tore off; before the Briars knew he was gone he had slipped between their legs and was running as fast as he could up the street. He heard a shout, a whinny, and the galloping grew even louder. He felt his mouth open in a terrified cry as he was hoisted off the ground and planted in the saddle of a charging horse. He struggled and kicked, fighting tooth and nail to break free, until he realized who was sitting behind him.

"Seiyariu!"

The vagabond was haggard almost beyond recognition. His filthy hair full of twigs and leaves, his face covered in unkempt fuzz and his whole body a mess of cuts and bruises, but his eyes still shone. He held Leo tight, beaming as they rode. The distant cries of the Briars were nothing now, as an unimaginable relief spread through Leo. He embraced the vagabond as best he could, sobbing uncontrollably into his bloody tunic. Leo was home again.

27

Blood and Water

THE DARK SURFACE of the lake stood pristine and clear, a prefect mirror, while the shallows lapping against the shore reflected a distorted and shifting image of the night sky. It sparkled with flickering stars and the elongated moon danced in the shifting waters.

They had barely made it a mile from Hunter's Hollow before the Briars cut them off. As their horse cantered across the shore, three men on horseback burst from the trees beyond, blocking their escape.

Seiyariu jerked the reigns, trying to turn around, but the Briars from the town had followed them on horses of their own. They swept around, forming a wall of men and animals. They were trapped, Briars on three sides and the lake at their backs. Seiyariu's horse reared and skittered, Leo doing his best to hang on as the Briars closed ranks, but he tumbled off the horse and landed painfully in the sand, his bandaged arm bursting with fresh pain.

The Briars were dismounting now, drawing their swords, their beaded tunics and brooches lit by the moon's reflection.

Leo fumbled for his knife as Seiyariu leapt from the saddle, planting himself between Leo and the Briars.

"Get behind me," he hissed, drawing his sword.

Leo did as he was told, moving back until the water lapped around his ankles.

The Briars advanced slowly, carefully. Whatever orders they had about keeping Leo alive, he was sure those didn't extend to the vagabond.

"Hold."

A voice rang out. Through the ranks of the Briars, Quinnel appeared, his white hair glowing in the light of the moon.

169

He gestured at his men to stand back, and they formed a semicircle around the beach, leaving Quinnel and Seiyariu alone. The icy man began to twirl his knives again, facing down Seiyariu.

"I'll offer one last time Leo," Quinnel called past Seiyariu. "Come with us, and we'll let your vagabond live."

Leo's knife was trembling in his hand. The pain in his bad arm even more present than before. They were surrounded and outnumbered. The Briars had them, there was no doubt about that. What else could he do?

Seiyariu didn't allow him to answer. The vagabond strode forward, clasping his sword in both hands. Leo could see the hunger in Quinnel's eyes, as they stared each other down.

"Our last encounter did not end as it should've. Please allow me to remedy that," said Seiyariu, calm as ever.

The men entered their joust. Seiyariu and Quinnel blurred as they grew nearer, each determined to strike first. Quinnel flicked his daggers and leapt at the vagabond. Seiyariu spun and knocked him out of the air. Blood flecked the speeding sword, but Quinnel's cut wasn't deep. He flipped his daggers and swiped twice at Seiyariu, ripping through his tunic and drawing blood as well. Then Quinnel flipped his blades again and caught Seiyariu's counter attack mid-stroke. He kicked him in the chest and Seiyariu fell backwards.

Seiyariu hit the sand and rolled backwards, spraying water in all directions; as it did, an idea suddenly occurred to Leo.

He pulled the vial of salt from his pocket, uncorked it with his teeth and hurled the whole thing behind him into the water. The lake hissed and bubbled green where the vial had landed, then lay still. The Briars paid him no mind, absorbed as they were by the fight.

Seiyariu was back on his feet driving Quinnel back towards his men. Quinnel made as though to block an attack, but instead ducked under Seiyariu's guard. Blood exploded onto the sand and Seiyariu staggered back, clutching at the red cross on his chest. He swayed, trying to keep his footing, but stumbled again, falling to his knees in the shallow water, staining it with his blood.

"Seiyariu!" Leo was by his side in an instant.

"Go," he growled. "Swim if you have to."

"I won't leave you."

"You're going to have to." His eyes rolled over and he nearly collapsed. Leo did his best to try and support him, but Seiyariu was a fully-grown man and Leo only had one good shoulder. The two of them drew back, deeper into the water, Leo supporting the barely injured Seiyariu.

"That's the end Leo," said Quinnel, gesturing to his men. They strode forward into the lake, weapons drawn, until they and Leo were up to their knees.

"You've nowhere to go," said Quinnel simply, standing on the shore with his arms crossed. "This is your last chance."

"You should've stayed in the well!" Leo shouted.

The Briars erupted in laughter. But even as they did, their voices were being drowned out by a bubbling, frothing noise. The water beneath them was churning and rising, as if something massive was about to surface. It burst from the water, just behind where Leo stood, so quickly; he only saw it as a shadow etched briefly against the moon moments before it splashed down beneath the water and vanished again.

The six men were on him now. One tried to seize him as the others looked around wildly for whatever had arrived. The first man vanished beneath the frothing lake, pulled under without so much as a scream. The remaining five closed ranks in alarm, Quinnel racing into the water, but he was too late.

Very slowly, a dark shape emerged from the water, standing between Leo and the Briars. The thing's eyes burned green, webbed hands grasping hungrily. Two Briars broke ranks and ran past Quinnel, making for the shore, but the water was too heavy. Kokaleth vanished beneath the surface again, and soon they did as well. He rose again on the other side of the remaining three Briars.

"Frightened little thorns, poking at things you shouldn't." The Mariner's gurgling tones echoed against the lake. He twisted around with a noise like the blast of a trumpet, and a gout of water erupted in the center of the trio, sending them flying in all directions. Kokaleth moved faster than thinking, his long, webbed fingers grasped one terrified man's face, and with a single twist, the Mariner broke his neck. Another man was on his feet and charging at Kokaleth, but the Mariner didn't even turn around, in a single motion he hurled the corpse at his attacker, burying him under the dead weight. Kokaleth sprang after them, launching himself from the water again. He came down on top of them hard, driving his webbed feet into the man's chest.

Then there was just one.

"What are you waiting for? Get him out of here!" roared Kokaleth. Cutting Quinnel off just as he just as he was making a grab for Leo's bad arm. The two of them crashed into the water, a flurry of steel and fists.

Leo was jolted from his trance. He turned his back on the fight and helped Seiyariu stumble out of the lake. The horses had scattered at the arrival of Kokaleth. If the vagabond hadn't been able to stand, Leo didn't know what he would've done. Together they managed to stagger into the woods, moving along as best they could.

Leo supported Seiyariu as far as he could, following a small stream. Finally, when his body refused to move further, he lay the vagabond down. All around him the woods were alive with the sounds of night. The silhouettes of the trees and stones cast long eerie shadows across the piles of fallen leaves.

Seiyariu was in a bad way, his face was pale and his breathing was ragged, but the cuts weren't as deep as Leo had feared. A twig broke behind him and Leo whirled around. One of the Black Briars stood there, sword in hand, eyes set. He remembered this man, the man with the dark hair and staring eyes. He hadn't been among the attackers at the lake. How could Leo have forgotten there were seven?

Leo held out his knife, standing between the Briar and Seiyariu just as the vagabond had done for him. The Briar paid no heed to his outstretched blade. He strode up and struck Leo with pommel of the sword on his bad arm. Leo screamed, his arm flaring in unimaginable pain just as it had with the takabran. His vision blurred as he collapsed to the ground, writhing in pain.

Through the haze, he saw the Briar standing over Seiyariu. The pain in his arm threatening to overwhelm him, Leo fought with all of his might against it. Seiyariu was going to die, if Leo did not stand, this instant, and do something. Leo clawed his way to his feet, then without hesitating he leapt up onto the man's back wrapping his good arm as tight as he could around his throat, just as Nea had done on the ship. Shocked, the briar stumbled back, Leo pulled even tighter, but the briar was a quick thinker. He slammed into a tree forcing Leo to break his grasp.

As Leo fell to the ground, the man seized him by his bad arm and wrenched him back to his feet. Pain overwhelmed his senses like a wild fire in his brain.

Seiyariu, Seiyariu, get to Seiyariu.

Something was bubbling up from inside Leo, something raw and powerful. A strength he didn't know he had. Leo was able to concentrate through the pain; he still had one hand free. He reacted on instinct, his blade flying as an extension of himself, claws of a cornered animal making one last attempt at escape. Then there was silence.

The man stared at Leo, blood running from his throat, eyes wide with shock. He let out one terrible, rattling breath and then stumbled and fell back against the tree. Leo looked on in horror, not believing what he'd done. It had all happened so quickly.

The dying man took the opal from around his neck. With what looked like tremendous effort, he raised the stone to his eyes. Leo saw a light reflected there, and the man's eyes rolled over blindly. He let out one last rattling breath, then nothing.

Leo stepped back, horrified. Without warning he was on his hands and knees heaving the contents of his stomach up onto the leaves. He wretched until there was nothing left.

He had killed a man. He, Leonardo Fortunato, had cut a man's throat and watched him bleed out like an animal. The gasp of the dying man, of the life he'd ended, danced before his view no matter how hard he tried to shut it out. It hadn't been skill, or even luck. The man simply hadn't believed Leo to be a killer. Well, he was wrong. Dreadful guilt sat like a weight on his chest.

The man still sat there, collapsed against the tree, covered in blood. Leo looked at his face, forcing himself to memorize it. Then something glinted in the briar's hand and Leo realized that he still held the opal.

He crouched down and gingerly removed it. Why had the man been so transfixed on this, even as he died? Leo saw something like fire, or light, flickering within the depths of the gem. He squinted and held the gem closer and found himself somewhere else entirely.

He was in the arms of a woman, his wife. They were dancing. Leo wasn't sure how he knew but he was certain this was his wife. He wasn't shy about the embrace, she was his and he was hers. She was so warm, so perfect, that he thought he would stay with her like this forever. All the darkness, all the cruelty of the world became fantasy when she held him like this. Like they were the only two on earth. He would—

"Leo!"

Leo was jarred from the embrace, and vaguely aware of slimy hands, prying the gem from his fingers. Gem? What gem? He was dancing with his wife.

"It's not real!" Kokaleth's voice came like thunder, bursting through his reverie as the gem was wrenched away. Reality came rushing back to meet him and he fell back, gasping. He was back on the forest floor. With a jolt he realized there were tears in his eyes. He stared at the corpse, the man he'd killed, his sadness so heavy it might just drag him down into the earth and bury him. Just outside his reach, the opal lay, glowing faintly in the moonlight.

28

Boiling Point

Nea couldn't sleep. Her mind was full of too many questions she didn't want to answer. A walk in the moonlight was as good a way as any to clear her head. She had drifted down the empty streets for a little while but eventually found herself in the cemetery. Always the quietest place in any town. It had been built beside a pond. The moonlight shone off the water and stone graves making Nea feel at peace.

Nea caught a glimpse of her reflection in the pond's surface and winced. She was amazed at how much longer her hair was, she'd forgotten to keep it short.

Too much else to think about.

Nea dipped her knife into the water, and started hacking away her bangs. She could've used scissors; Cain undoubtedly had some among her tools but Nea liked the jagged way her hair looked after the knife was through, like a boy who couldn't be arsed to do it properly.

When she was finished, Nea tugged at the wet locks, admiring her handy-work. Even she was astonished at how restless she felt. She wanted to run, burn away this energy and get some rest. Or…

She looked around, there wasn't a soul in sight. The town had long since gone to sleep. Carefully, Nea got to her feet.

Don't you dare.

The "education" aspects of life at Glatman had been little more than window dressing. Designed to teach them how to act and a few tricks to entertain. She hated every second of it. Almost. Ever since she was a little girl, Nea had loved to dance. Even before she'd been sent to that damn school. Their dance lessons at Glatman had been largely ceremonial, but the love of it hadn't left her. Nea had enjoyed the rhythm, it was liberating, there was freedom in it. And Nea had precious little of that at Glatman.

Nea hadn't danced in some time. It embarrassed her terribly, especially now. The needling voice in the back of her head mocking her for enjoying something so feminine. It was shameful, just another thing about her that was weak. Yet when she did dance, she didn't feel weak at all. She felt alive, happy and free, as though she'd never been sent to Glatman at all. As though she were still that happy little girl.

Movement – out of the corner of her eye – Nea stopped dancing, spinning around even as two large shapes collided with her. She was seized her by the arms, suddenly and violently jerking her down. She swept a kick into the knees of one of her assailants, hitting him hard. He lost his grip and she wrenched herself free and reached for her bow, but she was seized around the waist and dragged back. Nea whirled on the attacker. Then stopped, fists hanging limply in midair. She recognized the ginger-hair. It was Rupert, one of the boys from the pub.

That momentary hesitation was enough, the other boy, one of the brothers, was behind her again. He seized both of her arms behind her back and held them there. Rupert and the second brother held her shoulders. She flailed about madly in desperation, but it was no use. A howl escaped from her lips, again she was at the mercy of those more powerful.

No! Do something!

"Well, what do we have here?" asked Jason, stepping out from behind a tree. He looked her up and down, contempt on his face. "Lady Cain's little man, dancing in the moonlight?"

Weak! So weak!

"I'll kill you!" Nea snarled at him.

"I'm trembling," Jason laughed. "There was something funny about you, couldn't put me damn finger on it until we were fighting; bulges in the wrong spots." He lifted her shirt revealing her binding.

They can see you!

The rage from when she'd slammed that girl's face back in Limani, flared back up. Nea struggled fiercely but they locked her arms tight, laughing.

All she could do was stand there in her binding, not looking remotely like a boy now. It was coming back in waves. Glatman Finishing

School, the hours, days, weeks, years she'd spent, a walking corpse. Her mind was blank, filled with memory after terrible memory dragging her away from reality. It was like trying to swim up a waterfall. Jason was moving closer now.

"Don't have much to begin with," he laughed. "Why tie them up?"

"Little slut wanted to run around playing soldier," said one of the brothers.

A terribly familiar look came across Jason's leering face. "Did she? Well I think she needs to be taught a lesson, don't you?"

There was a murmur from the other boys.

Jason's eyes narrowed and he seized Nea by the chin. "What are you going to do now little man?"

Nea felt his hands on her body and a wave of white-hot madness engulfed her. She snapped at his wandering fingers. She tasted blood, but Jason struck her across the face with his free hand before she could bite any deeper.

"Hold her down," he ordered and Nea felt herself being pinned on her stomach. The rage boiled impotently, she thrashed and screamed but there were too many people holding her down.

No! No, you can't let them!

She wanted to die, to lose consciousness, to be anywhere but here. All around her was the sound of jeering laughter. She was so weak. Despite everything, these idiots had overpowered her.

Pathetic.

Then one of the boys let out a cry of alarm and the arms pinning her to the ground loosened. Nea exploded out of their grasp, scrambling away. The boys were in a panic, there was someone else in the clearing now. Jason was already on the ground, unconscious, his friends had swiftly broken ranks as the newcomer scattered them with her fists. And just like that it was over.

Cain stared at Nea and Nea stared back.

No, please not her too.

But there was no covering up now. Cain could see her for what she truly was, a weak, pathetic, scared little girl who couldn't even defend herself.

Nea staggered to her feet searching for the wave of anger. The feral rage that she'd had before, where had it gone? She needed it back. She needed that strength. For a long time they just stared at each other.

Run.

She'd been trussed up and helpless, just as she'd been at Glatman. Her disguise had done nothing, not a damn thing except given her the illusion that she was stronger. What an idiot she'd been, all of that talk, all of that swagger and she'd been brought back to where it all started. If it hadn't been for Cain...

Now Cain knew as well. Nea couldn't bear the knight looking at her like that. That terrible, tender, pity. It was worse than any pain on this earth.

Run.

"I knew," said Cain, her voice muffled.

"You...you what?"

"I knew from the minute I saw you. It's okay Nea, a lot of girls on the run—"

"You knew?" Nea said almost hysterically. "You knew the whole time and you just let me pretend?"

"Nea—"

"Shut up!" she screamed, driving her fists into the dirt. "You don't understand a damn thing. Nobody can see me like this! I trusted you! I trusted you and you're just like everyone else."

Cain refused to break the stare, her eyes shining. "I didn't realize... I thought you were just keeping yourself safe. I didn't realize it was so important."

Nea turned away, and her eyes fell on the crumpled form of Jason, knocked to the ground by one of Cain's punches.

Look at him, lying there all helpless.

The rage returned, filling her with renewed vigor and she pressed her foot to his throat. She could crush his neck under her boot just like she'd smashed that stupid girl's face back in Limani. And that had just been for seeing her binding – he had done far more than that.

They found you out. They touched you.

She was aware of hands again, this time pulling her away from the unconscious boy. She struggled and screamed, but Cain's grip was as strong as it had been their first night together and Nea was just as helpless.

"Let me go!"

"Nea…"

She struck Cain across the face, sending her staggering back.

Cain righted herself, eyes shining. Then Nea struck her again and again, knocking her to the ground. She wanted to beat that sympathetic look off of her damn face. But no matter how hard Nea hit her, the flood of old memories refused to stop.

She's letting you. She's letting you hit her because you're weak and she knows it.

Cain stared back her, her face bloodied but unharmed.

Run.

Nea ran.

"What are you doing?" Cain called behind her. "The grassers are still after you!"

But Nea didn't listen, she couldn't listen. She just ran, she wanted to get away, wanted to cover herself, but she could never hide it from the person it hurt the most.

You're not a boy or a girl. Just a monster.

She wanted to cry out again. But she had no more rage left in her; the fire had burned itself out. She was as docile as a drunk; her movements slow and awkward as she ran.

Why does it hurt so much?

She had run away before, it was part of who she was. The only reason she'd been traveling with Cain was because it had been a better alternative than the damn grassers.

You could've left any time you wanted to.

Cain. She couldn't lie to herself. It had always been Cain.

For hours she ran through the woods, blind and mad with grief. Unaware of how far she'd gone or what direction she was headed, all she knew was that she needed to get away. Nea stumbled into a clearing, halting to catch her breath, when a man on horseback came upon her like a shadow. She knew who it was instantly. He wore the same dark cloak held together by that unmistakable brooch, one of The Black Briars.

"You know where this road leads Nea," he said, his hood up so she couldn't see his face.

She narrowed her eyes. "What do you mean?"

"The slaving companies will find you. You'll be right back where you started, unless you come with us."

"Go to hell!" said Nea. "I don't want anything to do with you. I'm finished with all this."

"Are you?" The briar was unmoved by her protest.

Nea nodded. "I've had enough."

"Did we not show you enough injustice, enough of the misery? Would you have us send you the long route, past the mass graves of the Feryls, or show you the husks of those lost in the catacomb city? You see the horrors brought about by Chiron and his cowardice, and you turn away? Are you truly that selfish?"

Nea stared at him for a long time, "I don't know anymore. I don't blame you lot for being angry, hell I'll even wish you good luck. But you'll have to do this without me."

"Where will you go?"

"West," said Nea commanding herself to remember that which had been her goal all along.

"And you don't think that this misery will follow you?"

Nea stopped her horse. "What?"

"You can't outrun the darkness Nea. It's burned into your soul like that brand upon your finger, casting scars upon the mind. It's within us all. I see it in you clear as day; Quinnel, the father and Brumani saw it as well, else they wouldn't have sent you on."

Nea looked off, somewhere into the darkness. Was he right? Would this pain follow her everywhere? And because of Cain she no longer had the rage to keep it at bay.

"You really want me to come with you?"

"Now that Captain Cain is no longer a factor, we're willing to welcome you with open arms."

"The hell do you mean no longer a factor?"

"She knows our secrets, knows where our trail leads. We hadn't wanted to kill her yet, but you've left us no choice."

A chill ran down Nea's spine. "W… what?"

"Our agents are dealing with her as we speak."

Nea's drew her bow. "Get the hell out of my way."

"Nea you know that I can't—"

He hadn't expected Nea to shoot first, or perhaps to shoot him at all. She did, and fast, faster than she'd ever shot in her life. He was stunned for a moment, staring down at the arrow protruding from his stomach. Then the shaft broke off and the burrower began to drill its way into his gut. He fell from his horse in a crumpled pile.

Nea paid him no mind. Ignoring his cries, ignoring the voice in her head that screamed at her to stop, she mounted the Briar's horse. Her mind was made up. Every logical impulse ignored, Nea was not going to leave her friend to die. She would not run, not this time.

29
Boil Dry

THE CEMETERY WAS deserted. So she guided her horse back down the road towards the inn. Nea nearly crashed into the stable but she refused to slow down. She righted the animal, casting an eye around the stable. Cain's horse was nowhere to be seen but there were tracks, fresh ones. They were deep too, the horse had made a mad dash from the stables.

God don't let me be too late.

Nea followed the tracks down the road and east, the town giving way to farmlands ripe with the last harvest before winter. It was here that Nea saw the other tracks; she couldn't tell how many, but Cain's horse had not been alone.

A faint light caught her eye, six pinpricks dancing about in the darkness. As she drew closer she saw to her horror that they were torches.

Six riders were circling a massive field of rye, their torchlight casting the crop in an orange glow. She couldn't quite make them out from where she was, but Nea had little doubt in her mind who they were. Now where in the hell was Cain?

The knight's tracks transformed into a path of beaten down rye, leading into the field. But Nea couldn't see any sign of a horse. The light was growing, leaping up into the sky with a horrible crackling sound.

They're burning the field.

Her horse reared up in panic and Nea leapt from the saddle, crashing down into the rye, she hit the ground sprinting as fast as she could along the trail. The fire was closing in now, impossibly fast. The rye was being swept up in droves and devoured by the hungry blaze. Then she

182

caught sight of a figure at the end of the trail, slumped over and not moving.

No!

Cain's limp form was on the ground, not ten feet away, pinned under her horse's arrow riddled corpse.

"Cain!"

Please don't be dead, God please.

She'd hit her head, badly, her soft face covered in a scarlet mask of blood. "Wake up damn it," Nea shook her by the shoulders, but Cain didn't move. Was she breathing? For a few horrible moments, the only sound to be heard was the roar of the fire, drawing ever closer, then—

"N...Nea?"

"Cain!" For the briefest moment, Nea forgot everything and threw her arms around Cain's neck.

"You came back," she whispered.

"Can you move?"

Cain nodded and together they wrenched her legs free. Nea thanked every god she could think of that the lady knight's legs weren't in pieces. She helped Cain stand. Her movements were little more than unfocused twitches and she was in constant danger of falling over.

She's in a bad way.

"Lean on me," Nea told the knight. Cain nodded confusedly, and bent to let Nea help her. Together they moved through the rye step by step. "Come on," Nea said, half yelling, half crying.

You can't be weak now, you can't! You have to help her!

"Just another day for us," Cain murmured. Her head was still bleeding badly. "I failed you Nea,"

"Shut up."

The fire was getting out of control now, howling like a tornado. Nea could feel the white-hot blaze across her face. They needed to move faster but Cain was barely walking, and Nea's legs were about to give out.

Not yet!

"Tell me about your machines."

"What?"

"Go on! Pulleys, gyros, all that rubbish." Nea yelled, forcing herself onward. The path Cain had cut through the rye was their way out, through the flames licking at her legs and arms. The little voice in her head was screaming inside her head, driving her forward.

"I thought I'd apply the properties of the vise to a sword someday," said Cain distantly. "Make a pronged blade that can suddenly close, breaking other swords."

"Not a bad idea," said Nea heaving Cain forward again. "Give it to your guards?"

"Maybe, or it'll just gather dust in my workshop."

"You've got a workshop?"

"Oh it's wonderful," Cain muttered. "I'll have to show you."

Not far. You're not far now.

The door through the fire was all she could see. They would make it. They had to. She hadn't gotten this far just to let the pair of them burn to death. Then they were through, crashing down into the mud as the field was swept away in an inferno. Nea rolled about madly in the wet earth for a few moments, putting out any trace of the blaze clinging to her clothes, then did the same for Cain. The lady knight's head lolled to one side, eyes half-closed.

Oh no you don't!

"Come on now," she growled, slapping Cain's face. "Stay with me."

Nea took her by the arms and let the injured woman pull herself into a standing position. Cain tried her damndest to fight through the injury. When she was vertical again, Nea pushed her on. They couldn't stay here; the Briars could be anywhere, waiting for them.

Her heart leapt as she saw that the next field was full of corn, tall enough to conceal a full-grown man. That was a start. They slipped inside of it and finally Nea was able to let Cain rest. She helped Cain lie back, wiping the blood from her forehead.

Thank you. Thank you God.

"My little savior," Cain said, her fingers running across Nea's cheek.

Nea smiled, "Don't get used to it, I—"

A shadow flickered across their hiding place. Then, against the flames, there appeared the dark forms of horses. She heard the Briars coming, but she couldn't see them for the corn and the smoke. But she was certain the sound of galloping hooves was growing closer and closer. They would ride right through where she and Cain were hiding.

You have to stop them.

Nea stood up.

"Nea wait," Cain tried to grab at the leg of her pants, eyes wide now, illuminated with horror.

For one fleeting moment, their eyes met. Nea knew what she had to do. Hoping that she could say as much as she needed to with that look, Nea burst out of the corn, her arrows flying, startling the Briars and their horses. Nea scampered as fast as her legs would carry her, back towards the burning field.

Come on you bastards.

She let an arrow fly back towards the horsemen, not stopping to see if it had made contact. She could feel them now, running her down like a fox.

The wall of flames that awaited her was only emboldened by the changing winds. But Nea had no intention of running any farther. She wasn't going to die swept up in a fire; if she was going to die she would die on her terms. So she spun on her heel letting another arrow at the oncoming riders. The Briars' weapons were drawn, and they were closing in. Nea went for her quiver but a blinding pain erupted in the back of her head and she collapsed face first in the mud. Her last thoughts before fading into unconsciousness were of disappointment. How she would've liked to see that workshop.

30
The Vagabond Way

NOT FOR THE first time, Leo found himself walking through the desert. Nico was holding his hand, and Leo gripped it tighter as they went, for he didn't want to be alone again. He felt Nico's grip tightening and turned to see not his brother, but that horrible skeleton. It looked back at him, its head cocked to one side as if curious.

"Ni... Nico?"

The skeleton didn't answer, it just opened its mouth and let out a single rattling breath that echoed across the wasteland. The same sound that the man in black had made when Leo cut his throat.

Leo shot upright, covered in sweat. With a stab of horror he realized that the old dream had found him again.

Must you torment me too?

"Ah, back in the realm of the living I see."

"Kokaleth!" The Mariner was stretched out in the stream, letting the water flow around him. "Where's—"

"Here."

Leo breathed a sigh of relief. Seiyariu sat propped up against a tree, bandaged and bloody but with color in his face. He had a bushel of apples clutched in his cloak and was devouring them hungrily.

"Who is Nico?" asked Kokaleth suddenly.

"What?" Leo jumped at the mention of the name.

"You were mumbling the name in your sleep," Seiyariu said.

"I was?" Leo decided playing dumb would get him out of this situation the fastest. Then the memories from the previous night returned like a blow to the head. "Seiyariu I..."

"Yes, we saw him. I'm sorry for forcing you into that situation," Seiyariu mumbled. "I was careless and stupid. But you handled yourself well."

"I killed that man."

Seiyariu sighed. "Yes you did. As vagabonds sometimes must."

"Does that mean that I'll have to do it again?" Leo stared at the ground, commanding himself not to cry.

"Perhaps, perhaps not. It's a dirty aspect of life."

"I can't, Seiyariu. Everything hurts, I just—"

"Stop," Seiyariu ordered. "That's enough, you're a mess, and I want you to eat something. He handed Leo an apple. Leo gingerly took a bite, surprised he could keep it down. "Taking a life is not something to be celebrated Leo, but we are vagabonds, we survive, there is no shame in that."

"I was trying to get to you."

"And I'm very grateful."

"I didn't mean to kill him! I just… just reacted, it was so fast."

"It happened. We cannot undo that, merely carry it with us. Carry them with us if we must. Do not crucify yourself between regret of the past and fear of the future, live in the moment. That is what it means to be a vagabond."

Leo thought about this for a few moments. He had killed a man, ended a life. But it had been to save, not only his life, but Seiyariu's as well. And as Leo looked at Seiyariu he realized he would do it again.

"Something else happened," said Leo. "He had a stone."

"An Opal," said Kokaleth. "Housing an illusion."

"Illusion?"

Kokaleth nodded, "A projection of light that manipulates what the brain perceives."

"Light in the stone?" said Leo, confused.

Seiyariu nodded. "Fortuan Opals catch light and hold it inside."

"And that light altered what you believed you were seeing," said Kokaleth. "It's quite a rare practice, even in these parts."

"Obviously not as rare as all that if the Briars are carrying them," said Seiyariu.

"And the light makes you see things?" said Leo. "Where does it come from?"

"I can't say," said Seiyariu. "I've never encountered anything like this before.

"The Briars must have a powerful illusionist or delver, working among them," said Kokaleth, eyes narrowing. "Or both. Seiyariu do you thin—"

"If it was just light, how come it felt so real?" Leo interrupted.

Kokaleth scowled. "As far as your brain is concerned it *was* real. You are very lucky I arrived when I did or you might have wasted away in a fantasy created for someone else. Please for the love of all that is sacred, don't poke your nose into everything new you encounter or you're going to get it bitten off."

Leo blushed. "I'm sorry."

"I'm curious though, what kind of image motivates a man such as that?" Muttered Kokaleth.

"It was his wife, I think," said Leo thinking back. Having experienced memory of this woman, Leo felt a strange camaraderie with his victim and the guilt grew a little heavier.

"Do you think all the Briars brooches carry unique illusions Kokaleth?" Seiyariu was saying.

"If that's the case our enemy is far more powerful than we originally thought."

*

The sun was bright, so Leo and Seiyariu kept under the trees, but Kokaleth didn't mind, he swam beside them in the river, checking ahead, scouting behind, laughing and boasting, as he always did. The Mariner had said nothing further of the night before, perhaps doing his best to distract Leo. With some success, by midday he was talking again and by the afternoon he was firing a barrage of questions at the unsuspecting mariner. Questions he'd been dying to know the answers to since they'd met, but hadn't been able to ask.

"How do you find us, with that salt I mean?" Had been his first question.

Kokaleth rolled over onto his back and allowed the current to carry him. "I don't find you, I find the salt. It's a part of me, and the sea lets me know where it is."

"The sea talks to you then?" asked Leo.

"The sea talks to all, I merely know how to listen."

"Can you talk back?"

"Sometimes."

"Oh," Leo said lamely. Kokaleth's vagaries put even Seiyariu to shame. "Are you doing that right now?" He glanced at the water on which Kokaleth floated, but there wasn't anything unusual about it.

"Don't let him play games with you Leo," Seiyariu said, chuckling. "What you saw last night was the height of this one's power."

"Don't lie to the boy Seiyariu," Kokaleth spat.

"Take your nonsense elsewhere you old frog."

Finally, Leo ventured one of the most pressing questions on his mind. Throwing caution to the winds, he asked, "What exactly is Knail, Kokaleth? Seiyariu won't give me a straight answer."

Kokaleth shot him a funny look, "Yes, he can be quite cryptic sometimes can't he. Knail is a weapon under the protection of the vagabonds."

"I figured that much," said Leo pouting. "Can't you be a little more specific?"

"Before the Clash of Comets, there were many artifacts scattered across this land," said Seiyariu. "Weapons with powers that most humans couldn't understand. After the Clash, most of these artifacts vanished. With one exception."

"Knail," Leo offered.

"Indeed."

"That reminds me. I assume you two are still planning to go to Adis and recover it? Despite the Briars seeming very keen on getting their hands on you Leo."

"I wish I knew why."

"We'll deal with that when the time comes," Seiyariu said, resting a hand on Leo's shoulder. "For now, Knail must be the priority."

"Alright," said Kokaleth. "But you know I won't be able to help you once you're in Adis."

Soon the river veered off towards the edge of a cliff, where it fed into a great waterfall.

Kokaleth beamed at them, "This is where we part my friends. Seiyariu, I'll do some poking around and see if there are any stories of an illusionist in Fortuna, summon me once you've got your thieving hands on Knail and we'll get to putting things right." Kokaleth waved to the pair of them, before allowing the river to carry him over the waterfall and out of sight.

"I'd no idea we were up so high," said Leo.

"We aren't," Seiyariu replied. "That river runs into a valley, in which is housed the forest that the men of these parts call Styx. That's where we will find the entrance to Adis."

"Why aren't we going that way then?"

"I'd hoped to get us a guide," said Seiyariu. "I've never been into Adis myself. It's said to run for miles and miles under the earth, an endless maze of tombs."

"Who would build something like that?"

"Nobody is quite sure where it came from," Seiyariu replied. "Some people posit that it was here before mankind even made its home in the Archipelago. But I'm afraid my knowledge of it is scant at best."

"You?" Leo smirked.

Seiyariu smiled back and put an arm around Leo's shoulder as they walked. "I am happy to have you back with me."

"I'm happy to be back," said Leo savoring the contact. It hadn't quite sunk in yet; they'd reunited in such a panic. Leo wasn't sure what to say.

"Seiyariu?"

"Yes?"

"What you said before, about the past and the future. Is that why you don't like to talk about yourself, your past I mean?"

Seiyariu said nothing, and for a moment Leo was afraid he'd made him angry again, then simply, "Yes."

And the words he'd been dying to say to Seiyariu for what felt like ages finally came to his lips.

"I'm sorry, about how I was in the forest."

"As am I," said Seiyariu. "I was a fool to think the forest wouldn't play tricks on us and I'm afraid you paid the price for my mistake."

This wasn't what Leo meant to apologize for, but he was unsure of what else to say. Did Seiyariu even remember their argument? The wanderer was as unreadable as ever.

"Tell me Leo, what happened after we were separated?"

Leo frowned but launched into a brief summary of his adventures of the past week. Seiyariu did not interrupt, he waited patiently for Leo to reach his rescue on the streets, before saying, "I hadn't intended for our first trial apart to go like that. Still I'm proud of you. You fought well, defeating a takabran is no small feat."

"I didn't defeat it," he mumbled.

"And I didn't think you were as sly as to play on a poor innkeeper's sympathy." Seiyariu grinned at him and Leo managed a smile back. "This woman in the meadow," Seiyariu said, stretching. "It's good that she taught you of the Legacy Patches. I was going to, but it looks like she explained it far better than I could. Tell me, what was the lady's name?"

"Zhenamansa."

Seiyariu stiffened.

"What's wrong?"

"We've met." His voice was so cold, and his body language had shifted so quickly that Leo wanted to ask more, but he decided against it. He let himself be content in the fact that they were on the road together once again.

31
Strung Up

When Nea was a little girl her Da had often woken her up to go fishing before sunrise. She remembered him carrying her to their boat, remembered how she'd fall back asleep as they rowed out, lulled by the calm slapping of the water. This same rhythm brought her slowly back to reality, something to concentrate on amid the damnable pounding of her head.

Nea was on her back, lying in the front of a long rowboat. It was pitch dark and all around her was the open sea. The water was calm, but a thick fog obscured her view. Nea groaned as a fresh wave of pain swept over her, her head felt like it had been broken open, she tried to reach back to where she'd been hit only to discover her hands were tied behind her back.

She writhed about and struggled furiously but it was no use, the knots were tied expertly. She let out a scream of frustration and agony, but she'd been gagged. Bound and broken once again, trussed up and helpless.

Weak!

Three men sat at the oars of the long rowboat, hoods up and brooches shimmering in the foggy dark. She began to remember.

The fire, the riders, Cain.

Nea looked around for land but saw none, however there were many more of the boats on all sides of them, long black daggers cutting through the sea. Then from the fog there emerged a gargantuan shape. At first Nea thought it was a monster, some hell bound creature risen from the darkest depths of the ocean, nothing on the sea could be that large.

Mother of God!

Was it an island? Were they staring at the face of a cliff? No. As they drew closer, Nea saw that it was made of wood. It was a ship, but not like any ship Nea had ever seen or read about. The vessel was so long that she could not see the end, and so tall that she couldn't see the deck in this fog, or the masts and sail. Cabins protruded from all sides. They had windows that were glassed and every single one emitted the same soft orange glow.

This was the Briars' base of operation? How had nobody ever found it? Nobody would, nobody *could*, miss something so impossible. Nea couldn't even imagine how the thing was floating, let alone being crewed and piloted. She let herself be awestruck, there wasn't much else she could do in the shadow of this beast.

As they came abreast of the ship. Nea sat up, trying to get a better view. Ropes descended from out of the fog and the Briars fixed them to the ends of the boat, pulling three times. Slowly the boat began to rise from the water up towards the ship's unseen deck. In every window, every cabin, she saw people moving about inside.

Do they all live here? What about their families?

As they rose, a blindfold was forced over her eyes and a pair of hands hoisted her to her feet. She had stopped her thrashing; at this height, it'd just get her killed. Even if it didn't, she'd never make it to shore.

How the hell are you supposed to get away?

The boat finally came to a stop, but she couldn't see how high they were. The next thing she knew she was being pulled from the boat, slung over someone's shoulder and carried down a flight of stairs.

"More trouble than anything this one," said the man carrying her.

"It's over now though," said another, yawning. "About bloody time too."

"How long you been active?"

"Three months. And you lot?"

"Three," replied the man carrying her.

"Two," said another. "Can't wait to get a drink."

As they walked the Briars began to break off, making for their cabins she supposed.

"Alright boys," said a voice Nea recognized. "On your way, I'll take this one from here."

She was deposited on her feet, standing proving a difficult task at that moment. She stumbled, ready to collapse but a strong arm held her firm. "Have a drink for me, would you?"

"Yes sir!" said the last of the Briars, their voices sounding farther away.

"Damn it all Nea, what am I to do with you?" said Quinnel, removing the blindfold and gag. Nea breathed a sigh of relief at the freedom but didn't move, she kept staring at him, unsure of what to do. His pale face and silver hair were unmistakable along with those gigantic blue eyes. Though, he was covered in bruises and cuts, his arm in a sling.

"Welcome to headquarters," said Quinnel unbinding her hands.

Nea took in her surroundings. She was inside the great wooden leviathan now. A huge cavern of a hull full of ropes and bridges and walkways. They were standing on one of these, a walkway connecting the cabins and the main stairways. Farther below she could see the working men, amid a mess of machines that she didn't recognize, but that looked far too heavy to float. She saw a man hop onto a pole and slide his way down from his cabin to the bowels of the ship. There were many of these poles, as well as a good many lifts, fast way up, fast way down. There were even tubes through which she could see men shouting messages into the depths, the chain of command persisting regardless of distance.

The interior of the ship was kept lit by a series of mounted lanterns, though there wasn't any fire burning, just bright orange gemstones that hummed with a supernatural glow. The same glow she'd seen coming from the windows.

Nea wondered if this monster could fight; if it could the Royal Navy hadn't a prayer. What a sight this thing would be looming across the harbor at Equius.

Whole damn army might just surrender then and there.

Quinnel kept his hand pressed to the small of her back, urging her forward. He was still glaring at her. "You know I didn't give you that clue in Limani so that you could turn us in to the Royal Guard."

Nea had no idea what to say. It was a lot to deal with all at once, but the one thing on her mind was truly just, "Is Cain…"

"No idea," he scowled. "No body, we made sure that whole field went up in flames. So be proud of that if you like. I'm disappointed, I misjudged you."

Nea shrugged. "It wasn't personal, she offered me a way out and I took it."

"We offered you a way out," said Quinnel. "And you turn around and try to sell us out."

She glared back at him. "Doesn't matter now does it. What are you doing here anyway? I thought you were supposed to be looking for Leo."

Quinnel's face darkened. "I was. I've been reassigned. Got back here about a week ago."

Nea looked him up and down, taking in his injuries. "Reassigned?"

This time it was Quinnel's turn to glare at her. "Your little friend is slippery, latched himself to a vagabond."

Leo?

Nea had a difficult time imagining the sick boy with the bad arm dressed in the regalia of the vagabonds, but so long as he was safe. "Is he hurt? You said you wouldn't hurt him."

"Of course not, what you and the boy still fail to understand is that we're not your enemies."

"Well that's a damn shame, because you sure as hell are mine."

"Why's that?"

"You tried to hurt Cain."

"She wouldn't have been in that position if it wasn't for your little deal."

Nea scowled. "I needed to escape."

"And I presented to you an avenue for just that. Instead you kill my men. Want to go by their cabins, tell their wives, their children?"

"Don't try to guilt me," she spat.

"A little gratitude wouldn't go amiss. You'd be belly up in the ocean if it wasn't for me. I set you on the trail, you're my responsibility. And Mister Beljhar thinks you're too clever to kill."

"He's going to regret that."

"Very frightening. I'm sure he will throw down his sword the moment he sees what a terrible adversary he's acquired." Quinnel stopped and opened the door to one of the cabins. He gave Nea a shove inside. "This one's yours."

A pair of twin beds were lined up against a tiny window, out of which hardly anything could be seen. It was warm, lit by another glowing gemstone, mounted on the wall. It was inviting; Nea didn't trust it for a moment.

"Where are my things?"

"Safe," said Quinnel with a yawn. "I'll see that they get back to you, don't worry and please don't keep scowling at me like that. There's some food on the dresser over there. Eat something and rest, you've got a nasty lump on your head." With that, he was gone, the lock clicking behind him. Nea checked the door; indeed it wouldn't open. She slumped down on one of the beds, grimacing at the ceiling. The cabin was warm, inviting, and her bed was soft. But she took no comfort in any of this; she was a prisoner again.

32

The Ferryman

THOUGH HIS EXPERIENCE of cities was limited, Leo could tell from the outset that there was something strange about the town of Raeva. As they strode down the muddy road, the city wall appeared atop a hill through the trees. It had been fashioned from a thousand different types of wood, bound together then carved and painted with thousands of symbols and letters that covered the entire wall.

The streets sprawled about every which way like the web of a forgetful spider, and the houses had no consistent size or shape. The passersby wore thick coats and cloaks despite the heat: long robes, full pelts complete with teeth, or little to no clothing at all. The smell of spice and gin filled the air and the morning was full of buzzing talk.

Leo was so busy trying to absorb the atmosphere that he almost didn't notice the man sitting cross-legged on an old rug on the side of the street. A small crowd stood by to watch as he passed, what looked like, a flame back and forth between his hands. With a flick of his wrists the fire grew, then morphed into the shape of a flower, before exploding out in all directions. People screamed and covered their heads only to laugh in surprise as a host of tiny flaming flowers burned above.

"What…" Leo started to ask Seiyariu, but his mentor was already striding past the performer.

As they went deeper into the city, more and more of these people appeared. For every peddler and craftsmen there was at least two of these mysterious manipulators. Some tossed fire, some caused plants to grow into the shapes of men, and a few were making shadows dance against the walls.

Seiyariu just grinned at the performers and dodged passing carriages. Leo made to follow him when something slimy, wet, and enormous walked right past him. Leo yelped and fell back in the mud as the great lizard trotted by. It was the size of a pony, complete with a saddle and a rider, who shot Leo a look of puzzled amusement as he led his mount down the street.

"Who are these people?" asked Leo, scrambling over to Seiyariu's side.

Seiyariu laughed. "Surely you've heard of delving?"

"Delving?" He *had* heard of delving.

Stories of delvers had been in all of the epics that Leo had pored over back in his days in the abbey. For every hero, knight or monster there was a delver to match. They were said to have the power to reach into the very essence of nature itself and change what they wished. He'd always thought them flights of fancy on the part of the storyteller, but now that he was here, staring at them all around, there were no words to describe his astonished joy.

"This is a true city of Delvers, one of the last places in which men can commune with nature so freely."

"How does it work?" he asked, scurrying after Seiyariu. Shooting a glance at a man recreating famous sculptures with the smoke from his on-lookers' pipes.

"I'm no expert, try asking one of them."

Leo decided against this, and instead hovered behind Seiyariu as he chatted amiably with a street vendor. The vendor's cart was unassuming at first, but upon further inspection, Leo saw a Peregrine Rune shaped like a tongue, and another like a coin. Loose talker for the right price.

"Finest fabrics this side o' the green sea my friends, nobody beats my prices, not a soul."

"I'm afraid we've no space for fabrics, are you selling anything else? Information perhaps?"

The vendor gave Seiyiariu a searching look. "I might be. Depends what ye might be wanting to know."

"I'll be blunt." Seiyariu's eyes shot back and forth then refocused on the merchant. "We're going to Adis, we need a guide. Do you know anyone who has dealings in the area?"

"Aye," said the vendor rubbing his neck. "But them's not the sorts you'd *want* dealings with."

"What do you mean by that."

"Well, that lot. They're odd."

Seiyariu grinned, "I'm sure we'll get along. I'm rather odd myself."

The vendor laughed. "Not around these parts you're not vagabond."

Seiyariu produced a coin as if from nowhere and tossed it to the man. "Where would I find these exceptionally odd folk?"

"Loudest one spends most of his time at the Oculus, that's the tavern just down the way. Take this road until you reach Medici's then it'll be on the side street there. Strange bastard this one, goes by Pluto, though Lord knows if that's his real name. You'll know him when you see him."

Seiyariu nodded. "Your words," he drew out two more coins, "and your silence." Then with a swish of his cloak he was off, Leo at his side.

*

The Oculus immediately stood out from the rest of the buildings, even in a town like this. It was jet black and the entire outside of the pub had been painted with colored eyeballs whose gaze, by some trick of the light, seemed to follow whomever walked by. The inside was as dark as the outside, black walls, black tables, black counter, black clothes. Only a few candles burned, and the air hung heavy with smoke. Unlike the streets outside, the Oculus was deathly silent. There were only six patrons. One sat at the bar, seemingly asleep. Another was locked in a game of cards with his friend, while a fourth man stood and watched. The bartender himself, made five, not even glancing up as they entered. As for the sixth man, when Leo saw him, there was no doubt in his mind that this was who they were looking for.

He sat apart from the rest of the patrons, hanging like a ghost near the corner. A mop of matted grey and black hair hung around his face, which was smooth and free of lines making his age impossible to guess. He wore a tattered collection of black fabric in a state of such disrepair that the original shape had long been lost. These garments would occasionally flutter and bulge, emitting strange sounds, as if there was something underneath. His pale fingers were wrapped around a black wooden staff and his head hung low.

Without hesitating Seiyariu approached his table. The man's head instantly shot up, and Leo jumped. A thick black bandage had been bound across his eyes. He was blind.

"Mister Pluto?" Seiyariu asked, not flinching at this.

"Mister Seiyariu?" The man's voice was slow, with odd pauses between words.

How does he know his name?

Seiyariu took a seat without being invited and Leo followed. "Have we met?"

"I wouldn't say that."

"You'll forgive me, it's not often I'm recognized by a blind man."

"I'm sure you've encountered stranger things, vagabond."

That sent a chill down Leo's spine but Seiyariu maintained his composure.

"Very well then, I'll not pry."

"That's good of you." Pluto shifted in his seat, bored. "So then, tell me what brings the famous Seiyariu to this filthy place, filthy company perhaps?" His thin lips curled in the suggestion of a smile.

Leo glanced at the vagabond out of the corner of his eye. Famous? Seiyariu?

"We need a ferryman, to take us through Adis."

"Of course you do." Pluto sighed. "You've certainly found the right man, not a thing goes on in that place that I am not aware of. Where in Adis, exactly?"

"I was hoping you'd tell me," Seiyariu replied. "We seek an artifact of some power that was… misplaced."

"The Tomb of the Cupbearer."

"I beg your pardon?"

"It's a chamber, one of the deepest in the entire city. Over the past few months, people have been in and out of there, stashing strange trinkets from all across Fortuna."

"I see."

"I must ask." Pluto leaned in, whispering. "Does Djeng Beljhar know you plan to steal from him?"

Leo sat bolt upright. "Djeng Belj" Seiyariu put a hand on his shoulder to silence him. Leo's mind was racing and he frantically tried to catch Seiyariu's eye. Beljhar? The Beljhar, the one who was looking for him? He'd been the one to take Seiyariu's mysterious Knail? Why had the vagabond not said anything? Had he truly not known?

"You mean the leader of The Black Briars?" Seiyariu raised an eyebrow.

"Don't play dumb, it's unbecoming."

"You give me too much credit, I know of the man, but I am surprised to hear it is his hand in all of this."

"Oh? How interesting."

"And what would the Black Briars be doing with all of these trinkets?" Seiyariu asked, pointedly. "I wasn't under the impression they were collectors."

"I couldn't tell you vagabond," said Pluto. "But if your treasure has gone missing, that is where it will be."

"Will you take us?"

"Willing to throw your trust onto a stranger? This artifact of yours must be very important."

"More than you know."

"I doubt that." Pluto sat up a little straighter and rested his elbow on the table. "Tell me, what is the name of this artifact you are seeking."

"Is that necessary?"

"No, but when you pay for my services the questions come with them."

Seiyariu paused, thinking about this for a moment. "And how much would it cost for you to take us there with no questions at all?"

"More than you can—"

Seiyariu tossed a bag of coins on the table before Pluto got the words out. Leo blinked in confusion, he'd never seen Seiyariu carrying this before. Where had it come from?

"There's half."

Pluto inspected the bag, "I believe we have a deal. But I must ask, will this stripling be accompanying us?" He gestured at Leo, unseeing.

"This stripling is my student, and yes he will be accompanying us. He can handle himself, don't worry."

"Most people say that, often it turns out they can't. But for this much I suppose I'll take your word for it. You've hired yourself a boatman to take you to hell, vagabond." He grinned at Leo. "Take care not to fall overboard."

33
The Briar Patch

NEA LAY BACK on her bed and stared for what felt like the thousandth time out her window at the dreary cloud of nothing beyond. The fog never faded, not offering even a glimpse of the sea or sky to sate her restless mind. The reflection of light through the soupy fog suggested it was midday.

Not for the first time in her life, she imagined that she could fly, leave the world, leave her body behind and soar without a care, without fear, without pain. Nea remembered being a little girl and watching birds, always jealous of how simple it was for them.

What was it all for?

She'd asked herself this question time and time again, ever since she'd saved Leo half a lifetime ago. If she hadn't helped him get away she wouldn't be in this mess. That memory of his haunted stare, his scared little face, she couldn't escape it. Every time it came to her, it was accompanied by the image of Cain pinned under her horse, left to die. She'd saved them. Both of them, and both times it had cost her her freedom. Nea had worked so hard. She had broken herself out of Glatman, fought and killed to survive in the wilderness. All to escape and find a new life. Why was it then, that she was so quick to throw it away for people she barely even knew?

She felt the cold draft before anything else. With an entirely unnecessary knock, Quinnel let himself in.

"You forget you locked it?" Nea asked not looking at him.

"Force of habit," he said gruffly.

"Well piss off then, make that a habit."

"Shut up, I'm not exactly thrilled to be your babysitter." He sat on the other bed, spinning his daggers like a bored cat.

"That's really what they've got you doing?" She raised an eyebrow. "The left hand of Djeng Beljhar and all that rubbish?"

He scowled. "It's better than I deserve. Mister Beljhar says that the task has been given to other operatives."

"He replaced you."

"You're a shit, you know that? Do you want to sit here staring out the window all day? I thought I might show you around."

"Why?" she asked, eyes narrowed. "I thought I was a prisoner."

"Well you're not. As far as Mister Beljhar is concerned you're a recruit, and therefore you have the run of the ship."

A little hope surged inside of Nea.

Stupid idiot doesn't know the mistake he's making.

"Come on then," Quinnel grunted.

"What's the matter?" Nea sneered, trying to play coy. "Lonely?"

He sighed, "Yes I'm lonely, my men are off without me and my leader has lost faith in my ability to follow orders. I'm as lonely as you are."

"I'm not lonely."

"Spare me," said Quinnel. "Sneer all you like, but I can smell it on you. You're the same as me."

"The hell does that mean?"

"Oh, have I made *you* angry now?" He met Nea's gaze, without the faintest trace of emotion crossing his pale face. "Come on, you don't want to waste the whole day sitting on your ass."

She glared at him.

Bastard doesn't know anything about you.

"Fine," she said, unsure why. "Just make sure you show me the best places to sneak out of this barrel, right?"

"Yeah, fair enough. Good swimmer?"

As they stepped out onto the landing Nea felt herself struck dumb by the sheer size of the water bound fortress. Had the Briars built this themselves? By any standards the structure of the ship made no sense, Nea couldn't figure out why the whole thing didn't just sink, or split in two under the weight. Even Conoscenzian technology wasn't advanced enough to create something like this.

Wonder what Cain'd make of all this. Probably lose her mind and want to study everything.

The idea helped her smile a little. "How…?"

"How does the ship work?" Quinnel finished for her. "Sorry, privileged information."

"Can't imagine people are keen to stay here if you don't tell them how it is they're not sinking."

Quinnel shrugged, staring over the rail into the depths below. "It's their choice."

"And they all just chose to live here do they?" She narrowed her eyes.

"Yes," replied Quinnel. "For many of them, this is home. As it will be for you."

"Don't count on it," Nea murmured, staring at a few of the men walking by on the opposite gangway.

Floating madhouse this place.

"I thought I'd show you the baths first."

Nea blinked. "The baths?"

"Yes, it's a room where you wash yourself, I can tell you're not too familiar."

Nea ignored this. "You've got baths, on a ship?"

"They're on level three, come on."

Nea froze on the spot. "No, I'm fine."

"You smell terrible. You're washing."

If you smell bad they'll stay away.

"I'm a prisoner," said Nea, trying to maintain her composure. "I might as well smell like it."

"Mister Beljhar—"

"Forgive me if I'm not eager to clean up for Mister Beljhar, maybe I'll be in a better mood when the hole in my damn head is mended."

"Are you going to be this difficult the entire time?"

"Yes."

Quinnel scowled. "You're going to have to wash at some point."

"Gonna scrub me yourself, are you?" She folded her arms, trying to appear more confident than she was. "I'll just run away, then how's Mister Beljhar's ace gonna look, eh? Chasing a scrawny naked boy around the ship with a brush and soap?"

Quinnel looked away, the faintest hint of color showing in his cheeks. Nea laughed then, finally. For the first time since being shanghaied by these miserable revolutionaries, she managed to laugh.

"Library then," Quinnel muttered. He turned on his heel and started walking, trying to look as dignified as he could in the midst of Nea's snickering. Quinnel could put on all the scary faces he liked now. Nea had chipped his armor. She hadn't expected it to be that easy.

He stopped at one of the poles. "After you, just down two levels, don't miss it."

"Right." She approached the pole, hesitantly. But as she began to slide, she got a rather childish rush of excitement in the three second plunge to the levels below.

Nea took her brief moment alone to study the layout of the ship.

Maybe if you can make it up to the deck you can get one of those boats in the water.

She bit her lip, it was a hard job for just one person. Every staircase that presumably led to the deck had a guard posted there. Quinnel shot down, jumping off the pole and landing beside her with a bit more of a flourish. His feet had barely hit the ground before he was walking again.

"Did you say library?" she asked, picking up her stride to walk beside him. The walkways were all lit by the same orange stones, hung in sconces as though they were torches. They emitted enough light that she could see across to the other side with no trouble. Along the other side of the walkway, men were going about their day following orders. For a ship, Nea noticed there was a distinct lack of any real seamen, and none of the orders being barked through the message tubes seemed to have anything to do with the ship. No calls to adjust sails or repair leaks, just ordering soldiers from one place to another. That was strange.

Quinnel nodded, still not looking at her. "Does that surprise you?"

"Nothing's gonna surprise me now." Nea shrugged.

"We'll see."

They walked along quietly for a few minutes and Nea took the opportunity to gaze some more at the maddening complexity of the Briar's vessel. The more she studied it, the more its intricacies astounded her.

Baths, library, if he takes you past a stable then—

She couldn't finish this thought however; the two of them had come to the end of the walkway, presumably somewhere near the stern of this monster. They were greeted by a pair of oaken double doors, which Quinnel pushed open to reveal an incredible sight.

The room had a high ceiling, vaulted like a church. Like the walkway outside, this room too had a railing, overlooking a staircase that descended several levels deeper into the ship. Books adorned three sides of the slanted room. Shelves were stacked to the ceiling, peppered with ladders. The room was lit by a gigantic circular window of stained glass. It flowered out in every color of the rainbow, dying the stacks and books in new shades. Nea carefully leaned against the railing and looked below, to see more books, going so far down she couldn't see the bottom.

Quinnel stood behind her, pleased at the incredulity on her face. She would've liked not to give him the satisfaction, but there was no way to hide her amazement at this. It was such a raw display of power, of wealth and knowledge. It made her feel small. Perhaps that was the intention.

"Lots to read," she muttered, rather pathetically.

Quinnel shrugged, "I suppose, most of it's too dusty and old for me, but Mister Beljhar expects us to be well read."

"Lots of romance for those lonely nights I hope," she smirked at him, trying to get a reaction.

Quinnel ignored her again. "This place is open to you, as the rest of the ship will be, save the deck."

"You fine with me just walking around this place, learning all your secrets?"

"Beljhar doesn't fear us having knowledge Nea. You assume we're fools following out of sheer loyalty. There is not a man on this ship who doesn't believe in the cause to his very core. The Black Briars are not merely an army, we're a movement, and the more truth one learns, the more likely it is they will turn to side with us." He met her gaze then, his cold blue eyes boring into her. "It's only a matter of time."

"You really think that?"

"I do," said Quinnel solemnly, "You, and Leo."

34
Crossing The River

THERE WAS LITTLE green in the forest called Styx. Gnarled, twisted grey trunks curled up from the steely soil, utterly bare. The fog clung to the forest like a mass of cobwebs; they met not a soul on their trek deeper into the wood.

Pluto had instructed them on what they would need and Seiyariu's suspiciously ample purse had handled the rest. They'd returned to the road, their packs bulging with supplies. It was three days to the entrance to Adis. Then, according to their mysterious guide, they would spend around twenty hours underground – if they were lucky, he'd added with a sneer. Pluto had made sure they were stocked up on flint and rags, so that they could make torches. They used these now to light their way through the forest and fog.

Leo was dying to ask Seiyariu about what Pluto had said, but he didn't get a moment alone with the vagabond until their second evening in the wood. Pluto wandered off, muttering something about scouting ahead, and instructing the two of them to stay on the path. Leo found this very suspicious, but he didn't say anything. At last they could speak without their guide's sharp ears present. Seiyariu seemed to have been waiting for a moment alone with him as well.

"Are you still having nightmares about the lake?"

Leo nodded, indeed every time he rested his hand against his knife now he was back in the woods, cutting that man's throat and watching him die. The familiar anxieties and guilt pulled at him, an animal eating him from the inside out. There were moments where he felt as though he wanted to throw up, to take a sword to his gut and spill the darkness from his body, if only to be free of the weight.

"Does it… does it get easier?" he asked blankly.

"Unfortunetly," said Seiyariu.

Leo swallowed; this wasn't the time to cry. Seiyariu needed him strong; Leo would not be a burden now, not when the descent into Adis was so near. He forced himself to focus on the present. Finally, Leo asked the question that had been fighting to get out of him ever since they'd set out with their strange new guide. "You didn't tell me that this Beljhar person was the one who stole your treasure."

Seiyariu stared ahead into the fog, holding his torch aloft. "Truthfully that is because I didn't know. I had my suspicions, I grant you. There are few people in the land who can gather as many powerful trinkets as Kokaleth has said have gone missing. Beljhar, as commander of a private military force like the Briars would be in an ideal position to seize these items."

"Why though?" demanded Leo. "You still haven't told me what this Knail of yours does."

"What it does," Seiyariu raised an eyebrow, "is entirely up to the person using it."

"That's too vague."

"Yes, yes it is." Seiyariu nodded like they were having an argument with a third, very stubborn person. "Knail is ancient Leo, predating both the vagabond order and The Clash of Comets. It was discovered by Romulus Caloway."

"The first vagabond? Like from the story?"

Seiyariu nodded. "We were to be its keepers."

"Why, what's so dangerous about it?"

"I promise I'll tell you everything when we're back above ground."

"Why not now?"

"Because ours aren't the only ears in this forest."

Leo very much wanted to say, *then why didn't you tell me before*, but he remembered when they had last discussed it, in The Pinwheel Forest. Seiyariu hadn't been keen on answering him then either. What was the vagabond keeping from him?

"Why then are the Black Briars looking for me? Am I a rare trinket as well? Am I dangerous?" scowled Leo. He was unhappy with Seiyariu's calmness about the whole thing. Kokaleth had been positively livid about Knail's theft. But Seiyariu's feelings were buried far deeper than those of the mariner.

"I'm not sure," Seiyariu said, the tone in his voice stating that the subject was closed. "I want to go over the plan with you, before we reach our destination."

"What do you mean?"

"You swore to me that, if I brought you along, you would do what I said when I said it."

"I remember."

"Good. I want you to stay in between me and Pluto at all times. Never in front, never in back do you understand?"

"Yes," said Leo.

"When we get to this chamber," Seiyariu continued, "stay in my line of sight."

"Alright." Leo was growing more and more anxious. What did Seiyariu expect to find down there?

"If we are separated at any point, I don't expect this to happen but if it does, and you find yourself in the chamber without me, here is how you can identify Knail. It sits in a sealed box made of polished metal, upon which rests an inscription from the Vagabond's syntax, written in Peregrine Runes. 'Pain begets Power, The Blood of the Lamb'. Do you think you can remember that?"

"Yes," Leo said, unsure of what else he *could* say.

"Remember what?" Pluto said, looming from behind a tree, a dark smile playing about his face.

"Merely to keep our wits about us in the dark," Seiyariu replied pleasantly. "Are we ready, Mister Pluto?"

"Oh yes indeed." Pluto nodded clutching his staff. He walked with a limp, yet somehow his staff carried him faster than both of them, like a third leg.

Everything about their guide unnerved Leo; the way he moved, the rustling of his cloak. And there was just something wrong about the way he looked at people. A blind man shouldn't be able to look through a person like that. If felt as though he could see everything, even what Leo was trying to hide.

Leo hadn't believed that a forest on earth could be as frightening as Mavrodasos, until they came to the deepest part of Styx. Were it not for Seiyariu and Pluto's torches, Leo doubted he could've seen anything. Grey boney branches reached higher and higher clawing at the unseen sky. The ancient trees contorted into such cruel and impossible shapes, Leo refused to believe they had simply grown that way. No two were similar. They wound around each other, through their bows, into knots on the trunks and out, their branches reaching to snatch the unaware, a great, congealed horror, writhing with every flick of the torch. Most unnerving of all though, was the silence of it all. He heard no birds, no animals, it was as though the whole forest was empty.

"Here," said Pluto at last.

It came looming out of the dark all too quickly. A slab of white stone jutting out of the ground, inlaid in it was a clean, smooth piece of iron, with no handle or lock to be seen.

Pluto held out his staff and struck three times. Slowly the stone began to rumble and shake as the plate was pulled back to reveal a set of spiral stairs, unlit, winding down into the blackness of the earth.

"Are you ready?" asked Pluto.

For the first time that night Leo looked directly at Pluto and saw to his astonishment that the blind man was holding not a torch at all. Hovering above his hand was a ball of light. It grew dimmer and dimmer until Leo could see what it truly was, a firefly.

"Don't fret, you'll be far safer down there with me, than up here without," warned Pluto, as the firefly hovered around their heads.

"You… you're one of them? You're a delver?" Leo stumbled desperately to get the words out.

"Now's not the time, Leo," hissed Seiyariu.

"No it's not, I'd say it would be in everyone's best interest for us to keep moving," said Pluto, turning his head back towards the dark, looking for something. "Come now." He strode forward and vanished into the maw of Adis.

I won't slow Seiyariu down. I made him take me.

Leo swallowed, and went in after him. Seiyariu followed, the hatch slithering shut behind him.

35

All Hope Abandoned

LEO INHALED SHARPLY through his nose, the stench of decay flooding his senses. He didn't trust himself to open his mouth. The walls were packed so closely together, and the fireflies dancing light made them close in further still. Using the walls for balance, Leo took the stairs with Seiyariu following close behind. They were caked with something thick and slimy. Behind him, he could feel Seiyariu's tension; he was ready to spring at any moment.

He expects a battle.

They caught up with Pluto, whose black clothes made him identical to the dancing shadows all around them.

"Don't tarry anymore or you're liable to get left behind," said their guide, glancing back.

Leo was growing increasing uncomfortable with the idea of being led down a steep staircase by a man who couldn't see. He focused on his breathing, trying to keep his heart slow, trying not to imagine the tons and tons of earth packed in on all sides. He tried instead to focus on Pluto's firefly; it was resting on the blind man's shoulder like a trained bird.

"Mr Pluto, how exactly are you doing that?" Leo asked, trying to take his mind off the tightness of the stair. "With the firefly I mean."

"I'm surprised you need to ask," Pluto murmured, sounding bored. "I find it incredible you've never seen delving before, given where you found me."

"So you *are* a Delver."

"Naturally."

"And you can control fireflies?"

Pluto laughed. "Hardly, Leo, my boy. I am an EntoDelver, meaning anything that buzzes about or creeps and crawls on many legs is under my power."

"Anything?"

"Anything."

"How does it work?" Leo asked, rapidly becoming more interested in the conversation than distracting himself. "Do you talk to them?"

"Not quite. But explaining delving to someone who has no concept of the basic principles is a task for one wiser than me, it would take far too long."

"We're not going anywhere Mister Pluto," Seiyariu interjected. "Humor us."

"Very well," Pluto laughed. "Leo, I wish you to imagine something for me, can you do that?"

"I'll try."

"Imagine nature in all its glory and splendor, as a rhythm, a pulse. Composed of billions of tiny pieces, from this pulse we live our lives. It's the music that the world dances to. With me so far?"

Leo nodded.

"Delvers' brains are not quite like those of you and your vagabond. From our youngest days we feel the pulse, our own little aspect of it, calling to us, asking us to reach out and touch it. Eventually we do. Then we reach deeper and deeper, until not only can we touch it, we can change it."

"Like you're doing with the firefly."

"Yes. Though this is fairly shallow, hardly deeper than the second ring. I merely amplified the creature's natural abilities. Were I to reach deeper, well, who knows what I could do," he finished, his voice mischievous.

"The second ring?"

"The three ring of delving, the deeper you reach the more you can accomplish. The first ring is the power to suggest, to move the fire as you see fit, to tell a fly to cross a room. The second ring is that of amplification, increase the heat or size of the flame, and increase the light of the firefly, altering the properties that are already present. The third ring exists far beyond these two and can only be accessed by the strongest and most committed to the art. The power of manipulation, like taking hands to clay with nature itself, it is here where the most powerful miracles take place, as well as the most horrible mistakes."

Leo struggled to wrap his mind around this. It was so fantastical that this kind of power existed in human beings. "Why don't you always reach that deep then? All that power, you could have anything you wanted."

"So I could Leo, but remember this – there is no power in this world that does not come with a hefty price. Every single time we reach into this pulse, we take a great risk.

"I don't understand," Leo replied, frowning. "We saw people in Raeva doing it for coin, it can't be that dangerous."

"On the surface it isn't. But if one were to reach beyond the third ring, into the very essence of nature itself, they would be consumed by the very element they'd sought to control."

"Consumed?"

"Pulled into the pulse and converted; I'd be left as a pile of insects on the floor. Perhaps I'll be able to show you someday, but now is not the time; we must focus. Herein lies the city of the dead."

As the stairs leveled out, Leo stared out into a dark, endless corridor with arched doorways every few paces. Above these doorways were carved names as well as dates of birth and death. An unknown substance dripped from the ceiling and thick patches of mold had begun to form on the floor and walls. The slime of the staircase continued here, mixing with the grime to clog Leo's nose with a terrible onslaught of smells. As Pluto shot out his ball of light a bit farther, Leo caught a glimpse of the inside of the closest room. It was empty, save for a single stone box. Then it truly dawned on him, where they were. Leo was looking at catacombs.

"Careful," Pluto hissed back at him, taking a few steps forward. "If you lose me, that's the end of it."

Leo followed, careful to stay in the light cast by Pluto's firefly, wishing that the strange man would bring out a few more. Still, the farther in the light he stood, the more the shadows began to look like they were reaching out for him.

Their guide moved like one of those shadows, slithering around corners, leading them up stairs, then down. No matter how many turns they made or how many staircases they climbed, to Leo, the catacombs were just a series of identical hallways lined with their little rooms, an endless dormitory of corpses. It was throttling, as though he were underwater, the darkness threatening to swallow him up, drown him. His breath was coming in gasps in the dark, unnaturally loud and strained, making his heart race even more. Leo subconsciously went for his knife, only to be bombarded by the image of that Briar by the lake, his throat slashed, eyes staring blankly. He faltered.

Finally, the silence was simply too much for him and he had to ask, "Seiyariu?" he hissed as quietly as he could, to no avail. It echoed throughout the catacombs as though he had shouted it. "Are there… are there people here?"

"Living people?" Seiyariu replied.

Leo nodded, "You said it was a city."

"So it is," said Pluto, not looking back. "But its residents are much farther in."

"How far does it go?"

"Keep your voices down," Pluto snarled. "We're about to enter the foyer."

"The wha—" Leo was cut off by his own gasp as they stepped out onto a narrow landing cut of the same slimy stone. They were overlooking a chasm so large and so dark that their pathetic torchlight did nothing but illuminate the walls around them. They were in a cylindrical chamber, their little walkway wound its way down in a spiral through the cavern where countless more doors led off to even more sections of the catacombs. It was even more narrow than the corridors, and they had to nearly cling to the grimy wall as they made their way down. Leo could hear Seiyariu's breathing behind him, see the flicker of his torch. He tried to concentrate on those, and not on the pit mere inches from his feet. It felt as though they were circling an enormous well, sealed and forgotten about by its monstrous owners eons ago. He couldn't fight the feeling that something might rise up from the blackness at any moment,

As they walked, Pluto opened his cloak and another firefly darted out, Leo watched him closely this time but still couldn't see what it was that he actually did to it. The creature's light just began to glow brighter, and when it was bright enough, Pluto flicked his staff, sending it winding down the slimy walkway, illuminating the way forward. The other stayed near his shoulder, casting a pool of light around their feet.

Leo knew now why they had called it a city. The chamber Pluto referred to as the foyer was so incomparable in its size that Leo had no idea how anyone, no matter how much power or wealth they possessed, would be able to build something so large and intricate. He was reminded of a time when one of the sisters cut open an empty beehive to show them the inner workings.

With this newfound light doing its best to brighten the foyer, Leo found his eyes wandering once more. As they passed below one of the doors back into the city, he caught something moving. A shape, like that of a man, moving farther in. His heart jumped into his throat. He wanted to scream, to run, but he knew better.

"Don't worry, they won't trouble us just yet." Pluto's voice was soft, and it didn't carry like it had in the corridors.

What did that mean? Leo turned to look at Seiyariu. He was stiff as a board and staring forward determinedly, subtly pushing Leo to do the same.

"What are they?" Leo hissed. He could see more of them now, poking their misshapen heads out of the tombs, black on black, save for the empty space where eyes should be. "Are they... human?"

"Once," Pluto said grimly.

"What?"

"Calm down Leo," Seiyariu's voice was sharp even at its softest. "They won't approach us. They can't stand the light."

"They've been without it for so long." said Pluto. "They are what we call the Shadow People. Humans stranded in the dark, choked by it for so long that they are consumed by madness. They are the true citizens of Adis, not crumbling skeletons or slimy stone."

"My master once told me that Adis was a place that many considered a sanctuary," said Seiyariu. "The poor, the sick, those without homes, vagabonds and the young on the run from the slaving companies. But there was something they couldn't have anticipated."

"A poison," Pluto cut in.

Seiyariu nodded. "The people stayed down here longer and longer with each visit. Until eventually they stopped coming up."

"The dark gets inside them," Pluto hissed. "The air is filled with decayed flesh and bone. You breath it in for long enough, and it becomes difficult to stop. Once Adis has someone, it does not let go. Only madmen like me, people who are strong enough to see through the venomous dark, venture here now."

Leo shuddered, averting his gaze from the shadow people. The idea was sickening; it filled him with nearly as much pity as it had fear. "Why would Beljhar store all his artifacts in a place like this?" Leo asked.

Pluto laughed, "Perhaps the best guards for his treasures are those too mad to use them."

Pluto stopped their descent at an unmarked entrance. Leo didn't ask how he knew it was the right one. Off the foyer they entered a corridor exactly the same as those above, the darkness clung to the walls as much as the slime, and Pluto's fireflies only illuminated a little of their path. There was movement in these tombs. More dark forms loomed, roused from their hiding places.

Pluto began to sing. A slow, jovial tune that Leo thought he might've heard before, somewhere. He couldn't quite place where.

"Here's a health to the King and lasting peace.
To faction end and wealth increase."

The song howled through the catacombs like a winter wind. Leo couldn't tell if it was the echo or not, but he thought perhaps he heard several other pairs of lips joining in.

"Come let us a drink while we have breath,
for there's no drinking after death."

Leo's eyes darted about but he could see nothing. Seiyariu noticed his fidgeting and clasped a hand on his shoulder. Whispering in his ear. "The deeper we get, the more your senses will try to play tricks on you. What comes back is not always what's there."

"And he that will this health deny."

Leo nodded and focused his gaze instead on the back of their blind guide. His hand hovered over the hilt of his knife, his fear of the cloying dark overpowering his guilt and trepidation. But if the need came, could Leo take a second life, a third? What about his bad arm?

"Down among the dead men, down among the dead men."

Leo shook his head. He needed to escape from this dangerous introspection. He'd make himself feel more trapped than he already was.

"Down, down, down, down.

Leo lost all sense of time as they moved through Adis; seconds felt like minutes, felt like hours, felt like years. He had no idea how long they had been down here. The only thing that gave him a clue was the ache in his legs.

"Down among the dead men, let him lie."

A sound met his ears, the last sound he expected to hear in a place like this: rushing water. Pluto ducked under a low arch that led, not into a tunnel, but onto a bridge, beneath which flowed a small waterfall. The bridge was a straight slab of stone, with no rail on either side to keep them from falling. The water below rushed from a gate shaped like the mouth of some terrible demon, it flowed through the chamber and out into the same pure darkness that they'd seen in the foyer.

Pluto did not waste time, he led them through the waterfall chamber, across the slippery bridge, and into what Leo thought would be another corridor. But this room was far too large to be a tomb or hallway; the fireflies cast into light an amphitheater.

Six levels of stone seating, arranged in a half circle, overlooking the center of the room. A single stair cut its way from the door they had entered from, down onto the stage below.

"We're getting close," said Pluto, shuffling past the rows of seating and down the sloping stairway.

"What is this place?" Leo hissed, incredulously. He hadn't expected to find anything so unmistakably man-made this far down.

"Where they entertain guests I imagine," said Pluto, sneering back at him.

Leo's foot slipped on the slime and before he could react he crashed into Pluto and the two of them tumbled down the filth encrusted steps. Leo hit the center of the amphitheater hard, barely missing a head-on collision with the stone. Pluto wasn't as lucky, the blind man's walking stick fell out from under him and he hit the wet stone face first. The fireflies went out.

36
Amontillado

LEO CAME DOWN right on his bad arm, a haze of incendiary pain wiping out all of his senses at once. He screamed and thrashed, fighting not to black out from the pain.

From far a way, he thought he heard Seiyariu's voice, calling out something to him. Leo struggled to get a hold of himself. He could feel the rustling, sense the dark shapes surrounding them on all sides. They filled the theater with their ghostly forms, clinging to stairs, walls, standing everywhere they could fit, the rasping breath of the shadow people, all around him.

Leo couldn't move, couldn't breathe. He waited for the shadow people to descend on him and tear him apart. Just as their hissing grew nearer, there was a thunderous *crack* and light flooded the chamber, casting back the shrieking mass of shadows and forcing them to pour through the exit at the top of the stairs, out into Adis and away from the brilliant glow all around.

The light dimmed and Leo saw Pluto, clutching his staff for support. The burst of light had come from one of his fireflies, twin balls of light now circling his head. He stared around the amphitheater; not a single shadowy form remained. The monsters were nowhere to be seen, but neither, was Seiyariu.

"What..." he stammered, confused.

"If he had any sense, he's running," said Pluto grimly. "I'm sorry, they would've torn us apart if I hadn't."

"He was calling to me," said Leo softly. "I couldn't hear what he said." Despair such as Leo hadn't felt in a long time welled up inside him. He stared at the floor; he didn't want Pluto to see his tears. Pleas were the only thing in his mind now, pleas to anyone and anything to keep his teacher safe.

"Alright boy, now listen," Pluto hissed. "This is a bust and we're getting out of here now. Then, we'll try and find out where your teacher has gone to, yes?" He gestured with his staff to the hallway out of the amphitheater.

"But Seiyariu…"

"Will be fine," Pluto cooed in an oddly soft voice.

"No," there was an iron in his voice Leo hadn't heard before. "He told me to keep going."

"He what?"

"He wanted me to keep going, he told me to find it."

Pluto raised an eyebrow. "It's that important is it?" Leo nodded. "Well I've been paid to take you there, so if you plan to carry on, I'll do just that."

"I do."

Pluto turned on his heel and strode off in the glow of the firefly. Leo took one last look at the doorway Seiyariu had vanished through, then followed.

"I wouldn't worry yourself too much," Pluto said as they continued their trek, "if your Seiyariu is *the* Seiyariu then I'm sure he can take care of himself."

"*The* Seiyariu?" Leo had never heard anyone call him that before.

"Yes, *the* Seiyariu, the vagabond who killed the King of Inferno in a duel. He's rather infamous."

"What?" Seiyariu, Leo's teacher Seiyariu, a regicide? "No, you must be mistaken, he's never said anything about that."

"He didn't? How fascinating," said Pluto. "But tell me Leo, would you be so eager to tell your young apprentice that you murdered a king?"

"I… don't know," he muttered. After all, Seiyariu had a nasty habit of not telling Leo things he needed to know. "Why did he kill the King of Inferno?"

"Ah, now there is the question I was going to ask you. The story I know is simply that Heiro Al-Emani, Regent of the Twelve City-States of Inferno, was killed by a vagabond. His death threw the nation into a chaos it has never recovered from."

"Why do *you* think he would murder a king?" Leo frowned. All that couldn't be Seiyariu's doing, could it?

"Well in my experience there is generally little to be gained from simply murdering a king. There are succession laws to be considered, not to mention that the mere contemplation of such an act is enough to land you in a hangman's noose. So, for one man, no, I can't think of a reason to kill a king. But I can think of thousands of reasons for a man to kill another man."

"I don't understand."

"Your vagabond, Seiyariu, may not have cared whether Heiro Al-Emani was royalty; perhaps it was simply a duel between two gentlemen to settle a matter of honor. Perhaps over a woman."

"A woman?"

"It's said that Heiro Al-Emani's Queen, Aisha Al-Mubarak, was a most beautiful woman. Two men, one woman—it certainly wouldn't be the first time."

Leo chewed this over for a few moments, and then shut it away to ask Seiyariu later. Pluto wasn't quite done with interrogating him.

"This artifact you seek," the blind man continued. "Your teacher wouldn't do me the honors of telling me its name."

Knail. "I don't know it."

"You don't?" Pluto didn't sound convinced. "Your teacher sends you on an errand without even telling you what you're collecting, dear me. It seems like there's a great deal he's not telling you."

"Yes," said Leo, "I suppose there is."

Pluto was trying to bait him into revealing something. That much was obvious. But Seiyariu had been careful when discussing Knail; even around Leo, he knew better than to tell Pluto anything more. Seiyariu wasn't here, but that didn't mean Leo would let him down. The burden of the journey was now on Leo's shoulders. He was scared, more scared than he'd been perhaps ever, miles below fresh air and freedom. He pulled his green cloak a little bit tighter and continued down the dim corridors after the shuffling form of Pluto.

"Here we are." The blind man turned sharply and led Leo down a wide staircase that led to a vaulted chamber, complete with columns on either side of the towering door.

"This is the tomb?"

"Aye," Pluto stepped through the archway and into the dark beyond. As he did, his firefly buzzed about the chamber bathing it in light and Leo let out a small gasp. Of all the bizarre things that surely lurked in Adis, he hadn't expected beauty. Under the grim, ornate columns of white stone stretched out to a dais lay a marble casket, carved in the perfect shape of a man.

"Who's in there?" Leo asked.

"Hieronymus Ganymede," said Pluto simply. "The last man to be properly entombed here."

"Who was he?"

Pluto shrugged. "Just an old noble. Though his granddaughter, dead these fifteen years, was said to be a general in the King's army during his ill-advised conquest of Conoscenzia. It was she who convinced His Majesty that the slaving companies would make powerful allies and led a squadron of boys no older than you to be slaughtered."

Leo shivered. "Children?"

"Aye, the Dashing of the Innocents, they call it."

"How did she die?"

Pluto turned to him, his wicked smile stretched out by shadows. "It's said that one of the slaves, driven mad by the horrors of war, stuck a knife in her heart. But the stories about House Ganymede are vague at best. Still, it interested your friend Beljhar enough to use the tomb as his own personal armory. Ironic, perhaps."

"Where are the weapons?"

"They're tucked in with old Ganymede, I should think," said Pluto gesturing to the marble casket. "Help me get it open."

Together they forced the lid off, sending it sailing down across the dais with a loud crash. Leo's stomach turned at the thing that awaited them within. The body had long decayed into a half-formed skeleton, its blank eyes staring out at them, hollow and infinite. Leo drew in his breath; the sight of the corpse, it took him back to his dream of Nico.

What remained of the corpse was buried under a pile of the most eclectic collection of trinkets Leo had ever seen. The skull of an alligator with rubies inlaid into its eyes, a thin dueling saber, a set of scales, and a small metal box no bigger than a shoe. Leo snatched it up, careful not to touch anything else. It was locked, but sure enough, upon the metal was inlaid a set of Peregrine Runes.

A nail, the symbol for unnecessary pain with a line leading to a fist, the mark for power, beside that was the mark for blood, followed by the mark for livestock.

Pain Begets Power. The Blood of the Lamb.

Whatever Knail was, he now held it in his hands. Leo couldn't help but smile slightly. Their travels had been worth it; Seiyariu's artifact was safe now.

"I'll carry it," offered Pluto, placing his long fingers on the box but Leo jerked it out of his grip.

"I've got it." He tucked it under his good arm and turned to leave. "Let's get going."

Pluto drove his staff into Leo's bad arm with such force, he went flying off the dais. He hit the ground, skidding across the floor as the metal box flew from his grasp. His ears were ringing and bright lights were going off all around him. Agony ripped at his arm. He shook his head, and sat up, Pluto was standing atop the dais, twirling his staff.

"What…?"

"Oh, come now Leo." Pluto gave him that horrible smile once more, and slowly trilled the words, "If you ever see a body, strung up in your view, take care and leave it strung, else the Briars string up you."

The Briars. Pluto leapt from the dais with unbelievable agility, bringing his staff crashing down. Leo rolled to one side and bounced to his feet as Pluto swung the staff at him again. Leo made to dodge but the pain in his arm flared up once more, he stumbled and Pluto caught him in the gut, knocking him back along the floor. Leo felt the breath fly out of his lungs as he hit the ground. It had been a trick, all of it. Leo sank his teeth into his bottom lip and forced himself to his feet, his bad arm hanging limply at his side.

Pluto cocked his head to one side, a small smile playing about his lips. This wasn't the eerie grin he'd worn on the way down; no this was a calm, fixed glee that shook Leo to his core. For the first time he was certain that Pluto was looking directly at him.

"I'm sorry I carried on the charade as long as I did," Pluto said, drawing his staff behind him, readying his next strike. "My curiosity you understand. You have no idea what's in that box, do you?"

"I know enough to keep it from people like you." The gears in his mind were turning. He needed to move, and he needed to move now.

"You know nothing about people boy, let alone people like me." Pluto drew back the cloth that covered his eyes. Large, bulbous green orbs, faceted like those of an insect, stared at Leo without remorse.

Leo felt bile rise in his throat, "You're one of those, the ones you told me about. The ones who reached too deep."

"Of course," Pluto laughed, reaching into his cloak.

As he spoke, Leo made an effort to inch his way backwards, towards Knail's box and the door.

"I've reached further than anyone has ever dared, and come back to tell about it. I stared into that abyss, Leo, and I did not blink." He chuckled.

Leo dove for the box, snatching it up and tucking under his working arm. He spun around, expecting Pluto to have rushed him, staff raised for another assault. But he hadn't, the delver was just standing there, leering at him with those horrible insect eyes.

"Come now Leo. Let's not be rash." From within his cloak, Pluto pulled out something small Leo couldn't quite make out and placed it on the ground. "I'm torn, because on one hand I am supposed to deliver you to Mister Beljhar alive, on the other I've been ordered to kill anyone who attempts to take away his toys." Pluto's firefly buzzed down to the floor so Leo could see just what it was that he'd placed there. A centipede, a tiny little brown creature, all limbs and feelers, too frightened to move. Pluto gave Leo one last smile. "I suppose I won't leave it up to me." He cracked his staff against the stone and the centipede began to grow.

37
Arms and Legs

LEO'S MIND WENT blank at the terrible sight before him. The centipede was writhing in pain, clicking its pincers as it increased in size. It was as big around as a dog now and nearly fifteen feet long. Then twenty. Leo's mind finally caught up with him and he ran.

Leo skidded out of the tomb and up the stairs, desperate to put as much distance as possible between himself and that terrible clicking. He heard a scuttling sound, legs scratching at the stone floor. Leo looked back; the centipede was chasing him, moving from wall to floor to ceiling.

Clutching Knail tight, Leo sped up the stairs four at a time, as he reached the top he slid to one side and tore off down the hall. Leo's cloak billowed out behind him as he sprinted faster than he'd done in his life. Half-running, half-sliding down the slimy corridors, he had a split second to make a decision when the path forked; he tried as best he could to remember the way they'd come but everything looked the same.

It was then that Leo realized he wasn't in total darkness. Why was that? Then after a moment or two he realized that the box under his arm, the box that held Knail, was glowing. Producing a soft white light that spread out just enough for him to see.

He hurled himself to one side just as the corridor ended, barreling to the right just as the clicking caught up with him. The creature paid no mind its surroundings, desperately snapping at Leo with its pincers.

An idea sparked in his mind, and Leo forced himself to stop at the end of the hall. The centipede had no chance to slow down and as it reared up to strike, at the last moment, Leo rolled aside letting it smash into one of the tombs. Sure enough, he heard the wail of the shadow people as the centipede disturbed their hiding place. The centipede emerged from the tomb, only for its occupants to throw themselves on it, shrieking. The centipede smashed into the wall, trying to knock the shadow people off, but only succeeded in driving more of them out into the corridor. These too began attacking the monster.

Ignoring another spasm in his arm as best he could, Leo tore off down the corridor, left, then right, then left again. There was a great screaming and crashing from behind, but Leo dared not look back. He ran up another flight of stairs, taking the left path down into another hall lined with tombs. He couldn't keep running like this, his head was bleeding and his bad arm was screaming in protest. He heard, what sounded like, more shadow people descending on the centipede below, driving it back. As the sounds of battle raged from the floor below, Leo stumbled off the corridor into one of the tombs. Checking to make sure it was empty, he dove behind the stone casket, clutching Knail to his chest, praying.

His breath came in ragged gasps and his arm ached terribly. Still, adrenaline had taken over. Leo was beyond fear, beyond pain. Blood dripped into his eyebrows and his hands were caked in it. Some of it had fallen onto the box, which was glowing no longer.

"Lost in the dark with nowhere to go," Came the jeering voice of Pluto, echoing through the halls. "If you think you've escaped, don't be naive. My pet will be with you in a moment, after he's finished with his meal."

What was he to do? Use his dagger? The beast wouldn't even notice such a tiny thing. But what if... Seiyariu had said that Knail was a weapon. Slowly, Leo undid the clasps and raised the lid of the box. He frowned, unsure of what it was exactly that he was looking at. The box was filled with nothing but black sand.

He stared for a few moments, confused. Where had the light gone? A drop of blood slipped from his forehead and fell into the sand and it began to glow once more. It wasn't sharp or bright, but it filled the dark tomb Leo was sitting in, radiating out from within the strange mass.

What on earth...

Leo brushed his palm against the cut on his head again. Holding his hand out he let the blood drip down into the box once more. Sure enough the glow intensified, and he could feel warmth from inside the sand.

The sound of clicking met his ears again. Leo had to make a decision. This thing wanted his blood and Pluto wanted his life. He looked at the box, then at his bad arm, at the painful, useless lump of ruined flesh that served as a constant reminder of his own weakness. If Knail wanted blood, then by God Leo would give it blood. Gritting his teeth, he reached into the box.

Nothing happened, just the damnable throbbing, same as always. Then something brushed against his wrist. He froze, there was something moving.

Pain, pain such as he had never known in his life, lanced up Leo's arm, something was cutting, stabbing, digging into his flesh from all sides; it felt like there were thousands, millions of jaws snapping at his flesh. He screamed, an inhuman howl the likes of which he didn't know his body could produce. Through his streaming gaze, he could see the mass inside the box flowing back and forth, writhing down onto his exposed flesh. He yanked his arm back, but the dark form had its claws in him. Leo screamed again as he felt it tightening, digging its way into his ruined arm, deeper and deeper.

He fell, thrashing and flailing like a mad animal in a trap. He was dying, though his brain was on fire, Leo knew that much. There was nothing in this world that could survive a pain like this. For what felt like eons he lay twitching and screaming on the floor of the tomb, waiting to black out, for it all to end. And end it did. As suddenly as it had arrived, the pain ceased, and he was not dead.

Leo sat up against the wall, gasping for air. The burn of the pain was so fresh in his brain he wasn't even sure it was over. But the seconds began to gather, and it wasn't coming back. With his good arm, Leo dragged the box over to where he sat. It was empty. Leo looked around blearily, searching for where the black mass had gone and his gaze fell upon his own right hand.

It looked like he had put on a metal gauntlet. His right hand and forearm were covered with a shimmering black substance. It was hard, smooth, and cold to the touch. Leo raised his hand. He flexed his fingers and they obeyed. His arm was still there. But this thing was latched onto him. *No*, he realized as he saw the dark tendrils that wound their way to his elbow, it was embedded in his flesh. The only place where the metallic substance extended beyond his arm, was at the tips of his fingers where it curved off into five claws. Awed, Leo ran these along the wall, leaving five long scars in the stone. So sharp, his fingers had become like gigantic razors, his fingernails… fingernails…

"Knail."

The weapon they had searched for, the thing that Beljhar wanted, that Seiyariu had been so desperate to protect, was now fused to Leo's arm.

Leo flexed his fingers again and again. Knail's onyx coating was oddly flexible yet, when he rapped his knuckles against it, hard as any metal.

It was then he realized that the pain in his arm, the agony that had beset him for months and months, ever since he'd shredded it in his grief, was completely and utterly gone. He extended his arm, waved it about, but none of the familiar aches came to him. His arm felt healthy, strong. Leo's heart leapt with joy and confusion. How was this possible?

As soon as he thought this, a familiar sharp pain flashed across his arm along with a sensation like being pulled, but it only lasted for a moment. As it faded away he saw, to his amazement, that from the ridges in his new arm, something like smoke was emanating, a soft cloud of white light, pushing back the dark of the tomb.

Knail had not only healed him, it was helping him. Blood for light, a fair trade right about now. Leo got to his feet with some difficulty, digging his new claws into the wall for support.

His legs felt like jelly, but now that an opportunity had presented itself Leo wasn't going to waste it. Whatever Knail was, right now it was the best hope he had of getting out of Adis in one piece.

He stumbled from his hiding place, white light filling the corridor. Leo made his way down the tunnel, limping and clutching the wall, but moving. He wasn't clear on where he was headed, but whenever he saw stairs he took them up. The centipede was nowhere to be seen, he couldn't even hear it anymore. Where was the creature, where was its master?

After some time, Leo rounded a corner and felt his heart catch in his chest. It was the hall to the amphitheater, the way out. But in his way, stood several more of the shadow people, huddled just at the end of the hall. They were looking at him, at least he thought they were, all he could see was their outline. Leo took a deep breath and kept going, striding down towards the dancing faceless forms. He wasn't sure what stayed his nerves, but he felt certain that they couldn't hurt him, not now.

As he drew closer several of the figures rushed at him, but they scurried back in all directions as they met the dim, white light emanating from his hand. Try as they might, none were able to penetrate the soft bubble surrounding Leo. They let out howls of frustration, swarming around him with every step he took. Then, Leo heard something that sent him into a cold sweat – a deliberate, constant, clicking. With a collective scream, the shadow people retreated inside the tombs and Leo looked back to see Pluto's centipede barreling towards him.

Leo flung himself forward, tumbling into the amphitheater and crashing up the stairs as quickly as he'd fallen down them. The centipede scurried up the wall, trying to cut him off. Leo rolled through the door to the waterway, just missing the creature's pincers.

He ran across the bridge as fast as he could, but the stones were slick with water and slime and Leo's feet gave out halfway across. His muffled cry was drowned out as the centipede's clicking was upon him. He turned back to see the animal lunge at him, heaving it's mutated form across the bridge towards its prey.

On an impulse he threw his Knail out in front of him. It was his only weapon. In that instant Leo felt the twinge of pain in his arm, and the feeling of being drained. Light exploded from his hand in all directions, no longer soft but fierce and bright. It burst through unseen cracks and folds in Knail's armored shell. The release staggered Leo and the light spread like a wave, out towards the centipede, driving it back. It washed over the beast, whose clicking and writhing grew more frenzied as the otherworldly beam overwhelmed it. The centipede reared back, flailing madly but it had ventured too far out onto the bridge. The centipede crashed over the slippery stone and several of its legs gave way. The creature fell over the edge and was half submerged in the water, catching itself with what legs it had left. It scrambled against the stone, clicking furiously but to no avail. The current had it. The creature's massive form was carried off, over the falls and out into the abyss.

Leo got to his feet gingerly, a warm feeling of triumph washing over him. Then, from nowhere, emptiness took him. All energy left his body and Leo collapsed to the stone, gasping for air. He couldn't focus, he was starving, tired and barely able to move. He wasn't sure how long he lay there, too weak to stand. Waiting for one of the shadow people to come and carry his helpless form back into the darkness.

"Ah, Leo." Was that a voice? Surely it was just his imagination, his drained form playing tricks on him. Yet sure enough, he heard it again, louder this time. It was the voice of Pluto.

"What *have* you done?"

38

Ante

"Post."

"Pair, royal aces."

Nea swore and flicked her cards down, glaring at Quinnel from across the table. "You're cheating."

"Aren't you?"

Nea rolled her eyes, prisoner though she was, she'd found amusement in the last week, learning the layout of the ship. Quinnel was still busy with his day to day tasks, but when his duties were finished he would come and keep her company. He didn't smile, wasn't much for laughs or anything, and was ostensibly Nea's jailor, so she was surprised to find that she enjoyed the company. Despite him being a cold, miserable bastard it was nice to have someone around to kill the time.

What are you turning into?

True to his word, it appeared as though Nea had almost the complete run of the ship. She'd been looking for a way to escape the moment she'd had some time to explore. Despite the increasing familiarity of the layout, Nea couldn't find a single damn weakness. Not one crack through which she might slip out. Even if Nea managed to steal one of the boats she'd arrived in, she doubted she'd even make it to the water before they hoisted her up back again. Plus, the deck was the one area of the ship where she was forbidden to go.

Not like you could get past the guards anyway.

When Quinnel was off working and she'd grown tired of exploring, Nea would find a comfortable place in the library to pour over the old and obscure tomes that littered the ship. Her original goal was to find something relating to the ship itself. Having failed that, she'd fallen back on general shipbuilding and seamanship. The more of these volumes she read however, the more her prison ceased to make sense. It defied all laws of the ship craft and indeed carpentry and physics too. The Briar's fortress was a puzzle, one that she was determined to solve. Still the days passed, and she had little to show for her efforts other than bags under her eyes and a crumpled deck of playing cards.

"Go on then," she grumbled.

"Again?" Quinnel raised an eyebrow. They were in Quinnel's cabin. It wasn't much different from hers, a bit larger in places, but with the same beds and lit by the same stone lanterns. He'd a table in his chambers and it was here they'd set up their game. "If we were betting, I'd already have your shoes by now."

This gave Nea an idea. "Alright, you want to make this interesting?"

"You want to gamble? What with?" he said suspiciously.

"How about this, whoever wins the hand gets to ask a question."

"What kind of question?"

"The kinds of questions the loser doesn't want to answer."

Quinnel thought about this. "What's to keep you from lying?"

Nea pondered this for a moment, "You said you could tell if I was lying, back in Limani. That true or were you just trying to scare me?"

Quinnel unscrewed the top of the flask he carried everywhere, letting steam fill the room. "It's not hard to tell when someone's lying. Mister Beljhar teaches us to read people."

"Then read all you please. What's to keep *you* from lying?"

Quinnel sighed. "The fact that I am a member of the Black Briars. We are the truth, why should we hide from it?"

"Spare me." Nea rolled her eyes. "So you never lie?"

"No, we don't, not to our friends at least."

"I'm not your friend. What about Mister Beljhar, does he lie?"

Quinnel's face darkened. "He speaks greater truths than I'd thought possible. You're worried that I might learn all your secrets?"

"Maybe," Nea replied, taking the cards and shuffling them. "One way to find out."

Quinnel drew back on his steaming flask and nodded, "Fine."

The game progressed slowly, each of them was playing more cautiously now. Nea had been craving some answers; if she had to win them, so be it.

"Pair, Crimson Kings," she said finally.

"Post, Triple Queen."

Nea swore again and dropped her cards. Had this been a mistake? What was Quinnel going to ask her? Nea liked to think that she was decent at reading people as well; Quinnel had been dead set on what he said before, besides what did she really need to lie about besides—

"Why don't you bathe?"

Nea instantly broke eye contact. She hadn't been expecting that. What could she say? The truth? "I do bathe, just not a lot."

"Why is that?"

"One question per hand," she said with a grin. "Don't get greedy." She breathed a little sigh of relief as Quinnel began to deal the cards again; she'd gotten through that one all right, now all she needed to do was—

"Post, Queens and Aces. Why don't you bathe frequently?"

Damn! Gonna have to give him a proper answer this time.

She avoided looking at him, and answered almost under her breath. "People will stay away, if you're dirty."

Quinnel did his best not to let any reaction show on his face, but Nea caught the faintest hint of understanding, before he returned to the cards.

"Fair enough, I wasn't always fond of company myself."

"What changed?" Nea asked without thinking.

"I thought you had to win a hand to ask a question," Quinnel said. "It's no secret. I've gotten soft working with Mister Beljhar. So soft I'll even let a grimy kid stink up my chambers, just to pass the time."

Nea smiled a little bit and dealt the cards again.

"Pair, two and six," Quinnel yawned.

"Post, Royal Aces."

Quinnel grunted, "Suppose you were bound to win one eventually."

She knew what she wanted to ask for sure. It was a simple question, but one that had been driving her up the wall ever since they'd met. "You were a slave, tell me what happened."

"Runaway, I got picked up by the, what did you call them? Grassers, and sent to work for a few years. Found out I was pretty good in a fight. They wanted me to be one of their hunters. That was when Beljhar found me. I think you've got me again, just got a pair of nines here."

"Why is it so cold around you?" as she said it, and Quinnel again met her eyes, Nea felt a chill run down her spine.

"Are you familiar with delving?"

Nea was. She'd heard many stories with delvers in them, growing up. Like many of the stories from the Archipelago, she thought it was an exaggeration. But when she'd been living at Glatman, Nea had found three books on the subject tucked away in the library. These had been written by an actual delver, or so it said. It outlined the theories involved, the pulse of nature, the three rings, its power, rules and limitations. Still Nea had never actually seen it for herself.

"You're a delver then? What do you draw from, water, cold? How does it work? Can you do it now? Can I watch?"

Quinnel put up a hand and Nea became instantly aware of how childish she sounded. "I'm not a delver."

"But you said—"

"I'm from a family of delvers," he said busying himself with the cards. "CryoDelvers, from the far north. They're able to shift the properties of cold, or ice if you prefer. I never learned it myself, but my heritage is plain. My body temperature is much lower than an average person's, and my sweat glands work differently."

"I didn't think being a delver changed your body like that."

"It doesn't, but years of attempting to become a delver and coming up just shy can leave lasting effects." There was obviously more to this story but Nea shut her mouth and let him deal another hand.

Might as well play by the rules, if he's going to.

"Pair, two and four," said Nea. "Why did you run away from home?"

"My father," said Quinnel.

For a moment Nea thought he was going to leave it at that.

"When he realized I wasn't able to delve he began to push me. When that didn't work, he began to hurt me. At first, I thought it was to motivate me, but he became crueler, fiercer. The more I failed, the more he hurt me, until I began to change." He gestured at himself. "To better answer your previous question, that's why I'm like this."

"I'm... I'm sorry," said Nea. Suddenly she saw Quinnel in a very different light. Someone who'd been hurt so much that they'd run, even if it meant falling into the hands of the grassers; that was a story she was very familiar with.

He shrugged. "At the time I felt it was my fault. My father wanted me to inherit his gift, and when I couldn't, I was ashamed."

Nea shifted uncomfortably in her chair. The similarities between the two of them were growing by the minute.

The difference is, what happened to you was your own fault. You escaped didn't you? If you'd just done that from the start those two years at Glatman would've never have happened.

Quinnel caught her eye. "To blame yourself for someone else's evil acts is a diseased way of thinking. And it makes broken people. Beljhar taught me that." Before Nea could respond he threw down a winning hand. "Post, three of a kind. And what about you? Are your parents still alive?"

For a moment, Nea thought she hadn't heard him right. *What kind of daft question is that?* "My parents?"

"Yes, your parents. You don't strike me as someone that was raised especially proper."

She snorted. "I've no idea, I haven't seen them in years but…"

There was a knock at the door. "Enter," Quinnel barked. A Briar stepped inside, snapping to a salute as Quinnel got to his feet.

"Report."

"Sir, Mister Beljhar sends word that the child is under our protection at last. The vagabond as well."

Nea let her cards fall.

"Are you certain?" Quinnel asked.

"Yessir, they're on their way to us now."

No.

This was wrong; this wasn't supposed to happen.

How could that daft boy let himself get caught? What the hell kind of vagabond was he travelling with?

"Thank god," Quinnel said, collapsing back in his chair. "It's finally over, good news, eh Nea? Tell me soldier, who finally managed to capture them? I'd like to buy him a drink."

"It was Pluto sir, Mister Pluto."

Something darted across Quinnel's face, just for a fraction of a second. Nea couldn't quite make out what it was. "I thought he was guarding the vault?"

"Yes sir, it seems that the boy and the vagabond were attempting to steal something from it."

Quinnel's face went possibly even whiter. "The vagabond…"

"Yes sir…" The man shuffled on his feet slightly, dreading what was to come next. "Mister Pluto said they were after the Knail."

Quinnel shot to his feet, "But Pluto stopped them, didn't he? They didn't get it?"

The man was quaking now, and Nea watched fascinated. What was this about a vault? What had Leo and this vagabond been up to? And why was Quinnel so concerned about a nail?

"Mister Pluto captured them sir."

"That's not what I asked."

"In the report, he says that the boy…"

"The boy what?" Quinnel was towering over the terrified messenger.

"The boy… Mister Pluto says he opened it, sir."

For a moment, Nea thought Quinnel was going to strike the man, but he backed away, slowly turning his back on the soldier. "Has Mister Beljhar been informed of this?"

"No sir."

"Good, it should be me who tells him. Dismissed."

The man was gone before the words had finished leaving Quinnel's mouth, and the two of them were alone again. It was cold, dreadfully cold. Nea stared at Quinnel's back. She wasn't sure what had just happened, she'd never seen him like this. Nea cautiously got to her feet.

"Quinnel…"

"Leave me."

She did, darting out the door and back towards her quarters. Trying to process what she'd just seen. Leo would be coming here, and soon. Damn, but that complicated matters, now she had to come up with an escape plan for the two of them, No, the three of them, she supposed he'd want to bring that vagabond too.

Nea shook her head. She hadn't ever expected to see Leo again, let alone like this. And what was all that about a nail? And why had it made Quinnel so insane? She pored over this as best she could, but it took her in circles, there were no answers to be found now. She would have to wait, wait for a new hand to be dealt, and then maybe these secrets would come to light.

39
Back in Chains

WIND SWEPT ACROSS the desert, sand flying up in curtains, winding through the sky then settling again in the endless dunes. Thick clouds were beginning to gather overhead and a distant rumble of thunder could be heard. Still Leo and his companion walked on through the wild, storm-tossed wasteland. His skeletal friend held his hand tightly, too tightly. The skeleton was squeezing down on Leo's right arm with all the pressure of a vice, and it was only growing worse. Leo screamed and tried to rip himself free, struggling and thrashing.

Leo sat up with a start. His was in the back of some kind of prison wagon. His whole body felt numb with exhaustion, but he recognized a familiar pressure on his ankles – irons on his arms and legs.

Leo's eyes fixed on a patch of sunlight coming through the barred window. He was out of the dark; somehow he had gotten out in one piece. The ache from his dream hadn't faded. His bad arm still hurt, though not the way he was used to. Why was that? He looked down, and all the memories and sensations of the trek through Adis, returned in a violent wave. He stared at the twisted remains of his arm in a more decent light. It was completely set in his flesh now, no twisting or bleeding. Knail was simply inlaid there, like a gem upon the hilt of a sword.

All at once he became aware of his insane thirst and hunger. He looked around for a something, anything to drink.

"Here." Seiyariu tossed him a bit of dried pork.

"Seiyariu?" The vagabond was a mess, battered and bruised, his clothes stained with blood. He was similarly shackled and his hood was up, casting his face into shadow.

"Eat, you need to get your energy back." Leo obeyed scarfing down the meat like an animal. "You had me worried Leo. You've been sleeping for a day and a half."

No. How could he still be so weak, so tired? "What's happened to me?"

Seiyariu leaned forward and Leo saw dark bags under his eyes. "For God's sake Leo, why did you open it?"

"I… I had to. I would've died."

Seiyariu's voice was without affect. "I need you to tell me everything that happened after our separation in Adis."

Leo did just that, and when he reached the point where Pluto had turned on him, Seiyariu scowled.

"I left you with him, damn my eyes but I should've seen it. It was too convenient, all of it."

"What do you mean?"

"I thought it strange that we didn't encounter any sign whatsoever of the Black Briars on our trek through Styx and Adis. I didn't understand why Beljhar would simply leave all his treasures unprotected. It didn't occur to me that Pluto might be the guard I was unable to find. Beljhar has outsmarted me again, and this time it's cost us our freedom."

"Pluto got you too?"

"Once he had you, it wasn't a choice."

Leo felt these words dig into him, so it was his fault Seiyariu was in chains as well. The vagabond let Leo finish his story, all the way up to his killing the centipede on the bridge. Then he sat in silence for a few moments, running through the whole thing in his head.

"You were in danger and you made a choice. But choices have consequences Leo, devastating consequences."

"What do you mean?"

"Knail was never supposed to be used again, especially not by a child."

"I didn't even know what Knail was!" Leo protested angrily. "All you told me was that it was a weapon, and I needed a weapon."

Seiyariu slammed his fist against the wall. "Do you ever stop to consider that I may keep these secrets for your own good?"

"Does this look *good* to you?" Leo was astonished at the venom in his voice. "You didn't want this!? *I* didn't want this! This wouldn't have happened at all if you had told me the truth! You can't give me nothing but vagaries and expect me not to make mistakes." Only now did Leo realize just how much he'd wanted to say these words.

Seiyariu stiffened, for a moment Leo thought he was going to strike him, but the wanderer just slumped against the wall and put his head in his hands. "Leo, Knail is so dangerous I... well, I suppose that's the trouble, isn't it? I thought it would be safer not to tell you certain things. Clearly, I was wrong. So be it, no more secrets."

"Then tell me, what is Knail?"

Seiyariu's face darkened further. "Knail is indeed a weapon, but unlike a sword or a piece of armor, it is an organism, a living creature, more specifically a parasite. You see how it's latched onto your arm? It will feed on you, to sustain itself."

Leo's stomach twisted in horror. It was eating him? That's what that new sensation in his arm had been, that draining feeling. "Is there any way I can get it off?"

Seiyariu avoided his gaze. "It's rooted into your muscles and blood vessels at this point. Knail is a permanent arrangement, I suspect that's why Beljhar himself wasn't using it. The only thing you could do is cut your arm off, and I'd advise against that for now."

Leo felt tears again but he wiped them away; this was no time to be a child. "What can I do?"

"If your battle with Pluto's centipede is anything to go by, quite a bit." Seiyariu took Leo's new hand and examined it.

"The light?"

"Perhaps. Perhaps even more. But I believe that's why you were unconscious for so long."

Leo stared at the gnarled creature mimicking his arm. "It feels better; like I never hurt it."

"Knail has wormed its way into your flesh, altering its body to replace the damaged nerves and muscle."

"Amazing," said Leo. "Can you teach me to use it?"

"I'm afraid not."

"But I thought vagabonds—"

"We were its shepherds and its guardians but never its owners. When our order was founded, the weapon was entrusted to an organization of delvers we refer to as the Cabal. We ferried it between these men once a generation, while they worked their hardest to unlock its secrets. Only the Cabal know how it is truly controlled."

"So what can we do?"

"Well considering the most powerful and dangerous weapon on earth is now latched onto your arm, I think it is only fair that we pay His Majesty a visit and ensure he knows just who stole it and why."

"Erm…" said Leo glancing around.

"Oh this!" Seiyariu glanced around like he'd only just noticed where they were.

Leo at last managed a smile.

"We'll have to escape."

"You make it sound so simple."

"Come now Leo, have a little faith."

"And we go from there to the capital?"

Seiyariu nodded. "I believe that these artifacts, Knail and the others, are for some kind of war effort against Fortuna."

"A war…"

"Please don't preoccupy yourself with that. Focus on getting your strength back."

"I'll try," said Leo. "Listen Seiyariu, if we're not keeping secrets anymore, there are some things I want to ask you."

The vagabond raised an eyebrow. "Oh?"

"Pluto said something about you, after we'd gotten separated."

Seiyariu's expression didn't change. "What was it he said?"

"That you killed the King of Inferno."

For a moment Leo thought he wasn't going to answer, then, "No more secrets then. He's correct. When I was young I challenged and killed Heiro Al-Emani in a duel."

"Why?" Leo asked, amazed at this revelation. Not for the first time he had to ask himself, who *was* this man before him?

"Did Pluto not offer you further explanation?"

"He said that there aren't many reasons for one man to murder a king, but that there are hundreds for a man to murder another man."

Seiyariu raised an eyebrow. "He said that? Well that's rather sage. It's true; I didn't kill Heiro because he was the King. I killed him because of a woman."

"A woman?"

"Love often kills more people than it creates."

"Was it... the queen?"

He nodded. "I'm afraid so. Yes, Aisha Al-Mubarak and I were entwined, Heiro discovered it and challenged me. I won, but barely. Sadly enough, murdering her husband didn't endear me very much to the Queen and I fled for my life."

"Was that what you meant when you said you'd done many things wrong?"

Seiyariu nodded. "Under Heiro Al-Emani, the Twelve City-States of Inferno had been united for the first time in centuries. I shattered that alliance. Ever since they've been engaged in constant wars and in-fighting. So many lives lost, ruined, all because of me."

With that, a silence fell upon the two of them. Soon, Seiyariu turned up his hood and began to doze quietly. Leo didn't sleep, the dream was still haunting him and he didn't wish to return. Instead he practiced picking up and holding things with his clawed hand. Trying to get used to this thing that was now a part of him.

The hours passed, and their barred view of the sky was soon obfuscated by fog, followed by a light rain, rattling along with the carriage into a hypnotizing melody. Perhaps he let it carry him off to sleep once or twice, but it was never deep.

Several times he tried to get Knail to reproduce the blast of energy he'd used to kill the centipede. Perhaps Leo could blow a hole in the back of the carriage and they could just roll out. But no matter how hard he focused, all he managed to do was make his head spin. Knail was completely unresponsive and inanimate, to the point that he wondered if the encounter in Adis hadn't also been some fabulous dream. As it stood, the parasite latched to his arm may as well have just been a glove.

Leo was just about to drift off to sleep again when the carriage lurched to a halt. Leo looked at Seiyariu, terrified, and the vagabond did his best to make Leo feel at ease. The doors were flung open to reveal six Briars, all armed. The two of them marched from the carriage.

Leo kept his head down, he didn't struggle, didn't fight, he was used to this. As long as he could see Seiyariu, he could hold it together. There was a numb resolve in captivity. He remembered it well.

Leo was picked up bodily and placed inside a long thin boat. The Briars climbed in on all sides, and without so much as a word they shoved off. He lay there in shackles, as they pressed on through the water, the gentle pull of the waves, dreadfully familiar.

40

Lost Boys

One more bleeding second on this damnable ship and you might just throw yourself overboard.

Another interminable week had passed since she'd played cards in Quinnel's cabin. She hadn't seen him since. Hadn't seen much of anybody.

They must be getting things ready for Leo and the vagabond.

Eventually the boredom became too much to stomach and Nea made up her mind to return to Quinnel's cabin and pay him a visit. It was late and the ship's walkways were mostly deserted, still not a soul took notice of her. There was something infuriating about the carefree attitude the Briar's had towards their prisoners. Did they really think she was so little of a threat that she could just go where she pleased whenever?

They're right. What kind of a threat are you? Skinny little girl in pants.

Nea hesitated, hand on the knob. It was true, honestly – what could she do to get in their way?

"Oh my, and who is this?"

Nea sprang back, there was a man standing right beside her, a man she didn't recognize. Though he leant on a tall walking stick, it was rather hard to tell how old he was. Plenty of grey flecked his filthy hair, which was indistinguishable from the cloak, or jacket, or rags that covered every inch of him. The man's eyes were bound, like a blind beggar and he wore a smile that made Nea's stomach turn. The man exuded a power she'd never felt before.

"Didn't mean to frighten you my dear," he said, still grinning. "Looking for an evening's chat with Mister Quinnel?"

"I... I... " Nea stammered like an idiot, she didn't know what to say, what to do, her mind was blank. What was this fear?

Pull yourself together!

She found herself backing away slowly, something the blind man found amusing.

"No? Very well then, off you go. Be good now." Then, with a swish of his cloak, he swept through the door, leaving Nea in the passage, trembling, barely on her feet.

Nea collapsed against the wall and slid to the floor, catching her breath. The way he'd looked at her, like he could see her frantically beating heart, like it excited him.

Did he... did he say, 'my dear'?

She pressed an ear to Quinnel's door, terrified curiosity getting the better of her.

"Why in God's name did you even let the boy near it?"

This was Quinnel, voice raised.

"I wanted to see if he would make the choice he did," said the second man. His oily voice was slow, with strange pauses between words.

"Your twisted games always have to come first don't they? Every time Pluto, every damn time you're told to do a job you try and have your fun first."

Pluto. That's the one who captured Leo and his vagabond.

"And have I ever failed any of these jobs?"

"Worse, you went against Beljhar's direct orders."

"Oh and of course we wouldn't want to do that," Pluto laughed.

For a moment the voices were silent, then Quinnel spoke. "What are you implying?"

"I'm not implying anything," said Pluto flatly. "You're always following Beljhar's orders to the letter, that's why your father is still alive."

Quinnel didn't answer.

"Yes, I know about that. What kind of idiot do you take me for? You were ordered to kill him when you stole Knail, were you not? So don't lord over me with your talk of loyalty. I wonder what dear Mister Beljhar would say if he knew."

"He *does* know," said Quinnel, from far away. "I can't lie to him."

"Of course you can't. You're soft, I'm curious. That's the difference between the two of us boy. And before you think to run and tell tales on me, Mister Beljhar has naturally been informed of the boy's condition."

Nea could hear Quinnel shiver. "What did he say?"

"Truth be told, he seemed rather intrigued," said Pluto slyly, his voice drawing closer to the door. "Now get some rest, you look terrible."

The door swung open again and Pluto strode out. "He's all yours," he said giving Nea another of those horrible smiles and stumbled off down the walkway.

She gathered herself. Again, this nail, and Quinnel's father, what was all that about? He'd been ordered to kill his own father? She remembered what they'd spoken about over cards, how Quinnel's father had experimented on him, hurt him. Why wouldn't he kill a man like that?

You would. Wouldn't you?

Nea shook her head, now wasn't the time. She hoped Leo was all right, the way they'd been talking about him…

She knocked on the door. There was no reply. She knocked again, rapping her knuckles impatiently so Quinnel would know it was her. Still nothing. Cautiously, Nea turned the knob and found the door open. Quinnel was sitting at his desk, his back to the door. A familiar chill filled the room.

"Oi," she said awkwardly. He said nothing. Confused, Nea crept a little bit closer. Quinnel was slumped over his brooch, eyes locked on the small stone, unblinking. Nea watched for a few moments, but Quinnel didn't turn away. There was an unnatural shimmer in his eyes, the reflection of gem perfect inside those pale blue orbs.

Careful not to let any of the floorboards creak under her feet, Nea moved just close enough to peer over Quinnel's shoulder at the gemstone.

Then she was not on the ship at all. She was young, small, gathering wood outside a cabin in the snow. The chill bit into her bare cheeks but she ignored it, father had asked her to gather the firewood and she'd do just that. Carrying as much as she could in her little arms, she walked back towards the cabin. As she did the wind picked up and she stumbled. Nea fell face first into the snow, wood scattering. The warm trickle of blood combined with the stinging of the snow caused tears to form in her eyes. Then she felt her father's hand on her head. He stroked her hair and knelt to wipe her face. As she looked at him, she saw nothing but love in his eyes.

Nea lurched back, gasping for air. She was in Quinnel's room. There was no snow, no pain. Her father was gone.

Your father? That wasn't Da.

She slapped herself in the face, hard. She was on the Briar's ship, in Quinnel's room just as she remembered. But there had been snow, a cabin, what in the hell…

Then her eyes fell on Quinnel, staring into the gem. He'd heard nothing. The gem. Was that Quinnel, in the vision? Was *she* Quinnel? Had she seen what he was seeing now? Then something came drifting back into Nea's memory. A man in the crowd at Limani, a stone set in his forehead. She recalled the looks of terror on the faces of the oncoming soldiers, seeing some great horror that she could not.

At your interrogation, the soldier had said they'd seen things that weren't there.

Could something similar have happened to her? It had felt so real.

She shivered, the memory of snow still fresh in her mind, and watched Quinnel for a few minutes – there were tears in his eyes. She thought about what Pluto had said, about his father. Was that who she'd seen walking through the snow to comfort her? The same man he'd spoken about with such hate. Without thinking she rested a hand on his shoulder, overcome with an alien sympathy. A lump began to form in her throat and she turned away. She didn't have time for this. If what Pluto had said was true, then Leo was onboard. She needed to find him and get off this damn ship. Shaking her head clear again, Nea made for the door, stopping only to snatch the ring of keys from Quinnel's belt.

Get ahold of yourself!

She hated the emotion running through her, how vulnerable it made her feel. She wanted it to go away, leave her system like poison and let her think clearly again.

He's the last bloody person you need to feel sorry for on this damn ship.

Quinnel was her jailor, her enemy, yet she could feel the pain in his heart as if it was her own. She ruminated on this, making her way back up the stairs towards her room.

Cain made you soft. You were never like this before her.

As if in answer, she opened the door to her quarters and something inside her gave out. For lying on the bed, curled up in a ball, and wrapped in a dark green cloak, was Leo.

No...

For him to just be waiting for her there, it didn't seem real. He was covered in blood and dirt, but he wasn't injured. Sleeping peacefully as could be, Nea thought he looked different than when they'd met, in that other ship, in that other life. He looked healthier, older. His clothes were patched and worn but were unmistakably his own. The green cloak he wore was identical to the ones Nea had seen other vagabonds wearing in her trek across Fortuna. His bad arm was wrapped up in the cloak like a bandage.

"Seiyariu?"

At the sound of the door closing, Leo tried to sit up. He sat there blinking up at her confused and frightened. "Where am I? Who are...?" His eyes got very round. "Nea?"

"H... hey," she stammered, barely able to meet his gaze.

His big sad eyes brimmed with tears of disbelief. There was so much emotion in his face. It scared her. He looked like he wanted to throw his arms around her, but he was weak, terribly weak; as soon as he tried to get up he collapsed back on the bed.

"Here," said Nea grabbing the tray of food from the dresser. "Eat something."

He did, slowly, taking his eyes off Nea only to look around the cabin in bewilderment.

"Where are we?" He'd been brought aboard unconscious, she realized.

Nea sighed. "The Briar's floating city."

"How did you—"

"I'm a prisoner here," said Nea. "Like you."

"Oh," Leo looked around again. "It's a ship?"

Nea nodded, "I think so. Guess we can't meet anywhere else eh?"

"I never thought I'd see you again," he said desperately. "I... I wanted to, but..."

"Yeah me neither," she said awkwardly.

She wanted to do more, say more, but she didn't know what to say. What *could* she say? So much had happened since they last laid eyes on each other. They were different people now, maybe too different.

"I never got to thank you," he said, "I know how much you wanted to escape, all I did was slow you down."

Nea looked down at her feet. "I got away later, so don't worry about it."

"After I left you," Leo leaned back and stared at the ceiling. "I don't know, so much happened, it's as if…"

"As if we never really knew each other," Nea nodded.

Leo was bolstered by the fact that she felt the same. "How did you end up with the Briars?"

"Christ that's a long story,"

"Will you tell me it?"

"I dunno, I've heard you had a few adventures of your own. You want to tell me your story?"

"Then will you tell me yours?"

"Maybe," she smirked, "Depends on if yours is any good."

This got a real smile out of Leo; the warmth in his face was refreshing. Nea listened as he told her of Seiyariu, the strange but kind wanderer who spoke in riddles. He talked of the adventures they'd had wandering Fortuna, of the mariner Kokaleth, and his training as a vagabond. He told her of his dealings with Quinnel and the man who called himself Pluto, and the catacomb city of Adis, which was something Nea thought, existed only in stories to frighten children.

"That was when I got this," said Leo, removing his arm from the folds of his cloak.

Nea realized that what she'd taken as a bit of armor was actually Leo's hand. What had happened to it? She'd never seen any disease do that to a person.

"Are you… are you ok? What is that?"

"This is what we were looking for in Adis, it's a weapon, a parasite called Knail."

Knail. That was what those bastards were talking about.

"How'd it get stuck on your arm?"

"I had to make a choice," he said, picking up his story again, telling the entirety of his journey through Adis, Pluto's betrayal and the monster he'd brought forth.

"And you, this Knail… you gave it your arm?" she asked in amazement.

Leo nodded, "Not like I was really using it that much though."

"To make light?"

"Something like that, only denser, solid."

Nea shook her head. "Can you show me?"

Leo frowned, "I haven't been able to make it do anything since Adis. I'm so… so tired." With this he seemed to realize just how true the statement was. "I guess it doesn't matter much, they've got both me and Knail now, and Seiyariu too. I'm sorry. I'm happy to see you again," he muttered, his voice breaking. "But how could everything have gone so wrong?"

Nea moved over to sit beside him.

What in the hell are you doing?

Nea silenced the voice. She was the older one. Surely she could say something. "We're going to get out of here," she said lamely. And, with a great effort, Nea put an arm around his shoulder. He was embarrassed, but didn't pull away. "I'll be damned if they think they can keep both of us down."

Leo sniffed, "You think so?"

"Yeah I do. Should I tell my story now?"

"Will you?"

"Alright."

She made to pull away but the kid held on, so she did too. And she began to talk. Skirting around the more sensitive details, she gave Leo her story, as much as she could. He listened quietly through the whole thing. Despite everything, Nea felt a strange feeling of comfort that she hadn't felt in a long time. She wanted to blame the encounter with Quinnel's gem but that wasn't it. She'd been vulnerable, but that wasn't the reason she had her arm around the kid, spilling her guts. They were prisoners, trapped in an impossible machine, crewed by an army of murderers. But they were together and somehow that was enough.

41
Rekindling

Leo was dead tired but he didn't want to fade away into nightmares and wake up a prisoner again in the morning. He wanted to stay with Nea. When they'd first begun speaking it felt like there was a barrier between the two of them. He had wanted nothing more than to tear it down so they could talk as real friends, but they weren't friends. They knew so little about each other; all they had was the memory of a single week.

The more they shared, the more Leo felt the ice slowly beginning to melt. With the older boy's arm comfortably around his shoulders, Leo, despite everything that had happened, felt safer and more content than he had in ages.

Nea's story was an extravagant one, though Leo could tell he did his best to make it sound less exciting that it was.

Leo took a moment to digest all this. "You saved Lady Cain, just like you saved me."

"I suppose I did," he shifted awkwardly. "You'd have done the same for that vagabond of yours right?"

Leo nodded fervently. "And the Briars, they want to unify the Archipelago."

Nea nodded. "That's what that old ghoul in Ventain told me, yeah. That explains what all the weapons are for."

"Doesn't explain why they're looking for me though."

"Don't have a clue there, sorry."

"It's ok," said Leo. "How did you get in here anyway?"

"This is my room," Nea laughed. "Must've been their idea to leave you here."

"Where were you then?" Leo asked.

"They said I have the run of the place, don't try to stop me going anywhere except on deck," he replied.

"So you've explored?"

"Not much else to do."

"D… do you know where they might be keeping Seiyariu?"

The older boy thought about this. "I'd say he's probably in the brig. He sounds pretty dangerous, doubt they'll let him go where he pleases. If you tell me what he looks like I can find him, tell him where you are."

"Can I come with you?"

Nea raised an eyebrow. "You sure? You look like you're about to keel over."

Leo was sure, desperately sure. "I don't want to be by myself… here." He added just to get Nea to stop looking at him like that.

For a moment he expected the older boy to sneer in disbelief, or take it in stride and laugh it away like Seiyariu. So he was taken aback when Nea nodded and got to his feet. "Yeah, come on then."

The two of them crept out onto the landing, though there was no need, it was all but deserted.

"Can you believe this?" said Nea.

"It's huge," said Leo staring across the cavernous hold. He had no idea a ship could be this gigantic. The insides weren't consistent with anything he'd ever read or seen. Nea stopped to lean against the rail. Leo imitated him, staring over the edge open-mouthed; it was such a long way down. The lifts and walkways, rigging within the ship itself.

"You should've seen it from the outside," said Nea. "Doesn't make sense, the whole thing should just sink. Seems this Beljhar is a bit of a showoff."

Leo's stomach turned, he still hadn't quite come to terms with the fact that they were, in fact, captives of Djeng Beljhar, and that, whatever purpose Beljhar had in mind for him, he would find out soon enough.

Nea noticed his troubled expression and put a hand on his shoulder. "Hey, stop worrying, let's go find your vagabond."

"Do you think he's ok?"

"Sure!" said Nea, overselling his confidence ever so slightly. "Come on, we'll use those poles."

Leo looked down at the bowels of the ship, it was a terribly long way to anything resembling a floor. Then he looked back at Nea, all swagger, no fear to be seen, and smiled. He knew that the older boy was trying to help him, but he appreciated it nonetheless.

"Want me to go first, or do you?"

"I'll do it."

Nea's confidence, it was infectious.

"Know how to hold on?"

Leo blinked, "Is there a trick?"

"Kind of, you need to wrap your legs round it and keep your arms like this," he demonstrated. "Let yourself go but not too fast or stopping will hurt like a son of a bitch."

"Ok," Leo said, trying not to look nervous.

"Go on then, I'll meet you down there, remember to get off at the third landing. Get off mind, don't let go, that's important," he smiled.

It felt like miscounting stairs, the twist in the stomach as he began to fall. His new claws were a hindrance the entire way down, making a terrible screeching noise whenever they struck the metal on the way down and sending sparks flying if they scraped too much. But the ability to move and use his arm again, excused any hinderance the claws might've added.

When he reached the third landing, he pulled himself to a stop and hopped back onto the walkway, certain he'd probably woken up everyone on board. A couple seconds later Nea came speeding down, far more gracefully, to meet him.

"Brig's that way."

Leo kept pace, tired as he was, the idea of seeing his teacher was more than enough to keep him going. It was strange how brave he felt even though Seiyariu wasn't around.

Finally they reached a part of the ship with no poles, or lifts, and hardly any walkways. There were bars on the windows here, just slightly higher than he was, but Nea could see inside if he stood on his toes.

"That one's asleep, can't tell if it's him or not," said Nea, squinting.

"It's not."

"Your vagabond not sleep?"

"Not in a place like this he wouldn't."

"I've gotta tell you, I didn't believe it when they first told me you'd taken up with a vagabond," said Nea, peering through the bars of another door.

Leo smiled, remembering how he'd looked when Nea had first found him. What an odd way of remembering it that was, surely they'd just been in the same place. Nea hadn't *found* anybody.

"I'm different now."

"Too right," said Nea. "I'm glad, sounds like you had a hell of an adventure." He strode across the walkway to the other side of the brig. "Wish I could've been there to see it myself."

"Sounds like you had as much of an adventure as I did," said Leo, hurrying to keep up.

"Maybe," Nea shrugged and continued down the line.

They went up and down the cells for a half hour but Seiyariu was nowhere to be found. Leo was getting more and more tired and it wasn't lost on Nea.

"Hey, let's go back."

Leo frowned, "But…"

"Hold on," Nea frowned, staring into, what felt like, the thousandth room. "Your Seiyariu, is he tall? Dark hair? Scruffy like an old scarecrow?"

Leo nodded, eyes wide.

"Then I think this might be him. Hang on," Nea rattled the bars. "Oi! Wake up you old—"

"And who are you?" Came an unmistakable voice from within.

Leo tugged on Nea's shirt, "That's him!" he said, trying to keep his voice from breaking.

"Leo?" Came the vagabond's voice through the bards

"Seiyariu!" Leo called back.

"Are you sure?" Nea took another look the through the bars. "Doesn't look like much."

"Nea!" Leo said, half laughing as Nea took out a ring of keys and began fussing with the lock. "They're Quinnel's." He muttered with a little smile. "He's got a few but I'll bet… there we go." The lock clicked open and the two of them slipped inside.

Leo had expected a cell, but the room within was almost identical to theirs. Same twin beds, same dresser, illuminated by those mysterious gemstone lanterns. It had a tiny window looking out into the dark spray of the nighttime waves and, sitting on the bed, lost in thought, was—

"Seiyariu!"

Leo tackled the man out of bed, getting his teacher in a furious embrace, trying and failing to hide his tears from Nea.

"Leo, thank God you're unhurt." Seiyariu's eyes shot to Nea. "Hello," he said, looking the boy up and down. Nea shifted uncomfortably. "And who are you?"

"Seiyariu, this is Nea."

"Nea," Seiyariu said. "The one who helped you escape?"

Leo nodded, unsure what Seiyariu was going to do.

The vagabond was silent for a moment. Then Seiyariu let go of Leo and got to his feet. Nea stood his ground and offered a hand, which Seiyariu shook. "How can I ever thank you," he said, smiling.

"It's… it's nothing," said Nea.

"I am Seiyariu, I suppose Leo's told you that." Seiyariu sat down on the bed and Leo joined him. Nea planted himself on the floor. "So, Nea," said Seiyariu. "How was it that you came to be here?"

"Same as you I reckon, made some bad choices."

"He was tracking them," Leo offered.

Nea nodded. "I was in the auction the Briars ruined back in Limani. Got recruited by the Captain of the Royal Guard. She thought I could help her find where the Briars were operating from."

"Maria Cain?" Seiyariu raised an eyebrow.

Nea nodded. "You know her?"

"I do," Seiyariu replied.

"How?" asked Nea. "She told me vagabonds were nothing but criminals and vigilantes."

"Yes, that sounds like her. You see Kokaleth and I…" Seiyariu was determined to slide his way out of this line of questioning, "…let's say we've had a few run-ins with Maria over our storied careers."

"Running afoul of the army, vagabond?" Nea asked snidely. "I thought your type were supposed to be the beloved guardians of the downtrodden."

"Sometimes," Seiyariu laughed. "We do what we, as individuals, think is right, often that conflicts with the interests of the powers that be. You'd be amazed at how few Royal Guardsman appreciate having a group of dirty gadabouts serving vigilante justice wherever they go."

"You talking about the vagabonds or the Briars?" Nea asked.

Seiyariu's eyes sparkled. "Aren't you a clever thing?"

Leo let himself smile again, and even Nea gave an approving sort of sniff.

"Kokaleth, the mariner yeah? Want to explain to me how something this big slipped the watch of someone who spends all his time in the water?"

Seiyariu shrugged. "I wish I had a better answer for you, but in truth this is the first time I'm seeing this or any of its like before."

"Well then, how on earth did the... Leo what's that look mean?"

Leo became aware that his smile had become a rather hysterical smile. He looked away quickly. He wasn't sure what had come over him, but having both of them, together like this. It made him feel wonderful.

"How long have you been here Nea?" Seiyariu asked, ignoring Leo's grin.

Nea shrugged. "Long enough, but I haven't found any way out if that's what you're asking."

"Well I imagine you wouldn't be sitting with us here if you had," replied Seiyariu.

"I do have these," Nea offered, holding up the ring of keys.

"That's certainly a start," said Seiyariu.

Leo was watching them back and forth, doing his best to keep up. Prisoner? Was he really? It hadn't quite sunk in. He was a little bit too warm, comfortable, and happy to think about such things. He wanted to sleep, he could feel his body fighting him, calling him away, but he fought to stay awake and listen.

Sure enough, his eyes began fluttering as sleep finally overtook him. Nea and Seiyariu were still alert, still talking, but he had no strength left, so he slipped away.

42
First Impressions

"I think he's out."

"So he is," Seiyariu let Leo slide off of his shoulder and threw a blanket over him. "Knail's left him very weak."

Nea sized up the vagabond. He wasn't quite what she'd expected. He just looked like any of the hundreds of beggars and vagrants she'd seen over the course of her life, lanky, with sunken eyes, and long dirty hair. Still, there was a strange way about how he carried himself, she couldn't place it, but something about the man was steady, reliable. Perhaps that's why Leo had taken to him so quickly.

"Not what you expected?"

"How the hell did you know I was thinking that?"

"It's what everyone thinks," he said, not unkindly. "I'm an oddball sure, but I think you'll find the wandering lifestyle attracts oddballs."

Seiyariu stood up and crossed to his dresser, where a pitcher of wine had been left. She watched him pour a glass, silently wishing it was something stronger.

"Shall we go out to the landing?" asked Seiyariu, "I'd rather not wake him up."

"Sure."

There was something off about this wanderer, but she couldn't put her finger on what it was. He was like a caricature stepped clean from a book or a song. What was he hiding? What wasn't he hiding?

Give him a chance damn it, Leo likes him.

After all she wasn't in much of a position to judge someone for keeping secrets. So the two of them leaned against the railing, vagabond absently sipping at his wine.

"I want to thank you."

"Why's that?" asked Nea, unable to keep the suspicion from her voice.

"Because without you, I don't think Leo would've ever trusted anyone ever again."

Nea's face suddenly became very hot and she looked away. "All I did was give him a drink of water and a kick in the ass."

"Never mind sacrificing your own freedom so he could escape." Seiyariu shot her a look.

"You give me too much credit," she said, still avoiding Seiyariu's gaze.

"I don't think so." said Seiyariu. "I think that everything, absolutely everything that we do has meaning, both to ourselves and the world."

What's he getting at?

"You sound like a preacher."

"Maybe I do," Seiyariu shrugged. "You're not the first to say that. But think about it for a moment. Was that boy you met the same boy from the ship, truly?"

Nea thought about it, then shook her head. "You two have been through a lot."

"Every great fire needs a match, a spark. A kick in the ass, I believe you so aptly put it."

Nea blushed again. "Thanks."

"Not at all," Seiyariu beamed at her, "Just the truth. Now tell me Nea, where were you headed before Maria picked you up?"

Nea shrugged. "Conoscenzia." She wasn't sure why she was being so honest with this man. But despite his mysterious ways he was rather easy to talk to. "I've been trying to get there since before I even got picked up by the grassers back on the isles."

"Was it why you left home?"

Why answer? It's none of his damn business.

"I suppose," she said, ignoring the voice.

"What exactly is in Conoscenzia, if I might ask?"

Nea thought about this, the only real answer she had was, "Freedom."

"Seems to me like you'd gotten that already."

Nea shook her head. "Not, not that kind of freedom, I mean freedom to... to live you know?"

"Was someone keeping you from living back home?"

"I guess you could say that."

He didn't press the issue further, knowing that he was drawing near to a door that was locked far too tight for anyone to get in.

Be careful with this one, or else he'll see right through you.

"We create paradises in our minds when we're confined," he said, Nea stiffened but Seiyariu wasn't even looking at her. His eyes were glazed over, lost in some memory. It made him look like a completely different person. "Sometimes that paradise isn't all we make it out to be, once we finally get there."

"That happen to you, did it?"

"You could say that," Seiyariu nodded. "And I don't think I'd like it to happen to you. That's why, if I might be formal, I'll ask you come along with me and Leo."

"What?" Nea laughed. Her, go along with them on their mad adventure across Fortuna?

No chance in hell.

But that wasn't what she said. What she said instead was, "You want me to be a vagabond?"

"I suppose that would be part of it."

"I don't even know where you're going!" said Nea trying to make the idea sound more ludicrous than it was.

Stop considering it for God's sake.

"Well before we were sidetracked we were on our way to Equius, to visit the King, bring him news of Knail and the Briars, perhaps see Captain Cain…" he trailed off, eyebrows raised.

Nea glowered at him. "I see what you're doing. You want me to come along for his sake. Think it'll do him some good to have a friend?"

"It'd do us all some good to have a friend."

"Stop it."

"I'm very serious Nea. There is something about you that lights a fire under Leo and there is something about Leo that lights a fire under you. I saw it from the moment you two came in the room, even the way he moved was different."

"What makes you think *I'm* different?"

"He doesn't make you feel different?"

"I've only just seen him again," said Nea. "How in the hell am I supposed to answer something like that?"

"Because it's a question you answered the moment you handed him that water. You saw a pain down in his soul, and you recognized it."

Despite her trepidations about Seiyariu, the sincerity behind these words was palpable. He was right. She'd seen something familiar in Leo. Why hadn't she realized it? Nea remembered those sad dark eyes staring at her through the bars. They were like that of a wounded animal, alone and backed into a corner to die. She'd seen that look in the mirror many times.

"I'll think about it."

"That's all I ask. You don't have to answer until after we're out of this mess. For we will, of course, be out of this mess soon. Don't you think?"

Nea frowned. "I haven't had much luck so far I'm afraid."

"Could you walk me through what you've learned in your time here?"

"Bloody nothing," said Nea. "There's a library, baths, an armory."

"An armory?"

"Yeah, you reckon your sword and summoning salts are there?"

Seiyariu shook his head. "After his encounter with Kokaleth, Quinnel will no doubt have informed Beljhar we're working with a mariner. He's likely destroyed the salts."

"What makes you so sure?"

"I continue to underestimate him, I'm trying to correct that."

"So what are we going to do then?"

"I'll think of something. In the meantime, I want you to listen Nea. I am quite certain that you and Leo will be kept alive. But if I am not so lucky—"

"Whoa," Nea cut him off. "Where did this come from?"

"Just a precaution. If something happens to me, there is something I need to give to you."

She raised an eyebrow. "What do you mean?"

"Just something that needs safe keeping."

"Oh? And how come they didn't take it off you if it's so bloody important?"

"It is only important to the three of us." From his sleeve Seiyariu produced something tiny – a bit of bone hewn into a flute, barely longer than her middle finger.

She was even more confused now and more than a little skeptical. "What's it for?"

"I can't say," said Seiyariu. "But when it matters, I promise you both will know."

Nea narrowed her eyes, what was he playing at? Despite her trepidations she found herself taking the flute, "Just until we're away from this place, got it?"

"Naturally, once you're on the road with us I've no reason to leave it with you," Seiyariu said with a grin.

"You're a stubborn bastard you know that?" said Nea, rolling her eyes.

"So I've been told."

43
The Architect

No DREAMS OF deserts or skeletal children found Leo that night. It was strange that he should feel so content while having failed in his journey. All the same, he slept peacefully and couldn't help but smile to himself as he opened his eyes to see Nea, bustling around the room.

"Morning," he said, tossing Leo an apple. "Quinnel came by."

"What?" Leo took a bite of the rich fruit. How Beljhar managed to keep fruit fresh on this leviathan was beyond him but it tasted wonderful all the same.

"Yeah, while you were sleeping. I got rid of him, but he says he's coming by again in a bit and that you're to be presentable," he rolled his eyes. "Whatever that means."

Leo faltered slightly. "What do you think he wants?"

"Probably to introduce you to Beljhar."

Leo sat bolt upright, all sense of serenity escaping in an instant. "What?"

"Relax," Nea said, not unkindly. "We both knew this was going to happen sooner or later."

"Will you…"

"Yeah, I'll come with you," said Nea, averting his gaze coolly. "Can't have you getting into trouble and messing up my clever plans."

"You have clever plans?"

"Never you mind," he smirked. "The baths are down two levels, big wooden doors, you can't miss them."

"Baths?" Leo blinked, surely not.

"You'll see."

Leo shrugged and tumbled out of bed. At this point he doubted anything would surprise him.

"Thanks Nea," he said, but the other boy waved it away like it was nothing.

"Say Leo," Nea asked carefully, "Seiyariu ever mention anything about a flute to you?"

"A flute? No why? Did the two of you talk?"

"A little yeah, after you went to sleep."

Leo wanted to know more but he was acutely aware of just how much filth and grime he was coated in. He hadn't had a chance to get clean since before Adis. "Right, are you coming as well?"

"I went when you were asleep. Remember that pole from last night, it's two doors past that," said Nea, not looking at him.

"Alright, I'll be back soon," said Leo, closing the door behind him.

Leo knew he wasn't always the most perceptive person; he'd been getting better at it but still there were things that just slipped past him. But even he had noticed the grease and blood matting his friend's hair, the grime on his cheeks. He clearly hadn't washed in days. Leo didn't really care, but why would Nea lie to him about that?

He found the baths without much trouble. They were just as ornate and impossible as the rest of the ship; the wood glazed in white, giving the impression of marble, though it was probably to stop the boards from warping. A round metal tub, big enough for a dozen men and full of steaming hot water, was set into the floor, adding to the illusion of carved stone. Mirrors lined every inch of the wall and ceiling, giving the place an eerie, infinite feeling. Pumps, buckets, and drains were lined up around the mirrors. A bench, glazed like the floor, circled the room. A few sleepy looking souls were soaking in the boiling water, while another was dressing along-side the wall of mirrors.

Leo sat on the bench and began to undress. Knail made it far more difficult than it used to be, he had to make sure not to shred his shirt to pieces as he drew his arm out of it. He paused for a second, realizing just how sharp his claws were. The Briars had taken all their weapons, but this… If given the chance, Leo could fight back, even kill if he needed to. The idea made his stomach twist. Could he kill again to help them escape? Would he even get the chance?

The water that came out of the pump was freezing but wonderful. Leo hadn't realized how stiff his body had been. The icy water, then the boiling warmth of the tub invigorated every inch of him, letting all the tension flow out of his arms, legs, his back and finally his neck. He scrubbed until not a trace of the catacomb city remained on him, except for Knail. It felt so strange to be able to wash his right arm again without worrying about the pain. When he was done, Leo lay back, letting the water carry him somewhere else, anywhere else, with Nea, Seiyariu, Kokaleth. He was with his friends; he was safe and—

"Be careful now," the voice came drifting in, unwelcome in his reverie. "The water is quite relaxing, but take care not to drift off."

Leo opened his eyes, there was only one man left in the bath now, sitting at the bench, disrobing. He was slim of shoulder and waist, making him look almost like a woman. The man had dark almond shaped eyes, and the amber skin of a full-blooded Infernian. His face was soft, without lines or scars, his bottom lip curled ever so slightly. His slick, black hair pressed tight to his skull. Tossing his garments aside, he stepped over to the tub. In contrast to his face, his slender body was a tapestry of scars. As he sank into the water across from Leo, he saw the gemstone embedded in the man's forehead. A shard of onyx, pure black, it sat in the center of his brow sparkling like a third eye.

"You like that?" he laughed. His voice was rich like honey, and just as sweet.

"What?"

"The Urna, the gem, you're staring at it."

"Oh, I'm sorry."

He waved the apology away. "It's not quite something you see every day is it?" Leo shook his head, avoiding the man's gaze. "What is your name?"

"Leo."

The man's smile broadened, "I take it you're *the* Leo, yes?" Leo nodded. "How are you finding the place?"

Leo frowned, what a strange question. "I'm a prisoner," he said flatly.

"Oh, yes I suppose that puts a damper on things. We had wanted to invite you more politely…"

"You tried to kidnap me from the slave auctions in Limani?"

"Yes that, it would've been much smoother that way. But it doesn't do to dwell."

"Where…where are we?" Leo asked.

The man's smile didn't falter. "Safe. We're quite thrilled to have you aboard you know."

"This is where you all live then?"

"Yes, this is home," he said looking around. "For many here, it's the first place they've truly been able to call a home. And a good one. It could be yours too."

Leo narrowed his eyes. "I told Quinnel I wasn't interested. What do you all want from me?"

The stranger cocked an eyebrow. "No one has told you? How odd. You're supposed to be an honored guest."

"Pluto tried to kill me!"

The man's face darkened, "I'm very sorry about that."

He truly looked it too.

"I hope I can convince you that Mister Pluto does not represent all of us. He's a man of simple desires, and those desires can prevent him from seeing the larger picture."

"What picture is that?" Leo demanded.

The man didn't answer. Instead he looked Leo up and down, memorizing him. Leo shifted, uncomfortably aware of his nakedness. He sank a little deeper into the water, wishing that the man would stop.

"One of your parents was Infernian?"

Leo shrugged, that wasn't much of a secret. "I didn't know them."

"Ah, forgive me, I'm being tactless. It's a terrible thing, not to know your parents. I left my family when I was quite young too, you see."

"Why?" Leo couldn't keep from asking.

"For the same reason many other Briars did. I was taken."

He flashed the nuptial, a patch of pure black against his soft skin. "By the slaving companies, yes. When I was a child they ran rampant over the southwest coast of Inferno, picking off entire villages of people at once. We were put on boats, whipped, beaten, scared, and then sent west. Fortuna and Conoscenzia were at war, you see, and one of the King's generals suggested to his young majesty that perhaps a deal could be struck with the Grassen Trading Company, to throw numbers at a dreadful technological disadvantage. A little army of children, I and twenty thousand like me were marched to the western shores. That was where we died."

"The Dashing of the Innocents." Leo's eyes were wide, remembering Pluto's words. Was it all true? The King, the one he was going to meet with Seiyariu, had sent slaves, children, to die in his war? The idea made him sick. Did Seiyariu known about this? Did anyone? Leo couldn't imagine a population willing to serve a king who'd committed such atrocities. Despite himself the man across from him had at least earned his sympathy. "I'm sorry."

"It was a long time ago, but we must bear the scars of our pasts openly, if only as a warning."

"I can't believe anyone would do such a thing."

"Don't you? I find that people are capable of a great many fantastic cruelties. That is why we exist, you understand."

"We?"

"The Briars. That's why this place was built Leo, the Briars founded it. It is a refuge, an oasis for lost, enslaved souls like you and me."

"Nea told me that the Briars like to say things like that," he replied. "It's not going to work on me. I'm not lost and I'm not a slave anymore."

"Not in the literal sense perhaps, but tell me, is there not something else that curtails your freedom, prevents you from living as you want?"

"I don't know what you're talking about." Leo looked away. What did this man mean?

"It doesn't do to live in fear Leo, especially for one as young as you. You can throw up all the defenses you like but, in the end, you are still bound by the shackles of the mind." The gem on his forehead glinted.

It was time for him to leave. Leo pulled himself from the water when a flash of light erupted from the stone. Then Leo was sitting on the top of an old stone church looking over at the abbey that had been his entire world. A hand slipped into his and he turned to see that he wasn't alone at all. Nico was beside him, just as he always was, clasping his hand and smiling at him, as they watched the sunset together.

Then it was gone, all of it and he was on the floor of the baths, gasping and choking. He'd been swept away, just as he had when he looked inside the dying man's brooch. Only now, it was his own illusion that he had been wrenched out of. He wanted to go back, to feel his brother's hand in his once more.

"You... what... what did you do to me?"

"I gave you peace," said the man, standing up to dry off. "That's all. A little rest from the fear and confusion that lurks in the minds of men."

"It's a trick," gasped Leo. "That wasn't real."

"Wasn't it?" The man's gemstone flashed again.

This time Leo was in a darkened room with the curtains drawn. Nico was in the bed in front of him. He didn't look like Nico anymore. Leo saw none of his brother in that skeletal face. Slowly, one of the sisters drew the sheets up over his unmoving form.

Leo crashed back to reality again, tears streaming down his face. He swallowed, half-retching for air as he looked around madly.

The Infernian man stepped from the bath and began to dress. Leo just lay there on the floor, pulling his knees to his chest as if to hide from the world. He couldn't stop shaking. How? How could this man know about that? Leo had never told anyone.

"I don't mean to scare you Leo, merely to show you that I understand the pain you've gone through. I promise my intentions have never been to harm you. You are as important to my plan as Knail is. You're a boy after my own heart."

"Who are you?" Leo managed weakly.

His fingers clasping around the door, the strange man turned back and smiled again at Leo. "Welcome to my home." Then the door closed, and Djeng Beljhar was gone.

44
Omnivorous

Nea was busy with her breakfast when Leo burst back into the room. His face was white, and his eyes were staring blankly ahead, not seeing anything. He bumped into the wall and collapsed to the floor, shaking.

"Leo what in the hell happened to you?" She was beside him instantly. His hair was still wet, long red locks dripping in front of his face, but he didn't notice. Nea had never seen anyone like this bef—

No.

That was a lie, she had seen this exact expression before, on this ship. The glassy eyes. "Say something please," she whispered, her voice much too high.

"Nico," he whispered softly. "I saw Nico."

"Who is Nico?" Was Leo sick? She put her hand to his forehead without thinking and he threw himself back, resisting the touch.

"He was there."

"What are you talking about Leo?" said Nea, keeping her composure as best she could, "Who was there?"

"Beljhar," said Leo.

"What?"

"He's not like I thought. Nea, he knows me. He knows everything about me."

"Focus Leo," Nea grabbed him, forcing him to look her in the eye. "Slow down and tell me what happened."

Leo drew in a rasping breath. What on earth had he seen that could make him like this?

"Beljhar was in there, he was in the bath, w… waiting for me."

"Did he hurt you?" Nea could feel the beginnings of rage inside her.

"I'm afraid," whispered Leo. "He said that was why it worked on me."

"You don't have to be afraid of anything Leo, I'm here with you, okay, and nothing is going to hurt you."

"But I am," said Leo holding his head in his hands. "I'm afraid. I've been afraid my whole life."

"Enough," snapped Nea, dragging Leo to his feet and helping him to the bed. "You're not making any sense, here drink this." She passed him a glass of water. He did as she ordered, choking it down.

"Now," she sat down beside him and looked him dead in the eyes. "Concentrate on me, I'm real, I promise. What did Beljhar do to you? Did he make you look into one of those gems?"

This brought Leo's eyes back into focus. "Gems," he said hurriedly, worried he might lose his nerve. "Illusions, in the stones."

"Yes, that's right Leo, there are illusions in the Briar's brooches. Is that what he did to you? Made you look at one of those?"

Leo shook his head. "I don't really know, it wasn't the brooch like the others have, it was a light, from a stone in—"

"In his forehead," Nea finished, remembering that face in the crowd. The Infernian man with the gem who'd made the guards run from nothing.

"He… he kept talking about fear."

Nea gave Leo a hard look. He was still shaking, Beljhar must've shown him something bad, but she didn't ask what, the pain on his face was all the answer she needed.

Bastard better hope you don't get your hands on him!

"It's not just fear though," Leo continued, his voice deathly quiet. "He showed me something, something I've never told anyone."

Nea put a hand on Leo's shoulder. "Lie down and try to relax," she told Leo. "I'll be back."

"Where are you going?"

"To get your vagabond."

Nea was out of the room and running, she leapt onto the pole and slid down, as fast as she could. Her mind was racing.

His face, my god, the look on his face.

Nea dropped to the ground and sprinted along the walkway. She flew, pushing aside anyone and everyone that got in the way. The brig was as empty as it had been the night before, identical rooms lined up with not a soul in sight. Nea looked around frantically,

Which one was it? They all look the damn same. There!

She flung the door open. A man was standing against the wall, but it was not Seiyariu. Before she could react he was between her and the door.

"Close," said Pluto. He turned to look at her; rather, he pointed his face in her direction. Leo had said that Pluto just played at being blind, and that the walking stick he carried was actually a weapon. She was trapped in a room with a delver, an armed delver, and nothing but her fists.

"I'm glad we met last night, it saves us the trouble of introductions. All the better, I'm not particularly in the mood."

"What are you doing here? Where's the vagabond? The hell do you want?"

"I don't want anything," said Pluto, leaning on his staff. "Mister Beljhar is ready to see our little crimson mutt and I've been asked to ensure it goes off without any trouble."

Nea felt a sinking in the pit of her stomach.

Damn it all.

They had trapped her. Was Leo on his way to Beljhar now, alone? Nea dug her nails into her palms.

You promised him.

"If it's any comfort I've no desire to be a child-minder. This is likely to be the absolute nadir of my duties amongst the Briars, but I won't pretend I don't know why they chose me."

"What are you doing to him?" Nea desperately tried to keep her voice from shaking.

"Merely helping him to grow into his own man. Free from the worries of—"

"Stop playing!" Her nails bit into her palms even harder, drawing blood.

Pluto grinned. "I've seen the look in his eyes, the same one that resides in yours. The haunted look of a person who has seen too much, too soon."

"You don't know a damn thing about me, or him!"

"Perhaps, but how well do you know Leo, truly? What makes you think he won't fall to Mister Beljhar's influence, he's not nearly as stubborn as you."

"He's not a fool," Nea snarled. "He wouldn't…"

"Wouldn't he?" Pluto's head lolled to one side. "You don't think—"

Throwing caution to the winds Nea threw a right cross at Pluto's face. Only to have her legs cut out from under her with one swing of his staff. The next thing she knew she was on her back with the staff pressing hard into her chest.

"A word on polite conversation: generally it's rude to interrupt someone, particularly someone like me. Allow me to let you in on a bit of secret Nea. I'm nothing like that preening little albino you're so fond of. I would be more than happy to kill you this instant should you not cooperate."

"You'll wish you had!" spat Nea.

Pluto roared with laughter. "I think you and I are going to get on famousl—"

Nea kicked him hard in the knee. He stumbled back, and she sprang at him, trying to jam her finger into his concealed eyes. She was met with a blow to the gut and then one to the side of the head, sending her stumbling back to the foot of the bed in a daze.

"So," Pluto wiped a bit of blood from his face. She'd missed his eye, cut him just below it. "He told you about my condition."

Nea didn't answer. She stared at the delver, measuring the range of Pluto's staff. He wouldn't catch her with it again. She was about to move when she realized that a strange rustling sound could be heard coming from under the bed.

"What else did Leo tell you about me?" asked Pluto, a wicked smile on his lips. Nea's whole form tensed, every hair on her body standing on end.

Nea looked him right where his eyes should be – refusing to let him see her fear. "He told me you like to play with bugs."

Pluto laughed. "I do." Then he flicked his staff and cockroaches, thousands of them, came pouring out from under the bed, from the cracks of the floor, from inside the dresser, everywhere. They came scurrying from their hiding places, tumbling over each other in their eagerness. In a matter of seconds the room filled with a squirming mass of insects. They closed ranks around her; she was stranded on a tiny island in a sea of the little beasts. Pluto strode forward, the waves of insects parting to let him through. He walked right up to Nea, the cockroaches sealing the two of them in the center of the room.

This is mad, everything about it, mad!

Nea wanted to move, to strike again, but she was frozen where she stood, completely at the mercy of a power she didn't understand.

"You know, I find that my little many-legged friends aren't that different from you or me. Take these roaches for example, they're not predators, nor are they prey. They eat whatever is to be found in their environment, anything and everything." He leaned in close to whisper in her ear. "Even each other."

Nea shoved him off and threw another punch, all sense abandoned. She wanted his blood, wanted him to stop looking at her like that. Her fist caught him full in the face this time, moments before she was hit from all sides by a wave of roaches. She was buried beneath a sea of writhing insects, desperately keeping her mouth and eyes shut tight, she braced herself. The horrible sensations of tiny legs on her body, she was thrown this way and that, all the while thrashing about in desperation. Leo needed her. Seiyariu needed her. But Nea was afraid, she was afraid of the power behind them, the relentless force with which they moved, something that wasn't from the world, as she understood it. Something far stronger than she could ever hope to be. The thousands of roaches crawled, madly scratching and biting every bit of her they could reach. The contact was so violating, so overwhelming, that Nea felt her senses give out.

She wasn't sure how long this torture went on, only that, when it became too much, at the moment she was ready to give up and die, it stopped. Nea wasn't sure if she had passed out. She wasn't even sure which direction was up, but the crawling sensations on her skin were now only in her imagination. The room was empty.

Nea felt as though she was twelve years old again, all the helplessness rushing back.

Stupid little girl.

She was bleeding from a host of scratches and bites on her arms and legs, as well as a deep one on her forehead. The ring of keys she'd stolen from Quinnel was gone. She felt sick. She hugged her legs close to her chest, trying to think of what to do.

You weak, frightened little thing. You can't even help your friends when they need you. Dress up and bind all you want, you're still pathetic as you ever were.

45
Red

LEO'S MIND AND heart were racing in panic. Beljhar hadn't even lifted a finger but he'd taken Leo apart. An illusion, how in God's name did you fight something like that? What scared him was how much he longed to be back on that rooftop, with Nico, whether it was real or not. And the image of Nico's corpse... Leo wasn't sure he could ever face anything like that again. Leo didn't have to wait long for a knock on the door, but it was not Nea waiting for him on the landing.

"It's time," said Quinnel.

No.

Quinnel gave a signal and two men strode into the room and seized him by the shoulders – he tried to struggle but was no match. They marched him from the room. Leo was at the mercy of the Briars, utterly helpless. This was all happening too fast. He tried to get away but the grips of the Briars were just too strong. Leo cursed being small, being weak. With every fiber of his being he tried to ignite Knail as he had in Adis, to call on that power. But it was out of reach, Knail didn't so much as spark and the Briars escorted him onto a lift.

Quinnel stepped in after him and nodded to his men who stayed behind and started working the ropes that controlled their ascent. Leo watched the men below grow smaller as they rose up through the ship. He was alone with Quinnel now. His thoughts now frantic, energy or no energy Knail was sharp as any knife. What if...?

"Don't try it," Quinnel muttered. "You know I'm faster. Besides, remember what he showed you? Don't you want to go back there?" Leo did, more than anything else in the world.

The lift rose out of the innards of the ship and up past the deck. It was a grey, pale day, with no trace of the sky to be seen. There was so much fog he still couldn't see much of the forward and aft levels either. As they rose farther, past the sails, the rigging got in the way, blocking any view he might've had of the ship. The lift carried them up the mast towards the crow's nest, which was as big around as a castle turret. Quinnel tossed Leo in and climbed after him. The nest was pristine, polished, and deserted, save for one. Djeng Beljhar stood leaning against the rail, looking out across the dark foggy sea.

"Hello again Leo." His voice invited no fear, no panic, yet Leo found himself unable to move. "I'm sorry for the shock I gave you earlier," he said, not taking his eyes off the cloudy sky. "I'm dreadfully inept at first impressions."

Leo found he could barely speak. "Y … you made me see things, like in the stones."

"Leave us Quinnel." Beljhar smiled and bid Leo come stand by him.

Quinnel bowed. "Sir." He hopped back up onto the lift and tugged sharply on the ropes, dropping out of sight.

When they were alone, Beljhar continued, "Just my way of giving back." He pointed to the gem in his forehead, "An artifact of the old world, not unlike the one you have latched to your arm. It allows me to project images into the minds of others."

"Images?"

"Anything at all. Though I must imagine them myself first."

"How… how do you know about Nico?"

"I know a lot about you Leo, I've been searching for you for so long. Our agents went to the abbey, but you were already gone. It was there I learned what happened to Nico. I want you to know that I'm truly sorry. He would've been as welcome here as you. If you'd like, I can make you a stone to carry his image wherever you go."

"I…" Leo wanted all of these more than he could possibly admit, but that feeling of the gem flashing, fingers in his brain, it haunted him. "Why are you doing this? What do you want from me?"

"Quinnel and Nea have told you about my crusade I'm sure."

"What does it have to do with me?" Leo found himself pleading, desperate for an answer after all this time.

"I'm going to tell you," said Beljhar. "I don't believe in keeping secrets. But first, how is your arm?"

"It… it doesn't hurt anymore."

"I'm glad to hear it. Knail can reshape itself to replace damaged or wounded body parts, and that's merely a side-effect. A treasure if ever there was one. And I'm glad it found its way to you."

"You don't want it back?"

Beljhar shook his head. "If it has eased your suffering, then I would say it's served its purpose for now, wouldn't you? Your arm, to do that to yourself, you must have been so lost."

"Stop," Leo said shakily.

"It's ok Leo. Those days are behind you now. You're safe here."

"I don't believe you."

"Why not?"

"I…," Leo said, disarmed. "You… you're a criminal, you poison people's minds with your tricks."

"Their minds are already poisoned," replied Beljhar. "Just like yours, and mine."

"I'm not…," Leo trailed off.

"The tricks just ease the pain. After you lost your brother, I'm sure you know what it's like. To feel so much of it that you might like to leave this world all together."

He rested a hand on Leo's shoulder. "It's alright to feel like that Leo. But the distance it creates, it invites predators doesn't it."

Leo felt as though all the blood had left his body. "Wh… what did you say?"

"It's alright Leo," said Beljhar. "It wasn't your fault, what that woman did to you."

Leo fought the urge to vomit. It was as though Beljhar had looked right through him and seen everything he tried to hide. His pain and grief for his brother, and the incurable shame of what had happened after Nico had died.

"Let me ask this one last question? Just the one, I promise. How do you think things might've been different had you and Nico not been left at the abbey?"

The question took him a moment to process properly. He thought about it, about everything that happened there. "I don't understand."

"A family, a home – to deny someone that, it's dreadful," replied Beljhar. Leo was vaguely aware of the sound of the lift creaking its way back up the to the nest. "Wouldn't you agree Seiyariu?"

Leo turned around, sure enough, standing in the lift, flanked by Quinnel, with his hands bound, was Seiyariu.

Quinnel kicked the vagabond into the crow's nest and stepped inside over his prone body. Seiyariu struggled to his knees; he was sporting a nasty gash on his forehead, blood coating his face and hair. Leo ran to his teacher but Quinnel barred his way, pushing him back to stand alongside Beljhar.

"I'm delighted you could be with us," said Beljhar. "I was just getting to your role in all this."

"Please." Seiyariu's face was ash grey behind its crimson mask. "Don't do this."

His voice sent a sharp chill down Leo's spine. There was such terror in those words, such desperation. He'd never imagined Seiyariu could sound like that.

"Don't what? Tell him the truth?"

"Please!" His eyes locked on Beljhar's, hate and desperation, threats and pleas all etched there in horrible detail.

"S… Seiyariu," Leo's voice broke. He felt a sense of dread wash over him as he realized that those tears running down his master's cheeks were real.

"Leo whatever he tells you—" Seiyariu was silenced by another blow to the head.

"Stop!" Leo demanded, whirling on Beljhar.

"Enough," said Beljhar eyes flashing dangerously at Quinnel.

Quinnel instantly relented, stepping back from the prostrate form of Seiyariu as if he'd been bitten.

Leo pointed a claw at Beljhar. He tried his best to sound threatening despite the tears in his eyes. "Start making sense."

"Very well."

Beljhar spread his arms. There was a flash of light and the crow's nest melted away before Leo's eyes, replaced by a moonlit courtyard, surrounded by cream colored stone. It was deathly silent, not a sound descended upon the… was it a palace?

Two men stood facing each other on opposite ends of the courtyard. One of them was Seiyariu, Leo recognized him instantly, but he looked so young, his hair was short, and he wasn't wearing his headband. There were no lines on his face, nor scars on his bare arms and there were far fewer patches in his cloak. Seiyariu's eyes were fixed, staring right through Leo to the other side of the courtyard. There was a fire in those eyes, a madness that Leo hadn't known Seiyariu possessed. They were the eyes of a man who wanted blood.

Facing Seiyariu, his sword drawn, was a man Leo didn't recognize. He was an Infernian, tall, broad-shouldered with large, sad eyes and a thick unkempt mane of black hair, flecked with stormy grey. There was something about those eyes. Leo felt certain he'd seen them before. The man's black tunic was embroidered with yellow, and a long emerald green cloak trimmed with scarlet covered his massive shoulders. Around his forehead was a small band of gold with a single gemstone in the center.

Leo felt a foreboding chill run down his spine. He knew somehow that he was looking at Heiro Al-Emani, once king of Inferno. The King's dark eyes bore none of the fury that Seiyariu wore, he looked sad, disappointed.

Leo took a few steps back, taking it all in. Beljhar was showing him the duel, the one that Pluto had told him about. Leo was about to watch his teacher kill the King of Inferno.

A hush fell upon the courtyard, even the wind itself was holding its breath, waiting for a sign. Then in a voice soaked in misery, King Heiro said two words, "I'm sorry."

Seiyariu let out a howl of inhuman rage, and threw himself at the King, the larger man moved with a speed Leo wouldn't have thought possible and the two met in the center of the courtyard, trading blows with such ferocity that the sand on the floor stayed aloft while they moved. The King's blade leapt across Seiyariu's bare arms, but he took no notice. He stabbed at the King's left shoulder, drawing blood. Leo saw it slowly begin to dawn on the King, that this was not a fight he could win. Seiyariu was too young, too fast, and too monstrous.

Heiro whirled about and made to catch Seiyariu in his sword-arm, but the young Seiyariu saw it coming and darted forward, under the slash and through the King's defenses. In the moment before he died,

Heiro saw the blow coming, and for an instant his eyes flashed with… was that pride?

With both hands, Seiyariu brought his sword crashing down hard, cleaving a massive gash through the King's shoulder and into his chest. Heiro stared down at the sword for a moment. Then the light in his eyes vanished, and he slumped to the floor, staining the sand and stones bright red.

Seiyariu stood over him, breathing heavily. Tears were now streaming down his young face, his look of venom transformed into one of hopelessness. He fell to his knees beside the King's body and just sat there in a trance.

The sound of panicked voices met his ear and a pair of double doors flew open as two women stepped out into the courtyard. One, the smaller of the two, wore a simple robe and headscarf with a green cloak. The other was an older, dark-skinned woman, her hair concealed as well. She stayed by the door, hand at her mouth and eyes full of tears. The second woman ran, with great difficulty to the side of the dead king. She was pale and short, with a young face, closer to Seiyariu's age. She was a small framed woman but she was heavy with child, her every movement difficult. She threw her arms around the lifeless form of Heiro, sobbing and screaming like a wounded animal. She wailed into the night, pulling her headscarf off to wipe the blood from the dead king's face. And as she did, Leo felt his heart stop, for the long locks now strewn about the corpse of Heiro Al-Emani, were red, a deep familiar crimson.

46
No More Secrets

THE ILLUSION FADED away, the palace dissolving back into the crow's nest. The cloudy sky had grown darker, the air colder. Leo stood, absolutely motionless.

"I'm sorry to show you such things," Beljhar's voice, from far away. "But you deserve to know who you are, who your parents were. Resha Fortunato stole the heart of the King of Inferno, so much so that he all but abandoned his queen. The Queen in turn, took a lover of her own. A lover who struck down the King of Inferno and left his pregnant mistress to her death. And his nation to its ruin."

Leo wanted to cry, but he couldn't. His body refused to shake, refused to sob. It wasn't possible, it couldn't be! Surely Beljhar was just trying to trick him. Slowly, Leo turned to look Seiyariu in the eye.

Seiyariu stared back at him, his eyes red and swollen, his tear-stained face had none of that fire he'd worn as he drove his blade through Heiro's chest.

"If you tell me he's lying, I'll believe you."

He waited for Seiyariu to laugh, to say it was all a trick, or smile and give him one of those odd riddles about life that he dispensed whenever he could. But Seiyariu just looked at Leo with that terrible emptiness etched on his face.

"Please," Leo's voice wavered. "Say he's lying."

Still Seiyariu didn't answer.

"Please!"

He didn't look away, but something behind his eyes flickered out. "I'm sorry."

Leo fell to his knees, a despair, a grief, such as he had never felt before in his life, welling up inside him. His heart felt slow, tired and unwilling to continue. Was this what dying felt like? It was Seiyariu. Seiyariu was the reason for it all. He imagined the life that might have been, having a mother and father, still having Nico, thoughts of a life away from all this fear, all this hate. But they were dead. Leo was alone, and now he knew why. The kindest man Leo had ever known, the man who had been a mentor, a teacher and a best friend to him, was the architect of his miserable existence.

"But..." Leo couldn't quite find the words. "You said..."

"He said he wouldn't keep secrets from you," Beljhar whispered softly, placing a hand on Leo's shoulder. "He said nothing about lies. Seiyariu didn't run into you by accident that day in Limani."

"I was looking for you!" Seiyariu said desperately. "I'd planned to collect you when I thought you were old enough, but when I came to the orphanage you were gone, I didn't know where. I had to find you again."

"And then pretend you weren't looking for me?"

"Leo I—"

"Were you ever going to tell me?"

"If I had, would you have stayed with me?" Seiyariu asked, stumbling to his feet. "I merely wanted the chance to give you back a piece of what I stole from you and... and..."

"Say his name," Leo ordered.

"And Nico."

Leo struck him across the face with Knail. The wanderer staggered back as Leo let out a cry of rage and despair. He stared at Seiyariu, tears streaming down his face. Nico had gotten sick. Died with no mother or father to cradle him and tell him things would be all right. All because of this man. Leo had slipped into despair and faded away. That distance had made him easy prey. The incurable shame of that woman's hands on his body, it was etched into his soul. None of that would've happened, if it hadn't been for this man.

"You did this to me!" Leo screamed, hate for Seiyariu guiding his fists over and over, trying desperately to make some of the rage go away. But Seiyariu just let him punch him and the hate only grew. It grew every time he struck, until it became too much to bear. Leo let Seiyariu collapse to the ground, his face a bloody mess. "You're a coward."

Seiyariu's mangled face stared back at him, defiantly. "Yes, yes I am."

Leo raised his claws up to Seiyariu's throat. Seiyariu didn't recoil. He leaned his head back, exposing his throat.

He wanted to slash and rip Seiyariu into a thousand pieces, scatter him to the winds and never have to look at his pathetic face ever again, but he knew he couldn't. Leo pulled away and turned his back on Seiyariu, fixing his streaming eyes on the clouds, the dark expanse of the sea, anything but the man whom he had looked to as a father.

"What shall we do with him?" asked Beljhar.

Leo didn't look back, how was he supposed to know? He just wanted Seiyariu gone, away. "I don't care," he said finally. "Just so long as I never have to see him again."

"So be it," Beljhar said. "Quinnel, give him back his sword and send him on his way." Quinnel nodded and grabbed Seiyariu. Silently Leo turned and watched them go. The vagabond put up no resistance and stepped into the lift in front of Quinnel. His eyes were bloodshot and swollen but in them Leo saw something worse than fear, worse than regret, acceptance. Leo looked away as the lift began to descend, taking away Seiyariu, forever.

When he was gone, Leo sank onto the floor, clutching his knees to his chest. Every time his closed his eyes to try and clear the tears, he saw the murder of his father, his mother, Nico, and the frightened little red-haired boy so desperate to see his brother again, so ashamed at what had been done to him that he plunged his fist through a mirror, trying to make the pain end.

He was vaguely aware of Beljhar, sitting beside him. He didn't say a word, just sat there and let Leo cry, until he couldn't anymore.

"Leo," Beljhar said kindly, when at last Leo's crumpled form had no tears left. "Would you like to take your life back?"

"What do you mean?" said Leo, wiping his eyes.

"This is why we have searched for you. You, the lost heir to the throne of Inferno. You are the key to uniting the Archipelago. Be my prince and let's put this world right. So nobody will have to feel like this," he wiped a tear from Leo's cheek, "ever again."

47
Broken

NEA STAYED HUNCHED in the corner of the room long after the last bit of daylight had slunk away. Seiyariu hadn't come back. Nor was there any sign of Leo. She'd seen this all before, it was how they did things at Glatman. When a girl first arrived they would isolate her. It made people easy to break down. She thought about how it had been when she'd first arrived. Back when she'd first though it was just a fancy school. What easy prey she had been.

Despair smothered her in its dark embrace. What would happen to them now? How long would they keep her here? Long enough for them to turn Leo around to their way of thinking no doubt. What then, would it be her turn then?

It'll be your turn then.

As Nea was lost in thought, her hand brushed against the wall, and she felt something wrong, something out of place. Like a scar. She shifted a bit, and tried to make out what she had touched. In the dim light of the gem she could see a kind of etching, scratched into the wood, letters maybe, or pictures. Had Seiyariu left this? He must've, the cuts had been recent, loose shavings of the wood fluttered to the floor when she ran her hand across them.

What's that old scarecrow trying to say?

Nea could tell what the pictures were individually, a book, a bone, a harp or something. Perhaps this was some code that vagabonds used to talk to each other, something that would look inconspicuous or be overlooked entirely.

Leo can probably read them.

At the bottom of the message, was a bar of music, with a few more marks scribbled beside it. Music notes…

She'd had some training in music when she lived at Glatman. But, like most things she'd been taught there, she had no desire to remember it.

Clink

It was the first sound she'd heard in ages, a dull metallic shudder.

The lock! Nea stared at the door for a moment, waiting for someone to enter. When they didn't, she got to her feet and carefully crossed the room, still nothing. She grasped the handle and pulled. The door opened without protest, revealing the landing beyond. Nea looked around for her savior but the walkway was empty. Nea didn't wait to make sure, she ran, nearly falling over the edge. She needed to find Leo – now.

It was late and there weren't many people wandering the ship. Even the smallest little noise carried far in the silence, so she kept her footsteps as quiet as they could be. Thankfully the ship was so large it was easy to stay out of sight. As she climbed the stairs, Nea thought back to the last time she'd taken this route. How she'd seen Quinnel, crying as he watched the images of his father, just a lost little boy.

But that's what they are, aren't they?

These men were damaged, all of them. They'd walked the same path she had, been shown all the same horrors, until Mister Beljhar promised to take it all away. Leo had said that he could make people see things, feel things that weren't there. What a perfect way to gather those already in pain.

Nea wondered darkly what she'd do if Beljhar had offered to make her think she'd always been a boy, erase her life at Glatman and replace it with something, anything else. She would've taken it without a second thought.

When at last she stumbled onto her landing, Nea heard the trumping of boots and retreated into the shadows. Two Briars descended from the stairs at the other end of the walkway, escorting Leo between them. Nea drew in her breath sharply, she couldn't make out his face, but there was something terribly wrong about the way he was standing. He didn't resist or fight, his shoulders were slumped, his head bowed.

She waited until the Briars were gone and snuck across the landing, but she found herself unable to open the familiar door. Nea wasn't sure what she expected to find. It had been less than a day, could so much change in such a short time?

You know it can.

She had expected to find Leo huddled over, crying, maybe staring defeated at the wall like he had when she first met him. Sobbing meekly and clutching his knees to his chest to block out the whole world. What was waiting for her beyond the door was something far worse, something even she hadn't been prepared for.

He wasn't crying, at least not anymore. His face wore a strange, blank expression, devoid of emotion. He looked like a candle that had been burnt out.

"Leo?" she said, stepping inside tentatively.

"Nea?" Leo stared right past her.

"What's happened, did they hurt you?"

"I saw my parents."

Nea froze. "Is that what Beljhar showed you?"

Leo nodded. "He told me the truth. The truth about me, the truth about Seiyariu."

"What are…?"

"It was because of him Nea, every last bit of it."

"S…Seiyariu?"

"My father," Leo paused, struggling with the words. "My father was the King of Inferno." She might've laughed, but the look in his eye, she'd never seen anything like it, and she knew then that he was serious, every word. "He was killed by Seiyariu, over my father's queen. My mother, his mistress, was exiled, and died a few months later."

"That's garbage," said Nea. "Beljhar is probably—"

"He admitted it!" Leo's face contorted then, twisted in anger and confusion.

"Seiyariu said that he killed your father?"

"That's right."

"And all this time, he didn't tell you?" Nea felt a surge of anger towards the vagabond, her first impression of him had been right.

That son of a bitch. He was just using Leo, just like everybody else. He was no different from the grassers, no different from those bastards at Glatman.

"Everything he ever told me was a lie," Leo said, his voice cracking.

"And your father was the damn King of Inferno?" Something clicked into place in her head. "Of course, that's why Beljhar wanted you isn't it? A lost prince to sit on the throne for him."

Leo turned to look at her; she didn't like what she saw behind his eyes. "I think we may have been wrong about all this. It's not like we thought, Nea. Beljhar's different. He never wanted to hurt me. He's like we are!"

"He's nothing like we are." She shook her head, remembering all too well when she'd thought the exact same thing. How the Briars had made all the sense in the world at first. "He's manipulating your feelings Leo."

Leo scowled. "You can pick at him all you like, but you can't argue the horrors of this place. He was a slave, like us Nea. He knows how it feels to be helpless. He has the power to make it so nobody has to feel like that again!"

"Do you honestly believe that?"

"Do you not? Nea, this… this whole damn world is… it's just wrong."

"Leo—"

"And we can help him fix it, we can!"

Who is this boy?

"Leo listen to yourself!"

He turned away from her. "He said you wouldn't understand."

Nea wasn't sure what to do. Leo was acting insane. She had to reach him, she had to be strong.

You're not strong.

She bit her lip. Maybe she wasn't, but she needed to be. For him, for both of them.

"You're talking nonsense," she was shouting too, now. "Honeyed words and empty promises. All of it means nothing! If you can't see this place for what it is then maybe I over-estimated you."

"What if it's where I belong?"

"It's the same damn ship I found you on. Except now, you've locked *yourself* up and don't even want the damn keys! The Briars aren't bloody revolutionaries, they're not freedom fighters, they're not even terrorists! They're frightened children, all of them!"

"No, Nea, people can't help being afraid, you don't—"

"You're right they can't, and that means they're easy prey for some-one like Beljhar. These men are not what you think they are Leo, it's just window dressing, all of it."

"You're wrong."

"Do you know what they did with me, while you were meeting with sweet Mister Beljhar? They gave me to that delver, Pluto. Let him throw me around." She spread her arms, showing off the cuts and bruises. "Had a grand time of it too."

"What?"

This horrified him.

Good.

Nea drew herself up to her full height and stared Leo dead in the eye. "We have to get out of here. Where is Seiyariu?"

Leo looked away, "I've no idea. I told Beljhar I never wanted to see him again."

Nea felt the hairs stand up on the back of her neck. "You what?"

"I couldn't bear to look at his—"

"You threw him away? Just like that?" Nea hadn't expected his words to hurt quite like they did. She'd cursed Seiyariu herself just moments ago.

"He deserved it."

"Maybe he did. But you're better than that Leo, you have to be."

Leo shook his head. "Not anymore. Too many lies."

Nea let out a cry of frustration. "But look at what you're doing, trading lies for lies."

"No!" There was desperation about Leo now. He was fighting to convince himself as much as her.

"Listen Leo, there's a message carved in the wall of Seiyariu's room. Please, come read it with me."

"No! I don't give a damn what he's got to say. All of that… it was all because he wanted to clear his guilty conscious. He never cared about me!"

"Don't be an idiot." Even Nea was amazed at how quickly she leapt to the vagabond's defense. But she'd seen the way he treated Leo with her own eyes, and it was perhaps one of the only things she'd been sure was genuine. "Seiyariu may have kept secrets from you, might've lied right to your face every damn time he opened his mouth, but you know something that wasn't a lie? Seiyariu loves you. I knew that after spending thirty damnable seconds with the two of you. For God's sake, you should see the way he looks at you, like you're the most precious thing on earth. Leo…"

"It's his fault! All of it! The reason my mother died, the reason…" His voice broke, tears streaming down his face. "It's not fair."

"That's just how it is Leo, things don't turn out the way we want. We have to keep going, deal with the losses as they come."

He whirled on her, dark eyes blazing. "And what the hell would you know about loss?"

Slap! Nea struck him across the face with such force that he stumbled back. She was towering over him now, all tenderness forgotten. "Don't you dare. Don't you ever. You don't know a damn thing about me Leo, not one damn thing."

Leo looked back at her, the fire in his eyes replaced with more fear. "Beljhar…"

"Beljhar? Beljhar, Beljhar, Beljhar. Do you think Beljhar or his messiah complex cares for you? You think he loves you?"

"He said we were similar, that we could make a better world for people like us. Help make the world more free."

"Free?" Nea's voice was growing dangerously shrill but she didn't care. "You're being used Leo, Beljhar needs you and he'll play all the games he can to have you, tell you whatever stupid little lies you want to hear. Is that freedom? Look around! These men aren't free! They're slaves, children scrambling in the dark for opals, I would've thought you'd had enough of that."

Leo stared up at her in shock for a few moments, and behind his eyes she thought she saw something shatter. Tears began to pour and he buried his face in his hands. As emotion overtook him, Nea felt her heart lighten somewhat. She knew this boy.

48
Last Words

Leo had wanted to believe Beljhar's words so desperately. For hours they'd talked today, each word out of his mouth had made Leo more and more sure of his decision. How was it that Nea could come in and bring it all crashing down so quickly? Because despite everything Beljhar had told him, despite everything Leo wanted to believe, Nea was right.

"Come on then, let me show you these scribbles, see if you can make sense of them. Then let's get out of here."

He stared at Nea. "How?" He felt so small, so weak, what could he do, even if he wanted to escape. "I tried Nea, I tried to use this." He flailed his black arm in despair. "Blow a hole in the damn ship and just make a run for it, but I can't, no matter what I do."

"Then we'll have to make do without it," Nea said calmly. "Whatever it is Seiyariu wrote for you, I think it'll help."

Leo didn't move. "I can't believe anything he said. It's broken, whatever it was we had."

"I'm not asking you to believe him, just read it."

"Why though?" Leo choked. "There's no going back to how things were, not now."

"No, you're right, there isn't. But would you really want it to? At least now you know the truth."

Leo sniffed, desperately wishing he could have this last day taken away. "I'm scared Nea. I'm always scared. I'm not strong enough for this." Nico had always been the strong one.

"Listen Leo," said Nea. "I'm not going to lie to you. Things…" He frowned as though he were struggling to find the words. "Things change, that's just how the world is. Things have to change, and so do we."

Leo looked at Nea, remembering the first time he'd looked in his eyes. He'd seen something then, something familiar. It was like looking into a cracked mirror. For the longest time he thought that Nea reminded him of Nico, and that was what drew him to the older boy. But it wasn't Nico he saw in Nea, not anymore. Leo saw his own fears, his own anger etched in the face of the boy next to him.

"I'm sorry," he said, "I didn't mean to say those things to you. It's just… my home, my family…"

Nea then did something Leo hadn't been prepared for. The older boy took a deep breath and pulled him in a tight embrace.

"*This* is your home," said Nea. "I love you whether you like it or not and whatever happens Leo, I promise that's not changing."

Nea pulled him closer, tighter. It was strange. Leo couldn't remember ever being held like this. Nea's embrace, it was like an oasis in a desert. He felt Nea's breathing, heard the sound of his heart. The contact was soft, warm, and perfect.

"Come on," Nea said gently breaking away. "Let's go."

He took Leo by the hand and led him out of the room. Leo followed obediently, down the pole, across the way, the walk to the brig still utterly deserted. He didn't let go of Nea's hand the entire time. When at last they reached Seiyariu's empty room, they scrambled inside, shutting the door behind them. Sure enough, etched onto the wall were carvings, Peregrine Runes.

"I found these on my way out. Blends right into the woodwork, the Briars completely missed it. But you can read it, can't you?" said Nea.

"These are Peregrine Runes," Leo said in amazement.

"Vagabond signs?"

"Exactly." Leo stared at the markings, memorizing each symbol. The first was a book, meaning knowledge or secrets, followed by a single bone, indicating lack of wealth in the area. The next symbol was a person, a man.

I know I am a poor man

The words cut through him, but he forced himself to keep reading. An inverted palm, indicating that there was some kind of a catch, followed by a fire, which meant hospitality, kindness or affection. The message was becoming clearer. Then came the symbol for the individual, designed to address the reader. The next carving was a clock, simple enough, it was meant to signify a long amount of time. That left only one more rune carved into the wall. This was a symbol Leo didn't recognize at first. A single finger raised. He thought back to his lessons on the road, his time with Seiyariu, his heart aching at the happiness in those memories. The extended finger, that was the symbol for truth.

I know I am a poor man,
but my love was always true

Leo stared at the words left behind by his friend, his teacher. He was overcome again, Leo leaned against the wall, sobbing dryly, he didn't have any tears left. He didn't know if he could forgive Seiyariu, but whatever happened, he could not let it end like this. He needed to hear the truth, from Seiyariu and nobody else. For that, they needed to get out of this horrible place.

"And these," Nea pointed at a row of signs Leo had missed. "What about these, they look like music notes to me?"

Leo studied them, attempting to remember his choir days and what exactly music looked like when it was written down. There was nothing else it could be; the rune for music was a lyre so it wasn't part of the message.

Leo ran his hands along the carved notes, just beneath them, so faint he could've missed it, were two more marks. Leo reread these several times, certain he hadn't understood, but the marks read, unmistakably,

Play for the Wind

He reiterated this to Nea. "I'm not sure what he—"

But Nea cut him off; "Leo," he said simply. And pulled a tiny bone flute from the folds of his tunic, "I think he means this."

49
The Call

"What do you mean?" asked Leo, confused.

"I mean the scarecrow gave me this, told me to hang on to it."

"Play for the wind," Leo repeated, looking at the fourteen notes carved into the wall, then to the window to the foggy sea beyond.

"It's worth a try isn't it?" said Nea.

He nodded. "But I don't know…"

"I do," she said. "Let's just see what happens okay?"

"Okay."

The two of them opened the tiny window, only to be buffeted by a furious blast of salty air. Nea couldn't see through the fog but it must've been getting close to midnight judging by how dark it was out there. Leo sat cross legged on the bed and watched as Nea tried to remember where her fingers where supposed to go. It had been so many years, but everything was counting on her. Whatever mad scheme Seiyariu had put into motion needed her to play this music, play it for the wind, *Whatever the hell that means.*

She started to play, slowly at first, fumbling with the notes and forgetting where to put her fingers. After a few minutes of this however, muscle-memory set in and she may as well have been back at Glatman doing her scales. The flow of the tune across her lips was somehow soothing. The cold sea air, the smell of salt and brine and the wind flying about her, there was release in it all.

When the last note left the instrument, Nea shut the window and sat beside Leo on the bed.

"What do you think is going to happen?" said Leo.

Nea shrugged, she was asking herself the same question. "Dunnno. But he must've had a reason, right? I guess we'll just have to wait."

"Do you think the Briar will come looking for us?"

She shrugged. "You're Beljhar's prince now, I reckon you can do as you please, yeah?"

He winced, and she wished she'd said nothing. "You remember what we talked about on the ship, the first one I mean?"

Leo met her eyes, "Suject and Perora?"

"Yeah that's right, we were gonna go see the boulder and everything."

"If it's even real," said Leo with a small smile.

"You're telling me you've seen Mariners, giant centipedes, and all this nonsense, but a sliced boulder is a little too much to believe?" she laughed.

For a time they sat there together, talking until they drifted into an uneasy sleep. When Nea next opened her eyes, the world outside the window was still dark. She looked around confused, she thought for a moment she'd heard a tapping sound.

You really are losing your mind, aren't you?

But there it was again, an insistent rapping on the glass with what looked like... was that a claw?

Nea bolted up. There was something hovering just outside their window, something Nea couldn't process, though she was staring right at it. It was a bit like a bird, and a bit like a woman. It had the torso of a woman. Her chest was covered by a layer of bristling brown feathers, as was the top of her head. Taking the place of hair, the feathers gave her a strange, windswept appearance. The creature's arms and legs transformed at the elbow and the knee. The flesh became rough and scaly, arms and legs ending in sharp talons. Her legs were bent back like a bird and a pair of enormous brown wings erupted from her back. These beat rhythmically, keeping the creature aloft. Her ears were long and pointed, and her face was sharply angled with a beak-like nose and huge yellow eyes. She was dressed like a human, with a leather breastplate, a blue tunic that came down like a skirt and a long green scarf flecked with patches.

You've finally gone mad.

Had she really? Or had another of Beljhar's illusions slipped down to spirit them away. Was it possible that the stress of it all had just given way to madness. She stood there, debating what to do, when Leo yawned and sat up.

"Nea, what's wrong?"

"B… bird," said Nea pointing dumbstruck at the window.

Leo rolled out of bed and squinted sleepily at her, then out the window, his eyes getting round. Then without so much as a hesitation he hopped over and opened it.

"What are you doing?" Nea's voice shrill with panic.

"Seiyariu, are you mad?" the creature squawked in a shrill voice that made Nea certain Briars would be kicking down their door any minute. "What did I tell you about using the…?"

Her big hawkish eyes flitted about the room, finally settling on the two of them. "Where is Seiyariu? Who are you?"

Nea blinked in astonishment. "You can speak?"

The creature raised an eyebrow and gave Nea a very human look of exasperation. "So, it seems, can you. Though listening appears difficult. I'll ask again, slower this time…"

"Seiyariu isn't here," Leo said.

"Don't play games with me little boy, I heard Seiyariu's call. The call he was forbidden from using ever again may I add, and…" Her yellow eyes darted to Nea just as she realized she was still holding the flute.

"Ah," the creature muttered. "He gave you that, did he?"

Nea nodded.

"And taught you the call?"

"What's the call?"

The bird woman rolled her eyes, "The Call to the High Nests. Play it on a strong wind, and the Erinyes, to whom you have proven yourself a friend, despite your best efforts, will come to your aid."

"Erinyes?" Leo asked.

How the hell is he so calm?

The creature nodded, or attempted to, it was a difficult thing to do positioned as she was. "Yes, children of the sky, harpies, furies, whatever you like. You may call me Zephyr."

The names she'd given, had they been in one of Nea's books, sketched in loving detail in some ancient bestiary of imagined terrors of the Archipelago? Nea found her memory wasn't working all that well at the moment.

"And… and you've come to help us?" said Nea.

"Oh for heaven's sake. Yes, I'm honor bound to answer the call and help whoever played it. Now that call was given to Seiyariu, and it was a privilege he very much lost. Though I suppose since he didn't play it *himself*…" she groaned. "I cannot dutifully leave the two of you. Why have you played the call, what is it you need?"

Nea still couldn't find her words but Leo piped up. "We need to get off this ship."

"Then you two had best learn to swim, hadn't you?" She sneered.

Bit cheeky this one, isn't she?

Leo frowned, a look of concentration on his face. "Sorry, but you don't know someone named Kokaleth do you?"

The Erinye's face went scarlet. "W… what? What makes you say that, I've nothing to do with…"

"You talk like him," Leo said with a small smile.

"I do not!" she squawked.

"But you do know him then?"

"I… I…"

Nea found herself smiling lightly, amazed to see such an indignant expression on such a noble face.

At least it's not so different from you that it can't get flustered.

Zephyr let out a frustrated little screech. "No more questions, you want off the ship, so be it. Meet us on deck."

Then she was gone, blasting through the night sky, cutting a swath through the fog as she flew out and away, until they lost sight of her.

"Leo?" Nea asked finally.

"Yeah?"

"Was it like that? Meeting the Mariner?"

He nodded. "I didn't know what to think. I was always told they were just stories."

"Well," she yawned and stretched, still watching the sky. "Nice to be proven wrong I guess."

He smiled, "I guess it is."

"If things like that are possible, then we might just have a chance, eh?"

His smile widened and he nodded, "Yeah maybe."

Nea found herself downplaying the impossibility of it all more and more. They had a plan now, a strategy, and a way out. Confidence, unfamiliar but welcome, began to return to her and she clapped Leo on the shoulder.

"Let's get out of here."

*

Nea decided that the library would be the safest way to the deck, at least the one with fewer guards. But Nea was astonished when they met not a single Briar going their way. They reached the library, silent and unseen. Nea threw open the doors and they stepped inside, only to find a man waiting for them inside.

"Hello," he said, leaning against the rail and staring at the stained glass. Nea knew this man before he even turned around. She'd seen him before, in a crowd of people at a slave auction.

Beljhar.

He was not imposing, physically. He wasn't tall, nor broad, and his soft features gave him a feminine appearance.

Leo was rooted to the spot, paralyzed with fear.

"You two are quite resourceful," said Beljhar. "Though I have to say, I'm disappointed you are trying to leave us."

His voice echoed with such genuine sadness that Nea was taken aback. It was like poisoned honey, smooth and impossibly dangerous. In an instant she understood everything Leo had said about him. She could sense power emanating from this man. He controlled the room, the ship, everything with his words.

"Nea," Leo hissed, his face draining of all color.

"What makes you think we're leaving?" she asked, trying to sound calm.

"Don't play games dear," said another voice, one that made her go as rigid as Leo. Pluto hobbled his way out of the shadows, leering at them. He snapped his fingers and something leapt from Nea's shoulder. A cricket, a tiny little brown cricket. How had she not noticed?

"You… you can…" she stammered.

"Hear what it hears? Yes," Pluto said, picking up the cricket and pocketed it once more. "The Call to the High Nests was it? Seiyariu is more clever than we realized."

She barely heard him, her mind was working so furiously.

You stupid idiot, you didn't notice and now they've got you. Stupid weak pathetic—

Nea bit her lip to keep these thoughts at bay. Perhaps they could get down to the hold through the library, and then slip on a lift back—

But even as she thought this, the doors opened behind her. A line of soldiers entered, Quinnel at their head.

"Sir," said Quinnel, his eyes meeting Nea's for the briefest of moments.

"My prince," said Beljhar, clasping his hands together. "Please reconsider what you're doing." Leo said nothing, still paralyzed with fear.

"He's not your prince!" Nea shouted. "Stay out of his head you bloody—"

Beljhar's eyes flashed to her. And she instantly felt her mouth close.

"Nea is it?" He strode over to look her in the eyes. She drew back despite herself; his eyes were like pitch, scalding holes through her. "And does the prince have any idea of the secrets you keep from him?"

A shot of pure ice water rushed through her veins.

"What did you say?"

"I think we both know."

How in the hell could he know?

Rage flashed inside her and before she realized what she was doing Nea had thrown a punch at Beljhar's calm face. He sidestepped with ease, looking mildly amused.

He's going to tell Leo. You need to kill him. Kill him now!

Beljhar spread his arms. "How sad. He treats you like a human being and you reward his friendship with lies and deceit, don't you think he's had enough of that?"

Nea leapt at Beljhar without thinking. This time he didn't move. He just looked at her. Then there was a flash of light and the library, Beljhar and Leo, melted away.

50
Winds of Change

NEA STOPPED IN his tracks, blank eyes staring past Beljhar at a world only he could see. He turned around slowly, taking in whatever it was being shown to him. Then a look of unbridled horror filled his face and he screamed. His voice high and shrill, he fell to the ground stumbling back at the nameless terrors in his mind. Then he began to shake, twist, and writhe in great pain.

"No!" Leo tried to run to his side. But Beljhar made a gesture and suddenly two of the Briars seized him by the shoulders. He pulled as he had never in his life. He had to get to Nea. He had to be stronger. The person who'd done so much for him was in pain and all he could do was stand there and watch?

"Stop!" Leo screamed, throwing all his weight forward, ripping at his captors' grip. As he did, Leo felt a sharp pain in his right arm. "Let him go! You're hurting him!"

Beljhar shook his head, "No, I'm not. This pain was already there, I just brought it to the surface. Like I did with you and Nico."

"Please." Tears were running down Leo's cheeks. "Please let him go. I'll do anything."

"I know. How suddenly protective you are. Even after you were so willing to throw out the vagabond. Are you truly that lonely?"

Leo stopped struggling, "Wh…what? "

"I don't know why I ask, I know the answer. It's because of Nico. You weren't supposed to face all this alone."

The words were like a fiery dagger in his heart. He found himself trembling. In despair, in fear and in hatred of the power Beljhar had over him, over everyone.

"Pluto told me what this one said to you. Do you think ill of me for my tricks, my illusions? You think I lie to people? You're wrong. It's quite the opposite. The true illusions, those are the ones we make for ourselves." Beljhar strode back to Nea. He wasn't screaming anymore, just groaning, twitching, a line of foam dribbling from his lips. "This is an illusion." He seized a handful of Nea's hair and dragged him to his feet.

"Put him down!" Leo leapt at Beljhar, but the Briars held him fast.

"The person called Nea, as you know them, never existed."

With that, he seized the collar on Nea's doublet and ripped. A white cloth, hidden by his shirt, was wrapped around his chest binding what were unmistakably… Nea… Nea was a girl?

It was as though someone had flipped the world on its side. The curtain was drawn back as he finally saw things as they truly were. It all fell into place. His mind raced through every moment he'd spent with Nea since they'd met and, God help him, it made sense.

"Do you see now?" asked Beljhar, letting Nea tumble to the floor in a heap. "Lies. Just more secrets and lies. They all have been lying to you Leo. Every single one of them, except for me."

Leo stared at his friend lying in pain. Nea had lied to him. She'd held him, told him things would work out, helped him stand when standing was the hardest, but she'd lied to him. To his amazement Leo found he didn't give a damn.

"Is that all?"

"Excuse me?"

Leo glared right into Beljhar's face, not shrinking back. "Is that all?"

Beljhar's eyes flared. "This creature deceived you, don't you understand. She took advantage of your trust."

"And what?" Leo snapped back. "Saved me from being a slave for the rest of my life?"

"Prince—"

"Twice?"

"How dare you," Beljhar's voice was venomous. "I'm nothing like those brutes."

"You're right," Leo nodded, forcing some of Nea's swagger into his voice. "At least they're upfront about it."

Leo thought for a moment that Beljhar was going to strike him. Leo wished he would. Nea had done so much for him, maybe more than she realized, but never once did she ask for a single thing in return. What the hell did he care if she was a girl? It didn't affect him any, so let her pretend. Leo thought about Nico, about the hole in his heart. Nea would've listened, Nea would've understood. Seiyariu would've as well, but Leo hadn't told them. How dare he judge them for feeling the same way. He thought of Seiyariu, could he possibly…?

Beljhar was still speaking. "They lied to you! Didn't trust you enough to tell their secrets to."

Leo stared at Nea. "Neither did I. I don't think I'll be joining you. In fact," Leo stared at Beljhar, white-hot resolve burning in every inch of his body. "I will do everything I possibly can to stop you."

"What then? Do you plan to leave with your little slut? Perhaps find your cowardly vagabond and go on about your merry way as if nothing has changed?"

Leo shook his head. "Things have changed, but so have I."

For just a moment, a fraction of one, he was not aboard the Briar's ship, but in a much smaller room of crumbling dark-grey stone. There were no shelves, no high ceiling, the only familiar sight was the window. Where was he? Then it was gone, and he was back aboard the ship, with Beljhar and his men, in the library lit by the gemstone lamps. The gemstone lamps… opals…

"Very well." Beljhar straightened up and met Leo's gaze with a cold fire all his own. "Quinnel, take her. This will be your final chance."

"Sir…" Quinnel's voice was shaking. He was looking at Leo and Beljhar with a look far removed from his usual cold apathy.

"Now," said Beljhar, eyes flashing dangerously in Quinnel's direction.

He did as he was told, drawing his dagger and crouching down. Pluto watched, eyes hungry as Quinnel lifted Nea's unconscious form up, holding the blade to her throat.

"I can make this all stop Leo," said Beljhar. "All you have to do is give in."

"No," Leo's voice was shaking again. Not from fear, no, from something else entirely. This feeling, it was familiar. It was then that he felt the lancing pain of Knail erupting along his entire arm.

"Very well. Quinnel kill her."

Then, something inside Leo broke. The pain in his arm reached its limit and he let out a howl of rage and agony so fierce that Quinnel and Beljhar stopped. The Briars holding him let go in astonishment, and Leo threw out his black hand, the pain redoubling itself. Knail was glowing white, pulses of the white energy breaking free with every beat of his heart.

The force burst from Knail and leapt out across the room, it was no longer like smoke or vapor, it was pure, crackling, energy. It hovered in the center of the room for a few moments. An absolute silence falling around the library, as every eye watched it begin to take shape.

It rose and branched out, bending and twisting until a ghostly, humanoid shape was left floating before Leo. It had no real features, only the faintest suggestion of an outline, but it was unmistakably shaped like a person. Leo stared at this creation, this phantom made of light.

Slowly and deliberately, with one clawed finger, Leo pointed. For a moment, the phantom hesitated before him, then launched across the room, towards the glowing gems mounted on the wall. The light bounced from gem to gem in a wild dance, shattering each into a thousand iridescent pieces. As it burst free of the final gem, Leo saw something that might have been a smile on the thing's sparkling face, as it spun in the air, throwing its form at the window, which exploded. The phantom's light refracted across the shards of raining glass, filling the library with every color of the rainbow, then it was gone, everything was gone. He was again standing in a cold, stone chamber, littered with fragments of glass and crystal.

The Briars froze, staring open-mouthed at what had once been the library. In the aftermath of Knail's attack, the exhaustion hit Leo with full force, and he had to fight to keep from blacking out. He couldn't give in, he needed to fight. The window was gone, the roar of the wind and sea deafening now.

Just as Leo fell to his knees, the whole host of Erinyes came pouring through the hole. Leo's breath caught in his chest as they swarmed inside the library. In that moment they might as well have been angels. For the briefest of instants, his eyes met Beljhar's. The man wasn't angry, or sad, he merely stared at Leo, even as the room around him filled with the sounds of battle.

Someone seized him by the arms and the legs, someone with large, sharp fingers. Leo watched the floor vanishing beneath him as he was carried high into the air in the grip of an Erinye. Quinnel, Pluto, Beljhar and the Briars were locked in combat with the flock on the ground, falling back to the chamber doors. Nea's limp form still lay discarded, until a second Erinye swept down and gingerly took her in its clutches.

Leo's carrier spun about in the air, through the window and up over the massive black expanse of sea. The Erinyes raced out across the water, retreating to the horizon.

Leo expected to see the ship but there was no ship. Where the ship should have been, there was an island, upon which lay a run-down fortress, a mess of stone masonry that was in disrepair, like the corpse of a castle. A realization swept through Leo. His mind flashing back to every single one of those gems he'd seen mounted on the wall. They'd been projecting an image, just as the dying man's brooch had done. The ship had been just another illusion. And he had broken it. Leo closed his eyes at last and let the Erinyes carry him away from that hell and into tomorrow.

51

Nea and Nico

A COLD WIND rattled Nea's bones and she jolted awake. Blearily she looked around. She was resting on matted wood bound together into a wiry nest.

A bird's nest?

Someone had wrapped a blanket around her to keep out the chill. Why was it so damn cold? She sat up, looked around and immediately regretted it. She was indeed in a bird's nest set into the side of a gigantic jagged stone cliff

She held still for a few frightening moments, trying to wake from whatever mad dream she was having. When that didn't happen, she crept to the side and looked out. A range of mountains wound around a picturesque valley full of sparkling lakes and forests, all surrounded by towering peaks. Nea counted twelve of these jagged stone spires piercing through the earth. Like prongs on a crown, or bars of a cage.

Where the hell…

Then she saw the figures flying throughout the valley, up and around the mountains. They filled the skies, a host of angels with wings twice as long as a man. Had she died then? No, her head was pounding and her mind clouded, but she began to think more clearly. The Erinyes, they had saved them, brought them to… wherever this place was. As she watched them race along the wind so effortlessly, their high voices little more than a chirp on the evening breeze. Nea thought they were the most remarkable creatures she'd ever laid eyes on.

Her memories were a blur. She had rushed Beljhar, yes, but then what? The illusions. One moment she'd been in the library with Leo and the next she'd been back at Glatman, reliving all those old horrors as if they were brand new. She felt cold sweat on her face. How easily

Beljhar had broken her down, with a mere suggestion. She should never have given him the opportunity.

A half-formed memory of a hand ripping at her collar played at the edges of her mind. Had that been part of the illusion as well? Nea looked down at herself. To her horror, her shirt was torn, exposing her bindings. And as she pulled the blanket tight around herself to cover up, she realized it was not a blanket, but a green cloak. Leo's cloak…

"Nea?"

Her heart sank.

God, please not him. Not him too.

Leo was sitting across from her in the nest, his big eyes full of concern.

Nea felt her whole world come crashing in on itself. For the first time in ages, Nea wanted to cry, not out of rage, or desperation, but out of sheer genuine sadness. She wanted to bury her face in the rough nest and cry until her voice was gone. But she wouldn't. The thought of Leo seeing her in a state like that, hurt even more. She turned away, not wanting to see the disappointment in his eyes, the confusion.

You were keeping secrets from him, just like Seiyariu. But you had too, he can't know. He can't.

"Are you hurt?"

"What?" Nea faltered and looked back at Leo, into his face. She didn't see disappointment, or confusion.

"Beljhar was in your head for a while, are you feeling any better?"

This was too much, the tears couldn't be held back any longer. Nea slumped in defeat as she choked back the hoarse sobs. It was all wrong, everything. She would've preferred accusations, screams, anger, anything but this. She wanted to run from him, but he refused to give her anything to run from. "Dammit Leo," was all she could manage.

"Sorry."

"Shut up, and for God's sake stop pretending."

"Alright, sorry I thought that—"

"Was it Beljhar?" She stared at him through the tears, at his worried little face. He nodded. Then the memory was real. Leo moved to try and comfort her.

"Nea it's ok. I—"

"No it isn't!" she cried, scrambling back. "I didn't want you to know."

"Why?"

"Because I don't want anyone to know!" she said, shaking. "I didn't want you to think of me like that."

"Like what?"

The confusion was there now but not the kind she'd been expecting. Was it possible that he genuinely didn't understand what she was saying?

No it's not.

She shrugged, hopelessly. "Like a girl."

"Nea I don't care if you're a girl!"

"Well I do! I hate it! I hate being frightened, helpless, a fragile little idiot that can't do a damn thing for herself."

Leo scowled at her. "But you're not like that."

"But I am though!" she shouted, desperately. "I'm just like the others. So weak, and pathetic, it makes me want to die. I hate myself Leo, so much, sometimes it's like I'm two different people. But when I cut my hair, tie down these damnable things. I feel better, like… like the world is a place I'd like to live."

For a moment or two they sat in silence. Despair washed over Nea. She wanted to fade away into nothing, like she'd never been. It would have been better if Beljhar had just killed her. Then at least Leo's vision of her would be untainted.

"I can't stay with you now," she said softly. She had to leave, just like she'd had to leave Cain.

She nearly burst into tears again at the horrified look in Leo's eyes. She forced herself to turn away instead, she needed to do this.

"Please," he said, his voice barely more than a whisper. "Please I don't care if you're a girl, I need you."

"You need him," she said. "He's gone now."

Leo just stared at her. Finally, he asked the question she'd been dreading, the question she didn't know if she could answer. "Why?"

Don't tell him. You can't. He won't understand.

But despite all her instincts, all the fear and disgust that she felt. She felt she needed to tell him. She owed him at least that.

Nea took a deep breath. "When I was younger, I lived with my parents in a run-down little fishing village. I had to work to help my family, they didn't have a son, so I just slipped into the job, I didn't think anything of it. Until I was sent away…" she stumbled, struggling to find the words. "It was called Glatman. They told me it was a finishing school owned by a rich family, a place to train young ladies in etiquette. But when I got there…" She bit her lip, fighting through the pain of the words. "The owners would 'train' us, use us however they liked and then sell us off when they were done. It was nothing like a school, it was a farm."

She tried not to look at Leo, but she could feel the horror in his eyes. "The other girls, some nearly grown women even, they did nothing. The damn empty-headed cows never tried to fight back or anything either. Two years I was there, two damn years and not a single woman ever tried to break out, escape, or even hurt them. I was the first. One night, I dunno something inside me just broke. I cut my hair and killed people to get away. Didn't bother going home, I tried to get to Conoscenzia, barely made it five months on my own before those damn grassers caught me."

They sat there again in silence, until Nea worked up the courage to look Leo in the eyes once more. Now he knew. He knew how soiled she was, how twisted and ruined. She hoped that he would turn away in disgust, in fear. But to her astonishment, he didn't look frightened, or sad, not anymore.

"I understand."

"Do you?" she snapped, trying to be cruel, anything to make him go.

But Leo's face was set with a strange look of determination. "Yes, I do. And I understand why you didn't tell me."

"But—"

"Before anything else happens. There's something I haven't told you."

"What?"

What the hell could he have to tell you?

"Just listen to me for a few minutes, please. Then, if you want, you can leave, and you never have to see me again."

Nea nodded slowly, astonished at how much the suggestion wounded her.

But you have to leave. You have to. No matter what he says.

"I was furious at Seiyariu for keeping secrets. But I realize how much of a hypocrite I was being. I've got secrets too, secrets that I never wanted to share with anyone."

Leo.

"You and Beljhar both said I'm too easy to trust, I'm dependent, lonely, always lonely. You're not wrong."

Nea watched Leo speaking softly, something was different about him. There was a strength that she hadn't noticed before. She could see the fear in his eyes, the anxiety, but still he pressed on.

"It's not just you who feels wrong... I... I do too. Like there's a huge piece that everyone except me seems to have."

Even as words left his mouth she saw the pain they caused him, he looked to be fighting back tears and perhaps even the urge to run.

"It wasn't always that way," he muttered, talking slower now. "I wasn't always alone."

"What are you talking about?"

Leo took a deep breath, "Do you know why I ran away from the abbey? Despite everything they'd told me about the grassers? It's because I couldn't stand to walk alone down the halls anymore. I couldn't bear to look at my own reflection because I never saw me, it was always him." He took a deep breath. "Nea, I *am* missing something. Something really important." His voice broke but he pushed on, fighting to get the words out now. "His name was Nico, he was my twin."

He wasn't scared or careful, not like me. He was brave, and he made me feel brave too until... until one day he just started coughing."

He let the words hang in the air for a moment. Nea felt a stab of pity, genuine and raw. Leo shook his head and continued. "Then he was gone, I was alone. Beljhar was right, I wasn't supposed to face this alone." He sniffled. "This whole damn life of mine was designed for two. I'm not strong enough...," he trailed off.

Nea thought for a moment that this was the end of the story. But these next words, she could see how hard they were for him to get out.

"There was a sister at the abbey. Sister Roberta, she was young, pretty, kind to both of us. She'd bring us sweets and let us stay up telling stories. She kept me company while he was sick. After Nico died… I was so alone I hardly even knew who I was. There was so much empty space where he had been. She told me that she could help, that she could make the pain stop…" He locked eyes with her and in that instant she saw a pain, all too familiar. "She took me to an empty room, locked the door… and then…" He couldn't seem to get the rest of the words out not matter how hard he tried.

Nea stared at him for what felt like the first time. It made sense, God did it make sense. A morbid understanding came over Nea, so many of Leo's actions, his mannerisms, and his dumb little mistakes. If she had known, maybe… Nea had no idea what that maybe might've been.

"When… when it was over, I ran up to hide in the attic. There was an old mirror there. And I saw Nico in it, looking at me, dirty, ruined. And I couldn't bear it. I broke the glass and…"

"Tried to kill yourself. That's what was wrong with your arm." She remembered the scars.

He nodded, "When that didn't work, I ran away, right into the arms of the grassers. And that's where you found me."

He felt dirty, violated, and alone. Just like you.

Was that what she'd seen on the boat, herself? Had the pain in his heart resonated with the pain in hers, like the scarecrow had said?

She wanted to comfort him, she wanted to tell him that it wasn't his fault, that he was wrong, that he was more whole than she could ever hope to be. But all she managed to say was, "You didn't have to tell me that."

Leo shook his head. "Yes, I did. I can't expect others to be honest with me if I'm still keeping secrets. You've got my secret now and I've got yours." He smiled sadly and took her by the hand. "We're even, ok?"

"We're… even?"

Leo nodded. "You're safe with me, just like I know I'm safe with you. I don't care if you're a girl Nea, honest I don't. I'm your friend. You can be whatever you want," he whispered, gently pulling her into an embrace, "So long as it's you in there, I don't mind."

Impossible.

Nea almost broke the contact, she stared at him, hardly daring to believe it. One look in his big dumb eyes and she knew he was telling the truth. The voice in her head mercifully silent, she pulled him in closer and let herself cry. Never in her life had she felt so much gratitude, so much love.

"I'll stay," she whispered. "You big idiot. God, things are going to be so different now though."

He nodded. "I expect so yeah. But remember what you told me. Things change, but so do we."

52

Where Birds Tread

LEO WASN'T SURE whether it was the strain on his body or his heart, but he slept deeper and longer than he ever had in his life. Every so often a dream would try to sneak into his sleeping mind, and he woke in a cold sweat. He needed only see where he was and who was beside him and he was at peace once again. The nest kept the ferocious wind of the mountain and the chill of the late autumn air at bay as they rested peacefully.

When at last the sun refused to let him stay asleep, he wondered if it was truly the next morning, or if Knail had weakened him to the point that he'd slept for days. He turned to Nea. But Nea was nowhere to be found.

Leo was up instantly, all drowsiness forgotten. Fear coursed through his body; surely Nea wouldn't have just left him, would she? Leo let out a sigh of relief when he saw his friend standing on the edge of the nest, gazing out at the world below. She still looked hurt, exhausted but she was smiling ever so slightly as the cool morning wind rolled over her.

In the morning light Nea truly looked a different person. The Erinyes must've brought them supplies; Nea had a new shirt, bunched in the right places so that not a soul could tell that wasn't looking. But Leo was looking now, despite himself, he couldn't help but notice. Nea carried herself like a boy, moved like a boy, acted like a boy, but there were one or two little things that she simply couldn't change, her slim shoulders and long spindly legs in particular. Though Leo never would've picked up on any of this on his own.

He regretted nothing; keeping Nea at his side was worth a thousand secrets, a thousand humiliations. But telling Nea, it hadn't felt like he had imagined it would, his own shame and despair had faded; now there was someone helping him with the load.

Without warning Leo's stomach erupted in pain, sharp and vibrant, wiping away any trace of drowsiness. He'd never felt this hungry in his life, like he hadn't eaten for weeks.

"Leo!" Nea noticed him rolling around in pain. She scrambled over to him. "What's wrong?"

"Food," he muttered.

"Right, right." She tossed him a pack stuffed to bursting. Leo dove headfirst into it and pulled out the first things that looked edible, scarfing down two warm loaves of bread, a few apples, pears and a bit of salted meat. Leo leaned back, the pain in his stomach finally abating.

"What was all that?" Nea asked, a bemused expression playing about her face. "Is it your arm?"

He nodded. "Whatever I did last night."

"What *did* you do exactly?"

"Right you were unconscious. Well Beljhar showed me you were a girl and I told him I didn't care. When I did, I'm not sure what happened, but it was like the ship vanished."

"Vanished?"

"Yeah, just one moment we were there and the next we were somewhere else."

"I don't understand?"

"Do you remember what those lanterns were made of?"

"They were opals," she nodded, eyes getting round.

"I think it was an illusion. There was never a ship at all, just an old fortress in the fog dressed up to look like one."

"God…" she hissed under her breath. "It was a bloody impossible thing."

"The lanterns carried the illusion, the same way the brooches do. So I destroyed them. I ignited Knail again."

"How? I thought you said you couldn't do it."

Leo blushed and turned away. "They were about to kill you, and it just of exploded, like in Adis, but something was different. It wasn't just light this time. It was… I dunno, solid, kind of, I didn't get a great look at it, but…"

"But what?"

"The way it was shaped, it was almost like a person." Leo's brow furrowed. "What do you make of that?"

"Sounds like one more thing Seiyariu didn't tell you."

"I suppose." He wasn't sure he wanted to think about Seiyariu just yet.

"Are you sure you're alright though? I mean it is still... still eating you, right?"

Leo held up his hand, looking it over. "I think it just subsists on me. It only seems to tire me out when I use it."

"Is it..." She frowned, looking for the right words. "I mean, is it better than how your arm was?"

"Oh yes!" Leo didn't even need to think about it. "I can move without any problems now. It only hurts when I use it and even then it's not so bad."

"Leo," her voice was oddly timid. Things were still ginger between them after all, so much had happened. Not for the first time since reuniting with his friend, Leo wished time would move just a little bit slower. But it didn't and neither did they.

"Will you tell me more about Nico?"

Leo's heart jumped a little. "Why?"

She fidgeted on the spot for a moment as if unsure of what to say, "You kind of... light up, when you talk about him. It's nice."

Leo smiled, then, "He used to always call me little brother, even though neither of us knew who was born first. He just kind of decided he would be the older one." The memory made him feel warm. "So he was in charge of all the adventures. The crazy things we used to get up to in that old abbey, that was all his doing."

"Wasn't that hard for him to talk you into it though?"

Leo laughed. "Never. He inspired me, like you did on the ship."

Her face fell. "Why did you... I dunno. I mean you lost him, it sounds like the worst pain on earth. Why did some skinny girl in pants inspire you? Just by giving you a little water?"

Leo shook his head. "It wasn't the water. There was something about you, something brave, infectious. You reminded me a little bit of him, I think. I'm sorry I know that sounds strange but..."

"No, it doesn't. You know I'm not exactly the kind of person who goes around helping strangers. Or at least I wasn't. I thought I hated people, but when I saw you there was just something, something different."

"Something familiar."

"Yeah, how'd you know?"

"Seiyariu talks about it sometimes."

"He said as much to me on the ship, can't get it out of my head."

They sat quietly for a little while, staring out at the valley.

"You hate people because of what you saw at that place right? Glatman?"

Nea didn't answer but her body gave a kind of jerk that could've been a nod.

"I sometimes felt like that too, you know."

"When the grassers had you?"

Leo nodded. "We were small but we outnumbered the slavers, some were allowed to use tools and everything. Nobody who'd been there more than a month ever tried to escape, let alone hurt anyone."

"Grassers make a strong first impression," she muttered.

"I'm not sure it's just that," Leo replied frowning.

He thought back to the boys and girls he'd been kept with. Some, like him, had started out madly trying to escape, only to be curtailed with such ferocity that the next two behind them wouldn't get any ideas. A horrible system of abuse them kept them all in line.

"I'm not sure I would've left my cell if you hadn't made me. Like they had…" He remembered a phrase Beljhar had used, "… shackles on their minds."

"A sound theory," came a voice from behind them.

Leo turned to see the wide wings of Zephyr fluttering to rest at the edge of the nest. Leo was in awe at the impossibility of her. She was beautiful, and terrifying all at once. Fortuna delighted in surprising him at every turn.

"Glad to see you're up and about Leo," she said.

"Thank you, Zephyr, for everything."

The Erinye puffed out her chest feathers a little bit proudly. Nea had to stifle a laugh. Zephyr ignored her.

"So how do you know Seiyariu?" Leo asked.

She snorted. "I'm a vagabond. Can't you tell?"

Leo looked her up and down, confused, before his eyes settled on her green scarf. Indeed, it was patched, just like Kokaleth's seaweed cloak. Leo supposed she wouldn't have been able to wear a proper cloak with those wings of hers.

Zephyr continued. "I haven't seen him or that damn Mariner in some time. We had a bit of a falling out. But I figured I, or at least the Erinyes, would at least come up in conversation."

"He didn't tell me much," said Leo. "About my parents, about Knail. Nothing."

Zephyr shifted on her perch. "I'll not make excuses for his behavior. A vagabond's decisions are his own. Now I'm assuming the two of you want to go after Seiyariu? Or do you mean to impose on our hospitality further?"

"We don't know where Seiyariu is," Nea replied flatly.

Zephyr scowled at them. "I do. I took the liberty of summoning Kokaleth to find him. Find him he did, but there was nothing that soggy old fool could do."

"What?" All the worst thoughts in the world rushed to Leo at once.

"Now don't lose your minds, I don't mean it like that. He's not dead, but Kokaleth on his best day couldn't get to him now."

"Where is he?" asked Leo, terror mounting in his gut. Was this his fault?

"I can take you to him," said Zephyr tentatively. "But…"

"But what?"

"Whatever may have happened in the past, I still care for Seiyariu and Kokaleth. If you mean to take revenge on him for what happened to your mother and father…"

"Revenge?" said Leo. "God no, I just want him to tell me how it all happened."

"Not a subject he'll likely want to discuss."

"I have to try."

"Very well." Zephyr tossed one of the packs to Nea. "Take out that map, would you? I'd do it myself but I don't fancy shredding the damn thing, I'm sure your little friend understands."

"Why do you have a map you can't use?" Nea asked.

Zephyr looked at her as if this was the most ridiculous question she'd ever been asked. "Every so often a human traveler stumbles into our valley. Don't look at me like that, we don't hurt them. Just fly them high enough that they don't ever want to find their way back."

This got a laugh out of Nea and she unrolled the map of Fortuna. Leo let out a little gasp when he saw how detailed it was. Slowly, he traced the path he'd taken with Seiyariu with his eyes. The Pinwheel Forest, Hunter's Hollow, Styx, it was all there but this was the first time Leo had gotten the chance to really see how it all came together. Seiyariu, of course, never carried a map.

"Here is where the two of you met up," said Zephyr, pointing a claw at a patch of sea to the east. "The island we found you on, or ship, you'll have to explain that to me at some point, it was here." Then she traced a finger along the sea. "We took you up this way, and here you are now." Her claw came to rest on the mountains in the southwest.

"Where is here exactly?" asked Leo, glancing out at the valley and mountains beyond.

"The Roc's Crest, one of the high nests that my people call home." Zephyr's eyes darted between the two of them and she led her finger north from the mountains to a series of lowlands just south of the capital. "According to Kokaleth, Seiyariu is here, at a place called House Lambert. My people will take you and we'll give you provisions for the journey."

"House Lam—"

"I wasn't finished," she chirped, shutting Leo up instantly. "You were not given the Call by us, still I think that if the need arises, should you need us again, and I have a feeling you will, remember the Call and we will answer it, at least two times more."

"Why two?" said Nea, raising an eyebrow.

"You ask a lot of questions," Zephyr said glaring at her. "The Call, at least the version given to Seiyariu, has a finite number of uses. Seiyariu had three remaining. That puts you at four."

"Thank you," said Leo, Nea nodding along.

Zephyr's voice was fast now, as if she was afraid the emotion would be too much. "Listen to me children. I know that this may be hard to believe now, but Seiyariu is a good man. Despite his best efforts that fact will never go away. I ask you to keep that in your hearts."

"Why? What's at House Lambert?" asked Leo. "Should we be ready for a fight?"

Zephyr shook her head. "There is nothing there, only memories. But to a man like that, those are the greatest danger of all."

53

The Lost House of Lambert

THE FLIGHT UP the coast was incredible. Despite the bitter cold that accompanied the first true day of winter, Nea was happier than she could ever remember being. In the grip of Zephyr, she soared along, enjoying the breeze rushing by her face, holding her arms out and letting the air buffet her. As they skimmed along a riverbed, twisting up and across the sky, she felt free as anyone could possibly dream of.

Leo was just out of reach, clutched in the talons of a second Erinye. In truth Nea welcomed the morning of solitude. She had a lot on her mind that she needed to sort out. The words they'd shared in the night, it was like nothing else that had ever happened to her before. Not with Cain, not with anybody. It was a bond, a covenant. He trusted her with the darkest truths of his life, and Nea, despite everything, trusted him back. Was this what friendship, real friendship felt like?

It's... it's nice.

She turned her attention back to the rushing landscape. Just a couple days ago the idea of creatures like the Erinyes had been little more than fantasy, and now here she was, flying with them. The way they carried themselves, like the rest of the world was ridiculous and impossible, not them. Nea wondered if Leo's Mariner friend was the same.

What other mad adventures are you going to find now that you're staying with him?

Though doubt still clung to her, Nea had made up her mind; she was staying with Leo, wherever that may take her.

There was little sunshine to be had that day. The grey sky overhead was threatening rain, but all it did was billow the same cold wind throughout the morning.

Their journey came to a halt at a small and overgrown patch of forest on the outskirts of a silent town. At first Nea assumed they were landing at the edge of the wood to hide from view, but when their feet touched the ground and she was face to face with Zephyr again, the Erinye pointed one sharp claw towards a run-down old path. There may have once been a road, buried under all the greenery.

"Follow it to the end," said Zephyr had told them. "He'll be waiting there."

Without so much as a word, Zephyr and her companion took off once more, sailing up into the grey sky until they were out of sight.

"Goodbye, I guess," said Nea, scowling after them.

"She sure was quick get away from this place," said Leo warily. "Why do suppose that is?"

"Leave it to the scarecrow to chase off the birds," said Nea, only half joking.

The two of them set off down the abandoned trail into the woods, the dull grey sheen of the morning making navigation easy enough.

"He never mentioned anything about this House Lambert to you before then?" asked Nea, stepping gingerly around the overgrown roots.

"He never talked about himself." said Leo.

There was something wrong there. "He seemed like such a braggart when we met."

"I suppose he does talk rather grandly. But every time I tried to ask him about himself he'd say something mysterious and change the subject."

"Knowing what he did, it must've been painful for him to talk about, especially since he was trying to pull the wool over your eyes."

"Almost like I didn't really know him at all."

She was unsure of what to say to this. Nea wasn't even sure of how she felt about the scarecrow. She was angry at him for lying to her, lying to Leo, but there was something very familiar about his lies.

He's not the first person to pretend to be someone he's not. Still, if it wasn't for him, Leo's family might still be alive.

"It's ok," Leo said, peering over at her. "I don't know how to feel about him either."

"That obvious, am I?" She laughed and gave him a little shove, ruffling his mane of bright red hair. "It's a bloody miracle we can trust anyone even a little bit, eh?"

Leo managed to smile a little at this. Painful though it was, she had to admit that it was nice to finally be able to talk about the past with another human being.

An hour passed on the ruined back road. To her intense delight, Leo had as big an ear for stories as she did, perhaps bigger. The two swapped identical accounts of sneaking into the library to read until morning, leaving the world behind and reveling in those that existed between the pages. They joked and argued; retelling their favorites as best they could to pass the time, laughing when they got bits wrong. Soon enough they came to the end of the road, to the ruins of House Lambert.

The manor had likely once been a grand old thing, but it was falling to pieces now, eaten up by the forest and the relentless march of time. The surrounding wood was like some terrible sea creature trying to drag the house under. Long tendrils of ivy slithered into the doors and windows. Branches burst from holes in the wall and roof. Wealth and prosperity had given way to rot and ruin, like a filthy corpse in an expensive doublet.

Nea glanced over at Leo. He had that scared puppy expression that was already becoming so familiar. "Why would he be in a place like this?" he said softly.

Nea didn't have an answer. "Come on," she said, trying to motivate herself as much as Leo.

One of the double doors had been broken off its hinges long ago and lay discarded in the overgrown grass. The other hung limp on one hinge as if lonely. Mounted above the door frame was a bronze plaque now green with age. On it, was engraved a single letter L.

They crept through the doors. The landing had been all but buried by a collapsing staircase; the wood was rotted through and it filled their noses with the stench of decay. Pricking up her ears, Nea listened for any sign of humanity, but she heard nothing other than the creaks of the ancient floorboards. She reached for Leo's hand and found he was no longer beside her. "Leo," she hissed, unsure why she was whispering.

"Here," he'd stumbled into what had once been a parlor or a smoking room.

She could still make out the remnants of tables and chairs and even an old stone fireplace, but anything of value had long since been ransacked.

"God, nobody's lived here in—"

But she didn't get to finish. It was faint, but Leo heard it too, echoing from somewhere out behind the house, the unmistakable sound of running water.

Leo was already moving, through what were once the kitchens and out into the back garden. There he froze. Across the ruins of the garden, there was a small pond. Beside this stood a single tree, older than the rest. It was crooked, broken, deformed. Resting at its base was a crumpled human form.

They ran to him fast as they could. For one terrible moment, Nea thought that he was dead. He sat, staring unblinking across the water. But his lips were moving, mumbling the words to a song she didn't know. He was alive.

The vagabond was almost unrecognizable. His hair was filthy, as were his clothes, his eyes red and swollen. Seiyariu's face was a bruised mess, covered in cuts and scrapes, and Nea didn't have to see the litter of empty bottles around him to know that he was drunk. He reeked of it. He didn't even register that they were standing there.

Leo was muttering something to Seiyariu, but the vagabond ignored him, continuing to stare out across the water, singing his sad little tune.

What was your plan scarecrow? Give up and drink yourself to death?

He hadn't known if they'd found his message or not. He'd just given up, to wallow in… Nea bit her lip, this wasn't the time to get angry.

Leo brushed his hand across Seiyariu's forehead; the vagabond's eyes flickered slightly, and he stopped singing. Seiyariu's mouth curled in a smile, a confused mad smile that was so unlike him. "He's burning up," said Leo.

"Probably been out here all night," said Nea, filling an empty bottle with water from the pond. "That, or he doesn't believe his senses. I wouldn't either if I was that drunk."

"How long do you think he's been like this?"

"Dunno,"

"What're you—"

"My Da used get like this sometimes," she said. "Help me get him up. Better to do this inside, yeah?"

Somehow the two of them managed to haul Seiyariu back inside the old house. Leo made a wet compress for his forehead, that would help a little bit, but they needed to keep him warm. The fireplace in the parlor had been one thing in the old house that hadn't collapsed. So they lit a small blaze in the grate and lay the vagabond out in front of it. Nea set about boiling the water in a pot she found in the kitchen. They had some herbs in their pack. She could make some tea. That might help.

As they worked in silence on the floor, over the inebriated form of the vagabond Nea kept snatching glimpses of Leo's face. There was nothing in his eyes but horrible, pallid, fear and guilt.

Pull through scarecrow. For his sake.

The hours crawled by, Seiyariu was well and truly asleep now. His fever had broken now that he was warm and had something in his body other than booze. As the firelight played across his haggard face, Nea thought she might've seen a glimpse of the man she'd encountered on Beljhar's ship.

"What am I going to say to him?" said Leo, half to himself.

"Remember on the ship, or whatever it was, you said you wanted to hear the story in his words, you still do, right?"

"Yes of course…" He avoided looking at her.

"You can be angry, you know," said Nea, choosing her words carefully. She wasn't cut out for this kind of emotional talk.

Leo shook his head. "I don't want to be. Not anymore. You see those marks on Seiyariu's face, those cuts? That was me. After Beljhar told me the truth, I was so angry, I just wanted to hurt him. I could've killed him. Beljhar gave me the chance."

"But you didn't," she finished for him.

"But I could've," he said, looking at her with a desperation in his eyes.

"But you didn't," she repeated firmly. "That was a choice. You had the opportunity and you made a choice, just like with Knail, just like when you tried to escape with me. I wish I'd made that choice myself, but I didn't, I've hurt people. Sometimes people who didn't even do anything to me."

The hell are you thinking? You can't tell him about that. He'll think you're a monster.

"What do you mean?"

Shut up!

"There was this girl in Limani. She saw me stealing clothes, saw what I was, you know? She didn't mean to but when she did… I dunno, I just lost control. I guess she reminded me of the girls at Glatman."

He met her eyes, grasping for some kind of understanding but she had no excuse to offer him.

"Was she alright?"

Nea nodded, not meeting his gaze. "I hit Cain once too. Towards the end, she told me she knew I was a girl. Told me she'd known the whole time. Nea found herself clenching her fists at the memory. But her rage was not at Cain, not this time. "Whenever I feel weak, I feel like I'm Linnea again, it's like I turn into this monster."

"What's Linnea?"

She blinked and let out a little humorless laugh. "That's my name. My real name. Linnea Dúlaman."

That sweeping stare must've been another thing he'd picked up from his vagabond. "You aren't like that anymore."

"How do you know?"

"You didn't try to hurt me, when I found out," said Leo.

"N… no."

"Why not?"

Because…

Nea found she couldn't even finish the thought. "I don't… I didn't…"

Leo gave her a sad little smile. "I don't think we're the same people we were. You've changed, I've changed. You and Seiyariu, you both helped me be stronger. If it wasn't for you… I might've… I might've turned out just like Beljhar."

"Like… Beljhar?"

"Yes," said Leo, gazing into the fire. "But I didn't, and I won't. If that means giving Seiyariu a chance then…"

He trailed off but Nea took his hand in hers. She didn't know what to say, but the contact seemed right. Leo closed his eyes and held on to her tight as he could, as if convincing himself she was still there. And Nea sat with him, watching the fire until the night drifted in.

54
Atone

After a small supper, Leo and Nea made up their bedrolls in the parlor. They curled up close as they could to the fire, as the night grew cold outside. The battered walls of House Lambert kept the worst of the autumn wind out. Leo soon drifted off, Nea's hand still clasped in his. The soothing contact kept his dreams blissfully free of the usual horrors. He wasn't sure how long he slept, but far too soon he felt Nea shaking him awake.

"Leo. He's moving."

Leo was awake instantly. "What?"

Sure enough, Seiyariu let out a little groan and shifted slightly. His eyes flickering open, bringing some life back to his face. He looked up at Nea, confused. Then he turned and saw Leo.

"L… Leo?" he stammered, trying to sit up.

"Don't worry scarecrow, you're not drunk anymore," said Nea clearly trying to keep the venom out of her voice. "We're real. Got your message and everything."

"You… you came to find me?" said Seiyariu, as if unable to believe it was true.

"Seiyariu," said Leo, unable to look Seiyariu in the face. "Please. I want you to tell me the truth."

The man Leo saw before him looked like his old teacher, he was wearing his clothes, his skin, but the facade was gone. The sagely aura that surrounded Seiyariu had evaporated the moment Leo had emerged from the vision of his parents. He knew he would never see that Seiyariu again. That Seiyariu had been a construct, an illusion.

"I'm going to give you this one last chance. Tell me everything, absolutely everything. Starting with my parents."

There was a long silence, what color was left in Seiyariu's face retreated. "I'll not give you excuses," he said. "You know what happened."

Leo nodded, "But I want to hear it from you."

For a moment Leo thought he was going to refuse, dance around the question as he so often did. Or try and run like Nea had when he'd learned her secret. He did neither. His eyes darting back and forth between the two of them, he sighed.

"Very well." With a groan, Seiyariu propped himself against the stone of the chimney, letting the fire's warmth soak into his bones. "But it's something of a long story, so try and get comfortable."

"Take your time," Leo replied, still trying to keep any emotion from his words.

Seiyariu closed his eyes for a moment, collecting himself. "It begins when I first left home. Ran away from home, rather. I wasn't much older than you at the time. I didn't know the first thing about surviving on my own. You both know that the wild woods and back roads of the Archipelago are no place for a young person to wander alone. I was a mess, cold, hungry, and sick. I might've been picked up the grassers, or worse, if he hadn't found me."

"He?" Nea asked, her eyes wide with interest.

"A vagabond named Heiro Al-Emani," said Seiyariu.

Leo felt his hands shaking ever so slightly. "My father."

"Yes, a noble from the east on the run from his family line. I didn't know this at the time of course. He was quite a young man, but there was a wisdom about him beyond his years. He took pity on me and kept me safe. Never asked for anything in return. He taught me to fight, to read the world around me, much of what I teach you comes from him Leo. I thought you might like that."

Leo couldn't picture Seiyariu being anyone's student, much less his father's.

"We traveled together for a time, but it wasn't long before we met her." A shadow swept across Seiyariu's face. "Resha Fortunato."

Leo felt his heart jump ever so slightly in his chest. He had so rarely heard his mother's name spoken.

"She was a traveling performer, already used to the road. But she wanted to get away from her troupe and persuaded us to take her along.

From the first day we met, she and I were inseparable. Rather like the two of you I suppose."

Leo tried to imagine his mother, his father and Seiyariu side by side. Three vagabonds on the Green Road together, bound for a single, terrible fate. How had everything gone so wrong?

"The three of us traveled together for several years; that was when we met Kokaleth and Zephyr. I could tell you stories for weeks about all the adventures we had. But as I got older I grew more and more curious about my mentor's identity." Seiyariu averted his gaze now, staring into the dancing flames. "He was... a braver man than I. He told me the moment I asked him. He sat Resha and I down and revealed that he was the heir to the Twelfth City-State of Inferno. And that he had no desire to rule."

"He was running away," said Nea flatly.

"He wouldn't deny that, I don't think. The twelve city-states of Inferno have been at odds since their founding, and the nation was in a state of constant war. Attempting to corral that had driven his father, your grandfather, into an early grave. However, in Heiro's absence things grew worse. Eventually we heard so many reports of the war to the east that he could ignore it no longer. He made a decision to return to Inferno and attempt to end the fighting. At first he refused to bring Resha and me along, but we likewise refused to let him leave us behind. The three of us went east together."

"How old were all of you?" asked Nea, not looking at anyone.

"Let's see, if it was fourteen years ago I suppose I must've been seventeen, eighteen perhaps, I can't quite remember. Resha was my age and Heiro was fifteen years our senior."

Leo frowned, "Does that mean that...?"

"I'm getting there don't worry," Seiyariu assured him. "Heiro took command of his late father's state, trying to lead them out of the war. However, it soon became apparent that the fighting would never truly stop. So Heiro made a decision, leading his army to conquer the warring states and bring peace to his homeland."

"And you fought in the war with him?"

"Yes, for three long years. Resha and I served as his Lieutenants. As the war dragged on, Heiro arranged to marry the commander of an allied city-state. Her name was Aisha Al-Mubarak. We didn't know what to make of her at first. She'd broken tradition and fought in the war, leading her home to victory after victory. I think it's what made Heiro agree to the marriage. He married Aisha, and together the four of us led our allied states to victory. For the first time since its founding, the twelve city-states of Inferno were united under one banner, one king. It's quite something, heir, to vagabond, to king in just a few years. I found myself living in the palace of Inferno with all my friends, it should've been perfect…" He trailed off, staring up at the ceiling.

"Did you love her?" asked Nea suddenly. Leo and Seiyariu both looked at her in surprise.

"Love who? The Queen? I'm getting there don't worr—"

"No, not the Queen. Resha, Leo's mother."

Seiyariu's face went pale, and for a moment he said nothing, "What gave it away?"

Nea raised an eyebrow, "You're not as good a secret keeper as you think."

"No," Said Seiyariu, "No I must not be."

"You were in love with my mother?" Leo couldn't keep the emotion from his voice this time.

Seiyariu met his eyes and nodded, "I was, more than I had ever thought possible. From the day we met, at least, I like to think so. She had a love of life unlike anyone I'd ever known. She loved making people smile and laugh, it was infectious. Just being around her made you feel warm, as if her soul burned bright enough to keep yours lit." His eyes were shining now.

Leo was dumbstruck, struggling to process what he was hearing. *He loved her. Loved her.*

"But by the time I realized my own feelings, it was too late. She was in love with another, someone I'd considered my closest friend, my ally, my mentor, even my father. When I discovered Heiro and Resha were together I was crushed. I haunted the palace corridors, barely eating, barely sleeping. I wasn't the only one. The Queen, Aisha, was in a similar state. Despite her best efforts, she was deeply in love with her husband. But he had no eyes for her, no room in his heart. The two of us were unbearably distraught and lonely. We fell into each other's arms, two broken souls desperate to love someone we couldn't have."

Leo felt tears in his eyes as he listened. He knew the story from here, but he needed to hear it again.

"When I discovered Resha was pregnant. I lost myself. I confronted Heiro and revealed my dealings with Aisha." said Seiyariu, eyes hollow. "I invoked the holy right of the duel, Allahuain Twarta, the prescribed punishment for adulterers in Inferno. Heiro was a man of faith and I knew he would accept." Then Seiyariu finally looked back at Leo. His face was stained with tears. "I wish I could say that I did not intend to win, that it was some elaborate attempt at suicide, but I've told you enough lies. All I can offer is this, jealous men do dreadful things to one another. Don't ever forget that."

There was silence for a time. It was so sad, so unfair. Even Nea had tears in her eyes.

"I was ready to die, in the aftermath," Seiyariu finally continued. "Aisha was distraught. I'm sure she wanted me dead, but by rights I had exacted holy justice on an adulterer. So she gave me the smallest window of time to get away and take Resha with me. We fled the city together. Crushed by grief though she was, Resha went along with me, knowing that that in her condition, she couldn't travel alone. She was thinking of your well-being. We went south to the island where she had been born. She said I owed her at least that." Seiyariu gave a hysterical sort of laugh that faded almost instantly. "On the ship, Resha began to get sick. At first I thought it was the pregnancy, but she grew worse, even after we landed. It was becoming clear to both of us that she wasn't going to survive. You and Nico, that was all she cared about, making sure the two of you arrived safely. She was a strong woman, and she held onto life until the last moment. I was able to bring you and your brother into this world, though she did not live to see you."

Leo felt himself shaking; it was crashing over him like a waterfall. He wanted Seiyariu to stop talking; he couldn't listen to any more. "The two patches on your cloak, they were your mother and father's you know."

Leo brushed his fingers against these, savoring the touch. He'd carried them both with him, all along. Was this why Seiyariu hadn't told him, this pain? He felt Nea's hand on his shoulder and kept listening.

"It was before your time, so you were both very small," Seiyariu said, gathering himself. "And I couldn't trust myself to take you on the road. At least not then. I left you at the abbey. I told myself I'd return and collect you when I'd become someone I could stand to look at in the mirror. But when I returned, Nico was dead, and you were gone." He added, looking Leo in the eyes seriously. "I never should've left you there."

Leo's silent sobs were all he could manage, the despair of it all, the idea of Seiyariu holding Resha's cold hand. Of visiting Nico's little grave on the grounds of the old stone church. He realized he was crying as much for Seiyariu as he was for himself.

"Is that satisfactory?" Seiyariu asked, wiping his eyes.

"I wish you'd told me everything," Leo choked. "From the beginning."

"So do I. But I'd hoped we could live like Heiro and I had. I was terribly misguided. I think I always knew that it was a fantasy. It just took me this long to admit it."

"So what happens now?" asked Leo.

"If you'd like I'll leave you, and you'll never have to see or think about me ever again."

"No." Even Leo was amazed at how fast his answer came. Despite everything Seiyariu had done, this wouldn't be where their journey ended. He did not know if he had forgiven Seiyariu or if he just desperately wanted to, but he had made up his mind. "You can't go, not yet." He swallowed and righted himself, trying to put on his bravest face. "We've got to get to Equius, tell the King what we've learned about the Briars, and about Knail."

"We?"

"We."

"Very well," said Seiyariu. "But after that, I can understand if you'll want to part ways, I don't blame you."

"We'll deal with that when we get to it." With these words Leo felt an enormous weight lift off of his back, sudden exhaustion overtaking him.

"It's more than I deserve," said Seiyariu, his face in shadow. "This mask I've worn, I don't—"

"We all wear masks scarecrow," Nea muttered, breaking her silence. "You're not so bad."

55
Second Chances

THE MORNING CAME bright and cold, casting beams of light through the holes in the wall. Seiyariu must've had a wash and a shave while the two of them slept, for when Nea finally rolled over to face the chilly morning, she saw the old scarecrow as he'd been. Not a trace remained of the drunken wretch they nursed back to health the night before. He gave her a smile but said nothing, just went about packing his things. It was fine; enough had been said the night before for a life-time. However, Nea was caught off guard when Seiyariu tossed her an emerald green cloak.

"What's all this then?"

"For the road."

"But…"

"If it's too short let me know, I can adjust it."

Nea was shaking her head, a bemused smirk on her face. "So, I'm a vagabond now?"

Seiyariu shrugged. "If you so choose."

Nea took the cloak from Seiyariu; it was the same length as Leo's with the same two patches on the inside. "Was this supposed to be for Nico?"

"Yes it was. Do try it on, it would be such a shame to let this one go to waste."

Nea conceded and wound the cloak over her shoulders, it was a bit heavier than she'd thought but it kept the cold out something wonderful.

"Not bad," she said.

"I think it looks great." Leo had finally roused himself.

"Do you," Nea smiled at him and fiddled with the hood. "I suppose it'll do."

"Do you remember the syntax Leo?"

He nodded proudly and fastened it for her, saying, "You have to repeat after me alright?"

Nea nodded. "Don't go too fast all right?"

"I give you the Rite of the Vagabond. Until the Clash comes again, you will walk the green road, a wanderer and guardian. A son of Romulus. Not alone, but as the legacy of those who came before you. Do not shy away from pain, inside and out. For Pain begets Power."

Nea repeated it, savoring each word. There was so much meaning there, she could feel it.

"So you're coming with us then?" Seiyariu asked, raising an eyebrow.

Nea smirked at him, "Of course I bloody am, somebody has to keep you two alive."

They gathered their things and left House Lambert behind without fanfare. Words had been said, promises had been made, but they still had a mission to finish. There was something about three of them walking together, all in the vagabond colors.

Don't you look a sight.

These parts of Fortuna were heavily wooded, with trees taking over the rolling hills as great formations of rock protruded out from the earth. Countless small stonewalls had been built alongside houses, roads, and property boarders through the wild forests. Many of these were crumbing in disrepair, but many more were still standing firm.

Leaves had begun to fall more and more; decorating the roads they travelled a beautiful collage of red, yellow, and orange. The air was inviting, and the sky was free of clouds, probably the last time it would be this year. With winter here at last, it wouldn't be long before it grew too cold to stay outside. Inns however, were getting more common as they made their way north. There were far more people on the roads than there had been. In one day alone they passed through three towns, not small ones either. It was in one of these that they stopped for supplies. Though before they entered Nea had turned Leo's cloak, so that it covered his black hand.

"Don't fancy drawing any looks," she said, admiring her handi-work. "Vagabonds are supposed to be sneaky right?"

"Don't know what gave you that idea Nea," said Seiyariu with a laugh.

"I have a bit of a question scarecrow," said Nea, jogging to catch up with the vagabond as they crossed through the market.

"I'm sure you've got quite a few of them…" He gave Nea a thorough look up and down.

This wasn't the first time on their trip Nea felt certain he was looking right through her disguise. "If you're going to keep calling me that, I'm going to have come up with a suitably charming title for you don't you think?"

"Good luck." Nea laughed, breathing a sigh of relief.

"Ask away then."

"Where do you get your money?"

"Ah Nea, never ask a gentleman that ques—"

"I'd like to know that too," piped up Leo, appearing at Seiyariu's side, interested.

Once it was clear they weren't going to let him wriggle out of this one he sighed. "Well I suppose I might as well tell you, but you're both a little young. We call it the Wayfarer's Tax. In theory vagabonds are doing a service to Fortuna, roaming the land, keeping it safe and not asking for anything in return, so it's only natural for us to just… well… help ourselves."

"Help yourselves?" said Nea. "You steal all this, do you?"

"Steal is perhaps the wrong word, re-appropriate perhaps would be—"

"Seiyariu," Leo gave him a hurt look. "You didn't tell me about this."

"Well it's not something you learn as a vagabond until you're a little older,"

"That's how you got the money in Raeva," said Leo. "You stole it!"

Nea laughed, "This might be the life for me after all."

*

At the next pond, Seiyariu insisted on summoning Kokaleth to inform him of all that had happened. Nea watched this with bated breath. The scarecrow uncorked some of that strange salt Leo had told her about and poured around half the bottle into the water. For a moment nothing happened, then the water began to bubble and foam, churning back and forth. This continued for several full minutes during which Nea forgot to breath.

The oldest people in her little fishing village would often tell her and the other children stories of the mariners, the strange men in the sea. They'd spun legends of their great ancient underwater cities, of the beasts of the deep that they tamed and rode into battle, of the rare times that they would come and interact with the world above the waves. Nea had always imagined them as looking like gigantic fish with legs, but she was astonished by just how human Kokaleth looked.

"What. Were. You. Thinking?" he growled, striding from the water and advancing on Seiyariu, eyes bulging with rage. His gurgling voice was deep and menacing. His long, webbed fingers flexed dangerously and for a moment Nea was certain he was going to knock Seiyariu out.

"Kokaleth I—"

"Selfish idiot! Do you have any idea what might've happened to the children if it hadn't been for Zephyr?"

"I made sure she would find them," said Seiyariu avoiding the mariner's sweeping gaze.

"Drop the responsibility on someone else and run. It's becoming a tiresome pattern, Seiyariu." Kokaleth snarled and drew in even closer. "At least you've got that stink of liquor off you."

"Kokaleth, it's okay," said Leo putting a hand on the mariner's scaly forearm. "Everyone's safe. Seiyariu's not going to get like that again." He flashed a look at the vagabond, "Right?"

Seiyariu smiled at Leo and finally looked Kokaleth in the eye. "No, I think that was the last time."

"You say that," said Kokaleth, "and maybe it's true. But I promise you this, for me and Zephyr at least, that *was* the last time. Are we understood?"

"Perfectly."

"Good, now what the hell happened? Where were the three of you? Why didn't you summon me? Where is Kna—" And then the Mariner's eyes fell on Leo, more specifically, Leo's arm.

For a long moment, the mariner said nothing. Though the water behind him seemed to be frothing with barely controlled rage. Leo stared wide-eyed from Seiyariu to Kokaleth, then to Nea.

Don't bloody look over here! The hell does he expect you to say?

"Seiyariu," said Kokaleth finally, "Start talking."

Kokaleth's constant interruptions made the tale take forever, but once Seiyariu had convinced him that Leo had absolutely needed Knail, and that it was better in the hands of a vagabond than the Briars, Kokaleth settled down. Seiyariu launched into the tale of their imprisonment. Nea noticed that he didn't skirt around what had happened between him and Leo. Leo looked uncomfortable hearing all of this, especially under the eyes of Kokaleth, but Seiyariu was quick to get the gist of the story across.

"Well that certainly puts things in perspective." said Kokaleth when Seiyariu had finished. "Telling your king about this would be prudent. Especially now that you've dealt a powerful blow to the other side. They might try to retaliate with gusto, don't you think?"

"That's what I'm afraid of," said Seiyariu nodding.

"Though the use of Knail in such a way is tantamount to heresy."

"I'm sorry Kokaleth," said Leo. "I'd give it back if I could."

"I know, I know. Why's this one keep staring boggle-eyed at me?" Kokaleth stepped past Seiyariu, sizing up Nea. "Do I frighten you?"

"No," Nea said truthfully. "You… you're incredible."

Seiyariu groaned as Kokaleth's face cracked into a smile. "You have no idea child. I am master of the tides, lord of the sea."

"You've got him started now," said Seiyariu.

"Shut up, I am the rider of the arctic whales, the pariah, the vagabond, the last of the—"

"I believe you," Nea said grinning. "How do you know the scarecrow?"

"The scarecrow? Oh, you mean Seiyariu? That's a good name for him, he's got about as many birds nesting in his clothes."

"Don't let Zephyr hear you talk like that." Seiyariu laughed, and Kokaleth joined him.

"So," Nea wasn't quite sure what else to say. "You two traveled together?"

"You might say that," replied Kokaleth. "We trained under the same vagabond, a human, one of the good ones."

"Leo's father."

"Apparently. Zephyr too."

An image of a young Mariner, Erinye and Seiyariu flashed before her view and Nea began to smile. "You all just walked around together did you?"

"Yes, walking is something I'm capable of." Kokaleth said, sounding rather wounded, "I don't dry out in the sun and flop around 'til I'm dead if that's what you think."

This continued for a while, they ate while Kokaleth talked and laughed till it was time they parted ways. It was nice; the mariner was abrasive and dramatic but entertaining. Just before he left he gave them each a bottle with that same blue salt. Nea tucked hers into her shirt pocket along with the Erinyes flute. She silently vowed that she would keep these on her at all times, no matter where she went.

*

Over the next few days Nea had to keep reminding herself that she hadn't been with her new companions for long. Their nights were spent telling mad stories, laughing, as she hadn't done in ages. She caught herself smiling more. Perhaps a little companionship wasn't the worst thing in the world.

Still, there were a few downsides, like how she got looks from Seiyariu when she'd go into the woods to relieve herself instead of just off the path, or when she would insist on only bathing at night when they would come to a river. This was not aided by an oblivious Leo who followed her everywhere. He clung to her like a shadow during the day, and his bedroll was never in the same place he'd set it up come morning, either nestled closer to her or Seiyariu. He meant no harm by it of course, but Nea couldn't help but feel like a rock in the middle of a river that he had to cling to, to stay alive. When she thought about why this was though she didn't blame him too much.

Some nights they stayed in inns, some they slept under the stars. There were even a few occasions where they stayed in someone's house. This always unnerved Nea, but some of these people even knew Seiyariu by name. One woman's children even called him "Uncle Seiya."

"It's always good to know people," he'd said to the two of them. "Be kind and helpful and people will welcome you. Every vagabond should have a least a few homes where they're known and welcome."

Seiyariu's false confidence and cloak of pretend wisdom didn't bother her as it had when she first met him. She'd seen the burned husk of a man underneath. He was an inquisitive old fool and knew, or wanted to know, everyone. Especially, to her horror, the strangers they met on the road.

Still, having him back put that smile on Leo's face. She'd never seen him look that happy. Though they talked and acted like nothing had changed, Nea could sense just how careful they were being with each other. Seiyariu's revelations had hit Leo deep, and her as well. He'd bared his soul, not just to Leo but to her, a complete stranger. She didn't know how to feel about that. She didn't know how to feel about a lot of things.

Do you ever?

Her training as a vagabond was virtually non-existent. She already knew how to fight, fish, hunt, steal; all that was missing was her being able to read Peregrine Runes. There was a lot to cover, but she was a decent study and there were many chances to practice. Those strange symbols were everywhere, cut into trees, fences, the sides of houses, shops, bar stools, even on beds at the inn. How many damn vagabonds must there be to scribble all over everything in Fortuna like this?

The night before Seiyariu had said they would reach Equius, she and Leo found themselves nestled by the fireplace in a busy roadside inn. The vagabond had made himself scarce.

Probably off to re-appropriate for the rest of the journey.

Leo had grabbed some charcoal from the hearth and was testing Nea to see if she could recognize distinct peregrine runes. To her surprise she was actually doing fairly well.

"And this one?" asked Leo.

"Sympathetic," she said after a moment. "Someplace that'll take pity on filthy homeless drifters like us, yeah?"

He nodded, beaming. "I think you've got almost all the important ones."

"Let me see that for a second."

Leo obliged and handed her the charcoal. Nea had been trying to recall it for some time, a mark that she'd always just taken to be a signature or a blemish. She'd only seen it a few times, but she did her best to recreate it now, a circle with a line through the center protruding out and becoming arrows pointing in both directions.

"What's this mean?"

Leo's eyes darted to hers for a second, then back to the floor. "Where did you see that?"

"It was on the gate, leading into Glatman. It's one of them, isn't it?"

Leo nodded, "It's one of the advanced ones, Seiyariu told me a little about these, they're sayings, vagabond wisdom you know?"

"Why was one that far south?"

Leo shrugged. "There are vagabonds in the Southern Isles, just not as many. At least that's what Seiyariu told me."

"What's it say then?"

"It's…" he hesitated for a moment. "Evil lives here."

The words hung in the air for a moment as Nea took them in. "Yeah, that sounds about right, I think."

"Sorry."

"Don't be," she shrugged.

"What was it like, before all that?"

"Before Glatman?"

He nodded. "When you were with your mother and father."

Nea sighed, wondering about this for a moment. "It wasn't what you're imagining, I don't think."

"You said your father used to drink."

"Yeah, yeah he did. No more secrets after all," she said trying to keep the reluctance out of her voice. She'd avoided talking about her family for so long. "He would be cruel sometimes, when he was drunk I mean. As I got older it became clear he didn't trust my mother. Thought I might've been someone else's kid y'know? He never hit me, not hard, just yelled a lot. I felt bad because he worked all day, he really did, for me and for my mother. Who was I to get mad at him for having a drink or two?"

"Sounds like you're making excuses for him."

You are.

Nea blinked in surprise, "Other kids had it worse though. I think he treated drink the way Beljhar's men do those illusions, you know? An escape. Things weren't so bad. Until I was about twelve. That was when he left."

"Left?"

Nea nodded, "Just left. Woke up one morning and he was gone. I didn't understand at the time, now I bet he just wanted to get away from my mother."

"Is that a joke?"

Sounds like one doesn't it?

"Dunno. She was difficult."

"How do you mean?"

She could be bloody insane sometimes.

Nea groped vainly for the words but couldn't think of what to say except the truth.

You said no more secrets. Show him you meant it.

"She could be bloody insane sometimes." said Nea. "She would fly into these rages. It got worse after my Da left though."

"Was that when they took you to Glatman?" said Leo.

"Didn't even take me, Mum agreed to it." said Nea.

"What?" Rage flashed in Leo's eyes. "She didn't care about what… what was going to happen to you?"

"Probably didn't have a clue about any of it," Nea said with a shrug. "Thought I was getting an education."

More excuses.

"That's horrible."

They sat in silence for a few moments before Leo said, "Will you tell me a little more about Cain?"

Nea stiffened a little bit. She'd been doing her best not to think about Cain these past few days. Being around people again, people who cared about her, it made Nea miss Cain even more. But she didn't even know if the lady knight was alive or dead.

"It's ok," said Leo, as if reading her mind. "She'll be there. You said she was strong right?"

Nea snorted. "Strong, unbearable, self-righteous, stubborn and nosey." She leaned back closer to the warmth of the fire. "But yeah, she was strong, and kind, sometimes she was even clever. Not bad in a fight either."

"Was she a swordsman?"

"Would you believe me if I said her fists?"

"Wow," said Leo, glancing at his mutilated hand. "Do you think she'd…"

"Teach you?" Nea smiled. "No need, if you want to learn to fist fight I can help you with that. I've had lots of practice. Why do you want to learn fist fighting anyway? I thought Seiyariu would've shown you all his tricks with a sword by now."

"My arm kept getting in the way."

Seiyariu appeared at the bar, talking amicably with the barkeep. Leo looked over at him.

"I'm sorry about your dad."

"Yeah." She followed his gaze, taking in Seiyariu again in his entirety. "Sorry about yours too."

Leo stared at her for a moment, but before he could say anything else, the vagabond had returned clutching mugs of something warm and creamy.

"For you," he said jovially.

"Oh scarecrow you're the greatest," said Nea beaming as she took the mug from him. This enthusiasm died the moment she realized that there wasn't any alcohol to speak of in the drink.

"Sorry to disappoint you, but I can't afford to dull that barbed wit of yours, we'll need it tomorrow."

"Have it your way," she passed the mug to Leo. "I'm going to bed. Goodnight Leo, goodnight scarecrow."

Leo was still looking thoughtfully into the fire, but Seiyariu gave her a warm smile. "Goodnight, Dulcinea."

56
Kings and Vagabonds

Leo's first look at Equius came when they crested a large stone hill spattered with leaves. The wood gave way to a grand view of the city before them, and he couldn't help but gasp.

Atop a cliff, overlooking the sea, stood a castle so silent and cold that it may have been a part of the stone on which it sat. It was not a palace, no, this was a fortress, a great sentinel keeping watch over the land. Fierce towers pierced the sky, and Leo could just make out the dark blue Fortuan banners, blowing in the wind.

The city itself wound from the cliffside fortress down onto the plains before them and then back towards the sea. Gigantic walls wrapped the city in its secure embrace, its harbor all but consuming the coastline. The buildings by the sea were built from dark wood. As the cobblestone roads wound up through the districts nearer the castle, they became stone and brick. Leo's jaw was slack at the majesty of it all. It was an incredible display of wealth, design, and most of all, power.

"Damn," he heard Nea hiss.

On the southbound road into the harbor they could make out throngs of people queuing with horses and wagons spattered throughout, all trying to get through the city gate.

Seiyariu frowned, stroking his chin. "They didn't used to have such security on the south gate, that's supposed to be for riff-raff."

"Those people don't look like riff-raff," said Leo.

"No but we bloody well do," said Nea.

"Winter," Seiyariu muttered.

"What?"

"I got my dates wrong again. But this time it might be to our bene-fit," the vagabond said. "There's a market festival at the end of autumn, a large one, farmers all over the country come to buy and sell, ships make port, entertainers make coin. There's even a formal jubilee at the palace, though I doubt we'll be invited to that."

"Is that good for us?" asked Nea.

Seiyariu sighed. "This time of year the military police will be far too busy breaking up drunken scuffles over farmers' daughters to worry about us, particularly if we know where to go."

"And you know where to go scarecrow?"

"Naturally."

*

Leo and Nea gazed slack-jawed at the wall, like sailors eyeing an encroaching tidal wave. Men were patrolling atop the parapets, soldiers in crisp blue uniforms. Military police making the rounds between sets of cannon. Leo had only ever seen cannon before on military vessels in the harbor of Limani. The idea of such a powerful and dangerous weapon atop the walls of the city in such numbers made him wonder if there was a place on earth more secure than the city before them. How in God's name did Djeng Beljhar ever expect to take such a monster?

Leo had thought that they would be going through the gate, but instead Seiyariu led them farther down towards the coast. He ran his arm along the stone of the wall, looking for something. Until at last he stopped at, what Leo took to be, an abrasion in the stone, but was actually a series of Peregrine Runes.

"What are you—" Nea started.

"One in every city," said Leo, remembering Seiyariu's words. Sure enough, Seiyariu reached through a small hole in the stone and pulled open the hidden door. And the three of them crept through the passage and into Equius.

The seaside section they had emerged in wasn't that different from Limani, save for the size of the buildings. The police were patrolling the docks, checking papers and examining cargo. Law and order reigned supreme here. The sailors were well dressed and clean-shaven, rich traders and merchants, not the slavers, smugglers and fisherman he was used to.

As they pressed farther in, they passed through a thoroughfare that was midway through its transformation into the festival grounds.

Market stalls lined cobbled roads, with many early farmers already buying and selling. Leo kept bumping into people, there were so many of them. He'd never seen anything like it and stuck close to Seiyariu, afraid of getting swept up.

Nea darted between the packs of traders like she'd been doing it her whole life. Still, he could see the wonder in her eyes. Indeed, as they walked the clean streets of Equius, they felt so far away from slavery, that it was hard for him to believe they were even in the same country.

The streets were laid out in neat pattern like the spokes of a wheel, merging into large plazas with flowing crystal fountains and statues adorned with wild colorful plant life. Towards the center of the city there was even a section of land free of buildings, a little patch of nature in this great metropolis.

This common was the border to the third and most lavish section of Equius. Here the houses were larger, the clothes fancier, more carriages trundled along the streets than horses and a great many more suspicious gazes fixed on them.

Seiyariu paid no mind to this, however, and strode up the high street like he owned it. Oblivious to the stares of the townspeople, Seiyariu had eyes only for the approaching fortress.

"God," hissed Nea, as they found themselves in the shadow of the monstrous castle.

"It's a sight to behold for sure," Seiyariu said, not breaking stride. "If my timing is correct, His Majesty will be holding a town hall. He does this once or twice a month. It's just a formality at this point but it's one of the only times that the palace is accessible to the public, assuming we don't wait for the festival."

"If your timing is correct," Nea rolled her eyes. "Scarecrow you just said you didn't know what month it was."

"Do have a little faith in my Dulcinea, I've done this before."

"If you've been here before, won't the people in the palace recognize you?" asked Leo.

"That's what I'm afraid of," said Seiyariu sheepishly. "And why it's so important we arrive when the King is meeting with his subjects. Once we're in, Chiron will listen."

"What makes you so sure."

"There's a great many unkind things I could say about Wallace Chiron, but his respect for tradition is at least admirable. He's perhaps the one part of this city that has yet to be modernized. He knows the importance of the vagabonds and our old laws even if he doesn't approve."

The portcullis was up but the military police were maintaining a strict watch on the courtyard within. All of Hunter's Hollow could have fit inside it. Looking through the door, Leo could see that in its center was a fountain, where water cascaded around statues of rearing horses, expressions of defiance carved into their stone faces. Twin marble staircases swept up on either side of the fountain, towards a pair of great oak doors, reinforced with steel. Above them flew the flag of Fortuna, the horse in the tempest.

Before they could even enter this courtyard they would have to get past the outside guard, who instinctively closed ranks when Seiyariu's destination became clear.

"Vagabonds," grumbled a large man with a few more medals on his uniform than the others. "Never cease to amaze me, striding up to His Majesty's front door."

"Not without good reason I assure you, Lieutenant," said Seiyariu smartly. "I need to speak with the King."

"Hold on a minute. Aren't you that vagabond that gave us all the trouble in the markets a few years ago?" piped up one of the soldiers.

"Yeah, I thought I recognized you," said another. "You're lucky we don't clap you in irons."

"Did you bring that fish man with you this time?"

Leo was about to start preparing for the worst, when the lieutenant caught sight of him and Nea. A curious expression crossed his face for a moment, his eyes fixing on Nea.

"What's your name?"

Nea looked as though she wanted to say something smart but held her tongue. "Nea," she said slowly, eyes narrowed.

The lieutenant held up a hand to quiet his men and stepped aside, "Go on then." He gave the military police a firm gaze, daring any of them to question it, but none did. At his word they made way for the three of them to enter.

"My thanks," Seiyariu said, "Good day gentlemen."

"What was that about?" Nea hissed at Seiyariu as they strode up towards the palace doors, but Seiyariu wasn't listening.

With a sound like a thunderclap, the doors were opened and two of the soldiers led them into an entrance hall. Its ceiling stretched up so high Leo had to crane his neck to see it all. Columns lined the hall, making him feel as though he'd stepped into a forest. Three silk carpets ran up and down a walkway lined with statues, towards a raised platform at the end of the room where an empty throne sat.

A crowd was gathered in the room, listening in rapt attention to the words of the King. As the guards led them down towards the crowd, Leo saw Chiron for the first time. He was a much younger man than Leo had imagined; he couldn't have been older than forty years. His head had been shaved but he had a dark beard with lines of grey. A band of silver wound around his forehead; this would've been the only indicator of royalty had it not been the way he carried himself. He had a large nose, broad shoulders and thick muscular arms. His strong chest jutted forward, covered in the garments of a diplomat rather than a soldier. But there was something wrong about him. For a few moments Leo wondered what it was, then he realized that Chiron was towering over his subjects. Was he standing on something? No, that was impossible, he was moving around too much. Up and down the gathered throngs he marched, then he turned, and the second half of the King came into view. Leo's breath caught in his throat. Chiron was not a giant, he was sitting atop, or indeed located somewhere inside…

Leo couldn't put it into words. Starting just below the King's torso was a mass of steel, rotating, gyrating and whirring. He stood on four mechanical legs, each ending in a great metal hoof.

His artificial limbs moved as though they were truly a part of him. He was bonded to the machine. Leo shot a look at Nea, but she had eyes only for the wonder on display. As he came around, Chiron saw them and this machine came to a grinding halt, hissing and clicking furiously.

"Seiyariu," proclaimed Chiron. His voice was sharp and quick, but strong at the same time, the voice of one used to giving orders. "What business brings you here?"

"The old deal," Seiyariu said simply. Chiron's iron gaze swept over the three of them. His eyes cut like a knife. The way he stared, like he owned them.

"Very well. Guards, make sure they are comfortable," he said simply. Then returned to the crowd.

The military police took them off through a side passage way. Leo looked back and watched Chiron as he went, not once taking his eyes off the King until he was out of sight.

"Well that went better than expected," Seiyariu said with a grin. "Don't you think so?"

"What... what is he?" Leo asked, his voice hushed.

"He is the King," Seiyariu said simply.

Leo wanted to ask more questions but was having trouble forming the words. He had heard of the wonders of Conoscenzia his entire life, but he'd lacked the imagination required for something like Chiron.

"Wait!"

A voice, a woman's voice cut through the air behind them with such authority that Seiyariu stopped dead.

Leo's first thought was this could only be the Queen. She walked with that same authority. But she wasn't dressed like a queen, nor any of the other ladies in the court; instead she wore a ceremonial military uniform emblazoned with the royal seal. Seiyariu put on a bold smile as she approached, but the woman walked right past him and Leo like they weren't there.

Nea hadn't turned around. She was stock-still, frozen to the spot, her fists clenched, knuckles white. Then the woman put a hand on her shoulder, turning her gently and they were face to face. They stared at each other for a moment, then the lady's composure gave way, and she threw her arms around Nea, and pulled her close, sobbing uncontrollably. Nea just stood, rather limply in her arms. And Leo realized there was only one person this woman could be.

57
Knight and Squire

EVEN SHE DIDN'T expect to feel as much as she did the moment Cain's voice had met her ears again. And the way she'd held her. It wasn't like being hugged by Leo. It made her feel small, young. She didn't hate it. Leo and Seiyariu had let them be, thankfully; Nea wasn't sure she could've handled them seeing her like this.

"Come with me," she said softly. "Somewhere we can talk."

Nea nodded mutely as Cain gestured to the attending servants. "Take the vagabond and his charge, get them cleaned up. Chiron will want to meet with them tomorrow."

Nea let the lady knight lead her by the hand, catching Leo's eye as the servants led him and Seiyariu off. He gave her a reassuring look and she followed Cain down several flights of stairs, unable to think of anything to say.

"It used to be one of the dungeons," Cain cooed happily, unfazed by Nea's silence. "But Chiron let me have my run of the place and well." She flung a pair of ominous metal doors open. "I finally get to show you my workshop."

Cain's workshop was everything she'd imagined it to be and more. It was blisteringly hot, and stuffy. Tables were placed about the room without much rhyme or reason, each covered in bits of half-finished clockwork machinery and buried under stacks of paper covered with scribbled ideas.

A gigantic furnace and bellows took up much of the room, though Nea couldn't tell where all of the smoke was going. Was there a chimney this deep under the castle? At the door of the furnace, there extended a long stone table, along-side which mechanical claws stood immobile attached to operating levers.

Cain had a row of dummies along one wall. Some were full of holes from weapons testing. The others were decorated in more clockwork machinery than Nea had ever seen in her life.

"These are some of the things I've been working on," she said eagerly, showing them off one by one. The first wore armor that seemed to open out in several directions, like the legs of a spider.

"I thought that if you were in close combat with your opponent and you didn't think it possible to win, something like this might give you the edge. They release very quickly with a great deal of force." She demonstrated, opening and closing the armor. "Enough to knock someone off their guard."

Listen to her, going on as if you never left.

"And this one?" asked Nea, eyeballing the next dummy in line. It held a sword mounted to its arm with a skeletal brace.

"Support," she replied. "I'm hoping to invent a way to distribute force across the arm to prevent bones from breaking. A request from one of my men."

Let her show you all of them. Talk your ear off until the bloody sun comes up, daft lass. God it's good to see her again.

Nea wasn't sure she could face a discussion about anything else. What could they say; so much had happened since they'd last been together like this, Nea had been a completely different person in Cain's eyes.

"What did you do to the King? That's the most incredible thing I've ever— "

Nea stopped when she realized that Cain was staring at her, eyes were still red with tears. "God in heaven Nea I thought I'd never see you again."

Likewise.

Nea took a sudden interest in the floor. "No need to get all fussy."

She didn't laugh. "Nea you came back for me. You saved my life. Did the Briars take you?"

"Yeah they did but—"

"Did they hurt you?"

"No not really." said Nea. "I met some friends, we managed to get away."

"I'm so happy to hear that. Oh, Nea, you risked everything for me."

Only after you hurt her.

"I…" Nea had no idea what to say.

"When the guards told me there was a scrawny boy named Nea at the gate, I almost didn't believe them. How did you get away? How did you wind up with Seiyariu of all people?"

She told Cain everything from her capture to arriving in Equius. Nea told Cain about her companions, Beljhar, and all the secrets that had come crawling to the surface on that illusionary ship. It was a relief she found, to get the story out. Only hearing it again did she realize how exhausting the whole thing sounded. Cain listened, eyes wide, never once interrupting.

"Astonishing," she said, shaking her head. "An island hidden in the fog, dressed up as a ship. And you say he uses this illusion power to subdue his men as well?

Nea nodded. "I saw it myself. He even did it to me."

Cain closed her for a moment eyes as if in pain. "What was it like?"

Nea thought back, "Horrible. Like all the worst parts of your life come back torment you."

"I see. Beljhar preys upon the vulnerable, perhaps he sees something of that boy he once was in them."

"I'm sure he does," Nea said. "You should've heard the way he talks to them, like a priest and a father."

Cain nodded sadly, "You did well getting Leo to reject that life."

"It's because I had such a rough time rejecting it myself."

"The moment you came back from the church I knew something was wrong. The trail to find the Briars—"

"You were right. It's an indoctrination." said Nea simply. "They give you little clues to think it's a game, then send you to all the worst places in Fortuna, until you're ready to fight for them."

"Still I should've been more honest with you, about my suspicions and about all that had happened." Cain sighed.

"Yeah," Nea shifted in her chair. Try as she might, Nea couldn't keep the conversation away from it forever. "Sorry about that," she said awkwardly. "Keeping secrets, I mean."

Cain sighed and glanced around the room fondly. "You know I spend most of my time in here with my machines. So much so that I've come to see the world as a machine itself. Thinking about every little piece, and how it will work in tandem with the others. I'm so focused on the tiny details that I miss things that are standing right before my eyes."

"I don't understand," said Nea.

"I should've told you that I knew from the beginning," said Cain. "I didn't realize there was more to it than just survival. But I should have, the way you talked about your past. I should've been able to put the pieces together. But I didn't, and you almost got hurt."

"I would've gotten hurt either way."

She cocked an eyebrow. "If you honestly thought I'd judge you for being a girl—"

"No, it's not that," Nea bit her lip, God this never got easier. "It's for me. Does that make sense?"

"It's starting to. It's like armor."

"Yeah I suppose."

"But boy or girl Nea, you're still my squire," she said smiling. "I hope you don't think this somehow relieves you of your duties. Besides, someone's got to keep an eye on an empty-headed lass like me, right?"

Nea felt a wave of intense gratitude toward Cain then, and all the respect and camaraderie they'd built up on their travels together came rushing back.

"One more question and I'll say no more about it. Do they know? Leo and Seiyariu I mean?"

"Leo does," said Nea. "Seiyariu doesn't, at least I don't think he does."

"You could walk around in a lacy red frock and Seiyariu still wouldn't think anything of it. That man lives in a world all his own; the details of this one slip him by."

"You know him then? He mentioned you."

"Did he now?" she snorted. "I don't care for the vagabonds, but I've fought alongside Seiyariu and his strange allies and they're decent folk. Certainly the type to have on your side in a fight like what we may have on our hands."

"You think there's a fight coming then?"

"I do, and we must be ready."

58

Portrait In Starlight

THE SHEER SPLENDOR of the palace made Leo feel dizzy. As the guards led him and Seiyariu to their chambers, the ornate corridors lined with busts, painting and tapestries entranced him. They passed dozens of servants, men and women scuttling about to make sure everything looked its best. Some of them were barely older than he was.

The pair of them had been cleaned up, their hair and clothes scrubbed free of road's grime. And they'd been given formal dress for their audience with Chiron. Despite himself, he was anxious. Chiron's appearance was mythic and Leo couldn't help but feel tiny and helpless at the thought of standing before him again.

"A sight to behold isn't he?" the vagabond laughed. "I'll never forget the first time I saw him."

"Lady Cain, she did that to him?"

"So the story goes."

"Incredible." He couldn't think of anything else to say.

Lady Maria had been lovely, but Leo hadn't been prepared for the power he sensed from her. That was certainly what had earned her Nea's respect.

It was hard to imagine the two of them on the road together. But it was unmistakable in their eyes; there was a trust and love born of necessity there. A bond he recognized. So lost in his thoughts was Leo that he barely noticed that the guards had left them.

"Our rooms are here," Seiyariu said. "Come and sit. When Nea gets back I want us to go over just what it is we're going to say to Chiron."

"Right," said Leo, running his hands through his unusually clean hair.

The room was quite plain, likely quarters for the servants. But the beds were soft, and the blankets were thick. Not a trace of winter wind found its way through his window. A small table was erected in one corner and it was here that the two of them sat.

The servants brought plates of food, and Leo and Seiyariu busied themselves with a proper meal. Though they'd barely started when a knock came at the door. Leo expected Nea. He hadn't expected Cain to come with her. He shot to his feet stupidly, unsure of what to do in the presence of someone like her. Cain gave him a little smile.

"You must be Leo."

Despite her power and authority, she gave off a completely different feeling than Chiron. Cain seemed welcoming, warm, and instantly made Leo feel at ease.

"Yes Ma'am," he said softly.

Nea snorted but Cain ignored her. "It's a pleasure to finally meet you." She shook his hand. "And Seiyariu of course. It's been some time. How are you?"

"Still alive," said the vagabond, inclining his head but not getting up. He bid the three of them to sit and they did.

"I'm glad to hear it. Let's talk about tomorrow."

"Right," said Nea. Leo noticed that she too had been cleaned and relieved of her traveling clothes. "You gonna teach us to bow properly?"

"I've written that off as a lost cause I'm afraid," said Cain. "I'd prefer to talk strategy."

"Strategy?" asked Leo.

"Yes, Lord Chiron has been made aware of what Nea and I discovered during our investigation," said Cain. "But Nea has explained to me that there's a great deal that's happened since. I'll attempt to get him abreast of the situation by tomorrow. But the three of you need to know something. Chiron will expect your support and loyalty if he challenges the Briars."

Nea blinked. "What does he need us for?"

Cain's eyes fell on Leo. "You, specifically Leo."

"Me?" Leo replied, confused.

"You're the heir to the throne of Inferno," said Cain. "Have you considered that you have the same political value to Chiron as Beljhar?"

The table was silent for a few moments.

"No…," said Leo. "No, I haven't."

"Are you aware of what could be asked of you?"

Leo nodded.

"And would you be willing to do it?"

"Are you out of your mind?" Nea demanded. "This is the same king who sent children to their deaths and you want Leo to sign on with him?"

"I don't want Leo to do anything," said Cain. "I want him to be aware of the position he's in."

"I don't think that would be wise Leo," agreed Seiyariu. "You're not—"

"Damn right he's not," said Nea flatly.

"Please you two," said Cain. "I hope it doesn't come to that. But if it does, will you have an answer for him Leo?"

All eyes fell on Leo.

"I don't…" Leo avoided looking at them. What could he say? Who was he to shoulder that kind of responsibility? "I don't know."

Cain nodded grimly. "I'm afraid that's the one answer he won't accept."

"What's he supposed to do?"

"It depends," said Cain. "How far are you willing to go to stop Beljhar, Leo?"

Leo remembered his words to Beljhar on the ship, his vow that he would stop him no matter what. There had been a conviction in his words, a strength he wasn't used to. He'd been right, no matter what happened, he had to use whatever power he had to stop Beljhar. And he had power now, his blood was power. But would it be enough?

*

After an hour more of talking, discussions that went nowhere and circular ideas, they decided to get some rest and bid each other good night, splitting off to their separate rooms. Leo was still wrestling with the decision he needed to make.

He sank onto the bed with a sigh that was half-relief and half-anxiety. The past few days had taken so much from him, they might as well have been a decade. For the first time in his life, he thought that he understood how it must feel to be old.

He wished they could meet with Chiron now. He wanted tell him everything that had happened, put it all together so that it would stop spinning around in his head. And know what it was the King would ask of him. But that was the thinking of a child. Chiron was the ruler of Fortuna. It was astounding that he'd made any time to see a trio of homeless gadabouts at all.

He undressed, extinguished the lamp and crawled under the covers letting the exhaustion of the road overpower his anxious mind. He wanted it to wash away his thoughts and pull him into the embrace of sleep.

He was ready for the dream this time. Leo again walked the sands with Nico. His ghostly brother held his right hand, black and white, the parasite and the skeleton. Nico led the way, as he so often had on their adventures in the abbey, until suddenly, he stopped. Nico squeezed his hand once, sharply, and turned to look at him.

Leo forced himself to return his brother's gaze. The empty sockets were a void, cloying darkness that threatened to swallow him up. Then came a spark, a twinkle like that of a star in the center of his vision. It shone like a gemstone in the depths of the earth. He stared at the star for what felt like a lifetime. It grew brighter and brighter until he had to shut his eyes.

He couldn't quite tell when he woke up. Even after he was certain he was no longer dreaming, the light was still there, creeping in. Was it morning already? There was an ache in his arm again and he'd forgotten where it was that he was sleeping. With a small groan he opened his eyes to greet the day, but there was no day, the night still hung all around him. The light was standing beside his bed, looking down at him.

Leo let out a cry of surprise and shut his eyes again for a moment. Looking at him? Light? He opened them again, slowly this time. It was the star from his dream. Wasn't it? Why then was it shaped like a person? Its ghostly head cast towards him in silent gaze. Knail's phantom made of starlight.

The two stared at each other for an eternity and Leo found himself with the strangest sense of nostalgia. Why? Was that even possible?

Then through the white mist there came a faint knocking, Leo wanted to call out to whoever it was, but his body was still not obeying him. The door gave a little creak as it swung inwards and a slight figure entered, the strange light revealing Nea's face.

"Leo are you alright? I heard you shouting." Nea froze, her expression jarring Leo from whatever trance he was in. She stared at the specter by his bedside, eyes wide. For a moment the room was silent as a tomb. Then as Nea took a few hesitant steps forward, the specter began to fade. Its sparkling white outline blurring and dissipating through the air, carried off by a wind that wasn't there. Leaving the two of them alone.

"Was that? Was that Knail?"

He nodded slowly. "I was dreaming... I didn't..."

"Like a person," she hissed. "Just like you said. It was like that, wasn't it? Back at the ship?"

He nodded again.

"God Leo, look what you can do."

He sat up with some difficulty as Nea lit one of the oil lamps, Leo could see that her hands were shaking, and so were his. A sudden exhaustion hit him hard. His stomach was empty, his throat dry and his muscles felt limp and lifeless, Leo slumped against Nea. She caught him with a gasp, calling out for Seiyariu, but Leo barely heard her. His mind was filled with the image of that figure. The way it looked at him. That face, he'd seen that face before. *Nico.*

59
Fist of Fortune

BRIGHT SUNLIGHT STREAMED through the windows of the audience hall, catching Nea in the eye. The beams drifted over the stones, past the columns, onto the ornate red and gold carpets and up to the raised dais at the end of the room. Upon this sat an empty chair, just like the one in the great hall. The wall behind it was entirely taken up by an enormous floor to ceiling map of the Archipelago.

Nea shifted uncomfortably. The dress clothes they had given her were itchy and the collar was so high she thought she must've looked ridiculous. Still they were boy's clothes, so she wasn't about to complain. Leo and Seiyariu weren't any more comfortable. The scarecrow in particular seemed naked without his cloak and swords.

If Leo was frightened or alarmed about what had happened the previous night, he refused to show it. He stood waiting for the King, his face set, looking older than she had ever seen him. When he'd collapsed in her arms the night before, she'd truly thought him dying. He'd felt so frail, she worried he might break in her arms. She hadn't known what to do and it terrified her.

She'd wanted to run, get help. But she didn't dare leave him. Thankfully, Seiyariu had returned not long after that. They'd kept watch over him together all through the night. When Nea had demanded answers about what had happened, Seiyariu hadn't been able to give them to her. Nea wasn't sure if he was keeping secrets. But she needed to believe him in that moment.

He wouldn't lie about something if it meant Leo was in danger. Would he?

That light had walked like a man, it was like something from scripture, an angel standing over her friend, come to take him away. The whole experience had shaken her to her core.

Bloody thing blew a hole in Beljhar's fortress last time, who's to say what it could do next?

Nea was acutely aware of her beating heart. In the silence, she wondered if the others could hear it.

Calm down.

Nameless terror that she couldn't quite place pulled at the corners of her mind. She shook her head as the door swung inwards and Cain re-emerged. The lady knight was wearing her full uniform, complete with her gauntlets. As the King entered behind her with a hiss of pressure and lurch of steel, Nea realized that the fear gnawing at her heart wasn't entirely directed at Knail.

Chiron's broad form and barrel chest clashed strangely with his hairless face. His eyes were stony and his mouth never moved. She hadn't noticed it before but carved into the side of Chiron's metal form was a phrase, *"Pugno Fortunae."* Fist of Fortune.

The King came to a halt in front of them, Cain standing behind him at dutiful attention. Chiron's eyes swept over them slowly before he spoke.

"Captain Cain has told me some of what transpired on your journey." His voice was hoarse and sharp, like the sound his hooves made when they hit the stone floor. "But I would like to hear the account in full." His eyes darted to Leo. "From you."

Leo looked as though he was about to swallow his own tongue, but he managed to speak all the same. The king took in the most fantastical elements of Leo's story with stony faced acceptance. Beside him, Cain followed Leo's words just as she'd followed Nea's. When he finished, it was Cain who broke the silence.

"That puts things in perspective," she said. "It seems my investigations into the Black Briars were legitimate after all." There was a barb in these words that Chiron ignored.

"If I am correct in understanding," said the King slowly. "This cell of revolutionaries, who operate out of an illusory fortress, are led by the sole survivor of the Dashing of the Innocents. And in his crusade against me, they have been stealing artifacts of power, including snatching Knail from the vagabonds. All while hunting the lost heir to the throne of Inferno, taken in and sheltered by the same vagabonds. And who now serves as the human host for Knail."

"That gets most of the critical information I'd say," Seiyariu replied, speaking for the first time. "We thought that this situation has grown to the point that it merits your attention. Or at least your awareness."

"And if your Majesty requires—" Leo began carefully, "—you will have my pledge of support, if it comes to that."

No!

She shot a panicked look at him. Hadn't they talked about this? But Leo ignored her, eyes locked on Chiron.

Chiron's brow twitched a fraction of an inch. "A vow of loyalty, and from one already bound to the green road?"

"Heiro Al-Emani was bound to the green road as well. It didn't stop him from taking the throne."

"Very true," said Chiron. Nea desperately tried to read the King's body language but he was a wall of iron, looming and impenetrable. "Show me your hand."

Leo extended Knail.

"Your other hand," the King said.

Obediently, Leo removed the glove from his left hand and held it out to the King. The Nuptial gleamed almost as black as Knail against his flesh. Nea watched Chiron stare at it for a moment. But she didn't see any guilt on his face, any hesitation.

"You've escaped servitude twice now. What makes you so eager to pledge yourself to me?"

"Because your Majesty," Leo replied. "Beljhar must be stopped. At all costs."

It's not worth that!

"Leo—"

"Hold your tongue Seiyariu. Tell me boy," said Chiron, "If I asked for you to sit upon the throne of Inferno for me in exchange for my aid. What would you say?"

"I would accept your Majesty."

What are you doing! Remember who we're talking to here!

Chiron drummed his fingers against his metal frame. "And if I asked for something greater?"

356

"I don't understand."

"Your position as heir to the throne of Inferno was your most valuable bargaining chip," said Chiron, raising a finger. "Until you were bonded to Knail, that is. What would you say if I asked you for use of its power? For you to serve me as its wielder for the rest of your days?"

Like Cain.

Seiyariu could take no more of this. "Your Majesty this is a child—"

"Not anymore Seiyariu," the King snapped. "What if I told you that it was *your* power that was required, not mine?"

"My lord?"

"Beljhar wields a relic I do not fully understand, this gem. And if it is as influential and as dangerous as you say, then I fear we are left without a defense. Unless we find something to counter it, a weapon of even greater power. On this ship of his, you say that you used Knail's power to break his illusion. What power Beljhar has, it appears that Knail can resist it. Seiyariu, is Knail's guardian still alive?"

"Isa Votrow? I do not know your Majesty. We haven't heard from him in several years."

Nea's heart skipped a beat.

Votrow? As in Quinnel Votrow?

"How did you learn of Knail's theft then?"

"Kokaleth, sir."

"Ah I see," Chiron gestured at Leo's arm. "Yours and my knowledge of Knail is tertiary at best, but if Votrow is still alive, perhaps he can impart enough knowledge to the boy that we may be able to use it against Beljhar. I think it prudent that the three of you seek him out."

Nea frowned at Chiron, "You're saying, even you don't know what this thing can really do?"

For the first time the King's eyes turned to her. "No, I do not," he replied.

"The secrets of Knail were known only by the cabal," said Seiyariu. "It was a safety precaution."

Of course not. Vagabonds and their bloody secrets, what's this cabal?

"But if there is so much in place to keep Knail safe," said Leo. "How did Beljhar manage to steal it in the first place?"

You know.

"Quinnel," said Nea simply, drawing all eyes to her. "Beljhar has a lieutenant named Votrow, Quinnel Votrow. He told me he came from a family of delvers."

Chiron closed his eyes for a moment, "A son. That fills some of the gaps in the story."

Nea then told them of the strange conversation she'd overheard aboard the ship. "Pluto said Quinnel was supposed to kill his father but didn't."

"So Votrow is still there then," Leo muttered.

"Nea why didn't you tell us this earlier?" demanded Seiyariu.

She had no response. Why would she? Who was Seiyariu to chide her for withholding anything.

"If Votrow is alive then you should waste no more time. I want the three of you to make your way to him at once."

"I agree your Majesty," said Seiyariu. "These questions must be answered."

"This son," said Chiron, "Would he have been told the full extent of Knail's powers, Seiyariu?"

"Not until his father could be certain he was ready to safeguard it," said Seiyariu. "I've never seen this Quinnel perform any delving. Have you two?"

"He can't," said Nea. "At least that's what he told me. He never learned."

Chiron crossed his arms. "Then how is it, that Beljhar appears to know the extent of Knail's abilities, while we do not?"

That's a bloody good question!

The scarecrow was quiet, lost in thought. Cain said, "Perhaps Votrow will be able to shed some light on that as well."

"We're missing a vital piece of the puzzle I fear," said Chiron.

"Yes," Cain replied eagerly.

"Seiyariu," chimed in Leo. "Where does this Votrow person live?"

"Isa's last known location was Tidal Monadonock," Seiyariu said simply.

Chiron nodded. "A few days ride north from here. But be careful, it's said the mountain is fortified against intruders."

The scarecrow grinned, a bit of vigor back in his voice. "But not against vagabonds, Your Majesty."

60

Under the Traveler's Sky

"ARE YOU OUT of your bloody mind?" Nea shouted at him. She was fuming, unable to stand still for more than a few seconds. She strode back and forth across the room in a feverish rage, yelling all the while.

"Why didn't you tell me you were going to agree?"

"I wasn't even sure myself."

She cursed. "You don't have any idea how plowed you could've been do you? If he'd taken you up on that?"

"He didn't though," said Leo packing hurriedly and avoiding her gaze.

"What if he had?" she demanded. "Sending you off to find this Votrow isn't much better."

"He thinks I can use it to fight back."

"He didn't see you last night. But I did," said Nea. "Leo you don't understand, you didn't see what that thing on your arm did to you. I was…" She trailed off as if afraid of finishing the sentence. "What makes you so eager to serve Chiron? After what he did to those children. Beljhar wouldn't even exist if it wasn't for him."

"I'm not eager," said Leo. "But we have to stop Beljhar whatever it takes."

"Beljhar isn't worth your life!"

"Yes, he is Nea!" Leo snapped. "Chiron is right, I'm a part of this whether I want to be or not. Through blood or through this." He held up Knail. "And I cannot sit by and let Beljhar hurt people. Whatever horrible things Chiron has done, and I'm sure there are plenty, we have to be allies."

"Leo…" She turned away now, hiding her face. "I don't…"

He put a hand on her shoulder and she took it, squeezing it in hers. Finally she said, "This is the best I've ever felt in my life. These last few days I mean, with you and the scarecrow. I don't want…"

"You don't want things to change," Leo finished. "It's okay Nea. I'm not going anywhere if I can help it. You know I won't lie to you."

"Then just promise me. Promise you won't throw your life away."

He smiled at her, the way she always did for him. "I promise. We'll stop Beljhar together, you, me and Seiyariu."

She gave him a little shove. "I believe you. Now let's get our stuff and be on our way."

"Right," said Leo fastening his cloak. Though it had only been a month or so since he first wore it, he felt stronger with it around his shoulders. Adorned with the patches of his mother, father, and the dead vagabond from the wood. Vigor and resolve filling his body, he followed Nea down to the entrance hall.

Seiyariu was nowhere to be found, he'd muttered something about filling Kokaleth in on the plan after their meeting with Chiron. Leo wasn't sure if his words to the King had affected the vagabond as much as Nea. It was much harder to tell things like that with Seiyariu, even though they weren't keeping secrets anymore.

"Leo," said Nea as they descended a spiral staircase made of cream-colored stone.

"Yes?"

"What do you want to do? When this is over I mean?" There was so much doubt behind those words. As if Nea never truly believed this *would* be over.

"I want to keep traveling with you and Seiyariu of course," said Leo. "Be proper vagabonds, you know?"

"Where do you want to start I mean? Where will we go?"

"What about Conoscenzia, do you still want to go there?"

Nea paused for a moment. "I do but…"

"But what?"

"I feel like I'd be running away again," she said.

"From what?"

"From Fortuna, from the grassers, from all that."

"Isn't that a good thing?" asked Leo.

"It's like you said with Beljhar, not if other people are going to get hurt. The Briars are right about one thing. Fortuna is a bloody mess. Somebody's got to do something, so why not the vagabonds?"

"I think Seiyariu would agree with you."

"And I know we need Chiron's help, but it's hard to look him in the eyes knowing what he's done."

"With any luck this will be temporary. Then you and I can free every slave in Fortuna if you like."

She looked back up the stairs at him, grinning. "Yeah, I'd like that."

Lady Cain or Captain Cain, Leo still wasn't sure how to address her, was waiting for them in the main hall. She held a bow and a quiver of strange metal arrows.

"These are for you Nea," she said beaming. "After I finished briefing Chiron last night I stayed up to get the burrowers done, there's forty. The bow is from the armory, standard issue. I'd make you a more special one but that would take much longer. I would've done it before, but I just didn't..."

"Didn't know if you were going to see me again," said Nea slinging the quiver over her shoulder and testing the bow's weight. "Brilliant. Thank you so much."

"Are we all ready?" Seiyariu asked, appearing from nowhere.

Cain nodded. "Almost. I was hoping I could have a private word with Nea before you left," she looked at Nea, who looked at her back.

"Yeah," Nea muttered. Seiyariu clasped Leo on the shoulder, but Leo had picked up on it himself this time. He stepped back with the vagabond, leaving Cain and Nea to talk in peace.

"Why don't I show you the garden while we wait?" said Seiyariu.

"The garden?"

"Lady Cain keeps a garden. It's a sight to behold let me tell you."

He led Leo through a door behind the throne at the end of the great hall. Leo expected another chamber, but the door led out onto the edge of the cliff, the walls giving way to a small courtyard full of flowers looking out at the sea. It was so simple, Leo felt there could be nowhere on earth quite as beautiful.

"Peaceful, isn't it?" said Seiyariu, his eyes meeting the sea and the horizon.

"It's wonderful," said Leo, voice hushed. It felt like being inside a holy place.

"I wanted to talk a little bit. About what you said in the meeting with Chiron."

Leo's stomach twisted. Was Seiyariu angry with him?

"I told you not to pledge yourself to Chiron," the vagabond said slowly.

"I know. But I did." Leo didn't back down, he met his teachers gaze with that strange new strength.

"Why?"

"I thought I needed to."

Seiyariu clapped him on the shoulder. "You've grown so much Leo, and I'm proud of you. But please, be careful. I'm not thrilled about you having to learn to use Knail. But the alternative would have been far worse. I never want to see one of my friends sit on the throne of Inferno ever again."

"It was that bad?"

"Like you couldn't imagine," Seiyariu said, shaking his head. "Your father had barely been on the throne a year but by then I swear he'd aged ten. You're far too bright a soul to be sullied by politics."

Leo blushed a little. "Thank you. I think."

"You seem surprised."

"I suppose I'm just not used to you talking about all this so openly."

"Chiron was right, you're not a child anymore. I'm not going to treat you like one. That's part of not keeping secrets from one another."

"Thanks, Seiyariu," said Leo, feeling distinctly like a child in that moment. The distance between the two of them had never been smaller. Leo found himself looking back on those days on the road, those days where he barely knew Seiyariu and found they didn't gleam as brightly as they had before.

We're building something new. He thought to himself. *Something better.*

They returned to the hall, Leo eager to return to the road. Despite the brief comforts of the castle, it felt good to be carrying his bag, moving, doing something other than fretting. They had a goal now, something he could concentrate on.

Cain gave Nea a quick embrace and then the two of them joined up with Leo and Seiyariu.

"Outside the city wall there will be horses and supplies," said Cain, patting Leo on the head. "Do keep them safe Seiyariu."

"On the contrary Maria," he said with a coy grin. "It's usually them that keep me out of trouble."

61

Ghost of a Chance

NEA NEVER STOPPED being amazed at the changing landscape of Fortuna. After only two days on the northern road they might've been in a different country all together. The horses they'd been given were strong, fast and didn't falter at the freezing rain that started pelting them on the second day. The road north was harsh and it grew colder every day. Just before evening came on the third day, they crested a hill, and saw it for the first time. The mountain they'd been searching for, Tidal Monadonock. It loomed in the distance, almost lost amongst the clouds.

They'd entered the highlands. Hundreds of hills stretching out before them. They curved and twisted as though crashing down upon their comrades in the battle to be called a mountain. All were joined, and flowed into one another, waves in a storm. The shape of Tidal Monadonock looming before the setting sun like the grave of a titan. It was surrounded by thick dark clouds, obscuring its true height.

At the foot of the mountain lay thousands of gigantic stones. They jutted out of the grassy earth like knives. A forest of rock, packed tightly. It guarded the base of Tidal Monadonock like a line of pikemen.

A small town was built into the side of one of the larger hills. They rode past this and camped just a mile or so from of the stone forest.

They made camp quietly and got a fire going. Their provisions from the palace were still in good supply and they ate a hearty dinner as the sun began to set.

Nea had been stiff and quiet as they rode over the past few days. She was still turning over Leo's words back at the castle.

"Listen up you two," Seiyariu said pointedly. "Before we make our way up Tidal Monadonock I want to make sure that you are clear on just what we're dealing with."

That's different.

"Why don't you start by explaining what this cabal is," said Nea.

"Well aside from teachings of The Green Road, Romulus entrusted one more duty to the vagabonds. That was the safeguarding of Knail. Romulus was the one who found Knail you see. It's not known how. But whatever the reason, Romulus decided that it must be kept safe, else the system of protection he'd created for the Archipelago would be pointless."

Nea shook her head, confused. "I feel like I'm coming in late. Who's Romulus?"

"Romulus Caloway," said Leo helpfully. "He was the first vagabond. He defeated the Astrologue and stopped The Clash of Comets."

He what?

"Oh, is that all?" she replied with a laugh. "You lot never stop surprising me, do you?"

"You'll get used to it eventually," said Leo. "I think."

What had she gotten herself into? "Why wasn't that in any of the books I read?"

"Part of Romulus' plan involved decentralizing both power and information." Seiyariu explained. "We keep much of our history to ourselves and are duty bound not to record it on paper."

"And it's the same with Knail," chimed in Leo. "Neither the vagabonds nor the cabal are permitted to record everything."

Nea scowled. "For a bunch of homeless gadabouts you have an awful lot of rules."

"Those rules, Dulcinea, are precisely what keep us from being simple homeless gadabouts."

"And another thing," she said, her scowl deepening. "What the hell is a Dulcinea?"

"You are. Back to your question of what the cabal is. Vagabonds were given a basic understand of Knail's functions, its parasitic abilities and its destructive potential. But the true secrets of Knail, what it is, where it comes from, and how to work it, Romulus didn't want those secrets, or indeed Knail itself, to be drifting across the Archipelago with us. So he chose twelve delvers, the most powerful in the land. These were the cabal."

"And is that what Quinnel's Da is a part of then?"

"Yes. These delvers would keep Knail and study it, only they were never permitted to try and understand its true nature. Sealed away in remote places like Tidal Monadonock. The mountain is inaccessible to all but us vagabonds, for it was our duty to shepherd Knail from delver to delver once every generation."

"Are they permitted to write things down?" said Leo.

Seiyariu shook his head. "Their secrets are passed down verbally as well, father to son after they've completed their training."

"Then the old horse has a point," said Nea. "How is it that Beljhar knows all about Knail?"

"Perhaps Isa was right...," Seiyariu muttered to himself before continuing. "Around five years ago there were at least three living members of the cabal still being considered for the next rotation. But one by one, they began to disappear without a trace. Votrow began to fear for his life and rightly so I believe. He suspected there to be a traitor among the cabal and ceased all contact with them and the vagabonds."

"A traitor," said Leo, chewing the words thoughtfully. "I remember Kokaleth saying something about that."

"Yes," said Seiyariu. "He laughed Votrow off at the time, but now he's beginning to entertain the theory as well. It explains a great many things. It will be something I'd like to ask Votrow about when we see him."

"You sure we will see him? What makes you sure he's still up there?" asked Nea.

"If Quinnel left him alive, then there's nowhere else a man like him would be."

The hell does that mean?

Leo said nothing, staring into the fire. That determination in his eyes from their meeting with Chiron hadn't gone out.

"Alright you two," said the vagabond, getting to his feet. "I'm going to go into town and see if anyone has heard anything useful. I want you two to try and get some rest, we've been riding all day and you're going to need your strength for the climb tomorrow."

"Alright," said Leo.

"You got it scarecrow," Nea grinned. "Don't get yourself arrested."

"I'll do my best, Dulcinea." Seiyariu winked, then with a flutter of his cloak, he was off, making his way towards the distant lights.

"Damn," Nea muttered, lying back on her bedroll. "That's a lot to bloody digest all at once."

"Yeah," was all Leo said.

"Still," she said. "Better than all those secrets yeah?"

Leo nodded. "Seems like secrets come with the cloak, don't they?"

"You got that right," said Nea. She finally managed to catch his eye. "You're going to sleep tonight right?"

Leo shifted uncomfortably. "So you noticed?"

Nea had noticed. Leo had barely slept at all since they'd left Equius. She'd caught him lying there, but with his eyes open, as if far away.

"Is it because you think it'll happen again? Knail I mean?"

His face fell. "I'm not sure. I thought I had figured a pattern, but not anymore."

"Do you, want to talk about it?" she asked. "Maybe if we put our heads together we can parcel out how it's happening. Maybe it reacts to when you're in danger."

"Maybe," said Leo. "That was what happened in Adis, but we were in danger the entire time we were on Beljhar's ship and it only flared up at the last moment. But there was something about it on the ship and in the castle…"

"I saw. It was shaped like a person, just like you said."

"There was something more this time though, but you can't think I'm crazy alright?"

"Too late." She managed to get him to smile with that one. "Go on."

"Before you came into the room I thought that the light, I thought it had a face."

"A face… you mean like a person's face?"

Leo nodded, nervously glancing around. He bit his lip. Nea's mind quickly conjuring a thousand horrible things the face could be to fill the silence. "I'd been having that dream. The one I told you about."

"The desert?"

He nodded. "Nea what if this light… what if it's Nico?"

Nea stared at him, unable to hide the confusion in her eyes.

God, what do you say to something like that?

"Leo, you told me Nico was dead."

"I know I did, but what if that doesn't matter, maybe Knail is beyond all that, that's why everyone wants it so badly. Is it really that much more unbelievable than any of the things we've seen here?"

"I… I don't know what you want me to tell you." There was a silent plea in his big dark eyes, a plea for validation that she couldn't give. She would not lie to him again.

"Leo," she began. "I'm not gonna pretend I know what it's like to lose a twin. But do you think that maybe, between these dreams, and Knail, you're looking for something to hang on to, so you don't have to let go?"

She couldn't bear his wounded expression.

"You think I'm making this up?" he asked.

"I believe you saw something, hell I believe you saw Nico. But I also know there's one thing on earth you'd give everything to have back, and maybe that thing on your arm does too."

Nea wished he'd slapped her, cried, yelled at her, something, anything would be better than the betrayed look on his face. He just nodded and for the first time he retreated from her. Getting to his feet and striding back into the forest of jagged rocks. Leo didn't say a word, he just left her alone with her guilt, digging into her stomach like the roots of a weed. She thought for a moment about going after him.

What else could you say? Dead is dead, you can't force him to accept that.

Had she been careless? She had nobody to ask but herself. For what felt like the first time in her life Nea wished she wasn't alone.

62

Old Man Winter

FOR WHAT FELT like the first time in his life Leo wanted to be alone. The memory of his words from just the other day made him feel sick. All she had been was honest and he was running away like a child.

There wasn't a path so much as a series of gaps in the stone; sometimes these were so tight that he needed to go hand over hand on his stomach. Others pressed him between two vertical pillars so tight Leo felt like they might slam shut and crush him any moment. He'd no idea where he was going, but as the moon drifted out from behind a cloud, he could see that the walls were covered with Peregrine Runes. They read, continue, halt, turn, continue, and then turn again.

Worse, far worse than Nea doubting him, was the fact that she might be right. Perhaps all he was doing was conjuring the things his heart desired. Illusions.

Illusions. Scuttling in the dark for whatever shines through, his own private opal brooch. Beljhar had been right after all. Leo stopped and drove his right fist into the wall with every ounce of strength in his body. The shock and impact traveled up his arm but he felt no pain in his parasitic fist even as the rock splintered beneath his fingers. So he hit it again and again until he felt calm enough to keep going.

For what felt like hours he squirmed and wriggled through the narrow passages following the signs with hardly any visibility. The narrow path was strewn with corpses. Skeletons in various states of decay. Leo couldn't bear to look at them, he didn't want to be reminded of the dream. The corpses were dressed in all kinds of attire, everything from noble raiments to vagrant rags. But there wasn't a single green cloak among them. This gave Leo a bit more hope as he pressed on, the runes leading him into a series of corridors hewn from the same cobalt stone as the maze above.

While he hadn't been sure if the stone forest was natural or not, these halls were unmistakably man-made. The twists and turns eventually gave way to a vaulted chamber, rather like a church. But instead of a pulpit or stained glass, at the end of the room there were a set of oak doors. Above them, a massive Peregrine Rune had been carved. Though Leo did not recognize it, the symbol filled him with a strange kind of awe. It was the image of a spear pointed up with the streak of a comet behind it.

He moved to open the door, pulling hard with his black hand. The old wood creaked and groaned, giving way to his first real view of the slopes beyond. A gust of frigid wind filled the chamber, and Leo saw that Tidal Monadonock was covered in snow.

He'd only seen snow in books before, but Leo knew enough to understand that there was something otherworldly about this first fall. How was it that the white powder fell only on the mountain side? Was this part of Votrow's power?

His boots crunched through the fresh fallen snow as Leo wrapped his cloak about his shoulders. His breath fogged, his bones rattled. A hand-spun winter, another obstacle standing between travelers and the mountaintop.

The game trails hewn by centuries of wildlife were buried under the snowfall and the mountain slopes were overgrown with trees stripped bare by the cold. Upon the flesh of these trees were carved still more Peregrine Runes, guiding him up the mountain.

For the first time, Leo considered turning back. Seiyariu and Nea would surely be worried about him. But the memory of that look on Nea's face kept him pushing forward. He would find Votrow and he would have his answers. One way or another.

Then Leo saw him, a figure in the distance, almost obscured by the billowing snow. He raced forward, not thinking. All too quickly the figure grew larger, far larger than any man could possibly be. It turned, catching him in its hollow black eyes. Leo felt his heart falter in his chest. It wasn't a man at all, it was a skeleton, a gigantic skeleton. Carved not from bone, but from ice.

It stared at Leo, the same way Nico did in his dreams. Its eyes pits of endless dark that threatened to swallow him whole. The thing opened its mouth and a voice that cut like the winter wind came howling down to him.

"You trespass upon this mountain child."

"I... Isa Votrow?" Leo stuttered, shivering.

"And who are you?"

Leo wouldn't lie; he needed the delver to trust him. His teachings from Seiyariu, his gut instincts, everything told me that much. "I am... my name is Leonardo Fortunato." He held up his black hand. "And I believe you once were chosen to keep this safe."

The skeleton crouched low to the ground, leaning in towards him. Its skull was the size of Leo's entire body. "And how does one such as you come across the Knail?"

"I stole it, stole it from a man called Beljhar, he leads an army called the Black Briars. He's trying to take the Archipelago for himself, using Knail and me."

"And you seek to return it to its home in the mountain?"

Leo shook his head, fighting to keep his legs from shaking. "No. I came to ask you to teach me its secrets."

Votrow laughed, a freezing wind blowing down the trail, sinking its teeth into Leo. "You are not a vagabond."

"I am!"

"You wear the colors, but if you seek the power of Knail you have no idea what it means to walk the green road. Knail will never be used again."

"I'm the student of a vagabond named Seiyariu." he said. "And the son of Heiro Al-Emani, last King of Inferno."

"A fine pedigree indeed. But both of them should know better than to allow the Knail anywhere near human flesh."

"It was no one's fault but my own," Leo said. "I had to make a choice. I chose Knail."

"And now you will make another choice," said Votrow simply. "You will choose to return it to me. Where it belongs."

"I need it!"

"If you knew what it was you carried, you wouldn't be so eager. The Knail will never be used again."

A long boney arm extended towards him, wrapping its frozen fingers around his body.

"What are you doing?" Leo drew his knife and slashed in vain at the ice as his feet left the ground. He tried to call on Knail's power but the cold was overwhelming and he felt his mind going blank.

"You will come with me and together we will make sure of that."

63

One for One

Any footprints Leo had left were lost in the snowfall, but Seiyariu pressed on, following the Peregrine Runes up the through the woods with Nea hurrying behind him, both trying not to let the weather slow them down.

Though the village was small, it had taken Nea nearly an hour to find the scarecrow. When at last his green cloak came into sight, she nearly collapsed at his feet, red-faced and out of breath.

She hadn't been sure what to tell him other than the fact that Leo had gone on without them. But if Seiyariu was suspicious he didn't press her on it. They set off after him immediately, through the spiny maze of stones, through the grand hall and out onto the slopes of Tidal Monadonock.

The snow was up to her ankles, enough to slow their progress up the mountain. But it wasn't the snow that forced them back, it was the stinging cold wind. The trees offered some protection, as did their cloaks, but it bit at them all the same. There was something unnatural about that wind, something hostile, like an animal guarding its territory.

Nea ground her teeth as they walked. She should've done something to stop Leo, anything.

Just sat there like an idiot and let him run away. Who knows what bloody trouble he'll get into.

After nearly two hours of climbing, Seiyariu finally spoke "How are you holding up?"

"Worry about yourself," she muttered. "I can keep up."

"Not what I meant," he said. "What happened with you and Leo before he left?"

How the hell does he do that?

"What are you talking about?"

"Come on Dulcinea give me some credit. I know Leo wouldn't leave your side unless something happened."

She scowled at him. "Fine, if you must know. We… we'd been arguing."

He raised an eyebrow, "What about?"

"Knail," she said truthfully. "These images it conjures, he thought they were showing him his brother."

"Nico? That's very interesting. He told me that Knail's energy had taken on something of a human form during your battle on the ship, is that what he believes it to be?"

"Yeah."

"And you don't?"

"I don't know what I believe," said Nea with a shrug. "But I do know how he thinks, and praying for a way to go back to how things were, it'll hurt him."

"Do you say that from experience?"

"What if I do?"

"Nothing wrong with that. And after your disagreement he just left?"

She nodded, "I didn't follow him."

"Were you supposed to?"

"I'm… I'm just worried I pushed him away right when he needed me most."

"You know for someone who does their best to talk like an adult, you've got a very childish view of the world."

"What the hell does that mean?"

"Correct me if I'm wrong Dulcinea, but I don't believe you've had very many friends before." Nea said nothing. "That's alright, you're new to all of this. If you're going to be friends, then you and Leo are going to fight, a lot, and that's good."

"Good?"

"Friends who never argue are no friends at all."

"That some of your vagabond wisdom is it?"

"No, that's some of my human experience," he said with a bit of a laugh. "If you could've heard the way Kokaleth and I went at it when we were children. Kokaleth and Zephyr still never stop arguing and Resha, my God. Friends are there to challenge you, force you to re-think things."

Nea thought about this for a moment, her own inexperience evident even to her. "I'm bad at this."

"You're new at this. So is he. Take the advice of an old man, keeping silent for fear of conflict isn't something friends do, that's not a friendship, that's orthodoxy."

Nea remembered her words with Leo on the ship, how she'd slapped him, shouted, forced him to come around. That had hurt, but look at what it had done. "Thanks scarecrow, I guess. You're not that old though, are you?"

"Dulcinea, the fact that you need to ask is very telling, don't you think?"

"You sound older than you are," she said.

"As do you. Though, in your case I think it's mostly an act."

Nea was spared having to respond to this. A patch of orange, a light faint but unmistakable had emerged from out of the trees. Before long a small cabin came into view. The light glowed from within and a plume of smoke wafted from a stone chimney.

Nea realized with a shock that she had been here before. In Quinnel's illusion on the ship, she'd seen this house, tread in the snow outside it, fallen, been picked up. It still felt like a real memory.

The scarecrow strolled right up and hammered on the door as though he was off to a friend's for dinner. There was no reply. Cautiously, Seiyariu knocked again, this time forcing the door ajar.

The cabin was empty, but it didn't seem to have been that way for long. There was only one room. A table and chairs lay in the middle; scraps of meat still sitting on a solitary plate. Two beds stood on either side of a great stone hearth in which burned the remains of a fire, the only source of light. Every other surface in the cabin was taken up by bookshelves overflowing with ragged dusty volumes in every shape and color. God, but the smell, even with the strong wind Nea could recognize that scent anymore. That sick, honeyed odor.

Opium

Nea took a few steps inside, looking around. Was this where Quinnel grew up? There certainly didn't seem to be much evidence of that.

Bit odd for a mountain hermit to have two beds though isn't it?

"Why isn't he here?" she asked finally.

"Must be further up the mountain," Seiyariu replied, wincing at the smell. "We have to hurry."

"Right. Say, Scarecrow," Nea began as they started out the door.

"Dulcinea?" He closed the door behind them and they returned to the path.

"You know those brooches that the Briars wear, the ones that have the illusions inside of them. Well this," she gestured at the cabin, "was inside of Quinnel's."

"Fascinating," Seiyariu replied, stroking his chin. "Was Votrow a part of this vision?"

"I think so," said Nea. "Quinnel falls gathering firewood, someone, I guess his Da, helps him back up."

"That's the entire illusion?" asked Seiyariu.

Nea nodded. "I thought it was odd too. But I got to talking to Quinnel a bit and…" She bit her lip searching for the right words. "His dad, did things to him, because he couldn't delve. Quinnel wouldn't say what. But it sounded bloody terrible."

"I can only imagine."

"Well, after all he told me, it just seems weird for that to be what's inside of his stone. I thought it was supposed to be a motivator. Leo said that the poor bastard at Hunter's Hollow had his wife."

"Perhaps it takes Quinnel to a time when things weren't so bad."

She thought about this for a few minutes.

Scarecrow, if you had one of those stones. What would be inside of it?

But she didn't ask this question. The two of them pressed on in silence. Two more hours on the trail and the forests gave way to rocky slopes and ravines. They were nearing the top of the mountain, but there was still no sign of Leo or Votrow.

The two of them emerged onto an outcropping of stone overlooking a sharp ravine. A clumsy old bridge made of rope and rotting boards was the only means of crossing. But between them and the bridge, there stood a solitary figure in black.

"End of the line old man!" Quinnel snarled, his knives outstretched, blocking the only way forward. "You go no further."

"What in the hell are you doing here!" she yelled, reaching for her bow. Nea notched an arrow and drew back the bowstring, pointing it right at Quinnel's heart. She found her hand was shaking.

Hold still damn it.

Quinnel was her enemy, he *would* kill them, wouldn't he?

"Where's Leo?" Seiyariu demanded.

Nea caught a flash in Quinnel's eyes, pale blue globes darting back and forth for just a fraction of a second.

He doesn't know!

Quinnel quickly pretended to regain his composure. "I have orders. Neither of you are to reach the mountaintop." His gaze fell on her. "Are you going to shoot me Nea?" In his pale blue eyes, Nea saw that it wasn't a taunt but an honest question.

"You'll kill us if I don't," Nea replied, her voice now shaking.

Quinnel said nothing, instead he threw his dagger at full force. Nea ducked, but he seemed to have counted on it. The dagger missed her and her bow, but it sliced the string in two. Nea's bow tumbled uselessly from her hands and she stood before Quinnel utterly defenseless.

"There," said Quinnel. "I suppose that just leaves you and me old man."

"Dulcinea," Seiyariu stepped in front of her, his sword clutched tight in both hands. "Please stay where you are."

"What?"

"This is something I have to finish, wait there, until it's over."

"Scarecrow…" She stepped back silently grateful.

He stepped passed her, and as he did he whispered in her ear. "When the way is clear, I want you to run. Get to Leo, do you understand?"

He didn't wait for an answer. Seiyariu strode out onto the precipice. The two men stood opposite each other, frozen in time, staring forward. There was no movement, no sound. They were waiting for something.

"I believe this is our third encounter," Seiyariu said, throwing his cloak back.

"Our last."

"I don't doubt that."

"You humiliated me—"

"And you almost killed me. Sounds like we're at a draw."

"Are you prepared then?" Quinnel asked.

"Come."

They ran, disregarding the snow crunching below their feet. Both seemed to blur as they grew close, each determined to strike first. Quinnel darted past Seiyariu and struck at his exposed back but without even seeing the strike. Seiyariu brought his sword up and blocked it. The scarecrow twisted and, carrying the sword with his momentum, knocked Quinnel back. Seiyariu slashed, but Quinnel had seen it coming, crouching at the last moment. Ducking under the scarecrow's defenses. He flipped his daggers upside down and pressed forward with even more ferocity.

The scarecrow kicked Quinnel hard in the chest, sending him nearly spilling over into the abyss. He caught himself on a protruding stone and hoisted himself back to a decent footing.

Seiyariu rushed forward, sword coming down with a speed that could split the air. Quinnel rolled to one side. Nea realized what was about to happen a second before it did. Desperately she tried to call out but Quinnel's daggers were moving. He slashed at Seiyariu's legs, causing the vagabond to stumble. Quinnel shot forward to meet him, planting his knife in Seiyariu's gut.

No!

Quinnel pressed forward, making to stab again, to kill. As he did Seiyariu brought his sword arcing across the younger man's chest, spraying blood. Quinnel howled in pain, falling to his knees and the scarecrow followed, staining the snow a vivid red.

She wanted to stop, to help them, but Nea remembered Seiyariu's instructions. Before she could second guess herself, she was running as fast as she could across the rickety old bridge, staring back at the two wounded men standing to face each other once more.

Stay alive scarecrow, she whispered to herself, *please, for… for both of us.*

64

Sins of the Father

LEO COULDN'T FEEL his right arm at all, he tried to move his fingers, nothing. He opened his eyes. Leo was at the end a circular chamber. A cave lined with ice – frozen. From the vaulted entrance on the other side of the chamber, a faint beam of moonlight carried inside. It reflected off the walls and floor, giving the cave an eerie glow. As his vision swam into focus, he saw that his right arm was encased in the wall up to his elbow, locking Knail inside the ice.

Leo's heart started hammering and he tried to pull it out, but there wasn't even the faintest movement.

"I wouldn't bother."

Leo whirled around, nearly wrenching his arm out of socket, he'd been so focused on Knail he hadn't realized something was in there with him.

The skeleton of ice stepped from the shadows and crouched in the center of the chamber, staring down at Leo with those unblinking hollow eyes.

"It will be over soon," said the skeleton slowly.

Leo fought back the terror in his stomach. "Please, Votrow I—"

"I've nothing left to say. I will not permit the Knail to be taken again. Its secrets will stay with me. Locked away, as Romulus intended."

"They aren't secrets anymore," said Leo, his heart hammering in his chest. He needed to do something and fast or he was going to lose his arm. And with it, he would also lose any chance he had of stopping Beljhar. "Djeng Beljhar knows the truth, about Knail and about you! How else do you think he got to Quinnel?"

The skeleton's voice boomed through the cave, ringing off the walls and bombarding Leo from every direction. "What do you know of Quinnel?"

Leo saw the opening and latched onto it at once. "I know that he stole Knail from you. Beljhar used him, played on his fears to get him to do what they wanted, just like they do with so many other people."

Votrow was shaking his head. "Quinnel was a very troubled boy."

"It's more than that," Leo insisted. "Beljhar has power, a gem in his forehead, he uses it to make people see things that aren't there."

"A gem…?" The skeleton's voice trailed off with a very human fear.

"He uses the illusions to keep people in his thrall, even Quinnel."

"You are stalling."

"Knail's power can stop these illusions, I've seen it."

"I will hear this no longer, Knail will be under my protection again."

"Your protection?" Leo scoffed. "He's stolen it from you once, why shouldn't he be able to again?"

"I—"

"And I got it back! I got it away from them and I've kept it safe," Leo pushed on, confidence starting to return. "Beljhar's power isn't the only threat. Artifacts of power from all over Fortuna have been stolen by the Briars. There's no telling the destruction they will cause unless you help me stop them!"

For a long time the skeleton didn't say a word. Then, "So be it."

But this voice wasn't coming from the skeleton. A tapping met his ears and Leo became aware of another figure in the chamber, one he hadn't noticed. As this man approached, the giant skeleton began to crumble, a pile of empty snow and ice.

This newcomer stepped closer, an emaciated old man in a pale blue robe. His skin clung tight to his bones giving his face a skeletal appearance and he was barely able to stand. He carried a pipe, from which a sickly smelling smoke was wafting. He propped himself up on a clear white staff and hobbled towards Leo, until he was just out of reach. Leo saw that his eyes, tiny blue pricks of light in his gaunt face, were strikingly familiar. Quinnel's eyes.

"Y… you're…"

"Isa Votrow." The man looked at him very seriously. "I will give you one chance, tell me what has happened. Tell me of Quinnel and I'll consider your request."

Leo swallowed, and for what felt like the thousandth time he told his story. Highlighting only the most important details, the ship, the gem, the brooches, the visions, and how Knail had brought them all crashing down.

When Leo was finished, Votrow leant on his staff in silence. Leo waited, unable to read the man's expression. Silently, he prayed Votrow would listen, would understand. He needed to.

He wondered where Seiyariu and Nea were now; were they searching for him? How stupid he'd been to run off like that.

"Leo, before anything else you must understand that, should I give you the tools to control Knail, and you did manage to defeat Beljhar, you could become an even greater threat to this land than he is."

"I don't understand," said Leo.

"Knail has given you the power to hurt a great many people."

Leo's faltered. There was such fear in the old man's words. "I… I'd never hurt anyone."

"Never?" Votrow asked.

And Leo remembered slamming his black fist into Seiyariu's face over and over again. He remembered cutting that man's throat by the lake in Hunter's Hollow. He remembered how Knail made him feel, powerful, safe. It had healed his arm and given him the strength to fight back.

The old man leaned in close, "Then why has Beljhar allowed you to keep it?"

A shock ran through Leo's body. He remembered what Beljhar had said, "I'm glad it found its way to you."

"He knows that there's darkness in you boy, just like his men. He knows he can groom you, forge you into his weapon."

"Just like Quinnel," said Leo softly.

"Yes." said Votrow, no affectation in his voice at all. "From what I understand my son has become quite the monster."

Leo saw the sadness in Votrow's eyes. He'd seen that look before, a man torn apart by grief. He had a chance to make another point, but he hated the idea of taking advantage of that grief. It was manipulative, but he needed Votrow's help no matter what. Nea would do it.

"Tell me about him, before Beljhar I mean."

This caught Votrow off guard and for a moment Leo thought he was going to refuse, cut their conversation off and rip his arm off. But the old man braced himself on his walking stick, and stared at him, decades of emotion etched on his gaunt face. "He asked me a question you know, when he stole Knail. Do you know what that question was?"

"What?"

"He asked if I believed in evil."

"Oh?"

"And I do believe in evil, boy. Do you?"

"I… yes I do," said Leo, his thoughts drifting back to his days in the abbey.

"A quick answer. I take it you've seen a fair bit in your short life."

"I have."

"Do you believe evil is something men are, or something men do."

"I…," Leo paused. He couldn't answer so quickly, Beljhar had taught him that much. But he'd never really thought about it. He recalled his discussion with Nea at House Lambert. About the things that they had done to hurt others. Surely that was evil, wasn't it?

"I suppose it's something that people do."

"And why is that?"

Leo hadn't been prepared for this kind of cross-examination, but he considered his next words carefully. "Beljhar does evil things to people. But I believe that's because evil things were done to him. He was a child soldier, the only survivor of The Dashing of the Innocents. I think things like that can…" He wrestled for the right word.

"You believe people who do evil have had evil done to them in the past."

"Yes!"

"A nuanced view for someone so young. Seiyariu has taught you well. My son is like this man Beljhar, and in many ways I think, like you."

Quinnel is like me? Leo thought back to every interaction he'd had with the man. Was it possible?

"I'm not speaking of the killer you've encountered. He was a very different person once. When he was younger he was quite a bright boy, kind, happy even."

"What happened to him?" Leo asked, careful not to sound eager. This was his only chance, if he didn't win Votrow over now, it was all for nothing.

"Evil things where done to him." Votrow sighed. "By me."

"You?"

"Yes. You see Leo, Quinnel's mother left us when he was very small. And I was a very poor father. Not that I knew it at the time. That's one of the blessings of being isolated on this mountain for so many years, I have had the time to examine my life, the mistakes I made."

"What did you do to him?" It was becoming apparent to Leo that this was something the old man was desperate to talk about.

"Delving is a hereditary talent. At least it's supposed to be. Delvers are born of other delvers. My father was a delver, and his father, and his mother and her father, on and on into antiquity. In more ordinary circles this isn't especially significant, but in the cabal, we tutor our children in the arts and when they grow strong enough we pass on our responsibility. The guarding of Knail can only be entrusted to a delver who has reached a certain level of mastery. At first, I merely followed tradition, pressing Quinnel to uncover his latent abilities. But…" Votrow's face contorted in pain. He leaned against the wall, and Leo wondered for a moment if he was going to fall apart like his skeleton of ice had.

"As the years passed and Quinnel showed no sign of developing the talent, I grew more and more afraid. He was the future of the Cabal. We had never been fewer than we were at that time, and without our children, there would be no one to carry on our legacy. So I pressed him, insulted him, beat him, subjected him to experiment after experiment. Anything to get his power to come out. I justified it to myself, saying that I didn't realize that I was eroding that wonderful boy into something unrecognizable. He ran away from here when he was just fifteen. In the years since then I…" he brandished his pipe, "…wasted away. I couldn't bear what I'd done to him."

Leo listened to the unfolding story in silence, not interrupting Votrow. Leo found himself feeling sympathy, empathy even for Quinnel. He didn't want to, but there it was all the same.

"How did he get Knail from you?" asked Leo, despite himself. "When he came back I mean. You're more powerful than he is surely."

"Because when I saw the man he had become due to my actions, I thought it only fair to let him kill me."

"But he didn't."

"No, he stole Knail and was—"

"He was ordered to."

Votrow's shaking hands stopped and he looked at Leo with a hungry desperation. "What did you say?"

Leo saw the opportunity, the desperation in the old man's eyes. "Beljhar ordered him to kill you. But he didn't."

"But I...I ruined him," Votrow stammered.

A vision flashed before Leo's view. He remembered something Nea had told him, in passing ages ago. Something she'd learned from Quinnel on the ship.

"The Black Briars carry opals on them. Inside of each of these is a single illusion. Generally, an image of something, or someone, dear to the person it's made for. It soothes them. Would you like to know what Quinnel's illusion is?"

Votrow didn't answer, he just stared at Leo, as if terrified of both knowing the answer and not knowing it.

"It's an image of you. He's a child gathering firewood, he trips and hurts himself. But his father is there, he picks him back up and—"

"Stop this!" Votrow shouted, turning away. "You're lying."

"You know I'm not! He can be saved," said Leo. "But only with your help."

For a few terrible moments, Leo thought that it had all been in vain. Then Votrow struck the floor of the cave with his crystalline staff and Leo felt the ice retreating from his arm.

"You have convinced me. You may have the Knail, but first you have to know. Knail is the weapon that brought about The Clash of Comets."

65
Delving Beyond

AT FIRST, LEO wasn't certain he'd understood Votrow's words. He looked down at Knail. Holding it out as if it might attack. This thing, it had nearly destroyed the entire world.

"The... Clash of Comets..."

"Romulus Caloway killed the Astrologue, preventing the Clash from annihilating the entire planet. Afterwards he formed his vagabond order to defend the newly broken land and keep the Astrologue's weapon safe from those who sought to control its power.

"People like Beljhar," said Leo, eyes still locked on the shining black surface that coated his once useless arm.

"Now that you know this, are you still determined to keep it?"

Leo remembered the damaged mass his arm had once been. How he'd often wished the limb just wasn't there at all. Now was his chance. How could anyone be trusted with that power, let alone him?

But his thoughts returned to Beljhar and his illusions, the terrible power they afforded him. Despite everything, Leo knew his answer could not change.

"I am."

"Very well," said Votrow, "the parasite on your arm consumes your flesh and blood to generate energy."

"The light." Leo nodded

"You told me you've accessed this power before but never on purpose. All of my studies indicate that this energy can be—"

"It looked like my brother." Leo hadn't meant to say the words, he'd barely even thought of them before they were spilling out of his mouth.

"I beg your pardon?"

"The light. I thought it looked like my brother. Why is that? My brother is dead."

Votrow was overcome with an expression of such pity it was like a knife sliding between Leo's ribs. Votrow shook his head. "I'm… I'm afraid that reviving the dead is not something Knail is capable of."

And the knife slipped deeper inside his chest, piercing Leo's heart. He felt a horrible aching pain in his chest and despair threatened to swallow him up.

"Then why am I seeing him?"

"The best explanation I can give you for such an event is that Knail is connected to you. It is a part of your body and it responds to your commands in the same way as your other arm. You may have caused the energy to manifest in the form of your thoughts. In your case, a memory. In the case of the Astrologue it was the destruction of the world. If I am to be honest the thought reassures me, even with all that power, you just wanted to see your brother. Perhaps Knail will be safe with you after all."

"Will you teach me to control it?" Leo asked.

"I will but first, we must get—" Votrow staggered, clapping his hand to the back of his neck.

"What's wrong?"

"So… something bit me," said the old man, fighting to stay on his feet. "I can't…"

Leo rushed to catch the old man before he fell. And on his neck, Leo saw a swollen red mark, a bite – an insect bite.

"Sorry about that old friend. Can't have you getting in the way."

It was as though all light and warmth had left the world. The stars themselves snuffed out by that terrible, familiar voice. It was a voice that taunted and jeered at him from the darkest corner of his nightmares. Its prose made his skin crawl as though a thousand tiny insects were fighting to break out of his flesh and tear him apart from the inside. Standing in the entrance, draped in black and dragging a body behind him, was Pluto.

"I believe this is yours," said Pluto tossing the limp body at them.

As it rolled to a stop at their feet, Leo realized with a start of horror that it was Nea. He crouched down, listening for her breath, she was battered, bruised, but she was still breathing.

Votrow forced himself to his feet, his long white fingers wrapping tighter round his staff, voice quaking. "You."

"Me," he replied.

"You know each other?" Leo asked, confused. And then something clicked into place in Leo's mind, a missing piece. He stared at Pluto, realization dawning on him. "You're the traitor. The one he suspected. You were part of the cabal."

Pluto beamed, holding up a single boney finger, "Very good."

Leo's stomach twisted, of course, there had to have been someone in Beljhar's ranks who knew, knew where Knail was, where Votrow was, that he had a son. "You killed the others. You told Beljhar everything."

He inclined his head before returning his attention to Votrow. "Your boy and the vagabond will be around soon I imagine, but we'll be done by then. The poison in your veins works very quickly."

Votrow mumbled something incomprehensible, taking a shuddering step towards Pluto.

"Stop it," Leo said, planting himself between them. "We need to get you some help!"

"You know Quinnel doesn't enjoy talking about you Isa. You should have seen his face when Beljhar ordered him to recover the Knail. White as a sheet he was, well more than usual anyway. I'm amazed he didn't kill you."

Leo could feel the cave growing colder and colder.

"I suppose he wanted you to see the man he'd become." Pluto shrugged, that wicked smile still dancing on his pale lips. "That would hurt far more, wouldn't it?"

Votrow's face remained unchanged. "Leo," he rasped. "Stand aside."

"No! You can't—"

Something hit Leo in the back and his whole world went dark as he crashed to the ground beside Nea. Dazed, Leo fought to sit up.

"Give us a moment little boy," said Pluto. "This won't take long."

It was then Leo saw what had hit him. A centipede, nearly as large as the one that had chased him through Adis was winding its way across the floor towards Votrow.

The centipede reared up to strike. Votrow barely moved, a simple jerk of the hand, and a spear of ice shot up from the floor, impaling the squirming creature.

Pluto raised an eyebrow. "Well, isn't this interesting?" He spread his arms and a curtain of insects spilled form his cloak onto the cave floor. "Show me what you've got left."

Two centipedes grew from the pile of writhing bugs, they burst out towards Votrow, now the size of small dogs. He threw up his hand, and it was as though the cave itself was converging on the centipedes, the ice moving in to imprison them like Leo's arm. But even as it did, Pluto darted past his creations and struck Votrow in the side with his staff. Votrow cried out in pain, collapsing to floor.

The horrible smile still etched on his face, Pluto gestured to his centipedes and began to sing.

> "Here's a health to the King and lasting peace.
> To faction end and wealth increase."

Votrow tried to move, crawling across the chamber away from Pluto and his beasts. Pluto just kept singing.

> "Come let us drink while we have breath,
> for there's no drinking after death."

Votrow reached the wall of the cave and using it, together with his staff, he managed to get back on his feet.

Pluto was a cat toying with a mouse he was about to eat. Two more centipedes burst through the mass on the cave floor, hissing and clicking at Votrow, waiting for their orders. Votrow locked eyes with Leo. Terrible resolve and desperation carved into every inch of his face.

> "And he that will his health deny."

And Leo remembered, he remembered what Pluto had said as they probed into the depths of Adis. About a delver's power and the consequences of reaching too far.

"No!" Leo cried out.

> "Down among the dead men,
> down among the dead men."

The cave began to shake. Votrow's staff clattered to the floor, shattering like glass. He pressed his hands together; all the warmth being pulled from the air.

"Down, down, down, down."

Leo wanted to run, to stop him but the cave was shaking violently now, and he didn't dare leave Nea's side. "Please, don't!"

"Down among the—"

Votrow let out a final scream of agony as his whole body came apart in an explosion of unbound cold. The blast of ice, an avalanche, came crashing towards Pluto at an ungodly speed. His blindfold was blown away, revealing his bulbous insect eyes. For one incredible moment they pulsed with something like fear, before Pluto and his insects vanished in a storm of ice, wind, and snow.

The whole chamber shuddered as though it was coming apart. Chunks of ice fell from the ceiling and cracks began to form in the walls and floor. Leo threw himself over the unmoving form of Nea, until the chamber stopped shaking and everything was silent. Slowly, he got to his feet. Pluto was nowhere to be seen, no doubt buried under the mass of ice left by Votrow's final attack.

Leo looked around for the delver, but all that remained where he had stood was a mass of ice chiseled to perfection in the form of the man he had been, frozen and dead.

"Father!"

The voice ripped through the silence like a knife and Leo watched in numb shock as a bloody Quinnel staggered into the chamber, followed closely by an equally bloodstained Seiyariu.

"Thank God," said Seiyariu, making his way between the statue and the mountain of ice. "When we heard the explosion, I thought for sure—"

Seiyariu's words were lost on Leo. He was watching Quinnel now. He limped towards the ice that had moments ago been his father, stretching out a single desperate hand. As Quinnel's fingers brushed against it, he fell to his knees, letting out a howl of grief like that of a wounded animal. A high and shrill cry of despair that echoed through the cave and out across the mountainside, a cry the howled through Leo's insides as the weight of what had happened settled on him.

Votrow was dead. The last chance Leo had of learning how to use Knail, his last chance of stopping Beljhar. They were gone. It was all for nothing.

"How is she?" asked Seiyariu, bending down to check on Nea.

"She's alive. What happened to you?"

"Quinnel met us on the bridge, I fought him, and she ran. But never mind that. Where is—"

Crack!

The heap of snow and ice, the aftermath of Votrow's avalanche, began to move. Something burst free and a triumphant song met the winter air.

"Down among the dead men let him lie!"

66

Blood of the Lamb

LEO THOUGHT HIS legs might give out as he watched Pluto break free of the ice. Everything, Votrow had given everything he had, and it still hadn't been enough.

Pluto was wrapped in the frozen corpses of his centipedes. His insects must have leapt in front of him to take most of the blast. As he emerged from the mound of snow, the bodies broke away from him, shattering on the ground. His robes had been torn to shreds, exposing the lean hard muscle of a much younger man, but he was bruised and bloody. He clutched his staff tight as he surveyed the room. One of his insect eyes had burst and its contents spilled down over his mouth and chin like frothing drool.

Quinnel launched himself at Pluto with another of those terrible grief-filled cries. But he was still bleeding and Pluto, atop the remains of the avalanche, had the high ground. The delver leapt out of the way of Quinnel's attack and brought his staff down hard, right at the base of his spine.

Quinnel rolled back down the pile of ice and Pluto followed him. The delver wasn't smiling any longer. Quinnel tried to get back to his feet but Pluto was on him like a spider, striking him in the head with a devastating swing.

Seiyariu's blade flashed, a strike at Pluto's exposed back, but he too was slowed by his injuries. Pluto spun, flowing through Seiyariu's strike with an agility Leo hadn't thought him capable of. The staff connected with Seiyariu's wounded stomach driving him across the unmoving form of Quinnel and into one of the fallen pieces of the cave ceiling. Seiyariu collided hard, his head snapping back, he did not get back up.

"No!" Leo darted forward, swiping at Pluto with his claws, but Pluto just laughed and stepped back, knocking his hand aside with a single half-hearted jab. Leo stumbled, but regained his footing, ready for a counter attack that didn't come.

Pluto was just standing there looking at him. His shoulders shook with every breath, the veins bulged on his bare skin. Leo could smell the adrenaline coming off of him. Pluto's silence was somehow worse than his singing. His stare was unhinged, demonic, not trace of the old grin remaining on his ruined face.

Pluto struck again. He knocked Leo back, driving the butt of his staff into his chest, jabbing again and again. Leo moved to help but something hit him hard from the side, knocking him to the ground. a centipede! In all the chaos, Leo hadn't heard it creeping up on him. He rolled and thrashed but the creature held tight. Hooked legs dug into his flesh, pincers gnashing at his throat. Leo threw up his hand and the centipede's pincers cracked against Knail's armored hide. He rolled again, pinning it down under his knee. He pulled his hand free and slashed across the beast's thrashing midsection, decapitating it. For a few more moments the centipede continued fighting him, until the fight left its dead body and it went limp.

Leo staggered to his feet just as Pluto's staff came out of nowhere, plowing into his stomach. Leo collapsed in a pile, desperately trying to get some air back in his lungs. As Pluto bore down on him Nea leapt onto his back, just as she had done to the slaver on the ship. Fully conscious now, and with fire in her eyes, Nea held her knife to Pluto's throat. Pluto took her momentum and turned it against her, flipping her over onto the ground then catching her in the face with his staff. Nea flew back, she tried to recover but she'd been hit hard, and her footing was off. As she ran at him again, he sidestepped, bringing the staff down on the back of her head. Nea's body smacked into the ice, and Pluto struck her in the ribs again and again until blood burst from her mouth.

He was killing her. Pluto was killing her. Agony lanced up Leo's arm and his stomach clenched as though something was trying to pull it from his body. Nea bared her teeth in a snarl of defiance. As Pluto raised his staff to end it, Leo threw up his hand.

The light erupted from Knail, brighter and more solid than it had ever been before. The energy spilled out into the winter air and took shape. Legs appeared, then arms, a head, a bow. The light came together to form the shape of an archer, standing over Leo, its ethereal bow fixed on Pluto. The delver stared in awe, his faceted eye reflecting the phantom a thousand times over.

Leo had been certain, sure to his core that he was about to see Nico standing before him. But it wasn't Nico at all. It was Nea. Just not the same Nea that lay at Pluto's feet. She was taller, older, and unmistakably female, her face etched in an expression of boundless confidence. This was Nea as she appeared in Leo's mind, his truest understanding of the girl. She drew back the string of her bow, kissing it as it passed. Then she let the shot fly, a beam of white light, a comet, straight into Pluto's black heart.

Pluto looked down at the massive hole where his chest used to be, an incomprehensible look on his face. There was no toothy grin, no laugh, no song. There was only the faintest hint of satisfaction, as the delver collapsed to the ground, lifeless.

The phantom of Nea began to fade, dissipating in the air like smoke on the wind. And Leo felt the now familiar exhaustion that came from using Knail. But he ignored it as best he could, rushing to Nea's side.

She was alive, but her ribs had been damaged and he wasn't sure if she could be moved. Nea looked up at him, clearly fighting to stay conscious. It was a fight she couldn't win. She reached out for his hand as she slipped away, murmuring, "God Leo, look at what you can do."

Fear gripped him for a moment, but sure enough she was still breathing. Leo wanted to fall, to pass out as well, but something kept him on his feet, something he thought had died with Votrow. Hope.

67
Prodigal

As Nea regained consciousness, she felt her aching head and found it wrapped in a bandage, same with her ribs. The pungent smell of a healing salve filled her nostrils and her skull felt as though something had been trying to break out of it. The light hurt her eyes at first, dim though it was.

She was in Votrow's cabin. A small fire in the hearth fought to heat the room from the howling wind and billowing snow outside. The rattling of the window was the only sound she could hear besides the crackling of the fire.

The battered form of Seiyariu sprawled in front of the fireplace, covered in even more bandages than she was.

"He's alright," she jumped. Leo had been so quiet she'd barely noticed him. He was lying in the bed beside her, a bandage round his head, but otherwise he seemed alright. "Just resting. How do you feel?"

"Like I drank myself under the table," she grumbled, sinking back into the warmth of her bed. "Not a bad job this."

"Thank Quinnel," said Leo. "I'd never have been able to get you back myself."

"Quinnel?" Nea wasn't sure why but the news was strangely comforting.

Leo nodded. "He and I managed to get the two of you back here in one piece. I passed out a little while after that. Woke up while he was treating our wounds. He didn't say a word to me. Although…" he trailed off.

"What?"

"He seemed worried, about you at least."

Nea bit her lip. Her shirt had been taken off to bandage her ribs. "Does that mean he knows that—" She glanced at Seiyariu, checking to make sure he was truly asleep. "Does he know… about me?"

"He already did," said Leo simply. "He was in the room when Beljhar told me."

"Oh," was all she had in response to this.

Suppose that makes sense. Damn.

"Where is he now?"

"He vanished a few hours ago, not sure where he went," Leo smiled gently. "Do you remember what happened?"

Nea shook her head, it was all a blur. "I think I woke up after the explosion." She remembered Pluto, remembered jumping on his back. She remembered the archer, remembered its arrow blasting through Pluto's chest, but nothing before that. "I'm sorry I didn't get to you in time," she said, ashamed. "Pluto jumped me when I was making my way up to the cave."

"It's ok," Leo said reassuring her. "He can't hurt anyone anymore."

"Did you find Votrow?"

Leo's face instantly darkened.

That bad was it?

"I did. Well, he found me." Leo glanced around awkwardly.

"Tell me what happened?"

"He was going to cut my arm off."

"Christ."

"He stopped when I brought up Quinnel. Then he started asking me all these strange questions. He told me that he'd done terrible things to Quinnel when he was a boy, that he was the reason that Quinnel is the way he is."

"Quinnel said some stuff on the ship that made me wonder about that," said Nea.

"When he saw his father, did you hear him? He was in so much pain."

Don't know why.

If what he said about the old man was true, he sounded like a bloody monster. Nea wouldn't be crying like that if someone had killed her mum, or the Glatman family.

"How can you feel so strongly for someone who's hurt you so much?" She asked.

"I…" Leo glanced out the window. "I don't know."

Nea got the impression that Leo did know and was about to ask when Seiyariu groaned and rolled over in his sleep.

Oh.

"What else?"

"He was sick, gaunt, looked like a skeleton."

"Opium," Nea said out loud.

"What?"

"You know, the drug from the continent. It makes people like that after enough time. Ghouls. I've seen it before."

"He did say he fell in with the pipe after Quinnel ran away," said Leo. "He was no match for Pluto, not like that. Pluto had won the fight before he even got to the cave, stung Votrow with something poisonous."

"Then how did he cause that… whatever it was?"

"Desperation," Leo replied. "Pluto told me about it when we were in Adis. He said that if a delver reaches too deep, they're consumed by the element they were trying to control. That's why Pluto's eyes were like that. Votrow knew he was going to lose, so he reached beyond for something that would take Pluto with him."

"Christ, and the mad bastard actually survived it." Nea shook her head. "Did he have time to tell you about Knail, before Pluto got there?"

"Barely," said Leo looking down at his clawed hand in despair.

"Then I guess we came all this way for nothing," she said bitterly.

"If I'm still at all involved in the decision-making process," grumbled Seiyariu. "I think you're both being rather hard on yourselves."

"Scarecrow go back to sleep before you start bleeding again," Nea said, trying to sound like she wasn't relieved.

He scoffed at this and propped himself up on an elbow, giving the two of them that look that she hated. "You two managed to fight off and kill one of Beljhar's Lieutenants by yourselves!"

"Leo killed him," Nea grumbled. "I just got beat up."

"We all did Dulcinea, I've got a hole in my stomach and a lump on my head. What's important is that we survived. That could've been disastrous. When he burst out of the snow like that, I felt for sure, I mean with my stomach in that state I thought…"

"You thought we were goners?" Nea finished for him.

"For a moment or two," Seiyariu replied smiling. "How foolish of me."

"But Votrow is dead," said Leo. "We've learned nothing."

"Nothing?" Seiyariu cocked an eyebrow. "He told you nothing?"

"Well, not nothing," replied Leo. "He did tell me what Knail is."

The scarecrow's eyes got very wide. "And?"

"Knail caused the Clash of Comets."

Nea nearly swallowed her own tongue. "You what?" That thing on Leo's arm, it had nearly ended the bloody world. "He must've been lying."

Seiyariu closed his eyes. "I don't think he was. There were theories of course. But I hadn't thought that a single weapon could've brought about such terrible destruction."

"Does that mean that you can also…" She stopped when she saw the cold acceptance on his face.

"Yes," he replied simply. "It's horrible."

"Still, in your hands Leo, that may not be what comes of Knail. I saw your projection, the one you used to kill Pluto. There was nothing horrible about it. Whatever Votrow might have told you, you should know that he always thought the worst of people. Probably because there was so much darkness inside of him, he couldn't imagine anyone living without it."

"Who's to say I don't have that darkness in me?" asked Leo, voice breaking.

Nea looked him in the eyes, hard, and remembered the conversation they'd had by the fire at House Lambert. About the people they'd hurt.

"Me," said Seiyariu firmly. "Assuming my opinion is still being counted. I think that in spite of all that has happened to the two of you, perhaps even because of it, you will be stronger than that."

Leo swallowed, and Nea could see all the emotion he was holding back. She even felt a little touched herself by the scarecrow's words.

Crazy old bastard.

"If you can get your head around how you managed that, we may still be in luck. You must explore these abilities as best you can in the coming days. We have to return to Chiron with what we've found out, as soon as the storm clears. I want you both to get some sleep."

"Aye aye scarecrow," said Nea flopping back in her bed. The pain in her head was going to be hard to ignore but she was so incredibly tired. But just as Seiyariu's snores filled the cabin, Leo shook her awake.

Nea blinked groggily, trying to get herself back to reality. "What's wrong?"

"I'm sorry I ran away like that, it was stupid."

"Too right it was," said Nea with a yawn. "But I shouldn't have…"

"Told the truth?"

"I wasn't going to say that," she scowled.

He's right though.

"But you were right. Votrow told me it was just my imagination – that thing in the light. It was never Nico."

"What was it then?"

Leo stared at her for a minute, confused. "You didn't see?"

"Yeah it was a lady, an archer, right?"

"Nea…"

A thought suddenly occurred to her. "That wasn't… was that me?"

His eyes got even wider than usual. "I was so scared for you," Leo avoided her gaze. "It, kind of, pushed everything aside."

They were quiet for a few moments, "Why did I look like that?"

"I think…" he muttered, "I think it's because that's how you look to me, in my head. Votrow said Knail can be influenced by thoughts, like I thought I was doing with Nico."

"Th… I…" she couldn't find the words.

"I'm sorry if it upset you," he said, hanging his head.

"N-no it's just…" Nea didn't know how to finish the sentence. Her mind was a whirlpool of different feelings all at once.

What are you trying to say? What's he trying to say?

How could Leo have created an image of her that looked like that. It was so perfect, so beautiful, so…

Wrong.

*

At first Nea thought it was the rattling of the window that woke her up, but the sounds of the wind had settled, the storm calmed for the moment. She sat up, rubbing her eyes as a shadow loomed over her bed and a cold hand closed over her mouth.

"Nea," Quinnel hissed. "Please, I've got to talk to someone. I can't... I can't be alone anymore."

She met his bloodshot eyes; there was none of his menacing stance remaining. He looked younger, smaller even. There was hopelessness in him. Nea nodded slowly and he took his hand off her mouth. He gestured to the door and tossed Nea her cloak. She pulled it tight, ready to face the winter. The clouds overhead were thick and the snow was still falling.

"Where'd you get off to?" she asked.

"I buried him. What was left of him." Quinnel's face was in the shadow of his upturned hood. He spoke slowly, as though it was very difficult. "I know you've been asked this before, but tell me, do you think that evil is something men are or something men do?"

Nea remembered the first time she'd heard that question, back in the confessional in Foresbury. Had her answer changed since then? So much had happened, she wasn't sure anymore. "Something men are," she said, trying to sound more confident in the words than she truly felt.

Quinnel looked up and she saw that tears were streaming down his pale face. "Then why does it hurt so much? If he was evil, why do I feel like this? I thought I hated him."

Nea just stood there stupidly.

You're not cut out for this, Leo would know what to say.

"I saw him you know. In your opal I mean."

If Quinnel was shocked by this, he didn't show it. "Strange choice, other men choose their wives, their children. I wanted a fall, a bump on the head, stupid."

"It was... peaceful," she mumbled. "Didn't seem like you hated him."

"Not then, things were better."

"What changed?"

"I couldn't delve." Quinnel's nails dug into his palm. "No matter how hard I tried I couldn't. I made him angry, he..." his voice broke.

He's the same as you and Leo.

"I..." She wasn't sure what she had meant to say, would she have told him?

"Someone hurt you too," he said softly, "I know. I knew it the moment I saw you."

"Y... you did?" Her voice was shaking without her realizing it.

"There's not a lot of other reasons for how someone becomes like you."

"No, no I guess not." For once, Nea's wild thoughts had nothing to say in response.

"The boy too I'm guessing. Beljhar has a way of sensing it in people."

"People like that... people like us, we're easy prey," Nea said.

"You haven't been easy prey for him at all. It's strange, I would think that you of all people would want an escape from this world."

"I do," She glanced back at the cabin. "Or, at least I did. But not like that."

They stood in silence for a while, listening to the sound of the window blowing through the trees.

"Where will you go?"

"I don't know." Quinnel's sharp eyes were far away. "I just learned I'm not the man I thought. Everything before now seems... seems like it belonged to someone else."

"Yeah," she pulled her cloak tighter as the wind grew stronger. "I know what that's like."

"The Urna," said Quinnel suddenly.

"Sorry?"

"That is the name of the artifact in his forehead. The Urna, The Mind's Eye, is a weapon from before, just like Knail."

"Before what?"

"Before the Clash of Comets. He told me once that it's a spike driven into the host's brain from which he can cast out images. Sometimes he makes the images and sometimes we do. Like you said, people like us, we're easy prey for the Urna. It pulls on the fear in our hearts like the strings of a puppet."

"Why are you telling me this?"

"Why do you think? Because I believe you will stop him."

"How?" Nea pressed him. "The only people who knew how to bloody work Knail are dead now!"

"I am not going to pretend to know how, but if anyone can use the information it's the three of you. Tell them won't you, Leo and the vagabond?"

Nea nodded slowly. Quinnel set off down the mountainside, the storm picking up once more.

What does he honestly think you can do?

"Wait," she called after him. Quinnel stopped and looked back. "Will I see you again?"

Quinnel smiled at her. It was something she'd never seen him do. It was odd, forced, like he'd forgotten how, but she could tell it was genuine. "Hope so."

Nea watched him as long as she could, until he was swallowed up by the storm. The ice and snow singing a funeral dirge for Isa Votrow, and the son he'd thought he lost.

68

At One

DESPITE LEO'S INSISTENCE that Seiyariu stay in bed, the vagabond was up at the crack of dawn strolling about the woods. He met the gray morning with a smile, all injuries ignored.

"Seiyariu you shouldn't be walking around," said Leo, hurrying after him.

"Nonsense Leo, no vagabond ever recovered by sitting still. Walk with me, I want to talk."

"You do?"

"I feel like the two of us haven't spoken in ages, not alone anyway. Where's Nea?"

"Back at the cabin," said Leo. "I... I'm worried he's upset with me."

Seiyariu gave him a knowing look. "Why is that?"

"The phantom I made to kill Pluto." said Leo, choosing his words carefully. "It wasn't Nico, it was Nea. When I told him that, he just seemed... I dunno like I'd done something to hurt him."

"What about it upsets him?"

"Votrow told me that Knail can respond to my thoughts. I guess that's what Nea looks like to me, deep down."

"I imagine it's hard to see yourself through someone else's eyes. I'm sure Nea will talk to you about it when she's ready. After all, it seems as though you two are past keeping secrets from each other."

Leo wondered about this for a moment, then what Seiyariu just said caused him to stop in his tracks. The vagabond continued trudging through the snow for a moment before he realized Leo wasn't alongside him.

"She?" Leo said accusingly.

"What?" Seiyariu raised an eyebrow.

"You said she."

"Did I?"

"Don't." Leo glared at him. "How long have you known?"

Seiyariu sighed, casting his eyes about rather shamefully. "I'd like to say since she strolled into our cabin aboard Beljhar's ship but that would be giving myself a bit too much credit. In reality I figured it out on the road to Equius. You don't spend as many years as I have on the road and not recognize a few signs."

"Are you going to tell her?"

"She will tell me, when she's ready."

"So, more secrets then?" He hadn't meant for the words to sound like an accusation but they did nevertheless.

"Actually, I thought that perhaps this wasn't my secret to know." Seiyariu turned back to the path and began to walk again. Leo hurried after him.

"What do you mean?"

"Well at first I wasn't sure if you knew, and if she didn't tell you, I wasn't going to. I wouldn't do that to Nea, I hope you know that. When it became apparent that you did know, well I thought it was something shared between the two of you. Something she told you in confidence."

Leo looked away. "It was."

"And I would've let it stay between the two of you if my tongue hadn't slipped just now. I'm telling you because I trust you. And I'm not telling Nea because I trust her. Does that make sense?"

Leo felt a sudden wave of gratitude towards his teacher. "I'm sorry, I thought—"

"You thought I was keeping things from you again?"

"Sorry," Leo felt terrible. Was he truly so quick to judge Seiyariu even after all they'd been through?

"It's not like I haven't given you reason to be suspicious. Would you have me tell her?"

"I don't know," said Leo honestly. They continued on in silence for a little while. But the silence didn't weigh as heavily on him as it had been, and Seiyariu's good mood hadn't changed.

"That name you call her, what does it mean?"

"Dulcinea? It means a princess or a noblewoman."

Leo bit his lip. "She's not gonna like that."

"No, I suspect not. But it's more a reflection on me, than it is on her."

"What do you mean?"

Seiyariu looked up at the sky, like how he used to pretend not to hear. "It comes from a story about a madman who believes himself to be a knight. He's delusional of course, a laughing stock. But he has a way of seeing virtue and nobility in people, particularly in those who believe themselves to be without either."

"And… that's you?" Leo didn't need to ask.

"I like to think so." The vagabond gave Leo one of his old familiar smiles. "That's the most flattering way I can look at myself."

Something was gnawing at the back of Leo's mind, something he'd wanted to avoid asking. But he knew now he couldn't keep it inside. "Do you think that you and I could've been like them? Quinnel and his father I mean, if things had been different?"

This time it was the vagabond's turn to stop. "I'm not your father Leo."

"You could've been."

Seiyariu put a hand on his head, the touch was comforting, familiar. "I would've been very proud." The vagabond pulled him close and they walked like that together for a while. "Leo, I think it's about time I told you my name."

Leo laughed. "I know your name."

Seiyariu gave him that old mysterious look again. "You know the name I use. But Seiyariu was not the name my parents gave me. Occasionally, when pledging himself to the green road, a vagabond will discard his birth name and take on something more powerful, more iconic."

"Seiyariu is—"

"An old word from the continent. It means watcher, overseer, and guardian."

Leo was speechless. "So all this time, I didn't even know your name?"

Seiyariu smiled sadly, "As much as I'd like to hide behind the excuse of tradition, my taking this name was rooted more in shame than in ceremony. I was born Serge Lambert."

Serge Lambert, the words echoed through his head. Did they truly belong to the man walking beside him? "You mean like House Lambert?"

Seiyariu nodded, "That old manor where you found me, I was born there. I was a child of privilege and wealth.

"You?"

He laughed again, though the pained expression didn't leave his eyes. "Hard to imagine I know, but my brother and I wanted for very little during our formative years."

"What was your brother's name?"

"Ernesto," he said simply. "He was older than me by three years. We grew up having incredible adventures, learning, exploring, failing, fighting. I imagine it wasn't that different from you and Nico, was it?"

"No, not that different all," said Leo. "Why did you leave?"

"When I was your age, my brother took his own life."

Leo felt a chill from somewhere deep inside his heart, "He what?"

Seiyariu's voice broke, lost in memory. "I didn't understand, he had seemed fine just that morning. I'd seen him laughing and joking as he'd done every day I'd known him. Yet still that day I found him…" He bit his lip, unable to finish. "There was a pain inside me after he passed, I couldn't stay in that house, not without him. Ernesto had always fantasized about the world beyond House Lambert, always told me stories about it. He'd planned to leave as soon as he came of age. But now… now he could never go on that adventure he wanted. So, I decided to, in his place. I ran away from home, never saw my parents again. When I eventually returned, the house was as you found it."

Leo was unsure whether to hug Seiyariu or not. He settled for holding the hem of the vagabond's cloak, as he had when they'd first started traveling together. "I'm sorry," there were tears forming in his eyes. "I don't… I didn't…"

"It's alright Leo," Seiyariu said clasping him on the shoulder. "Just one more thing we've got in common."

"Why didn't you tell me back then?" Leo asked. He didn't want to cry; he wanted to be stoic, like Seiyariu, but dead brothers, it was too much for him to bear.

"Because if you were to forgive me for what I'd done to your mother and father, I wanted it to be a decision you made yourself. I didn't want sympathy to play into that at all. I needed to be judged by you, and I knew that would sway your choice. But I swore I'd tell you, should you choose to keep me around of course,"

"Does it ever stop hurting? I mean, losing him, does the pain ever stop?"

"No."

The vagabond's response was like a white-hot poker into his stomach. There was no trace of emotion in the word, no despair, just truth. Leo felt the tears again, this time he let them come. The emptiness he felt, the hole in his heart, it would never be healed.

"However, there is something that can be done to keep it at bay."

"What is it?" Leo asked, still afraid to look in Seiyariu's eyes.

"People die, often suddenly, tragically and with no chance to say goodbye or guarantee they'll be remembered. When that happens, their legacy instead comes to rest on the shoulders of those whose lives they touched. We become that person's legacy. I am my brother's legacy, for he was denied his. You are your brother's legacy, for he was denied his. That is why we wear the patches and carry our lost comrades with us forever. Perhaps that's what drew me to the green road most of all, the fact that the dead will walk it with us, that we will never truly be alone."

"That doesn't mean I'll stop missing him," said Leo.

"Of course not, but nor should you." Seiyariu took Leo by the chin and raised his head so that he could see Leo's eyes. Leo saw that Seiyariu's eyes were sparkling with tears of his own. "Carrying him with you means carrying the pain of his loss. But it also means pushing forward, building something. A legacy he can be proud of. If you were ever to believe anything I tell you Leo, let it be this, your brother would be so proud of the person you've become."

69
Dancing in the Calm

A FESTIVE MOOD had descended over Equius. Thousands of tiny lanterns were hung throughout the capital city. They'd been mounted in the harbor, from wires above the streets, even outside the cathedral. The three arrived back in the city the night the winter festival was scheduled to begin. The thoroughfare in the city center had been decorated and was now swarming with people. The military police paid Leo, Nea and Seiyariu little mind as they entered, occupied as they were with keeping everything under control. There was a wonderful warm atmosphere about the place, reminding Nea that Christmas wasn't far off.

Their rooms at the castle were waiting for them, but there was no sign of Chiron or Cain. Nea wasn't surprised; everyone from servants to soldiers could be seen preparing for the festivities. The winter jubilee would be held in the great hall tonight, open to all the merchants and traveling performers that had journeyed there for the season. The castle was even more glamorous than it had been before, glowing with high spirits.

Nea's feelings about this time of year were mixed. She recalled fondly the season falling upon her small fishing village. The day's work having finished, the townsfolk all gathered together to sing and listen to gospel and dance. That had been her favorite part by far. And when she was too tired to dance anymore, she and her parents returned to their little house by the water. There had sometimes been a tree, barely a few leafy twigs, but she'd thought it as beautiful as any. The three would sit close and listen to her Da tell stories from his book. She wasn't sure if they were gospel, but she liked to listen to them, his voice lulling her off to sleep as she watched the tiny glowing tree. Then it was business as usual come morning.

Yule time at Glatman had been a far more extravagant affair. Many friends of the family that owned the compound came in to celebrate the holiday. The extravagant mansion and grounds were transformed into a veritable cornucopia. There was food, drinking, laughter and music from dawn until dusk. At least, that was what she could hear from her quarters as the older women fussed with her dress and make-up, making sure she looked her best. As the sun went down, she and the other girls were paraded down into the main hall, Nea took little notice of the decorations then, she kept her eyes on the ground, not wanting to catch the wandering eyes of any of the visitors.

They'd had a winter ball there as well but there was no joy to be found in a dance on these evenings. Only the leering eyes and rough hands of her partners and the pale painted faces of the women staring lifelessly. Nea always thought they looked rather like ghosts.

So Nea was nervous when the night of the jubilee arrived and had resolved to stay upstairs in her room as long as she could get away with.

Still, bet the food's good.

A knock at the door broke her concentration and she rose grumpily to see who it was.

A soldier stood in the doorway in full uniform. He snapped to a salute, "Captain Cain wishes to see you."

Relief and confusion hit her at the same time.

Rather late notice isn't it?

She hadn't expected a summons until the celebrations had moved out into the town market the next day, and the castle could return to normal. Still, she followed the guard who, to her surprise, did not lead her to Cain's workshop in the dungeons, but to a large room in the eastern wing of the palace. He rapped smartly on the door and stood to attention.

"Send him in," came a familiar voice from inside. The guard held the door open and Nea entered.

Nea realized immediately that these must be Cain's private chambers. They had the look, fancy and clean, but with enough oddities strewn about to raise a few questions. She found the knight standing in front of a series of mirrors, surrounded by ladies in waiting. She was dressed in a bright blue dress that fell all the way to the floor. Her blond hair was held back on one side with a pin emblazoned with sapphires, and she wore a tight gold necklace. She was beautiful; the dress, it held her perfectly.

"Hello!" she beamed. "I'm sorry I didn't get a chance to send for you earlier, but you know how mad things are around here."

"You look…" Nea swallowed her sarcasm. "You look nice."

"Well thank you," said Maria spinning around once for show. "I should hope so, it's taken me about an hour and a half to put this ridiculous thing on."

"I'm sure His Majesty will appreciate it." Nea smirked.

One of the ladies in waiting presented Nea with a small package.

"These are for you," said Cain. "Get dressed and let's go down."

"H…here?" Nea asked looking around at the servant girls. They eyed her with equal suspicion.

No wonder, what's this boy doing in the lady's private quarters eh?

"No, not here, go into the parlor and be quick about it. They're expecting us."

"Us?"

"Yes, I told them we were coming. Seiyariu's already downstairs. I thought this whole thing might overwhelm him, but he seemed to be enjoying himself when I left."

"And Leo?"

"Not sure, I hope he got the clothes I sent him, if the three of you are going to wear those ragged cloaks at least… Nea what's wrong?"

Go on, ask her.

"I'll get dressed," she muttered, stepping off to one of the adjoining chambers.

What she wanted to talk to Cain about was more complicated than she could put into words. She felt like a selfish child. Leo had reached into his heart and let the parasite take what it needed to save her life, and it had. She was grateful, proud even, but the image upset her no matter how she thought of it.

How could something so beautiful, so strong, be a reflection of you?

The clothes were similar to the ones Cain had given her on the road, just formal. A purple doublet and white shirt, long black trousers and high boots. Aside from her vagabond cloak, she might have been any steward boy attending the festival. The thought was comforting at least. She tucked Kokaleth's bottle and Zephyr's flute inside her doublet, she wasn't sure why. Having them there gave her a kind of security. Especially when she didn't have her weapons.

"Dashing," said Cain, looking Nea up and down as she reemerged. She'd shooed off her attendants while Nea was changing, leaving the two of them alone. "I suspect the girls won't give you a moment's rest."

Nea smiled awkwardly, the thought secretly terrified her. "Are we going then?"

"In a moment," said Cain, sitting in front of one of the smaller mirrors to touch up her face. "Before we head down, won't you tell me what's on your mind? You seem troubled."

"I… I am." And Nea told her everything that had happened, an abridged and condensed version but enough to get the important bits across. She omitted the revelation about The Clash of Comets, there would be time to fret about that later.

"I see," said Cain when Nea had finished. "Votrow's passing is unfortunate, but the way you tell the story it seemed to be unavoidable." Cain's eyes flashed. "But if Leo can truly use Knail, that gives me some hope to be sure."

"Cain," Nea muttered.

"Yes?"

"Why is he… why would he use Knail to make an image of me?"

Cain frowned, "That's what bothers you? Even in the face of all this?"

"I…" Nea felt stupid as soon as the words left her mouth.

"I don't mind telling you how short sighted it is Nea, to focus on something like that. The boy has achieved a miracle, who cares what shape it took."

"I know." Nea couldn't look Cain in the eyes now. "But just, why, why did I look like that? It was… wrong."

"To you perhaps." Cain said, getting to her feet. "But this is not the time to let your own insecurities, however genuine they may be, distract you from the gravity of this situation. If you think you're troubled by what took place, imagine how Leo feels. He has just been given a terrible burden to bear. The fate of the entire world now rests on his shoulders."

"I know that, I'm just… I don't understand."

Cain thought about this for a moment. "Regardless of the shape this phantom took, it was you was it not?"

"It was supposed to be, yeah."

"So in the darkest, most critical moment, the one thing Leo wanted by his sid—"

"Was me."

"And I'm sure he needs you now. I think you might need him as well. Let's go downstairs and join them, do you think you can do that?"

Nea glanced beyond Cain at her reflection in the mirror. For once, she was able to hold its gaze. "Yeah, let's go."

*

The hall was filled with merry couples, servants, soldiers, merchants, performers and nobles, a rare gathering indeed. As they entered the hall, Cain pointed out Seiyariu waltzing past with a servant girl in his arms. He winked at them, his face aglow. Nea smiled and looked around the room. Musicians and cooks were spread here and there adding to the happy noise filling the hall. Hundreds of lanterns hung from the ceiling, filling the room with cheerful light. The whole effect made her feel content inside. Cain happily slipped off into the busy crowd of dancing people as Nea felt a tug on her sleeve.

"Leo!"

He smiled rather awkwardly at her. "Hello."

Nea grinned, looking him up and down. He wore a dark green tunic that complimented his hair and matched his cloak, as well as a maroon shirt and the same black leggings as her.

"Looks better on you than on me."

"I thought I looked a little silly," he said, sounding relieved.

"Oh don't worry, you do." They laughed.

"Lady Cain looks so beautiful," said Leo, watching her moving through the crowd, shaking hands and smiling.

Nea shot him a look. "Listen to you, why don't you go and ask her for a dance?"

Leo blushed. "I'm fine."

"Strange that the common folk and nobles mix like this," said Nea, not wanting to tease him further. They almost had to shout to be heard over the music.

"I like it."

Together they located a table groaning under the weight of food from every corner of Fortuna. Nea stacked herself a plate with as much as she could fit, and the two of them made their way to an empty table away from the center of the hall.

"Listen Leo," she said sitting down. "There's something I've gotta tell you. Remember how I told you Quinnel came to say goodbye while you were asleep?"

Leo nodded.

"Well he told me something about Beljhar. About how his power works."

"Why didn't you say something earlier?" Leo asked more concerned than angry.

"Because I was being stupid about the phantom alright? I'm telling you now, so listen up. Quinnel said Beljhar's illusions come from something called the Urna. That's the gem in his forehead. He said that it plays on the fears inside our hearts, that's how our minds are susceptible to the illusions."

Leo turned this over in his head. It made sense. "But everyone's got fear in their hearts, don't they? How are we supposed to fight that?"

"That's what I said," Nea replied. "But of course, he didn't have an answer."

Leo sat, lost in thought for a moment. "Remember what happened on the ship? When I said there was a moment where I could see through the illusion, before I used Knail to destroy it I mean."

"Yeah, what about it?"

"It was right after Beljhar showed me you were a girl. When I realized that we were all keeping secrets from each other, and I felt strong, determined. Like even though I was afraid, I would keep going."

"That's when you saw through it?"

"Yes," said Leo, seeing now where Nea was going. "Do you think it's is a way for us to fight back?"

"Could be. But—"

The music abruptly ceased and all the voices slowly fell silent. The only sound that remained was a creaking, mechanical trot. They threw a worried glance at each other and looked through the crowd to see Chiron, standing tall above the solitary form of Cain. The King looked coldly down on Cain, but she stared defiantly back. For a moment everything was deathly quiet.

"If you would do me the honor Lady Cain," said Chiron, bowing his head.

He held out his hand. Cain's face exploded with joy. Eagerly she took the King's hand. The music began again, and slowly they began to dance. Cain rested her head on Chiron's chest, her face so peaceful that Nea couldn't even pretend to roll her eyes. It was such a beautiful sight that, for a moment, the entire populous of the hall stood enraptured. To her astonishment, Nea found herself tearing up, her vision blurring slightly. Others joined in and soon the whole hall was winding around each other. The minstrels were singing of isolation and love, their voices carrying over everything else.

Leo nudged her, "Do you want to?"

"Want to what?"

"You know…"

"Oh." Nea was about to come up with some excuse but when her eyes fell again upon Chiron and Cain, her heart softened.

Are you out of your mind? What are you thinking?

"Yeah alright then," Nea replied, silencing the voice. "But I get to lead."

"What does that mean?"

Nea laughed and that was it, they were dancing. Nea felt the blood rush to her face as she saw how close they were. Quietly, avoiding each other's gaze, they began to step together as Chiron and Cain did. She guided Leo through the movements, careful not get nicked by his claws. Before long, the awkward embarrassment passed, time slowed, the men and women surrounding them blurred together into a single mass of whirling shapes and color. They forgot everyone but themselves. Leo kept stumbling over his own feet and Nea wasn't breathing, but the simple act of being together, surrounded by all this happiness, all this peace, was more than enough.

70
The Change

LEO HAD ALWAYS loved this time of year. The soft lights, the crackling fires, the trees everywhere. It brought a blanket of happiness over the abbey. He remembered the hymns and the gospel, he could sing as loud as he wanted and the sound of all the voices together made the holiday feel more real. Especially with his brother's hand clasped in his. As he danced with Nea, he felt this comfort again. Leo wished the dance could've gone on forever. He loved the closeness, the contact, it was as though the wound in his heart was being sewn shut, like the world was a place he'd like to live in after all.

All too soon the song ended, but they didn't notice. They kept going, through the next song and then the one after that. Leo was grateful; he knew it couldn't have been easy for Nea. She wasn't looking at him, but she was smiling in that way she had, brighter than any torch in the hall.

When at last they came to a stop, faces red and out of breath, the two of them made their way to a table.

"That was nice," she mumbled.

"Yeah," was all Leo could think to could say. "Are you—?"

"I'm fine. I like dancing, probably always have. It's nice to do it again. Feels... right."

"Yes, it does."

"Nea?" Cain emerged from the crowd. Leo was floored by how beautiful she looked. The whole hall must have felt the same, nobody could take their eyes off her. She may as well have been the queen.

"May I have a word?" she asked. "Just the two of us?"

"Oh," Nea shot Leo a confused look. He just shrugged. "Yeah that's fine, where do you want to..."

Cain took Nea by the hand and dragged her off, and just like that, Leo found himself alone. He stood listening to the music for a while, but when he saw Seiyariu step from the crowd and disappear through the doors to the garden, he followed.

The music echoed quietly in the little glade, joining with the lapping of the waves. The flowers hadn't yet wilted despite the encroaching winter, they still flaunted their colors. A gardener was silently working, despite the late hour, oblivious to the noise from the hall. Seiyariu stood on the edge of the cliff, looking out at the sea, a far-away look in his tired eyes.

"Are you alright?" Leo asked, taking up beside him.

Seiyariu sighed and smiled at Leo. "Just nostalgic. Did you enjoy your dance?"

Leo's face went red as his hair and the vagabond laughed. "Don't be embarrassed, you'll thank God for moments like that when you're as old as I am."

"You're not that old."

"On nights like this, I don't mind telling you I feel ancient. You know I met Resha for the first time at this festival."

"My… my mother?" The words were always difficult for Leo.

"She was staggering. I was only a few years older than you, but I remember it so perfectly. She was one of the performers."

"Singing?"

"Juggling actually. But she did a lot of different tricks at celebrations like this, she could throw knives, I even caught her trying to do that fire-breathing trick once," he laughed. "She loved making people smile."

Seiyariu's words were fond, but there was an impossible weight behind them, years of grief and regret pressing up against a dam of bright memories. In that moment Leo thought Seiyariu looked quite old indeed.

Their talk was shattered by a scream. Crashes, and the sounds of battle were coming from the great hall. Leo bolted for the door. *Nea.* At first Leo wasn't quite certain what he was looking at. Chaos had broken out, tables were flipped, glass shattered. The guards standing watch over the hall had been stabbed and were now lying dead in pools of their own blood. But as his eyes flashed across the scene, Leo could tell there was more to it than simply a riot. Most of the civilians were running this way and that in a panic, but there were some that weren't. Several of these guests barricaded the door to the hall. There were around a hundred of them, moving about with a purpose, weapons drawn. Servants, musicians, traders, with nothing in common between them, until they shed their civilian disguises, revealing black cloaks, leather armor and opal brooches.

Leo turned back, "Seiyariu! It's the Briars; they—"

He froze in the doorway. The man Leo had thought to be a gardener had gotten to his feet now.

"It's good to see you again prince," said Djeng Beljhar, striding across the flowerbeds. "I was sorry to hear about what happened on the mountain, but I had no doubt you would persevere."

"You." Seiyariu was quaking with anger, hand at his sword.

"I wouldn't bother vagabond," said Beljhar. "It's already over."

The screams and cries from the main hall grew louder. His eyes wide, Leo stared at Beljhar in horror. "Why?"

He turned, cocking his head to one side a look of genuine sympathy on his face. "Because you left me no other choice. You rejected my offer, my help."

"Stop lying," said Leo, his voice quiet. "You don't care about me."

Beljhar's face remained unchanged. "On the contrary Leo. The wanderer saved you out of guilt, the girl out of loneliness. I am the only one who ever *truly* cared for you."

Pain and grief flared up in Leo's chest again. Seiyariu locked eyes with him, silent instructions in the gaze. This was it, the critical point. They had been through so much together; it was time to see what their bond was worth. They moved as one, darting forward, claws and sword. The Urna flashed in Beljhar's forehead and he ducked the strike from Seiyariu. Leo slashed at him, reaching into his mind he probed for the well of power that was Knail.

Please, I need you.

Beljhar dodged his attack and kicked him hard in the ribs, knocking the air from his lungs. Leo collapsed on the ground, coughing and gasping, furious at himself that he wasn't a better fighter.

Please.

In one swift motion Beljhar drew his own sword. A long, thin, dueling saber. Seiyariu swung at Beljhar again but he feigned to the side and parried the blow, pushing Seiyariu back and aiming a stroke at his heart. But Seiyariu was a better swordsman, Leo could see that instantly. The vagabond caught Beljhar's sword on his own and threw him into the wall of the castle.

Leo saw his opening. He thought of Nea and of Seiyariu, of Cain, Kokaleth, Zephyr, of all the people who had helped him, all the people he wanted to protect. He let the well of energy flow from Knail, pooling and collecting around his hand. He could feel it fighting to get free. Behind him, the ghost of Nea appeared, her starlight phantom with its bow at the ready. Leo let the arrow fly straight through Beljhar's chest.

Silence fell upon the garden. Djeng Beljhar slumped against the wall, painted red with his insides. His whole form was limp, his eyes wide open. The great hole in his chest seeping blood among the flowers. Leo let out a noise that was half exhaustion and half joy. He'd done it! Djeng Beljhar was dead. It was finally over.

"Leo!" Nea screamed from the door. Leo looked at her, his eyes full of pride, until he saw the abject terror on her face. Slowly, Leo turned his gaze back to Beljhar, horror mounting in the pit of his stomach. The illusion faded. Beljhar was standing some feet away, a sad look in his eyes. The dead man, slumped against the wall, was Seiyariu. His eyes that had been so full of life just a moment ago stared blankly past Leo, a trickle of blood running from his lips.

No, no it couldn't end like this. No final words, no goodbye, no… nothing? As he looked at the body of the man who'd loved him more than anything else in the world, a pain unlike anything he'd had ever felt before ripped throughout his being. Leo felt as though a piece of his heart had been torn out, yet again, leaving an empty void, pulling everything else inside of it. He had no idea who he was, or what he was doing, the only truth in the world was that Seiyariu was dead, gone, and Leo would never see him again. Never see him smile; never hear his voice, never again. And it was all because of him.

From far away, Leo heard Beljhar's voice. "You see little prince, every being on this earth is a slave to fear and to me."

Nea let out a grief-racked scream and ran at Beljhar, all strategy and sense forgotten. Perhaps she just wanted it to end as well. Leo wanted to help her, to fight, but he couldn't even move. He'd only ever felt this once before. In a small room in the back of the abbey, watching his brother slip away.

Beljhar sidestepped Nea's attack and seized her by the throat. Then in one terrible motion he hurled her off the edge of the cliff. Leo watched her fall, heard her cries all the way down. He stared up at Beljhar; he wanted to scream, to turn his power on Beljhar, to take revenge. But the only rage in Leo's heart was at himself.

"Please," he said simply. "Please, let it end."

Beljhar looked him in the eyes, the Urna flashing once more. Illusion washed over his entire being, and Leo let himself be carried away. He submitted to it, anything to stop the pain.

71

Shackles of the Mind

"Leo? Leo, wake up!"

He groaned, his dreams of the sea calling him back to sleep. But Leo forced himself to sit up, blinking in the bright sunlight. It had been so warm he must've drifted off.

He was lying in a sandstone courtyard open to the sky. It was one of his favorite spots in the palace, here the desert winds blew harmlessly overhead, clouds of sand painting abstract pictures in that sea of perfect blue. The Infernian sun shone brilliantly, but the shadows of the stone columns offered him just enough shade to stay comfortable.

"Are you alright? It's not like you to go off on your own like that." said Nico, grinning down at him.

Leo smiled back and let his brother help him to his feet. "I was just tired. I had the strangest dream."

"Well tell me about it later," Nico replied. "Father's back!"

"What?" Said Leo. "When?"

Nico laughed, "No idea, he must've gotten back sometime in the night."

"Where is he?"

"In the garden, come on!" said Nico, taking him by the hand. Leo noticed that his right arm was clean, strong, why did that seem so unusual?

The halls of the Royal Palace were carved with pictograms, some depicting historical scenes, some mythological. Often the two would blend together on the same column or wall, telling a story all their own. The corridors were rich with the smell of spice. Some courtyards were open to the sky like the one Leo had been napping in, others held pools of full of crystal-clear water that carried the sun's sparkling rays through every inch of the ancient court.

They passed servants as they went, most were boys and girls no older than them. Father had a policy of accepting the abandoned youth of Inferno into his palace. He said that it was to keep them from the hands of the slaving companies. The more traditional nobles of the Infernian court didn't think much of allowing the twin princes to have street urchins as playmates. But Heiro Al-Emani had always upset them, ever since he'd taken their mother, a common Fortuan woman, to be his Queen. Set in their ways as they were, there was little they could do to oppose the King.

The nobles spoke of Heiro as if he were a figure from the stories etched into the palace walls, a legend, more than human. The boy's tutors said that this was because King Heiro was the first man to unify the Twelve City-States since the Clash of Comets.

To keep this fragile alliance intact, their father was often called to visit the capitals of the other City-States, negotiating treaties between them and putting down rebellion. For the past two weeks he'd been in the southern cities to great the Alfresian Monks on their pilgrimage to the holy city of Oliantar.

The princes took a long spiral staircase carved of ochre stone, that wound up to the roof of the palace. It was here that their mother had her garden. The whole roof was covered in greenery, flowers and plants from all across the Archipelago. Resha Fortunato collected them, reveling in the challenge of raising the blooms in the arid Infernian weather.

The gardens looked down across the Infernian capital. Countless buildings hewn from sandstone spread out at their feet. Beyond that the desert stretched to the horizon, vast and unchanging as the sea.

Heiro and Resha were there, looking out upon the kingdom and holding each other close. Resha Fortunato usually kept her hair concealed for the nobles and dignitaries but whenever she was with her family, she always wore it down. A curtain of dark crimson locks, billowing in the desert wind.

She turned as they crossed the garden, her face aglow with that smile she always wore when they were all together.

"Leonardo!"

His mother held out her arms and Leo ran to embrace her. There was a safety in her arms, reassurance. Surely his mother had held him like this a thousand times or more, why then did it feel so new?

Leo reluctantly broke the contact, confused. His mother didn't seem to notice. She was a slight woman, dressed in purple silks from the continent, contrasting rather dramatically with his father. Heiro Al-Emani was tall and broad-shouldered. He wasn't a cold man, but he was stoic and quiet. Still, whenever he saw his boys his face softened.

He smiled, striding forward and placing his hands on their heads. Pulling them in close. He was still in his traveling clothes and smelled of the desert. His mother and father couldn't have been more different from one another. The one thing they shared in common, was that they both wore the same patchy green cloak. Regardless of occasion, no matter how fine their other clothes may be, these cloaks were always with them.

Green... Green cloaks.

Leo stumbled back from his father, confused. His head was spinning, his mind cloudy.

"Leonardo, what's the matter?" asked Resha, concerned.

Leo opened his mouth, but no words came out. He met the gaze of his parents. There was something wrong, he could feel it, as though from far away. As he realized this, their faces slipped out of focus.

It's not real. This thought took root in his mind. Slowly, Leo began to remember. He had never been to the palace in Inferno. He'd never known the man and woman standing before him.

"Leo?" Nico took his hand, looking him in the eyes. His face hadn't changed, it was just as Leo remembered it. "Leo it's going to be okay."

"No..." said Leo shaking his head. "No, it's not real. None of it!"

"I see." said a soft voice, as if from nowhere. It was distant, echoing through his mind, dreadfully familiar.

"Beljhar?"

"If it's the truth you prefer, then so be it."

Reality seemed to shake, darkness and silence descending over the rooftop. Then there was no rooftop and the two boys were floating in an abyss, an endless sea of infinite black. Leo clung to Nico's hand, desperate not to let him go. There was a great lurch, as shape and color began to wash back over them, and the world righted itself.

They were in a candlelit hallway of cold grey stone. A hallway Leo had walked countless times before. They were back in the abbey on Meridus, the place that had been their entire world.

"No…"

Leo felt Nico's grip on his hand loosen and his brother collapsed to the floor. Coughing violently and shaking like a frightened animal.

Not again! Leo threw his arms around Nico. He knew the story from here, knew what was coming. Still he held onto Nico as though there was nothing else in the world, illusion or not, he couldn't lose him a second time. He remembered holding his brother close like this, praying that the disease would take him too. That way he could follow Nico; he wouldn't have to be alone.

Now they were in a room, removed from the rest of the abbey. Silent forms watching over Nico's lifeless body. He was as Leo had seen him last, sickly thin, his eyes empty and dark, like those of a skeleton.

Leo held his dead brother's hand; his mind was so aware yet helpless to do anything but scream into the void. He felt the grief all over again. He was one of two, joined with Nico through everything. Now his brother was gone, and Leo was alone, incomplete forever.

He was walking the corridors of the abbey, like a ghost. He felt so far away from the rest of the world. So empty. Terror rose inside his chest, she would be here soon. He wanted to run, to fight, but he was forced to let it play out just as it had before.

He heard her footsteps, felt her breath on his neck.

"You're hurting so much," she whispered, her long fingers gripping him like a vice. "Come with me, I'll make the pain go away." She had called him her little prince.

72
All For Nothing

NEA HEAVED UP the contents of her stomach, as well as what felt like half the ocean. Her eyes opened blearily as she drew in heavy breaths, desperate to fill her lungs with air. She was soaked, and chilled to the bone, but she was alive. How was that possible? The last thing she remembered was Beljhar throwing her from the cliff. Nea wanted to try and stand up, but couldn't get her legs to obey. So she just lay there. Every part of her body hurt, her injuries from Pluto most of all.

Nea was lying on a rocky beach covered in white sand. Not even a mile in the distance, she could make out the shape of Equius, etched against the night sky.

It took her a moment to realize she was crying.

Scarecrow, God I'm so sorry.

Seiyariu's limp lifeless form was all she could see when she closed her eyes. Nea had felt loss before, even grief, but never anything like this. There was a hollow emptiness in her chest, like something had been pulled clean and taken away, something she desperately needed. Seiyariu had been a good man, in spite of everything. She knew that. He had shown her a tenderness and understanding that at times made her angry. She could stomach hate, block out abuse, but love, that was something else entirely. Seiyariu had loved her. Just like Cain, and just like Leo. And what the hell had she done about it? She'd sneered, called him names, laughed at his oddness, and let him die.

Not a boy, or a girl, just a monster.

Leo. His face when he saw what he had done would haunt her forever. Where was he now? What was Beljhar doing to him? He'd seen her fall, if Leo thought she was dead too...

Despair ruled her every thought. A thousand possible scenarios playing out before her, all ending in tragedy. Beljhar had Leo and Knail. The Briars had gotten into the castle. By the time the military police could get inside…

Nea imagined Cain and Chiron, back to back against the hoards. Cain still in that silly dress, ready to die with her King. She let out a miserable howl, driving her fist into the sand.

Here you are at last then. The scared little girl who could do nothing to help her friends. You're just going to let them all die.

"What can I do?" Nea asked aloud, choking out the words.

Nothing. You're pathetic, just like you were back then.

"Shut up!" Nea screamed her voice high and shrill, not remotely like a boy's now.

Wouldn't it be better if you'd never met them at all?

"No!" she screamed.

The three of them had been gifts. Cain had shown her how wrong she was about strength and weakness. Seiyariu had brought back her smile. And Leo, Leo had given her a piece of his heart and taught her how to use hers again.

There's nothing you can do.

"You're wrong," she forced herself up, onto her knees. "I'm not going to let anyone else die."

"Then I guess you'll be wanting these."

A bow and quiver tumbled to the sand in front of her.

Nea looked up, eyes still streaming, into the last face she'd expected to see. "Quinnel?"

"Yeah," he said, striding out of the darkness. "Now get up, we can mourn later."

Nea got to her feet, shaking whether from cold or rage she couldn't be sure. "Quinnel they—"

"I know what they did, saw the whole thing. You're lucky I was there when I was."

"You saved me?" She noticed then that his clothes were drenched as well.

"Aye," he muttered, looking away. "I'm sorry, about the vagabond. He… he deserved better."

"What are the Briars doing, do you know?"

He nodded, "I wrote most of the plan myself. But it was supposed to come later, much later. We had men on the inside already, working as guards and servants for so long, nobody would've suspected. With their help, we would get as large a force as possible inside the castle, disguised. From there we'd barricade the police outside and kill the King."

"I can't let that happen," said Nea, taking up the weapons, and pushing past Quinnel.

"You plan to take the whole castle back on your own then?" he asked.

Nea held up her hands. In one there was a crystal bottle full of blue salt, in the other a tiny flute covered in carved symbols.

"Not on my own."

*

Kokaleth was the first to arrive. He burst from the waves, landing on the beach with a flourish. He looked around for someone to appreciate this, but gave up when he realized it was just her. It might've made her laugh at one point. Now she couldn't remember what that felt like. How did she begin to tell Kokaleth what had happened?

Quinnel watched him appear, if he was surprised by the creature's arrival, he didn't show it. In fact, Quinnel approached Kokaleth first, offering his hand. "Mariner," he grunted.

Kokaleth didn't move. "You're the one from the lake, aren't you?"

"I am."

"What are you doing with Nea?"

"Right now? I've no idea," said Quinnel.

"Kokaleth," Nea started weakly. "Something's happened."

Suspicion vanished from the mariner's face, replaced with genuine concern. "What?"

"The Briars attacked Equius," she said. "Leo's been taken and Seiyariu... he's dead."

Everything behind the mariner's face shattered. His brash and powerful confidence was gone, replaced only with shock. But Kokaleth did his best to rally himself; he kept his face solemn and simply asked, "How?"

"Beljhar," said Nea, omitting the dreadful truth.

Kokaleth turned away, looking out at the sea. For a long time he was silent. Then, in a voice quite unlike his own, Kokaleth said, "I knew him from when he was barely older than you. Never could hold still. Always trying to help other people, when he was the one who really needed it." Kokaleth let out a roar and slammed his scaly fist into the sand. "Stupid, he was so stupid!" The waves moved back and forth like a pair of shoulders shaking in sorrow. She wanted to join in his mourning, but Nea knew that if she did there was no return.

He turned back to her, eyes still full of pain and rage. "And the boy?"

"Leo's still in the castle, Cain and Chiron too. Kokaleth listen to me. I have a plan, but I need your help."

Kokaleth straightened. "Plan?" His voice no longer rang with its familiar edge. She told him her plan in its entirety. For a few long moments, Kokaleth looked at her aghast. "Are you mad! We've no army—"

"We've a much better chance than any army would have," said Nea, her confidence rising.

"She's not wrong," said Quinnel. "Beljhar has had to initiate this plan earlier than expected. He won't have as many men. No doubt the battle is still going on as we speak."

"We can get the drop on everyone."

"How many are there?" asked Kokaleth.

Quinnel thought about this. "We had fifty sleeper agents throughout the castle, and we'd planned to smuggle at least two hundred more on the night of the Jubilee."

"Madness." Kokaleth paused, deep in thought. "But at this point, I'm sure Seiyariu would give me some flowery speech and bring me around to his way of thinking."

"I'm not as good with words as he was," said Nea.

"Fair enough," said Kokaleth, folding his arms. "I'll do it."

"Thank you."

"Will this one be coming with us?" asked Kokaleth, pointing one of his webbed fingers in Quinnel's direction.

"Do you know what you're asking Mariner?" replied Quinnel, his voice as cold as it had ever been. "I fought for years alongside those men, I bled with them."

"So, your loyalty stays with the Briars does it?" Kokaleth growled.

"My loyalty to them died with my father," said Quinnel. "If I need to, I will kill every man in that castle, so long as I can get my hands on Beljhar."

"How treacherous," Kokaleth inclined his head. "How can we be certain you won't extend us the same mercy?"

"You can't," he replied flatly. "But you need me, you can't do this just the two of you."

"He's right," Nea murmured.

"Don't get the wrong idea. It's not for you," Quinnel folded his arms and stared up the cliff. "It's for me."

Suddenly there came a shrill shrieking voice from just above their heads. The sound of beating wings filled their ears as Zephyr swooped down onto the ground. She was just as Nea remembered her, everything about her sharp, but her feathers were tensed. "What have you summoned me for Nea?" she demanded. "Where are the others?"

Nea opened her mouth stupidly but Kokaleth cut her off.

"Zephyr."

He took her by the hand and led her out of earshot. Nea had never heard either speak of the other with anything short of derision, but now they spoke so gently, they might have been children again. Kokaleth rested his hand on Zephyr's wing as her expression shifted to one of terrified disbelief. Zephyr didn't cry or scream. She just hid her face into her wings, trembling.

"I'm sorry," Nea told her when they returned. "I knew the three of you used to travel together."

"The five of us," replied Zephyr her voice broken and far away.

How strange it must've felt, to be the last left alive of their childhood friends. The thought tore at her. "Zephyr," she said imploringly. "Leo is inside Equius."

Zephyr gave Nea a sweeping look. "Seiyariu was a great friend to the Erinyes, despite what he may have told you." Her wing muscles tensed. "He was a good man. I will fight for him and you. What's the plan?"

"Oh, this one has a grand strategy," Kokaleth gave a humorless laugh. "Tell her child."

73
By Wind and Water

The sunrise broke across the sea and fell upon Equius as Zephyr drew in over the city, cresting a gust of wind. Atop the battlements of the castle, legions of Beljhar's men were ripping through the thinly spread Fortuan forces pushing them back on every front. The only people to stand against the Briars were those soldiers that had been in the castle at the time of the attack. At the gate, the military police were still trying to batter down the blocked door with huge siege ram, but the doors refused to give way.

The remaining Fortuan soldiers were making a final stand in the north courtyard. The Briars were beating them back into a corner, there couldn't have been more than a few dozen left alive. Bodies of their comrades littered the ground at their feet, but they were still fighting. As Nea watched the carnage, the true weight of what she was doing hit her. She found herself silently whispering a prayer, not to anyone or anything in particular, she just needed to say it.

"I'm going to drop you," screeched Zephyr. "Roll or you'll break your neck."

Zephyr swooped in closer over the wall overlooking the courtyard, unnoticed in the chaos. Nea felt the talons let go and she heaved her body forward, colliding painfully with the stone. On her way back around Zephyr seized an unlucky briar in her claws, hefting him over the side. Then she was off to get Quinnel. Both the Briars and the Fortuan army stared in astonishment at Zephyr's retreating form; perhaps they thought they were going mad.

During this lull, a spout of water erupted over the sea, all the way up the cliff to the top of the castle walls. Kokaleth landed, dripping wet and clutching a boat anchor on a chain. Before the Briars could react, he slammed his weapon with inhuman strength into the nearest man. The briar went flying down into the courtyard, his chest completely caved in. Kokaleth's anchor crashed to the ground and shards of stone flew out in all directions. Then, like a wave upon the shore, Kokaleth spun, catching another man and sending him careening over the cliffside wall. The Briars barely had time to call out before he was on them, battering through armor and shields and bones.

The battle in the courtyard had almost come to an almost complete stop at the arrival of these strange creatures. A soldier in the center of the melee caught Nea's eye for the briefest moment. Cain had gotten her hands on some armor, which she was wearing over the tattered remains of her dress. Nea saw the shock, the disbelief in her eyes.

"Fortuna!" Nea yelled, opening fire into the crowd of Briars. It came from the voice of a child, but it rang like an order; a cry of opportunity.

In answer, Cain slammed into the Briar's line, battering man after man with her iron fists. The soldiers beside her following suit, rallying as it became clear whose side these newcomers were on.

Give 'em hell, M'lady.

As the Briars atop the wall rushed her, a shadow passed overhead and Quinnel crashed to the ground beside Nea, his knives out and ready. The oncoming Briars stopped at the sight of him.

"L… lieutenant?" One of them asked, stepping forward.

"Fall back," said Quinnel, shouting over the din of combat. "That's an order."

He's giving them a chance to run.

"Don't listen to him!" cried another of the Briars. "He's betrayed us. Kill him. *That's* an order."

Some hesitated, unsure of who to listen to. Three had already made up their mind, they advanced on Quinnel, swords raised. Nea saw a flash of hesitation on Quinnel's face. Then it was gone, replaced with a cold fury she'd never seen before. The Briars saw it too and they tried to cut him down, but their swords were too long and Quinnel was too fast. He tore through his former comrades unflinchingly and leapt over their corpses into the mass of fighting men.

On the other side of the courtyard Kokaleth was gaining ground. Zephyr flew to join him, hurling anyone she could get her claws around over the edge of the wall to the mercy of the sea. Beljhar's men were faltering now, their formation broken. They had not been prepared for anything like this. Soldiers were packed shoulder to shoulder along the wall, each of them engaged in single combat, while the body of the Fortuan troops still fought to hold the courtyard below.

Will it be enough?

Nea kept her position atop the wall, shooting like mad. She clutched the arrows in her hand, quiver forgotten; she needed to the extra speed. Quinnel was keeping them back on the north side, giving her just the one flank to worry about. For once, Nea was grateful that she was such a slip of a girl; it meant that the crossbow bolts flying up at her had a narrow target and she was able to dodge or take cover.

In the courtyard, Cain had stopped pressing forward, she and her men weren't losing ground but they weren't gaining it either. She was tired, Nea could see that even from this distance. Cain had been fighting for hours and her body was about to give out on her. Then the door to the courtyard burst open and nearly two dozen more Briars emerged.

No!

Despair threatened to overtake Nea, but in that instant she realized something was chasing them. Then she heard it, a metallic, grinding, roar. The mechanical form of Chiron galloped into the courtyard wielding a spear in each hand. Blood stained his clothes and the steel of the legs; his grey eyes bore down upon the Briars.

Nice timing Your Majesty!

He met the opposite flank, stabbing, slashing and kicking. He reared up onto his hind legs and let out a war cry that rang through the morning air like a church bell. The Briars in the courtyard were now pinned between Cain's forces and the King himself.

Nea renewed her efforts, putting a shaft into the shoulder of an oncoming Briar. But it wasn't enough to keep him down, she needed her burrowers. Nea let a second shot fly, this time catching him in the stomach, but he barely noticed it. The man was barreling towards her like a raging bull, arrows protruding from his body. Her third shot found only air as the Briar slammed into her so hard the two of them crashed over the wall and down into the courtyard.

They fell twenty feet to the ground. Nea managed to separate herself from the Briar, but as she collided with the stone floor, her arm snapped. Nea screamed in pain, clutching at the useless limb. The briar staggered up, some feet away. The arrow shafts still protruding from his body, adrenaline making his injuries seem meaningless.

Dammit don't just lie there, do something!

She wanted to move, to run but the pain was so intense she could barely see, let alone fight. The Briar raised his sword, but before it could fall Quinnel leapt from the wall like a bolt of lightning, driving both his daggers into the base of the man's neck. Quinnel let the corpse tumble to the ground, as he knelt beside her.

Forget about me! Defend yourself you idiot!

"You're done here." He forced her to her to her feet, slapping her across the face with his cold hands. "Get somewhere safe."

"No," she snapped, pushing through the pain. "I'm not going anywhere." She held out her good arm. "Give me a sword."

Nea didn't care if every damn bone in her body was broken. She wasn't going to run. She wasn't going to helpless, wasn't going to be weak. Not anymore.

Quinnel looked at her, then at the battle. "You stay beside me, are we clear?"

"Try to keep up," she said grimacing.

Quinnel tossed her a sword and together the two of them entered the battle in the courtyard.

Nea hadn't used a sword since she was very young. Her father had given her a few lessons. She remembered those mornings, fencing with sticks under the gray sky, feeling the cold sand between her toes. The memory somehow helped her focus.

Overhead Nea saw Zephyr flying along the wall, slashing and biting with primal ferocity like some terrible avenging angel. Then she lurched, losing altitude. Nea saw the arrows sticking from her wings. Zephyr crashed to the ground, Briars drawing in to finish her off.

Kokaleth vaulted the battlements in a single motion and fell upon them, sending Zephyr's attackers flying in all directions with a swing of his anchor. He ran to the aid of the wounded Erinye even as soldiers surrounded them on all sides. Out of the door to the courtyard poured even more Briars.

Shit, how many did he say there were?

The newcomers pushed them back, forcing Chiron to circle around and join the Fortuan soldiers. The tide was turning in the Briar's favor. Quinnel and Nea fought with everything they had, but it made little difference, Nea's injuries were too great and Quinnel couldn't fight at full strength if he was busy guarding her. The Briars pressed in and Nea felt despair take hold once again.

Is this it then?

74

Tooth and Knail

LEO SAT ALONE in the attic, among the crates and piles of dusty books, holding his knees to his chest. He felt sick and dirty, as if his flesh was marked with stains that would never come off. It was happening all over again. Beljhar was giving him what he'd asked for. The truth.

What was to become of him? Was this his new life, trapped in his worst memories, unable to change a thing? He felt the pain in his heart as if it were brand new. The realization that Nico had been protecting him, shielding him from the truth about the darker things in this world. And that there was now nothing standing between them. The dark things would sweep him up, do what they pleased with him and there was nothing he could do stop it. Be it Sister Roberta or Djeng Beljhar, Leo was nothing but prey.

His eyes fell upon a mirror, old and covered in filth. Leo screamed at himself to leave it, not look. But he knew it was hopeless. What he was looking at had already happened. Leo wiped the grime off the mirror, staring at his reflection, at the face of his brother. Even he hadn't been prepared for how much pain the reflection caused him. He couldn't bear to look at Nico now. But in seeing Nico, Leo felt as though Nico could see him. That his brother could somehow see what Sister Roberta had done to him. Shame and grief, twin agonies that pierced his heart.

Don't do it. He pleaded to himself. *It won't make things better.*

Leo drove his fist through the glass, trying to break the mirror's gaze. But as he did, the glass dug into the flesh of his arm. That burning pain, for a moment it seemed to block out everything else, even his grief. How quickly that horrible decision had come. And it came again. Even now, knowing Beljhar was tormenting him, Leo was prepared to end his life. He twisted his arm, the glass digging deeper and deeper, anything to make it stop. There was so much blood.

He was sitting in the infirmary, his arm wrapped in bandages. He'd pretended to be asleep, listened to the sisters whispering about him. Some of them thought he'd gone mad, losing Nico. Maybe they were right.

Sister Roberta came to visit him, cooing over his injury and stroking his hair. He wanted to push her away, to bite her fingers, but he had just sat there. Nico had always been the brave one. When she had gone, Leo thought about telling another of the sisters. Would they believe him? Would they think he was mad? Would they blame him?

He couldn't stay at the abbey any longer.

As the illusion shifted, Leo was running through a forest, the sharp glow of torches following him wherever he went. Men's voices and the bark of dogs closed in all around him. The grassers will catch you, they always do. Leo felt irons around his legs, felt a brand being applied to his finger. He was property now, their property. Then he and the other children were being beaten by the drunken shadows mercilessly. Only their grins could be seen. Leo watched children being dragged away screaming while he did nothing. It was happening faster now, the scenery changing again and again.

He was chained up in the hold of a slave ship. He was running through the streets of Limani, the grassers chasing after him. Then through the forests of Mavrodasos, lost and scared. He was underground, in the tunnels of Adis, Pluto's monstrous centipede on his heels. He was in the crow's nest of Beljhar's illusory ship, battering Seiyariu's face with Knail. In the garden, Leo let a blast of energy fly at the man he thought was Djeng Beljhar.

No!

It ripped through Seiyariu's chest, sending him flying into the wall where he collapsed, dead.

"I gave you a choice," came Beljhar's voice. "You chose truth."

"No." Tears streamed down his cheeks as he fought against Beljhar's mental hold, but it was no use. There was nothing in the world but this, the worst moments of his existence replayed endlessly. Binding him, wrapped around his mind like a thousand iron shackles. Shackles of the Mind.

The attic before him faded, his vision faltered for a moment, a glimpse of a garden from far away. But this wasn't the illusion. Leo could feel it. He could see Seiyariu's limp body lying just a few feet away. Leo reached out for the vagabond's hand, but fell forward, back into the attic.

No!

"Leo."

Leo froze, eyes slowly fixing on his reflection. Only this time, it wasn't his own face that stared out of the mirror, it truly was Nico.

"It's over now," Nico whispered gently. "Don't keep doing this to yourself. Don't you want to be with me again?"

Leo stared into his brother's eyes. "Yes."

And before he realized what was happening Nico was standing over him. He smiled and held out his hand. "Then let it end, let's be together."

Leo nodded and reached out, letting Nico help him to his feet. As he did the attic seemed to blow away. They were in the desert, the desert he'd walked a thousand times in his dreams. Bonfires alighting upon the dunes, music in the distance. Nico was standing beside him. He looked just as he had in the illusion of the palace, healthy, alive.

"There you go," said Nico smiling. "Let's get out of here. Let's go home."

"Home." The word echoed in his mind. His hand froze.

Shackles of the Mind.

A memory. A memory of a smile, a subtle smile on the face of a boy that was not, that smile that warmed every inch of him. He remembered sipping a bowl of soup with the strange man who'd saved his life. Sitting around a campfire with Seiyariu and Nea, talking, laughing. These images poured out from the depths of his soul, truth drowning out illusion. All at once, Leo knew what it was he had to do. He looked at Nico, tears pouring down his cheeks.

"I'm sorry."

And he let go of his brother's hand.

Everything went mad. The desert, the world, his body, it was all torn away. He was alone, truly and terribly alone. Drifting in a void. Was this an illusion too? The hand Nico had been holding stretched out to into the endless darkness. Reaching desperately for something, anything. There came a light. Then another. Stars in the black, the ones he shared a name with. Leo felt strength swelling inside of him. He reached out and the sky folded in on him, wrapping around his hand, turning it black. He closed his fingers around the stars, feeling energy from beyond his understanding fighting to get free.

Leo was awake, and he was not afraid.

The wind kissed his face; the salt on the air was bitter, cold, and real. He was on his feet in the garden, light pulsing from his black hand.

Beljhar had been watching the sea but as Leo got up he turned, eyes wide in disbelief. "Impossible."

The energy burst free, taking shape, the shape of the man who had been his hero. His savior. His father. His friend. Like his phantom of Nea, this Seiyariu was taller, broader, clutching a shining sword. An idealized, faceless version of the man lying dead against the wall. No, not faceless, it was wearing a mask.

The Urna flashed but the garden remained unchanged. Beljhar lunged forward, it was then Leo saw that he was holding Seiyariu's sword. The sight filled him with rage and he brought up his black hand to block the strike. As he did, the phantom struck, reacting to Leo's thoughts. The gleaming sword slashed across Beljhar's chest drawing blood and sending him tumbling back. But it wasn't deep enough, Leo could tell right away. Beljhar was on his feet again in an instant.

"How did you—?"

"Your tricks won't work on me anymore," said Leo, the phantom Seiyariu pointing his blade at Beljhar.

"So it would appear," said Beljhar, staring down at his wound. "What was it you found in those memories Leo? Strength? How fascinating. You know, I find that my memories give me strength too. Strength unimaginable."

Before Leo could react, Beljhar drew Seiyariu's sword up to eye level. The Urna flashed, its light reflecting off the steel and into Beljhar's eyes.

He threw back his head as the illusion hit him. Staggering under its power. What was happening? Leo couldn't afford to wait and find out. He lunged at Beljhar, slashing at him with burning white claws as the ghostly Seiyariu stabbed forward. Even as he did Beljhar's head shot back up, pupils tiny black holes in a sea of insane white.

There was a glint of steel and Beljhar seemed to vanish before Leo's eyes, closing the distance between the two of them in an instant. Leo made to dodge, at the same time trying to block with the phantom's blade. The blow sent him tumbling back across the garden. Leo scrambled back up, bracing himself for the coming assault.

Beljhar had stopped moving. His head lolled to one side, sword hanging limply next to him as he stared around the garden. There was such detached horror in his eyes. Leo knew where Beljhar was in his mind. There was only one place he could be. Among his fellow child soldiers as they were slaughtered. He was back at the Dashing of the Innocents.

Calmly, like a walking corpse, he strode over to Seiyariu's body and drew the vagabond's short sword in his free hand. Pushing the limp form of Leo's teacher away with the heel of his boot.

Leo roared and threw himself at Beljhar with everything he had, slashing at him with his claws. Beljhar parried the claws with the short sword and brought the vagabond's other blade crashing down on the phantom. Leo ordered it to block, barely having time to roll away himself.

How strong was Beljhar? Wielding both of Seiyariu's swords as though they were nothing but daggers. The madness of his memories giving him an inhuman strength. The unbending will of someone who refused to die.

Leo had barely righted himself when Beljhar was on him again, swinging both blades down in an arc towards him. He sidestepped the attack, rolling with his momentum the way he'd seen Seiyariu do and commanded the phantom to strike. It and Beljhar exchanged a flurry of furious blows, sparks flying in all directions. Finally, the phantom was able to throw off the assault and stagger Beljhar.

Seizing this opportunity, Leo brought his claws up, making to rake Beljhar across the face. And the phantom's sword flew past the side of Leo's head, right at Beljhar's exposed throat. Neither blow connected. Beljhar's free hand came twisting around, burying the vagabond's short sword in Leo's unarmored elbow joint.

A bout of white-hot agony exploded throughout Leo's arm. It was as though he'd struck the mirror again, all his nerves on fire. Beljhar twisted the blade and ripped it free. The pain was too much all at once, Leo had to fight to stay conscious. The phantom of Seiyariu began to flicker, and Leo staggered back, falling to his knees, blinded and leaking blood onto the flowers.

Beljhar tossed the short sword aside and delivered a devasting two handed blow, knocking the phantom back, its light fading away.

Don't leave me!

Beljhar's mad eyes fixed with a supernatural glee, and he brought Seiyariu's blade down to cleave off Leo's arm. Leo watched it speed towards him. Was this the end? Would all the sacrifice, all the suffering, be for nothing?

No!

The fragments of light, the remains of the phantom, they retreated inside of Knail. Leo felt another wave of pain overtake him as his arm began to glow white. What was happening to him? Leo's senses overloaded, making time slow to a crawl. The armored flesh of the parasite slithered up his arm, sealing the wound left by Beljhar's attack. He could feel his fingers, his claws, again. The pain was fading away. Leo shot up, throwing Knail past the oncoming blade. And in that instant he saw something in Beljhar's eyes, something familiar.

Fear.

Beljhar's strike glanced off of Knail, sending crimson sparks flying as Leo wrapped his blazing claws around the Urna. And, with the last bit of strength in his body, Leo ripped the stone from Beljhar's forehead, and crushed it.

75
Ashes of the Rainbow

A SCREAM RENT the air. So loud and sharp it could be heard even over the din of battle. It echoed through the castle, over the parapets and towers, and over the northern courtyard where Nea was still locked in combat. The fighting faltered for a moment, the unearthly scream giving pause to both sides. Suddenly every brooch on the throat of every briar, shattered into a thousand iridescent shards. The Briars stared down in shock at the pieces of opal now sprinkling the courtyard. Looking back and forth to one another in confusion and fear.

What in the hell?

The sight was enough. Cain shouted an order and Chiron, Kokaleth, Zephyr, Quinnel and Nea all threw themselves at the enemy line.

Some of the Briars seemed to forget where they were, falling to their knees pathetically grasping at the pieces, all thoughts of war forgotten. Still others merely dropped their weapons at the sight of all this. Those that did try to fight were no match for this last charge. When it became clear that the battle was lost, many of the Briars turned to flee, only to be cut off at the gate by Chiron and Zephyr. They were corralled. And, once the last of the Briars were killed or captured, Nea felt an impossible relief wash over her.

How?

Only then, as the adrenaline faded, did she truly become aware of the pain in her arm. She leant against a column, breathing heavily.

"Captain," said the King, cantering up to Cain. "I believe the day is yours."

Nea could see it in the lady knight's eyes, she wanted to throw her arms around him. But Cain settled for a smart salute. As the prisoners were led off and the bells began to ring, Kokaleth let out a triumphant roar, joined by birdsong from Zephyr and the soldier's cries of victory. The day brightened; the whole world came to rest. After everything that had happened, the fighting was over. The wind picked up, billowing the remains of the opals around the courtyard, the dust sparkling like the ashes of the rainbow.

Leo? Was that you?

Nea caught sight of Quinnel slipping out a side door and hurried after him as fast as she could manage. "Wait," she hissed through clenched teeth.

"You need to lie down," he said, not looking back at her. "Go join the rest of the wounded."

"Go to hell," she snarled. "I need to find Leo."

"And I need to find Beljhar," said Quinnel. "Something's happened to him, to the Urna. That scream…"

"You're not running away?"

"Not yet."

He's really got his mind made up, hasn't he?

"They were in the garden," she said. "Both of them."

"Then that's where we'll start," said Quinnel, offering his arm to help her walk.

"I don't need…"

"Shut up, you're barely standing."

Nea glowered at him but took his cold arm all the same, using it to prop herself up as they made their way through the halls of Equius. It was a strange feeling, sharing victory with so many people. Perhaps Leo would be able to appreciate it better than her.

Still, you did it.

"Yeah I suppose I did."

"What's that?" asked Quinnel absently.

"Nothing," she said, smiling to herself. "Mind your business."

*

Nea's heart nearly stopped when she saw how much blood now coated the garden. Beljhar was kneeling among the flowers, eyes utterly blank, a think trickle of blood running from his forehead. The scarecrow's corpse was still there, but he was wrapped in his cloak now, his eyes closed. Standing over him, was—

"Leo!" Nea nearly shrieked as she fell to her knees beside him, pulling him tighter than she'd ever held anyone in her life.

Leo said nothing, just stared at her. He reached out to touch her face, as if unable to believe she was real.

"Nea?"

Nea nodded, fighting back tears. Then it was Leo's eyes that began to stream and he pulled her close again, shaking quietly. "I thought you were dead."

"Take more than a fall to kill me, you know that."

"You stopped him," said Quinnel, looking over the scene. "Where's—"

"Here," said Leo, holding out the shards of the Urna. "It's over."

"You saved us," Nea whispered. "You saved all of us."

"I what?"

"We were going to be overwhelmed before you shattered the Urna," continued Quinnel. "When it was destroyed, its illusions went with it. Including the ones we kept around our necks. Most of my brothers didn't have the will to keep fighting after that."

"You... you were fighting?"

"The little miss brought your friends to help in the battle," grunted Quinnel. "The bird and the fish. It was a nice idea."

And him. Couldn't have done it without him.

"Kokaleth and Zephyr are here too?"

Nea nodded eagerly. "They all came."

The joyful look of pride in Leo's eyes was enough to make her start crying again. She looked away, eyes falling on the unmoving form of Beljhar. "Is he dead?"

Leo shook his head. "He'd used the Urna on himself just before I broke it. I don't know what's happened to him."

"The hell did all this blood come from then?" said Nea, looking around.

"He stabbed me."

"What? Where?" Nea leapt back into a panic.

Leo just smiled and held out his black arm. Nea saw that the armored flesh of Knail had moved further up Leo's forearm, all the way to his elbow.

"It healed me. Just like before."

Nea couldn't help it, she hugged him again.

"What happened to *your* arm?" asked Leo.

"I fell on it like a bloody idiot," she laughed. "No parasite to make this one better."

"Just one thing left," said Quinnel softly, turning his attention to Beljhar. He seized him by the throat, hauling him off the ground. Nea watched in astonishment as a tiny line of ice began to form around his former master's neck.

"Stop!" Leo cried scrambling to his feet. "He's no harm to anyone now!"

"My father…"

"Quinnel," said Leo gently. "He doesn't deserve it. Wherever he is right now, it's worse than being dead."

Quinnel slowly loosened his hold on Beljhar, tossing him back to the ground. As he did a troop of armed Fortuan soldiers came rushing into the garden.

"You!" They ordered, blades trained on Quinnel. "Throw down your weapons and surrender."

"Wait!" said Nea, rushing between him and the soldiers. "He's not—"

Quinnel brushed her aside gently, dropping his knives at the guards' feet, and splaying his hands.

"What are you—?"

"Your boy is right," said Quinnel, looking back at her as they clapped him in irons. "It's over. And I've crimes to answer for."

"You can't…" Nea stammered. "You helped me."

"Suppose we're even then," he said with one of his awkward smiles. He let the soldiers lead both him and Beljhar from the garden.

Nea made to run after him, but only then did she become truly aware of her injuries. Leo caught before she fell, helping her to sit.

Nothing you can do for him now.

"I'm fine," she grumbled, her vision flickering.

For a time they sat there, holding each other up. Leo seemed on the verge of collapsing as well, Knail having taken its toll on his body.

"Nea, I'm so sorry," Leo said finally as though from far away. "It's my fault. I killed him."

She looked into Leo's eyes, consciousness slipping away from her. Tears were streaming down his face, he didn't even bother to hide it. Nor did she. Before Nea blacked out, she reached out and put a hand on Seiyariu's cold body.

Goodbye, scarecrow.

She closed her eyes, holding Leo tight. The three of them together, one last time.

76
Dulcinea

"I'm fine alright! Stop fussing."

"I'm not fussing," said Cain, rolling her eyes. "You've got a broken arm, now sit down before I make you."

Nea grumbled and sat back on the stool. One of the barracks had been converted into a makeshift hospital. Healers from the city were bustling about, attending to all the wounded men. Two days had passed since the battle had ended. During which, everyone had treated Nea like a bloody child. The healers wanted to check on her splint every few hours to make sure she didn't get an infection. So Nea was spending a lot of time popping in and out of the sick-ward.

Like nobody ever broke their damn arm before.

Nea's complaints were mostly playful, and her heart had leapt when she'd found Cain waiting for her in the ward that morning. The lady knight's teasing put Nea's heart at ease. She knew that it meant the worst of the soldiers' injuries were dealt with. And indeed, most of them were sitting up, talking, laughing. The king had spent much of the first day among them shaking hands and thanking the wounded for their service.

Shifted that onto Cain now that he's sure nobody's dying.

But Nea knew that Cain would've been among her soldiers the whole time, whether Chiron asked her to or not.

"They said I won't be able to use it for at least a month," said Nea.

"I'd say that's being conservative," said Cain with a sigh.

Nea stared at the splint.

This what it felt like for Leo?

"Have you seen Leo?" asked Cain, as if reading her mind.

Nea shrugged. "Not today."

Indeed he'd been keeping odd hours in the days since the battle. She was worried about him truly, but honestly wasn't sure what to do. Grief had consumed her these past few days. She'd never experienced anything like it.

Must be even worse for him. Probably why he's keeping to himself.

"Well His Majesty wants to speak with the two of you bright and early tomorrow," said Cain.

Nea raised an eyebrow. "He gonna give me a medal or something? Thank me for my clever plans."

Cain gave her a stern look. "That was not a clever plan."

"Worked didn't it? Besides, don't tell me you wouldn't have tried it."

Cain let herself laugh. "I suppose none of us really know what we're capable of until the very last moment." She gave Nea a knowing look. "You saved us."

"Leo saved us," she mumbled, embarrassed.

"If you hadn't come when you did, I think I and every one of these men would've died. That's twice I owe you my life."

"Suppose we're even then," said Nea, her mind drifting back to Quinnel. He was still imprisoned with the rest of the Briars, she hadn't been allowed to go see him. "What does Chiron want to talk about?"

"Perhaps, if you're very good, Chiron will put you on a ship to Conoscenzia," said Cain, eyes sparkling.

"Conoscenzia." How long had it been since she'd thought about that?

"What's wrong? Do you still plan to make your way there?"

Nea didn't know what to say. In truth, she had no idea what was next for her, for Leo, for anyone. "I don't know anymore. Listen." She looked Cain in the eyes. It was easier than she thought it'd be. "You remember when you told me you saw the whole world as a machine, all moving parts working together?"

"I do."

"Well I was thinking. When I was on that beach, and I didn't know if you lot were alive. Whatever my part in that machine was, I don't think it worked properly until you came around."

Cain clasped Nea's hand and she thought for a moment she saw tears in the lady knight's eyes. She couldn't find the right words. Nea didn't mind. They had made it through this together, in one piece. For that, she would never stop being grateful.

"I've got something for you," said Cain, trying to compose herself.

"You want to give me a medal too?"

Cain snorted and from under her chair she produced a small brown package bound with a length of purple string.

"What's this?" asked Nea, taking it gingerly. She could already tell it was a book, it felt bloody expensive.

"It's a gift," said Cain, her eyes suddenly sad. "Seiyariu wanted you to have it."

Nea looked at her, confused. "Just me? Not Leo too?"

Cain shook her head. "He just said it was for you. We're going to have a service for him, in the wood tomorrow night. I think he would've liked that."

Nea nodded, trying not to meet Cain's gaze. "Yeah, I think he would too."

Nea returned to her room in the eastern wing of the castle. Leo still wasn't back yet, so she stretched out on the bed and opened the package. As she'd thought, it was a book. A leather-bound classic, the kind wealthy aristocrats payed a great deal of money for. How in the hell had Seiyariu gotten his hands on it?

Probably stole it. But why me? What are you playing at scarecrow?

Curiosity piqued, Nea made herself comfortable and cracked the book open. She'd been reading a lot over the past few days, there wasn't much else she could do with her arm the way it was. And it gave her an escape. The world felt so much colder without the scarecrow in it. Nea found herself longing to escape between the pages and spend a few hours as someone else.

The book was a translated work from the continent. The author and the characters all had strange names she couldn't quite pronounce, and the story was set on the mainland. It was about a crazed old man who ran off and pretended to be a knight. Nea read on for hours, a light rain falling on the window outside, until she came to a passage that made her stop dead. She read it again and again, her hand shaking.

The mad knight had a lady, or at least he said he did. A lady of great beauty and elegance. A lady he called Dulcinea. She appeared to the knight as this perfect woman, but that was merely a product of his deluded mind. In reality she was only a filthy peasant whore, cruel and jaded, fed up with the world.

Nea suddenly realized there were tears running down her cheeks.

So that's it, scarecrow? You knew the whole time?

Not only had he known she was a girl, he'd known how she felt, filthy and ruined, just like that whore. Yet still he'd called her Dulcinea. He was as mad as the knight in the story. How insane must a man have to be to see beauty in someone so ruined?

She read on, fighting through the emotion that threatened to overwhelm her. Nea read until she couldn't see through her tears. Every new page was like agony, but she needed to keep going. The crazed old knight, in her head he spoke with Seiyariu's voice and she needed to follow him to the end of his story.

77

By Deed of the King

LEO ARRIVED LATE to his audience with Chiron. He'd kept to himself much of the past few days. He hadn't wanted to, but he didn't think he could bear to look Nea in the eyes right now. He couldn't face himself in the mirror, how could he face her? She'd watched him murder Seiyariu. Would she ever be able to look at him as she had before?

Every morning since the battle, Leo had found himself praying that he would wake and that it would all be a dream. That Seiyariu would stride in with some grand new adventure for them to undertake and they would leave Equius together, at peace.

Leo had murdered him, just as he had murdered that man by the lake, just as he had murdered Pluto. He wanted to put the blame on Beljhar, but try as he might he couldn't. He'd broken free of the Urna hadn't he? Why couldn't he have done it when it mattered most?

Every day since Nico died, Leo had lived with grief. It never got smaller. When he'd found Nea and Seiyariu it had felt easier to carry somehow. Now Seiyariu was gone and a new grief ate at him, and the one person who could help him bear this burden, he didn't have the courage to face.

But there she was, waiting for him in the audience chamber, her arm in a splint, talking animatedly to the King. As Leo shut the door behind both pairs of eyes settled on him.

"Mister Fortunato," said Chiron. His voice was soft and neutral, preventing Leo from getting any kind of sense of his mood.

Nea didn't say anything, but she tried to catch his eye. Leo avoided this and hurried to stand before the King. "Forgive me Your Majesty I was—"

"It's unimportant," said Chiron with a wave of his hand. "This won't take long."

His metal half gave a great lurch as he started to pace back and forth. "I wish to thank both of you. Had it not been for your efforts, it's likely the Briars would've overrun us."

"Quinnel said that they had men pretending to work here for years," said Nea.

"So it appears. Beljhar's indoctrination was powerful even for some of the most loyal members of this house." A shadow fell across his face. "But we will rebuild. Never again will we allow something like this to happen."

"Nice words," said Nea folding her arms.

"What are you going to change?" asked Leo.

"Well, for a start, I believe I'll begin to heed the advice of vagabonds again. My own distaste for the profession notwithstanding, it's clear they have more knowledge of what goes on in my kingdom than I do. And I don't intend things to stay that way. I thought about awarding the two of you with some kind of medal, but I imagine the less you have to take with you on the green road the better." Chiron continued. "I'm prepared to grant you each one request. Anything within my power to do."

Leo stared at the King in disbelief for a moment. "A... anything?"

Nea's jaw was slack, "You're havin' a laugh."

"I assure you I'm not," said Chiron, cocking an eyebrow. "Whatever you wish, provided it doesn't impede the rights of my people. You can take what you will from the royal treasury or armory. I can have The Nuptial removed or I can give you land or titles, a place in my court, even a home within the walls of this castle. I leave it to you."

Leo and Nea shot a look at one another, Leo's uneasiness forgotten in the shock moment. His mind was racing. One request, within Chiron's power. He thought about all he could ask the King for. The idea of staying in the palace would've appealed to him once, but now he couldn't wait to get away from Equius; too much had happened for him to call this place home. No, all Leo wanted was to return to the road. He didn't need a weapon, he had Knail. Money didn't hold much sway. Lands and titles, Leo wouldn't know what to do with those in the first place.

Losing the Nuptial. It would make wandering the roads of Fortuna easier certainly, but they'd gotten by fine with it so far. This made Leo think of the children still toiling away, enslaved in the opal mines. Leo would've liked to ask Chiron to march the Fortuan Army south and liberate every last one of those poor souls, but he knew that was one thing outside of the King's power. The slaving companies, technically they were Chiron's people too. The King couldn't just take them apart because Leo asked. Leo would have to do that himself, one day.

Finally, a thought occurred to him. It was so simple that it had almost completely slipped his mind. What had caused all of this suffering? The conflict with Beljhar, the Briars? The same thing that had cut that rift between Leo and Seiyariu. Too many secrets.

"Will you tell your people about the Dashing of the Innocents?" asked Leo, looking right into Chiron's cold grey eyes.

"An interesting request," said Chiron slowly. "I offer you so many possibilities, yet all you request is truth. You fascinate me boy, you really do."

"So does that mean—" Nea started.

"Yes, if that's your request I will honor it. I'll make an address before the week is over."

"Just like that?" she said. "What if they…"

"Turn on me? Demand my abdication?" Chiron crossed his arms. "I will fulfill Leo's request, the consequences of that will be mine to deal with, not his. Besides, I believe it's time my people knew the truth anyway. When they do, we can let them judge of whether or not I'm fit to rule."

"Thank you, Your Majesty," said Leo, bowing his head. "I think… I think it's better like this, without secrets."

"I imagine your vagabond would agree," Chiron replied, a knowing look in his flinty eyes.

Leo felt his heart ache. "So do I, sir."

"And you?" said Chiron turning to Nea.

Nea bit her lip, "Nice as money sounds. There's a prisoner in your dungeon. Quinnel Votrow."

"Yes?"

"I'd like you to pardon him. Let him go on his way. If it hadn't been for him, I dunno if any of us would talking right now. He fought for us, against his own comrades."

"Another unorthodox request. But who am I to refuse something so simple. I was on the battlefield with you child, I saw what that man did, but the law is the law."

"Never was much good with the law, Majesty," said Nea with a little smile.

"Very well, I'll have someone escort you down to the dungeons, I imagine he'd like to hear it from you."

"Now sir?"

"I don't see why not? Leo will you be joining them?"

Nea shot Leo a surprised look. Leo wanted to go with her truly, he just couldn't bring himself to. He gave her a fake little smile but shook his head. "No, forgive me Your Majesty, I've some things to take care of."

"Ah, yes," said Chiron knowingly. "But I will see you for the service in the wood tonight yes?"

"Yes, my lord," Leo said.

"Very well, you're both dismissed."

Leo turned on his heel and left the audience chamber, not looking back. He didn't want to think about the service in the wood. The idea of going was more than he could bear, but the idea of not going was even worse. It was strange, all his life he wanted to be around people, and now that Seiyariu was gone, Leo found he was almost afraid to be. All except Nea of course, and even then, he'd let her down. She was suffering too, and he was just letting her do it by herself. What the hell kind of a friend did that make him?

78

Diamond Dust

WELL THAT WAS bloody stupid.

A pair of soldiers escorted Nea down the winding staircases of Equius Castle into the dungeons below. Leading her to where the prisoners were being kept.

You got a chance to ask for any damn thing you wanted, and you choose him? The hell is wrong with you?

But Nea ignored the voice, a small smile playing on her lips. In truth, she probably would've asked for something similar to Leo if she'd gotten the chance. The Dashing was what had caused all of this and with it public, perhaps people might finally start to stand up to the slaving companies.

Leo was making her more and more nervous. She wanted to be with him, but she also was old enough to tell when someone wanted to be left alone. He truly blamed himself for the scarecrow's death and nothing she said would be able to change that.

Do you blame him?

Nea shook her head. She'd been under those illusions before, it was impossible to tell what was real and what wasn't. Even if Leo had managed to break out eventually, what he'd done under the influence of Beljhar's power wasn't his fault. Not even that snide voice in her head could disagree with that. She could tell Leo wanted to be gone from this place and so did she. The sooner they got away from it all the better.

There you go running away again.

"Not alone though," she said under her breath.

Where will you go?

452

Nea was spared having to answer this question, because at that moment her escort passed Cain's workshop and made their way to a room lined with iron cells built into the wall. Not a trace of the morning light could be found down here, the only illumination came from a few oil lamps set in sconces on the stone wall. It was colder down in these chambers, perhaps there was a place where the sea air was getting in, or perhaps it was the white-haired man in black, leaning against the wall of his cell.

"What in the hell are you doing here?" Quinnel groaned, but he was smiling.

"Nice to see you too," said Nea, folding her arms. "Got you locked up good and proper, don't they?"

"I should say," said Quinnel. "Though, I'm grateful they don't have me sharing a cell with my former brothers. Don't fancy being beaten to death as a traitor."

Too right.

"Where's Beljhar?" Nea asked.

Quinnel gestured down to the last cell on the block. "In there, silent as the grave. Haven't gotten a word out of him since the battle. Imagine it'll make it easier for them to execute him though, don't you?"

Gallows humor

"Seems cruel to execute a madman."

"Or a mercy, however you look at it," he replied.

"Thank you," said Nea. "For helping us."

"I told you, that was for me."

"You saved my life."

Was that for you too?

"Yes, I suppose I did."

"And you said we were even," Nea said with a frown. "How does that work, I never saved your life."

Quinnel shrugged. "No, you didn't. But you helped me all the same. Don't think any of this would've happened if it hadn't been for your prodding."

"I'm good at that," she grinned at him. "But if that's the case, I don't think we're even anymore."

She gestured to the guards. They shuffled forward and unlocked the door to Quinnel's cell.

He stared at her, ice blue eyes fixed in shock. "What is this?"

"Majesty said I could have one request. So here it is," said Nea. "Best be on your way, before I decide I'd rather have something else."

She winked at him and Quinnel took a few hesitant steps out of the cell, hardly daring to believe it. "You chose me?"

Don't go getting all emotional now.

She looked away, hands on her hips. "It doesn't do anyone any good if you swing. Not after coming around like that. Be better to spend your days doing something worthwhile. Well? Stop gawking at me like an idiot and say something!"

Quinnel's face broke into a smile and slowly, he began to laugh. It was the strangest sound Nea had ever heard, high and fleeting, a boy's laugh. Like his smile, it seemed as though he'd forgotten how to do it. Mirth still echoing about the chamber, Quinnel leaned against the wall breathing heavily. "You are a strange one."

"You're one to talk," she said, unable to help herself from laughing along.

"It's funny," said Quinnel drawing himself back up. "I could've sworn you told me that evil was something men were, not merely something they did."

Nea blushed. "Yeah, I suppose I did. Still do, kinda."

"Then why?"

Because you're not evil

"Because you're not evil," she said firmly.

"I've done plenty of evil things."

"So have I! That doesn't mean…" Nea trailed off, realizing just what it was she was saying.

"It's alright," said Quinnel putting a hand on her head. "I don't think that question has a truly right answer anyway."

Nea met his gaze, smiling. His hand was cold but reassuring. Even she was surprised at how comforting the contact was.

Maybe you're learning to be human after all.

"Thank you Nea, for everything."

"Go on now, no need to make a scene," she said looking away, embarrassed. "For what it's worth I think your Da would've been proud, if he could see what you've done now."

Quinnel's smile slipped, and Nea caught the hint of a faraway look in his eye. "Would he?"

She nodded, "You turned around and saved a lot of people. In spite of what that old man did to you."

Sound familiar?

Nea gave a little gasp of realization. It wasn't just Quinnel she was talking about, not just Quinnel she was proud of. There was another person who she'd thought was beyond hope. Someone who'd had horrible things done to her. But even that little monster was able to turn around and help people in the end. She bit her lip, not wanting to show all the different emotions this stirred up inside her.

She just took Quinnel by his cold hand and smiled again. "Do you know where you're going this time?" she asked.

"I do," he said, with a peaceful sigh. "I'm going home."

79
A Vagabond's Legacy

A FEW MILES south of Equius in a forgotten part of the wood, there stood the remains of an old stone fort. It was here that Seiyariu was going to be sent on his way. A small crowd gathered within its crumbled walls, standing silently around the pyre, waiting. It was Zephyr who carried the body, wrapped in black. She laid it to rest atop the pyre, then settled on the remains of the fort beside Kokaleth, folding her wings. Leo had seen very little of them since the battle. No doubt they were mourning Seiyariu in their own ways.

Cain and Chiron were among the crowd as well, solemnly holding hands. Nea gripped his tightly as the two of them strode forward, holding the torch together. It was all Leo could do to keep from running away, he didn't want to say goodbye, didn't want to burn away his friend, but he knew it was what Seiyariu would've wanted.

As the flames leapt up around the body and the plumes of smoke drifted up into the clear night sky, Leo let himself cry. He felt as though he'd cried enough to last his entire life, but he needed to. He needed to feel this. It was because of him, after all.

The two of them stood beside Cain and watched as the fire grew higher. Crackling sparks etched against the night sky like blood red stars. Nea had said she wasn't going to cry but Leo knew that wasn't true either. Her shoulders shook silently as she clutched his hand like it was the only real thing in the world.

Leo reached out and pulled her close, holding on as if she too might be swept up by the fire.

He'd been a fool to keep his distance. Why didn't he realize she would be hurting just as much as him? Yes, he'd killed Seiyariu, that was something he'd have to live with for the rest of his life, but Leo couldn't let that shame prevent him from being there for his best friend. Seiyariu would've told him the exact same thing.

Leo didn't spot them immediately, with their green cloaks they blended into the surrounding trees. There must have been over a hundred of them, vagabonds, all standing in silent reverence for the man they'd called Seiyariu. They stepped over the ruined sections of wall to join the crowd before the pyre. The gathered people parting to let them in. Leo saw to his astonishment that Zhenamansa was at their head. Beside her stood a small girl. She looked about Leo's age, with shoulder length black hair and the same olive complexion as him. Their eyes met, and she stared at him for a few seconds, her sad eyes sweeping over him with a mix of fear and surprise.

As the fire burned on through the night, Kokaleth brought forward Seiyariu's cloak. It was divided among the gathered vagabonds. Each sewing a legacy patch of his cloak into theirs. Leo shook with every turn of the needle, but he pressed on, placing Seiyariu besides his mother and father, a trio of vagabonds reunited once again.

As the night drew on the vagabonds drifted into the dark one by one, returning to the road. After the fire finally burned itself out, Leo and Nea got ready to leave. They'd brought their packs with them, deciding together not to wait around Equius after the funeral. Both of them felt an incurable desire to be on the road once more. Though Leo could tell how much it hurt Nea to say goodbye to Cain.

"Take care of yourself," Cain whispered, embracing her one last time. "I don't suppose I can convince you to stay."

Nea glanced at Leo. "We'll come back whenever we can."

He nodded, smiling.

"Please do. And Leo, do keep her out of trouble."

Leo laughed for what felt like the first time in years. "That's impossible."

Cain beamed at them, then took her king by the arm and together they and their guards began making their way back to distant lights of Equius.

"Leo."

He turned to see Zhenamansa and her young companion. "I wanted to speak with you," she said. "I thought perhaps I owed you some kind of explanation."

"Why would you owe me anything?" asked Leo. "You saved my life."

"Did Seiyariu ever tell you his real name?"

Nea shot him a confused look. "Leo who—?"

"Y… yes, we promised each other we wouldn't keep secrets. What does that have to do with you?"

"I cannot tell you how much I would've liked to have shared a similar promise with him," Zhenamansa said wearily.

"What are you talking about?" Leo was starting to get angry now.

"It's not uncommon for vagabonds to take special names after a time, names like Seiyariu or Zhenamansa."

"That's not your name?"

She shook her head. "In the oldest writings of my country, our country I should say, the word refers to the separation of lovers. Leo, my true name is Aisha Al-Mubarak. I am the former Queen of Inferno. Your father's wife."

A moment of stunned silence passed between them, as Zhenamansa let these words sink into him. His father's wife, his queen. Zhenamansa was the woman who… the woman who'd been with Seiyariu. The woman he'd run to when Resha had found another.

Nea's mouth was hanging open and she looked from Zhenamansa to her young companion and back again, as if waiting for one of them to start laughing, but they did no such thing.

"It's strange," Zhenamansa's voice was so sad. "For years I pretended you didn't exist. You're a constant reminder of my husband's love for another. Yet when I learned you were traveling with Seiyariu, I found I simply needed to see you. Perhaps I thought I'd see some of Heiro looking back at me. I loved your father very much you know. I miss him terribly to this day, as I told you. Had you not been in danger, I doubt I would've revealed myself that day in the woods."

"Why are you telling me this now?" asked Leo. "I don't understand."

"Because I knew that Seiyariu would not."

"Seiyariu…"

"Seiyariu murdered my husband," Zhenamansa replied coldly. "Any feelings I had for him became… unwelcome after that day. But they were real, I am certain of that. I regret not seeing him at least once more."

"I'm sorry," said Leo.

"For what child?"

"For taking him away from you, from everyone. He was…"

"He was," she replied simply. "I don't seek atonement from you Leo. Nor, I think, would Seiyariu. But I'm sure you knew that already, you knew him best."

"I… I'm not sure I even knew him at all sometimes," said Leo.

"I am certain that you knew him better than anyone on this earth ever has. And for that I believe you are uniquely blessed. Goodbye Leo." Zhenamansa turned on her heel, gesturing for the girl to follow her. "Come Yashri."

"Yes Mother."

"Wait," said Leo, his eyes now fixed on this girl. He saw the resemblance between the two of them. Yashri had some of Zhenamansa's long, regal features, her sharp nose and high cheekbones. But her eyes, Leo couldn't look away from her eyes. He'd seen them before. Seiyariu's eyes.

Leo was overcome with a strange mix of grief and joy as he realized who he was looking at. The daughter of the man he'd loved, who'd loved him, so terribly. Of the man who had taken everything from him and tried his hardest to give it back. What could he say to her? Was there anything?

"I'm… I'm so sorry," he said limply. "He…"

Nea's eyes got very round as she realized the same thing he had. Yashri stepped forward, offering her hand to Leo. Zhenamansa looked as if she wanted to stop this, but she relented, stepping out of earshot so the two of them could speak. Nea did the same, though Leo could see on her face that she was dying to listen.

"Mother didn't want you to meet me," said Yashri, eyes on the ground. "She said it would cause you too much pain."

"I killed your father," Leo said.

Yashri frowned at him, and in an instant her timidness vanished. "Is that truly what you want to take away from this? More guilt?"

"But I…"

"I bear you no ill will Leo. I never knew my father, I have nothing to grieve." Leo was lost for words, but Yashri continued. "My mother says that this Seiyariu raised you like his own, protected you. Is that true?"

Leo nodded.

"Then he was more a father to you than to me," said Yashri. "Please do not torment yourself, like mother says he did. I know he would want better for you."

Leo had no tears left, and he could feel the truth in Yashri's words. It was so strange, she was his age, yet she spoke like someone years older. "You're right," he said, putting a hand on her shoulder. "Please, take these." He held out Seiyariu's swords.

"I cannot—"

"Take them, please. I'm no good with them." It was agony to give away yet another piece of his teacher, but Leo knew the swords would be better off with Seiyariu's daughter.

She took them, smiling at him. "Thank you."

"I hope you can forgive me."

"It's not from me you need seek forgiveness."

Leo's eyes flashed to Zhenamansa but Yashri shook her head.

"Not my mother either. Please Leo, try to forgive yourself." Then she hugged him.

"You gonna be alright?" asked Nea, coming out of nowhere to clap Yashri on the back. "That sword's bigger than you are."

Yashri and Nea looked at one another for the first time and Yashri's cheeks got very red. She let out a shrill little yelp and scurried off to her mother. Zhenamansa gave Leo a little salute, and she led her daughter off up the trail and out of sight.

"What was wrong with her?" asked Nea, confused.

"I think she's rather taken with you," Leo replied.

Nea went scarlet with indignation. "You're teasing me."

"Might be." Leo laughed as Nea shoved him.

"I knew that kid was the scarecrow's though," said Nea, looking off at where she'd gone. "Minute I saw her."

Leo nodded. "It's amazing."

"It's those eyes, I half expected her to call me Dulcinea," Nea laughed.

Leo stared up at his constellation, the one Seiyariu had shown him on their first night on the road. "I killed her father Nea. Just like Seiyariu killed mine."

Nea's face got very serious. "What did she say to you?"

Leo shrugged, "Said I need to forgive myself."

"Listen Leo, she's right. And you didn't mean to do it. We both know that, and so does the scarecrow."

Leo didn't answer.

"You know," she continued. "I don't feel like he's gone. Not all the way I mean. We carry him with us forever, right?"

"Sewn upon the hearts of your kin that you may walk the green road forever," he said, reciting the words Zhenamansa had used. They stood there in silence for a little while, watching the stars. "Nea?" he asked finally, not looking at her.

"Yeah?"

"I think I know what I want to do. Where I want to go, I mean."

She gave him an odd look. "Where's that?"

"Seiyariu told me something about the patches, the reason we wear them. He said we become their legacy. I want to be worthy of that. I want to find people like us, like Beljhar and Quinnel and I want to help them, just like Seiyariu did."

"Every slave in Fortuna."

"What?"

"You promised me, back at the castle. That when it was all over we'd free every slave in Fortuna." Nea's misty eyes were fixed on the sky. "I think... I think I'd like that."

It felt so strange, this world without him in it. Everything was so distant now, so cold. Nea took him by the hand. Well, not everything. She smiled that special smile of hers and Leo felt light return to his heart once again. He gripped her hand tightly and together they watched their breath drift up into the starry winter sky. The bright sentinels stared down at the two of them. The only true constants in their ever-changing world.

About the Author

A MYSTERIOUS WRITER from North Carolina, William Hastings was born in New Orleans. He has been telling stories since he first learned to talk. In 2009 he started what would one day become The Crimson Spark. After graduating from Eastern Connecticut State University, Hastings began to pursue his dreams of writing professionally. In 2019 he finally completed The Crimson Spark, his debut novel. Hastings writes predominantly for a YA audience, and includes mature themes and subject matter inspired by his work in education. Visit his website and subscribe to his mailing list for more information on the future adventures of Leo and Nea.

Because a spark is always just the beginning.

https://www.williamhastingsgreenroad.com

Twitter: @MrWillHastings
Instagram: @mrwillhastings
Facebook: mrwillhastings2

Made in the USA
Middletown, DE
13 November 2019